Forgive Me Father, For I Have Loved

Written by Tiana Laveen
Edited by Natalie G. Owens
Book Cover Design by Travis Pennington

COPYRIGHT

This book was originally written in 2013, but has had notable revisions, modifications, and updates in 2024 which include, but are not limited to: the cover, added dialogue, formatting, and grammatical corrections.

The book plot and characters are the same as when it was originally published.

Print Edition

TRIGGER WARNING

Please Note: Though this book is a contemporary romance based on the journey of a Catholic priest, it does involve the following subject matters/topics/ideals, which may be offensive to some audiences: religion — particularly the Catholic faith as it pertains to priesthood. It also includes detailed intimate depictions of a consenting couple engaging in sexual activities, and a host of situations that are adult in nature. This book is not intended to encourage or discourage those in the Catholic faith. It is a love story that deals with the human experience in its totality.

DEDICATION

This book is dedicated to all the laicized Catholic priests, Catholic support groups that tackle the delicate subject of priests and marriage, women and priests who have fallen in love but were unable to stay together due to religious regulations or fear of stigma, and to everyone who wishes for these rules to be removed. Man-made laws are not always beneficial, and sometimes, we have to put our pride aside, look at the bigger picture and see what love *truly* is, with new eyes and insight. When you *know* better, you *do* better…

TABLE OF CONTENTS

COPYRIGHT   ii

TRIGGER WARNING   iii

DEDICATION   iv

PRELUDE   1

CHAPTER ONE   3

CHAPTER TWO   14

CHAPTER THREE   24

CHAPTER FOUR   39

CHAPTER FIVE   45

CHAPTER SIX   56

CHAPTER SEVEN   73

CHAPTER EIGHT   87

CHAPTER NINE   99

CHAPTER TEN   107

CHAPTER ELEVEN   128

CHAPTER TWELVE   138

CHAPTER THIRTEEN   149

CHAPTER FOURTEEN   157

CHAPTER FIFTEEN   171

CHAPTER SIXTEEN   182

CHAPTER SEVENTEEN   197

CHAPTER EIGHTEEN   214

CHAPTER NINETEEN   235

CHAPTER TWENTY   246

CHAPTER TWENTY-ONE   257

CHAPTER TWENTY-TWO   266

CHAPTER TWENTY-THREE   278

CHAPTER TWENTY-FOUR   297

CHAPTER TWENTY-FIVE   315

CHAPTER TWENTY-SIX   335

CHAPTER TWENTY-SEVEN   344

CHAPTER TWENTY-EIGHT   361

CHAPTER TWENTY-NINE   378

CHAPTER THIRTY   394

A WORD WITH THE READER   397

AUTHOR BIOGRAPHY   399

PRELUDE

THERE SHE IS again, her hair giftwrapped in that thickly enfolded black fabric that smells like my incense and wafts past me while I'm on my knees…

Yes, I'm on my knees again, God. This time, praying not for you to forgive me, but to release me from the demons that make me second guess myself. I have a feeling I should be praying for something else, but of exactly what that should be, I'm not sure. All I can do is think about her. She now interrupts my dreams. One dream in particular stands out the most…

I knelt before her, at the altar of her lap while Amel Larrieux sang, 'For Real'. She was singing that song one day in the park, and it became the soundtrack for this odd fantasy. Running her soft, brown fingers through my hair, real slow, she laughed…you know the laugh, the one that is light and airy, like she doesn't have a care in the world. A laugh that is loose and free, like invisible birds flying off into the sunset. I looked up at her, God, and I saw her smiling down at me, like she'd found some lost money and couldn't wait to spend it. I've never felt as weak as the moment I looked into her dark eyes, and realized, *she had me.*

My God, she has me, *all* of me, and my only prayer to you, Lord, is please don't *ever* let her let me go…

When I am afraid, I put my trust in you.
Psalm 56:3

CHAPTER ONE

THE CRACKED CONCRETE walls and the sound of plopping water drops hitting worn linoleum in the time-worn gymnasium shower created the perfect ambiance for Dane to start his ritualistic torment of the newbie. Not actually *torment*, but an initiation of sorts—an act of kindness disguised as fraternal mockery. The guy was close, and fear was eating him alive as if he were a two-legged buffet fit for a famished tiger. Dane needed to help—he'd seen this hurdle one too many times before from so many of the men right before they finished seminary study. Cold feet, fright and the adrenaline rush sent more than a few into an emotional frenzy.

Dane ran a finger along his chin, feeling the prickly hairs he'd shave away as soon as he returned to the parish rectory. Or perhaps this time around he'd let his beard grow out. That was still up in the air. He cocked his head to the side, watching the man in front of him move jerkily, his nerves appearing to be getting the best of him. Assessing the situation, he devised a plan on how to proceed, waffling between two approaches—humor as an icebreaker or bravado? He scanned the pale, bright-eyed young man from the corner of his eye and caught his own reflection in the water streaked mirror several feet away before turning back to speak to Douglass.

"I see what you have there, a Playboy magazine. You actually brought that in here? That sure is a lot of nerve." Dane's shrouded his face with his warm, moist palm, hiding a massive grin. The soapy scent on his hand infiltrated his nostrils as he absorbed the moment he had perfectly laid out for his own pleasure to open the flood gates of productive discussion.

Good, a laugh. Perfect icebreaker.

"Fr. Caruso!" Douglass hooted, turning crimson as he leaned against the silver gym locker with the rolled periodical under his arm. "This is Time magazine, thank you. I'm a man of distinction. I like to read it while on the treadmill." He pointed toward the closed door that led to the exercise equipment. His green eyes sparkled as he flaunted a coy smile.

"Call me Fr. Dane," he reminded. "Yeah, ya don't say?" Dane smirked as he tightened the white, stiff towel around his wet frame, the trickles of cool water from the shower beginning to dry. "Are you meeting up with all of us at the restaurant tomorrow night?"

The tall, lanky and freckled Douglass looked over his shoulder. His eyes dimmed as he shook his head and gave a half-hearted grin. "I don't have a choice," he shrugged. "I finish seminary classes in one month, Fr. Caruso, I mean, Fr. Dane. I know I am expected there. I can't rock the boat."

"Mmmm hmmm…So, what is the scariest part of it for you?"

Douglass sighed. "The bishop will be there."

Dane nodded. "Yes, Bishop Thayer will be in attendance."

"I'm afraid I'll be so nervous in front of him, I'll say something stupid. I have to stay on top of this, I want to make a good impression, you know? I want this so bad, I can taste it."

Dane shrugged. "Well, what do you think would happen if you didn't show up? You could opt out and save yourself the ribbing." Dane opened his locker and removed the small container of roll-on deodorant.

"Nah, I can't." The twenty-three-year-old shook his head. "It would look bad."

"Probably," Dane said. "That's my point though. Don't run away, run toward the unknown when you know you are doing the right thing. It's scary; I was in your shoes, but you've got nothing to be afraid of. Bishop Thayer is a really nice man. Relax. Believe it or not, we have a heck of a lot of fun." Dane smiled as he ran his fingers over the back of his head.

Douglass shoulders slumped as he took a few deep breaths, then gave a nervous grin and grabbed his beaten and bruised navy blue gym bag.

Dane turned away and quickly dressed, sliding a dark sweater over his bare chest, and repositioning the golden crucifix on a matching gold chain over his torso. He tossed a glance back Douglass' way. The guy was sick with worry, even after the pep talk. The archdiocese had a way of causing fear even in the most brave, and here the poor guy would be with the bishop and all the priests, under their watchful eye, in one room.

"Look." He placed his hand on Douglass' arm. "All jokes aside, you will do just fine. You've proven yourself. You've shown you are serious. You've been preparing for this for a long time and now it is almost over."

"Thanks. It *is* almost over, and I thought this day would never come but now that it is almost here," he shrugged and exhaled loudly, "you'd think I'd never known it was on its way. I want to start helping the community, go on retreats." Douglass' lips curved in a smile, but it was tense, tight, as if it would shatter if his face were gently touched with a single fingertip. He placed his worn yellow terry cloth wrists bands into his bag. "I just, I dunno, I guess my nerves are getting the best of me today." He slumped on the nearby bench, defeated, and cupped his chin while looking down at the drab floor. He reminded Dane of *Le Penseur,* 'the thinking man' bronze statue from Paris. Dane sighed and sat beside him quietly. He rubbed his palms against the thick fabric of smoky gray jogging pants.

"Fr. Dane, I mean, you and I haven't talked much about your personal story. You've been a great teacher to me, though. Do you mind if I ask you about, you know…how you did it? What was it like?"

"I don't mind at all."

Dane grinned and scratched his eyebrow after running his fingers through slick, damp waves. "Honestly?" he said in almost a whisper, capturing Douglass' attention. "I was petrified. I think my friends were shocked when I told them I believed God was calling on my life to become a priest. I just didn't seem the type, according to them, but God chooses all sorts of people." He laughed lightly. "God calls all guys from all walks of life. We are all different; we all have something special to offer. Right before I went into the seminary, I said goodbye to the secular things. I got rid of my friends that were discouraging, the ones that were negative. Some people that I really enjoyed got rid of me as well. They didn't like that I was changing. I removed my earring, I loved that thing." Dane grinned. "Things were different. It was time for me to be different, too. When I was in the seminary, there were about fourteen of us, all unique, from diverse backgrounds. But, I prayed a lot, and I had some really good men around me, helping me, encouraging me, just like I am doing with you right now. I had struggles, we all did. That is why by the end of the time for me, there were only five us left out of the fourteen that began."

"Same here. I made it this far. I know this is what I am supposed to be doing." Douglass said with conviction. "Did you always know, too?"

"You know, at first I didn't." Dane paused as he relived those archived moments in time. "Some guys say they knew at like…five!" He laughed. "That is not common, but definitely a possibility, although it isn't my story. I was on the high school football team, popular, made pretty good grades when I wasn't goofin' off… I thought I'd get some big corporate job after college and get married but during my studies, it struck me, Douglass. This was what I was supposed to be doing." Dane pointed to his heart with conviction. "In college, the thoughts would drift in and out. I wasn't happy. I should've been."

"What do you mean?" Douglass's eyes squinted as he held onto every word.

"Well, I had it all, or so people thought. You know, a great family, supportive and loving parents, a nice group of friends. I had a football scholarship to college and a nice girlfriend. All I kept hearing was, 'Why would you throw that away?' I had to tell 'em, 'I'm not throwing anything away; I am giving my heart to the Church, to serve.' As a priest, I am a gift to the people, and this is about sacrifice. I was called," Dane answered, filling with emotion as each word left his mouth. "And I answered. I could feel the calling on my life. I was called to do this—the vocation chose me, God *chose* me." Douglass nodded, as if falling deeper into understanding while the spirit of comradeship weaved between them.

"The Church has been a positive part of my entire life. I've been active in it since I could remember. My entire family, actually, all of us went to church. I've seen miracles, too." He smiled as he drifted into thoughts of children surviving traumas through prayer vigils and people in the clutches of financial destitution suddenly finding new employment or receiving a loan that saved them in the nick of time. Dane's faith was strong, and he loved speaking to the new guys about to graduate the seminary, especially ones like Douglass who showed tremendous potential.

"I graduated right here, at Michigan State and—"

"Really? I didn't know you were native here and that you'd gotten your degree. You don't…you don't act like some of the other guys."

Dane paused. He'd heard that before, but for some reason, it always took him off guard. He leaned back and nodded.

"Yeah, born and raised right here in Livonia. Was an altar boy at Sacred Heart Byzantine Catholic Church."

"Oh wow!" Douglass said, his eyes widening on an impressed, joyful laugh.

"Yeah, my parents made sure that I and my two brothers and sister were there at Sacred Heart, every Sunday, and we attended the youth programs and participated in liturgies. I was one of the few kids who actually looked forward to going," Dane looked down into his lap and laughed. "I see that in you as well."

Douglass nodded. A look of peace covered his face, and he

seemed to relax. He shifted in his seat. "I'm almost there, or, I hope."

"You really are. I have the utmost confidence in you. Of course, it isn't my decision, but, I've not heard one negative thing mentioned about you. The day you are ordained will be one of the best, if not *thee best* day of your life." He put his hand on Douglass' shoulder. "And you're going to make it. I know you will. We're not all a bunch of uptight guys shaking our finger at the parishioners, Douglass. At St. Michael's, that is one of our emphases. I've been at this parish for two years, and that's one of the things I love about it. We just," Dane exhaled and slowly shook his head, overcome with truly how blessed he was to serve at the church, "treat everyone the same."

"I know, I love it at St. Michael's and I hope I will eventually be assigned to this location. But, you earned that spot. It takes a while, but that's fine, I'm game." He smiled back at Dane, optimism coating each syllable.

"It is a great church and yeah, a lot of the newer, younger guys want to serve here. And it is because of what I said—we are open. Whoever comes off the street," Dane pointed to the door, "is welcome with open arms. We don't care what they're dressed like, where they've been or what they've been doing. When they come inside this place, they are in God's house, and that is how we treat them. As for me, and the rest of us, Fr. Thomas, Fr. Kirkpatrick, Fr. Brier, all of them, we are everyday men. We have dreams, goals and plans. None of that stops us—you just keep God first. We are servants of God. You can still be hip and cool like me." Dane raised his arm, pretending to flex his muscles.

Douglass' eyes gleamed with humor.

"We are all unique. Never lose yourself, you don't have to. That is what it is all about. Like I said, and remember this, because it's important."

Douglass nodded, showing his understanding.

"We all bring different things to the table and you will, too. We are made differently, all of us, and we all have something to contribute, something new, a gift to bring to the people."

"Yes." Douglass looked to be deep in thought, mulling over Dane's words for a while. "That's what I like about you, Fr. Caruso, I mean, Dane. It's like…talking to my big brother instead of another priest. Like, when I was a kid, I looked up to the priests, but sometimes they seemed untouchable and that is why I wanted to do this, too."

Douglass straightened his posture, fired up with excitement as he turned to face Dane, his hands on his knees.

"I wanted to be approachable, and *really* get in the trenches. So many people have left the Church, left God, when it isn't the Lord they're running from. They are running from the dogma. Like, I don't want that. I just want everyone to see that we're just—"

"Regular people." Dane grinned, finishing his sentence.

"That's right! And that is why, when I first met you, the way you joked with me and a couple of the other guys, I just couldn't believe how cool and laid back you were. Man," Douglass shook his head, "you are *exactly* the kind of priest I want to be."

"Thank you, but I'm sure your own personality will shine just fine." Dane bent down to tie his shoe, trying to remain impassive although feeling pleasure at Douglass' appreciation. He liked making people feel better, but for selfish reasons. When the new guys smiled, the guys he helped train and teach, he got something from it—it put him on a high because they'd have reached a new plateau of understanding. God used him to restore their confidence, and being the instrument that helped them achieve that gave him a great sense of satisfaction. This conversation was part of Douglass' preparation for Fr. Brier to take the young man under his wing. Dane had a special way with young people; he made them want to listen. Perhaps because he was so down to earth—not being past the occasional profane word leaving his lips, or a slightly sexually construed joke used more times than not to lighten the mood during heavy discussions. It wasn't the first time he'd been the recipient of shocked looks from teens and young adults for this reason.

"Fr. Dane, I want to first, thank you for speaking to me. I know you have things to do, but you sat here and took time out of your schedule to talk to me anyway. Because of all of this, I want to let you in on something. Everyone thinks really highly of you. I should tell you what we say about you, when you're not around just so you know how important you are to all of us."

"There's no need, Douglass," Dane waved him off, "I'm just doing what—"

"No, I want you to hear what we say—what we talk about when it comes to you. I really don't think you realize the full magnitude you have on our lives."

"Okay, shoot." Dane resolved as he prepared to listen.

"Not just me, all of us, every single one of us talks about you. We know what your aim is, and you've been successful. You want to keep the humanity in the faith—let all of us be reminded that we are men in a modern world. Men of God, yes, but our hearts pumped blood just like everyone else's." he said with passion. "You never got on a high horse and you help us get over our hurdles."

"Well, thank you, Douglass." he could feel the heat, the warmth taking over his face. He undoubtedly was blushing.

"No, it's true. I know you don't want to be on anyone's pedestal."

"You are right about that. I don't. If Jesus could hang with delinquents, thieves and prostitutes, then neither I nor anyone else is too good to get eye level with a so-called outcast or derelict."

"We know some of the other priests tease you, call you Rambo."

Dane studied Douglass, a bit of confusion became him as he tried to figure out what he meant.

"You haven't heard?" Douglass said full of surprise.

"No," Dane earnestly grinned, "What does that mean?"

"Well, it's a compliment—at least we think so. It means you aren't afraid to do your job, like go to some places that others won't."

"Oh," Dane nodded in understanding and smiled. "You mean like the bad parts of town. I've been accused of throwing caution to the wind. Yeah, some say I'm crazy."

"I don't think so. You're there to do the Lord's work, you shouldn't stop dropping off meals, offering prayer to the lost."

Dane thought about what Douglass was saying. He never gave any of it a second thought. It just came naturally. All the late nights he'd spent in the bristling wind, clutching heavy boxes with canned goods, school supplies and sanitary materials. These were the moments he lived for—moments that made his vocation worthwhile. For every person that shunned him, another welcomed him with open arms. The cracked spirits poured open like the alcohol going down the throats of those who needed his help the most. He didn't hate the sinner, he hated the sin, and that was how he conducted his business.

"Thank you for the talk, Dane."

Dane nodded, stood and grabbed his dusty gray Nike duffle bag, tossing it leisurely over his shoulder.

"No problem, Douglass. Just remember, keep asking God to speak to your spirit, to keep giving you strength. Don't give in to the fears; you know the path you are on. You can do this and you've got a support system."

"Thank you, thanks so much, Fr. Dane."

Don't let them change you.

"You're more than welcome and I'll see you at the dinner tomorrow night, Douglass. We'll have a great time and if you want to get in good with Fr. Kirkpatrick, he is the toughest and—"

"Tell me about it! He scares me to death!" Douglass laughed nervously as he clutched his bag.

"Right, well, here is something to help you. Tell him you want to serve at Juniper Turns, the nursing home, and make sure you follow through. It holds a special place in his heart. I'll let him tell you why after you say it."

He winked at the man who now had renewed faith and headed outside into the sunlight...

CHAPTER TWO

R HAPSODY CARESSED THE black and white keys of the piano, as if they were the tepid flesh of a brand-new lover. Oh, how she adored the grand instrument that stood alone in the vast, majestic room, the stage still aglow with warm yellow overhead lights. The mahogany and blue velvet theater chairs were now empty, but the energy inside the grand space remained.

Like a nomad, she drifted from place to place to play, sing, and teach musical wisdom. Now, she was all alone with her paramour—coveting the seconds, savoring the stolen moments. This particular piano was exquisite: an Italian handmade Fazioli, one she'd never be able to afford on her derisory income. She relished her time at the Michigan Music Palace due to the eclectic, vibrant audiences it attracted and the seasoned, learned and fun musicians she met here. Also, she treasured this gorgeous instrument she'd come to know so well, so much it had become a beloved friend.

When she was invited to play here, she knew that, be it before or after the performance, she'd have her special time with the wide-backed man dressed in black and white. His four short legs were small but sturdy, and his voice—my oh my, he created stirrings in her that were damn near orgasmic. She stood for a moment and looked around, ensuring she was all alone before beginning another phase of the lurid harmonious affair. Adjusting her flowing midnight blue dress, she took her seat at the bench. She smiled and ran her fingers along the keys once more, reminding the wooden man that she was ready...and then, she opened her mouth and began to sing, Alicia Keys' rendition of 'New York.'

"...there are sirens all around and the streets are meeeaaan..."

She closed her eyes, disappearing inside of herself as she performed one of her most favorite melodies. Each note grew a thumping heartbeat from her being, coming alive as the song picked up speed and her fingers flew across the smooth keys. In her mind, she imagined other instruments accompanying her, and it sounded oh, so sweet. Slowly opening her eyes, she looked up at the ceiling, and in the near distance out her peripheral vision, she saw a figure, then another and another...

Her deep, soulful voice boomed, testing the acoustics in the auditorium. While she sang and let the emotions flow, she caught movement beyond the stage and realized people were pooling in the theatre and coming up the steps toward her. She'd thought the orchestra was gone for the evening, but they were still there, surrounding her as she performed. Their faces showed awe and before long, several picked up their instruments they'd carefully packed away earlier and joined her. They jumped right into the song and its strong, rhythmically addictive rifts, hitting their notes just right and letting her voice rise above the harmony with little to no effort.

When it was all said and done, Rhapsody gave a husky laugh and clapped her hands as she looked around the stage and thanked them for participating. The troop of performers acknowledged her with bright smiles. Nori, a lanky man with a purple Mohawk adorned with bright green tips, who played the violin like his life was on the line, observed her from behind gold rimmed sunglasses.

"You've got serious skills, Rhapsody. We love it when you perform with us. Your voice, the way you play," he said, shaking his head in wonder, "you make all of us your bitch, and we love every minute of it!"

This caused laughter throughout the stage.

Rhapsody grinned and winked at him as she prepared to leave. She looked wistfully at the piano, her secret lover. *Until next time…*

She blew a kiss at the small crowd then made her way down the stage steps, through the side aisle past the darkened rows of ghostly auditorium seats, away from her beloved instrument, her timber sweetheart always dressed to impress. The troop waved goodbye, and she responded in like, only, her final wave was also for the beloved piano…

DANE GAZED AT the coiling, gray incense out of the corner of his eye. He stayed in his stooped position, his knees partially numb. The quiet had become his best friend as the multitude of pirouetting hot flames flickered in the red candle holders surrounding him. He closed his eyes, swallowing deeply as a slight breeze brought in the scent of jasmine through the stingy, cracked high rafter window. The window also invited the hushed sounds of roving cars and the familiar, muted tunes of Detroit nightlife, alive and breathing with urban mystery as soon as the sun set. It was two in the morning, but in his mind, it felt more like eight o'clock. Feeling alert, he enjoyed his favorite time to pray, especially when sleep evaded him.

He'd had trouble slumbering as of late, and early morning prayer proved to be a welcomed reprieve. He ran his hands over the fabric of his tan pants until the palms warmed up, then pressed his hands together to pray before the crucified Christ carved in gold above the altar. He looked up at the crown of thorns, and the blood around the nailed hands and feet, and felt his heart swell.

"God, our Father, You divulge your omnipotence in the abundance of your compassion, transferred into the world through the wounds of your Son, and our Savior. I pray that your sacred ministers may be a clear reflection of your mercy. May they, with every expression and endeavor of their life, illuminate humankind taken over by sin, and bring it back to You, Lord, for You are love. I ask this, Father, through your Son, our Lord Jesus Christ, who subsists and governs with you in the unity of the Holy Spirit, forever and ever. Amen."

On a deep breath, Dane gripped his rosary and stood to his feet just as a knock sounded at the door in the back of the chapel. He had his suspicions as to who it could be—possibly a wayward person in need of a place to sleep, or the criminal element could have drifted close. They were no longer open late at night. Crime had migrated even toward their semi-safe corner of the city and vandals paraded the streets and fairways looking for an easy hit. No place was safe, not even local churches, mosques and synagogues.

Nevertheless, he made his way toward the entrance, opened the lens on the peephole and peered out, seeing a man that most would deem was up to nothing good. Regardless, Dane trusted his gut. He opened the hefty double doors for the man, who stood shrouded in shadows as light rain fell on him. A car with muffled music pouring out of a partially cracked passenger window drove slowly past, casting brief light on the tall, rugged form before him. Dane kept his watchful eye on him, waiting patiently as the man slowly stepped closer. The rainfall had increased, and his light hooded sweater seemed to offer little to no protection under the now torrential conditions.

Dane stood straighter, trying to get a read on the fellow. The man's dark clothing hung loosely on his frame, his lips were drawn tight, and his movements irregular and spasmodic. The man drew close with unbalanced steps and bumped Dane's shoulder as he attempted to push past him onto the red-carpeted aisle. But Dane gripped him firmly, telling him with an open expression that the man was welcome in this house of peace—yet, should there be an ulterior motive for his presence, the situation may end differently than he'd planned. The man paused as Dane dug his fingers a bit deeper into his slumped, wet shoulder.

Has he been drinking? Is he high? Does he need a place to stay tonight?

"Son, may I assist you in some way?"

The man hesitated, then lifted his face, allowing Dane to clearly see all of his features. The dark eyes did little to hide the troubled heart of their owner.

"Is...is the church open tonight?" The man fiddled with his coat sleeve, lifting it up to expose an old, brown leather strapped watch. He looked down at the shiny face. "I know it's late, but somethin' happened and this was the only place I could think of to come to." The man's voice cracked and the desperation came through rich and sharp.

"We aren't open, but is there something I can help you with?" Dane stepped back and closed the door, crossing his arms over his chest and keeping his guard up.

"Are you a priest? You dress like one ... You look young though. I need to speak to a priest."

"I'm a priest." Dane smiled, offering comfort in his expression, trying to put the stranger's mind at ease.

"Are you doin' confessions? It's been so long. I haven't been to church in years." The man removed the hood from his head, exposing dirty blond chin length hair.

"Well," Dane put his hands on his waist, "if I have you come back during our normal hours, I have a funny feeling I won't see you again. So...follow me." He stood shoulder to shoulder with the man, their steps in sync as they walked over to the confessional booth. Dane made the sign of the cross and sat down, pulling the thick red curtain closed behind him. He heard the stranger clear his throat and could see his silhouette clearly from the other side.

Father, I trust you. Please ensure my safety as I try to help this man. He is professing to needing assistance, and possibly needs more than that. Once again, I've taken a gamble, so I'd appreciate a hedge of protection during this interaction.

He knew that welcoming this man wasn't the safest choice, and once again, he played the role of rebel without a cause, but he did have a cause. This man was a child of God, no different from him, and sometimes chances had to be taken, just like now.

The stranger morphed into the penitent, and he choked out the familiar words that Dane had heard thousands of times.

"Fuh…forgive me father, for I have sinned. It's been years since I last confessed. I don't even remember how long or how."

He heard the man sigh. Strong emotions carried on the air between them, like invisible fingers grasping at their throats and hearts. A muffled cry from the stranger told Dane just how much that stray heart was bleeding.

"I don't even know where to start…"

"Start at the beginning."

"Okay. Uh, I have an anger problem."

"Mmm hmmm…tell me about how this anger problem has interrupted the productivity of your life."

Dane listened intently.

"I've been having trouble at work, at my job. The boss has been giving me trouble, wrote me up for being late. I am usually on time, most of the time early! I know I'm going to lose my job and I need this damn job, man! Sorry about the cursing, I mean, Father. No one else will hire me. I'm a felon. He hired me, I thought to help me out, but he doesn't pay me overtime, makes me work long hours and I was only two minutes late, and he docked me anyway. He knows I need this job, and he is takin' advantage. I…I waited for him outside of the building tonight. I had…a knife."

Dane remained calm. He'd heard worse, much worse, and a sense of peace had come over him, despite the realization that the man more than likely still had the sharp, serrated weapon on him. He did as he always did, careful to not show shock in his intonation.

"I see. And you were thinking of attacking him? Scaring him? What was your plan?"

"I don't even know, Father, but I know that it wouldn't

have ended too good. I thought he was alone. I saw everyone leave and just as I was gettin' ready to confront him, the back door to the warehouse swung open and the foreman, Henry, came walking out, talking about paint or something. I could hear him speaking, and it agitated me. I was in a state of shock, knocked me back into what was really happenin'. My hands were trembling. I looked at myself in the car mirror, and couldn't believe it, what I was aiming to do. What's worse, I'm *still* mad…all knotted up inside, but I know I did wrong. I don't have it in me to take another man's life, or so I thought, until today. It scares me…and I drank a bit too much tonight, to try to make it not feel as bad as it did. I wanna hurt him; I wanna hurt him real bad. I know that's wrong, but it's how I feel and now it is all trapped inside of me. I still feel rotten, and I'm mad about that, too."

"It appears to me that God gave you a second chance. That foreman came out of the door, interrupting your intentions. That is a saving grace."

"…Yeah, I think so, too. A lot of stuff has happened over the years, and I just want to ask for forgiveness. Let me see if I remember this right."

Dane clasped his hands together and waited patiently.

"For these, and all of the sins of my life, I ask for forgiveness… I'm finished, Father."

Dane briefly deliberated.

I am not going to give him two or three 'Hail Mary's.' He needs to pull his strength, to face what has been tormenting him all of these years.

"I want you to think about how you thought the warehouse was empty, and God sent out that foreman to save your life. God doesn't want you in prison, but you're *still* in prison, inside *here*." Dane tapped his temple. "Inside of your mind. You're a slave to your impulses. You are not the first person to want to hurt someone because they hurt you, but the true test of character is how we respond to things like this. It is normal to get angry, especially when there has been an injustice, but there is a lesson here that I don't want you to overlook."

"Okay, I understand, I'm listening, Father." the man responded quietly, taking it all in.

"I want you to think about the fact that your past hasn't always been a testament of your true potential, and how, despite that, you landed a job, albeit with a difficult employer who may have underhanded motivations. Never mind him— leave it to God to sort that out. You are here, in his house, after all of these years. He led you right here, Son. You are exactly where you are supposed to be—spared, saved and ready to embark on a new day, thanks to our Savior's love, mercy and grace. You are special, you are important. He made concessions for you this evening.

"Your life is more significant than *anything* your boss could do or say to you that will anger you to the point that you'd consider physically harming him, or worse, taking his life. That man may be your overseer at that warehouse, but he is not your boss in heaven—God *is,* and that is who you clock in with every morning and owe your life to. This is a brand new beginning, and your *real* Superior is asking you to not throw it away… Take this second chance, don't squander it."

"Yes…yes…you are right. It's true!"

Dane heard the man softly weeping, but he didn't dare move the partition. He had a good idea of what was happening on the other side of the panel. The flesh had lost a battle, and now the restrained spirit was exposed, shining under that dark clothing and broken heart. The man suffered and ran from the fears that dwelled inside of his mind, trying to stop him from being the very best he could be.

"So, here is what I want you to do." Dane clasped his hands together. "I want you to start attending church again. At first, just get acclimated, then get involved. It doesn't have to be *this* church, but you are more than welcome to attend here. I want you to go to your job knowing that you are in charge of your own life—that no man will cause you to do things that will cost you the very reason you were created. I want you to forgive yourself for all of your past sins, and not allow anyone to hold them over your head. Walk the path laid out for you, and the Lord will never lead you astray. Your penance is to pray for your Supervisor, every morning, while you are under his management. Do you agree to this?"

He heard the man sniff. "Yes. This confession stuff is coming back to me now."

Dane grinned as he heard the smile in the man's voice.

"I firmly resolve, with the help of thy grace, to avoid sin. Amen," the man added in a clearer, firmer tone.

"God, the father of mercies, through the death and resurrection of His Son, has reconciled the world to Himself and sent the Holy Spirit among us for the forgiveness of sins, in the name of the Father, the Son and the Holy Spirit. Amen."

Seconds later, the man stood and exited the booth. He heard the front doors open then close. Dane sighed and leaned back in the chair for several moments before walking out, blowing out the candles and locking the church front door. After a while, he made his way back to his comfortable apartment inside of the church rectory, with a smile on his face and peace in his heart…

CHAPTER THREE

*T*HROW ALL HIS *shit out… Lousy ass!*

Rhapsody lifted a large black trash bag bursting with all of her ex-boyfriend's old clothing, and hurled it as hard as she could into the smelly dumpster behind the grocery store down the street from her home. She grunted upon hearing the loud thud as it hit the trash heap, causing corrugated boxes and plastic wrap to crush under its weight. It had been months since they'd been together, so she did a bit of pre-emptive spring cleaning, deciding once and for all that Raul's artifacts were no longer welcome in her home. She'd sent a courtesy text, letting him know his time was up, and she was only met with, "Awww baby, you know we'll get back together," via voicemail… *Voicemail,* for heaven's sake!

He called immediately, per her warning, but she didn't dare answer. She'd had enough of him and his Latin bravado; he had stung her for the final damn time. She'd met the man while in California, two summers before when she'd been invited to sing at the San Diego State University, at the graduation ceremony. It was a once in a lifetime opportunity, and she'd graciously accepted. Raul had been on stage playing the piano—a walking piece of eye candy, dreamy in every sense of the word. Dark, alluring eyes, jet black smooth hair and dimples... Goodness, dimples so deep they could practically be seen from miles away as he cracked that crooked, sneaky grin he was known for.

After the graduation ceremony was over, they'd struck up a conversation and before long, the handsome, charismatic devil moved in with her...but that's *all* he did. The rest of the time, he was playing here and there at local bars, doing penny ante gigs around Detroit, and garnishing the attention of resident women—some of whom he had no qualms cheating on her with. Nevertheless, Rhapsody had been in love with the fool, until she found the text messages he'd received from three other women, all of whom seemed to believe he was their 'man'. That was the final straw. Proof of infidelity was not something she'd been willing to ignore. She'd had it. She'd been taking care of the sloth, believing his sugar-coated lies that he was a changed man, faithful, promising her he'd change his wicked ways, but Rhapsody was done living in denial, no matter how comfortable of a bed it was to pretend the truth hadn't been revealed from under the sheets.

This was the bad thing about being in her skin. Rhapsody was many things—not the least of which, a dedicated musician. She could hear a tune twice, and play it exactly chord for chord. She also had the voice that afforded her work for commercials and independent films. Some of her efforts included love songs she'd written and recorded herself for a soap opera or two. Landing a record contract was her dream, but she wouldn't sell out to get it. She'd been told to show a bit more skin, do something about her long, crazy, coiled natural hair, and wear a push-up bra for goodness sake. She refused. This was who she was. Take it or leave it. She had intelligence, quirkiness and ethics…but bad taste in men. It seemed the more inaccessible they were, the more guarded, secretive and mysterious, the more she wanted them and it had cost her dearly. Now, at the age of twenty-seven, she'd fully seen the error of her ways, and wanted a fresh start.

In this new chapter in her life was a testament, she'd swear off men. No dates, no flirting, nothing of the sort, unless she was with someone she felt comfortable with—which meant an old friend. All she wanted was to focus on her career and though it still stung a bit when she reminisced of happier times with Raul, she had to let him go. Him, and all the crap he'd left at her house, thinking she'd take him back.

But it was time for something new, and she deserved some peace.

A few hours had passed since she stood behind the grocery store tossing away memories of what once was and she decided to paint the living room wall. She stood tall with a brush, roller and an open tin of gray-blue triple gloss paint. Oh, it was on. She would capture serenity back, make it all hers, all on her own. She thought about her recent self-improvement, and it did not only her body, but her soul good. She'd also started exercising again, though she was already in great shape with a naturally high metabolism. She attended yoga classes and decided she'd return to her favorite Detroit park—Mies. Such a grand place, big enough to get lost in should she desire alone time among nature and people.

Yes, it was time to start anew, to listen to her heart. So she brushed on the paint, stroke by stroke, grinning a mile wide as she hummed, *"Goodbye Raul! And good riddance!"*

DANE WORKED THE dry, tough roast beef around in his mouth, wishing on a prayer that the mashed potatoes would soften the leathery meat, make it fit for consumption.

This is worse than expired beef jerky.

Forcing a smile, he glanced at his two brothers and sister who sat around the table with their spouses and children. The room bustled with noise and conversation.

"I can't eat this!" his six year old nephew called out as he pivoted around in his chair, his cheeks stuffed full of food and a look of disgust on his small, peach shaped face. "It tastes like rocks!"

Ahhhh, the honesty of innocence of babes.

A brief silence ensued when a whisper would have sounded like a scream, then, as if a light switch were turned on, the bustling laughter resumed, filling the dining room. Meanwhile, his mother stood silent in the dining room doorway, looking both embarrassed and amused.

"Jacob, Grandma did the best she could! I overcooked the roast tonight," she offered as people kept eating and passing plates filled with rolls and peas. The laughter soon died down, replaced by new conversations regarding sports and local gossip.

"Everything is delicious, Mom," Dane offered, causing her to point a knobby finger at him and roll her heavily hooded blue eyes. He burst out laughing, causing an avalanche of laughter once again.

"You can't lie with a straight face, you never could," she

chastised as she disappeared into the kitchen.

"So," his father began from his seat next to Dane. He shot his son a glance out the corner of his hazel eye as he carefully scooped up a spoonful of chopped baby carrots and popped them in his mouth. "How has everything been going? Haven't spoken to you in a couple of days," he said around a mouth full of food.

"Great, things are going really well. One of the guys in seminary class just got ordained by Bishop Lourdes. Really great fella, I know he'll do well. I'm heading up the youth ministries this month, and we painted a mural on Jackson Street, near the YMCA. We are doing another one next week, and a fund raiser for the new recreational center."

His father smiled and nodded as he smeared a pat of warm butter on his roll.

"Keepin' the kids out of trouble. Proactive. I like it."

He glanced up at the large oil painting of his grandfather, hanging smack dab in the middle of the wall. The elaborate gold frame caught the reflection of the low hanging chandelier, the one he'd hung for his parents a few years earlier. He quickly turned away from the sight.

"Oh, guess who is in town? Josh." Dane couldn't curb his enthusiasm as he grabbed his gold linen napkin off of his lap and used it to pat the side of his mouth clean. "We're going to have dinner together before he heads out again to Sacramento. He is back home on business."

"Well, you tell him to stop by here before he leaves, if he has time. Hell, he *better* make time! Time flies." His father stabbed a dollop of mashed potatoes with his spoon and the extra dark brown beef gravy trickled down the sides of the lumpy mound. "It seems like just yesterday that you two were out in the backyard, horsin' around with your brothers and those other guys. Now, he is some fancy medical sales director and you're a priest! Making me feel old!" He laughed.

Dane looked into the older man's face, the chewing mouth, the red cheeks, as the lovely sounds of merriment boomed through the room. Then he took another survey of the table, watching everyone talk, eat and drink. Meanwhile, Heidi, the senior Golden Retriever, made her begging rounds as she shamelessly solicited everyone who dared to cast her a glance for a morsel. Few could resist her soulful eyes.

"You're only as old as you feel, Dad, and to me," Dane raised a brow, "you look great."

His father grinned and coughed into his napkin, then glared at his son with obvious suspicion. "You are actually not being a smart ass! It must be the apocalypse!"

Dane burst out laughing and lightly tapped the table with his fingertips as he caught a glimpse of his sister wiping crumbs away from her daughter's mouth.

"No, seriously, I hope I look good as you when I turn one hundred."

They shared a brief pause then both burst out laughing. His father shook his finger at him.

"I knew it. I knew there was a punch line coming, Mr. Funny Guy."

After a few hours filled with catching up with the old man, playing portable video games with his nephew, more kisses to his forehead and several bags of unwanted leftovers shoved into his arms from his mother, Dane hugged everyone goodbye and left the house. It felt good to visit home. Moments like this helped his soul; his spirit fed off of his family's closeness, not only the family meal. He made his way to his car, which he'd parked in front of the suburban Cape Cod style house with white shingles and windows covered in thick cream curtains. As he started the car, he said a silent 'Thank You' for having such a warm, loving family, especially since he knew that so many people didn't have such a blessing, and nowhere to call their very own. Even if deep down some wires were loose, and some pain remained unresolved, he still felt grateful and positive, for he'd seen much worse in his vocational travels.

But as soon as he left the warmth of his family home, the truth inside him would come to light, and tempt him with temporary solutions. He fought the darkness, the negativity— the truth in its sinister, cold, nasty natural form. Dark secrets lived inside him, stuffed away in dank recesses of a vivid remembrance. Nothing he couldn't handle…he *had* to handle it because it wasn't a choice. Too many people were depending on him to be strong, to be the rock, the backbone—and he was, regardless of the emotional weight that threatened to break him in two…

A few days later…

DANE COULDN'T PART with his grin. The expression had completely taken over his face, broad-siding him and making his cheeks ache as they arched upward—freezing his happiness in place, for all patrons to see. He watched closely out the frosted restaurant window, gripping the table as he sat at the two-seater bar style table right at the front of the restaurant. He observed as his best friend, Josh Perkins, made his way across the street toward him, a newspaper covering his head as he dodged the raindrops and oncoming traffic. Josh pushed through the front doors, his light brown eyes darting around the place, searching for Dane.

"Josh!" Dane called out, waving to him. With a smile, Josh walked to the table and took a seat. Dane gave his friend the once over.

What in the world? He doesn't look right…

Dane looked the man directly in the eye and hugged him tightly, hardly able to hide his concern. The rain seeped through Josh's dark brown leather jacket down to his striped blue and white Polo shirt. But the man was entirely too frail, as if he'd evaporated, leaving only a shell and a memory of what he once was. He stood back and again scanned the man from head to toe. Josh's face appeared distended, the muscle tone lost. When Dane had first spotted him crossing the street, he'd hoped somehow that the downpour was distorting his friend's image through the window, that the man had simply lost a few pounds, nothing too severe. No, this was something more than the results of a low-carb or Keto diet.

The once attractive, six foot two fellow high school football star was a mere shadow of his former self. His straight, sandy brown hair clung to his forehead, and the glimmer that once shone in his mischievous golden eyes was gone. Cracked, dry lips—near bleeding—stood out in a pale face, tinged with blue. Dane braced himself for a story he didn't want to hear for this was his friend, his *brother,* the man who knew everything in the world about him…

Both men took their seats. Dane sat down slowly, his eyes still focused on the man before him.

"Nice to see you, Dane. So good to see you, bro."

Dane coughed into his fist and looked around—anywhere but at his friend. His heart sank. He considered himself a bit of an intuitive—it helped with the job, and he realized that this dinner with a long-time friend was going to hurt him to his core.

"Yes," Dane said quietly as he sat back in his seat, re-signed. "Good to see you too, Josh. Uh, you've lost some weight." He decided to take the bull by the horns and not dilly-dally any longer. Besides, it wasn't his style.

"Yeah, uh," Josh looked down, rubbing long, thin fingers across the maroon leather-bound menu, "I've wanted to speak to you about that…"

"We talk every week on the phone…*every* week," Dane said in almost a whisper. He attempted to dismiss the bubble of anger growing inside the pit of his stomach, seeping into his tone, the one that clawed at his throat—the one that threat-ened to scream, *Why in the hell didn't you tell me anything a long time ago?!*

He hadn't laid eyes on Josh in over six months, and at that time, the man was still strapping—a perfect, walking and talking bill of health. Typically, they'd see each other every three to four months. One of them would fly to meet the other, but Josh's schedule had been hectic as of late, or Dane would have a conflict in the timetable as well. Now, he looked at him and simply wondered where the truth began and the cover-up ended. He felt deceived. Turning away from that dismal sight, he tried not to judge the man before he even had a chance to talk.

"I…I know, Dane. That's why I'm here actually—to speak to you about what has been going on."

"So, there is no business trip? You aren't here for work?" Dane asked, taking a sip of his iced water. Most of the ice in his glass had melted, and he felt suddenly parched, dry, as if someone had poured flour on his tongue, thick and heavy, that would turn anything he could possibly say at that moment into gelatinous gravy.

"Well." Josh clasped his hands together nervously and shifted his body on the bar seat. "Yes, I had some business to take care of, but it could've waited. I escalated the visit."

Escalated. Like this is dire. Oh, dear God…

A waiter with choppy blond hair and a pierced eyebrow came up to the table, speaking with a pronounced lisp.

"…Broccoli and cheese and potato and bacon…and then there is the clam chowder made fresh daily…"

Outside the window, the rain fell hard like bullets onto the street. Cars and passersby moved in a blur to and fro—a symphony of activity carefully orchestrated around the rain. Yes, the rain, like tears from the heavens, tears of a God who is crying for His children. Someone paid a meter while holding a teetering dark umbrella with the word 'Paris' printed on it in bold, elegant calligraphy, while another person screamed 'Shit!' as the relentless shower drenched the poor guy from head to toe.

"Dane?" Josh called out, tearing him away from his wayward thoughts. "Are you ready to order?" The waiter and his thin friend were looking at him, waiting.

"Uh, yeah, I'll just have the Chicken Caesar salad, please." He handed his menu to the man and looked back at Josh who was now rubbing the back of his nape and staring contemplatively into space.

"Just tell me, Josh," he said. The words tumbled out, unbidden, and he waited for acknowledgement.

"Okay. Here it is." Josh sighed as he planted his hands on the table. "I have cancer. Lung cancer."

Dane looked at him for a moment while his legs got heavy, as if they'd been dipped in cement in preparation for him to be thrown off a plank into icy Michigan river waters. His heart cracked, then he tried to summon all his strength just so he could get through the darn conversation. He felt light headed, as if he may pass out right then and there, but he needed to keep his cool, not fall apart. He'd heard of people getting sick from cancer all the time, and even visited them and prayed over their beds, as well as gave them and their families words of encouragement as the end drew near. But looking at Josh was like looking at himself—like looking at a torn page from his most favorite book, and he refused to believe it could be ripped away and burned with little to no regard. After all, this particular page, and book, meant *everything* to him.

"You don't smoke anymore. You haven't smoked in years…just…God." Dane's head dropped as he stared down at his lap, feeling destroyed by the implications of Josh's admission. Barely, he held a slippery grip on his reserve and composure.

"I know. Imagine my own surprise. It all started about four months ago." Their eyes met, saying unspoken things to one another, so much more than their mouths ever would. "I was…feeling tired. Margie insisted I go to the doctor. I figured," he shrugged, "it was just the stress from work, you know, the new position. Then, I started coughing a lot, coughing up blood, and I knew I had to see someone. It…it doesn't look good, Dane. I needed to *see* you, to tell you face to face. You're my best friend. This isn't something I could email ya or tell you over the phone."

"But *four* months, man? You've known all this time." Dane tempered himself, the screaming in his head becoming so loud, he had to tell it to shut up. It would be so easy to go off, to point a finger at Josh and let him have it for his blatant disregard, but it wouldn't change anything, so why even bother?

"No, I was in treatment, not believing what was happening to me. It took me a while to even fully accept the diagnosis. I wanted to tell you, 'Hey man! I beat cancer.'" He laughed; a sad, sorry laugh that left his mouth sounding like a sickly little white ghost then disappeared into thin air. "But I know now that won't happen. I am here against doctor's orders. I haven't quit my job, either." He sighed. "I tried to fight but—"

"Please, don't." Dane put his hand up. "We can't afford to think that way, to just give up. With God all things are possible, Josh. The body and mind, when working in agreement, can do some phenomenal things, but if you ever want to see those possibilities, you must keep fighting!" Dane caught the glances from people nearby as his voice rose. He didn't care; his heart had accepted the words, and now he just wanted to fix the problem, make it right. He was the rock...he had to make it all go away, make it all right. Reaching across the pub table, he tightly grasped Josh's wrist.

"Dane, I need you to—"

"We will pray right here, right now, we will ask for—"

"Dane, damn it!" Josh snatched his hand away angrily, his voice, though weakened, ragged with irritation and hoarse undertones. "Don't you think I've been praying?!"

He hastily turned away and stared at the people milling about, eating, enjoying themselves...carefree. The laughter and chatter seemed to mock the somber mood hanging over them, and the invisible murderer called grief went unnoticed as it slinked about, under the radar, delivering packages of pulsating pain.

That pain was beginning to eat him alive, right there front and center, starting with his bleeding heart. Josh's eyes welled with moisture and tears cascaded down his sunken cheeks. He was angry with God—Dane was familiar with the look. So many that stood before him during mass had the same mask on. One of disappointment and unbelievable resentment that drove them to the depths of hatred for the Heavenly Father, for leaving them in a world that was destroying them, among people who simply didn't give a damn.

"I'm going to pray for you, because I know God can heal you," Dane said calmly as their food arrived. He nodded at the waiter, clasped his hands and turned back to his friend, who was now slumped in his chair, his arms loosely by his side, as if his tenacity and will to live had melted right then and there like a prayer candle burned down to its pitiful blackened wick.

"You can pray all you want," Josh said gruffly as he looked down at his plate. "It won't change anything, Dane." He shook his head, his tone still fueled with fury, but Dane knew it wasn't anger toward *him;* but toward God and the world, in general. Josh admitted he was exhausted from fighting the tormenting emotions, the back-to-back doctor appointments and everything else that this downward spiral to hell entailed.

"This is the reality, Dane. Take it or leave it. I'm in stage 3B, the chemo and radiation is making me even sicker! I am going to die from this. It could be tonight, it could be months from now, but I'm going to die sooner than I'd like. I've gotten past the shock, I'm angry as hell, but," he gulped, "I've accepted it. My affairs are in order," he said matter-of-factly before coughing harshly into his napkin. His face reddened from the exertion and pain that twisted his expression with each outburst.

"God is stronger than cancer."

Josh rolled his eyes dramatically.

"You've always seen the glass half full, Dane. You were the class clown, the calm guy all rolled into one. You kept order in our group of misfits." He managed a genuine smile. "But I'm sorry, Dane, that won't change anything this time. No jokes will make this disease run away from my body. No prayers, resilience, none of that will change one…damn…thing. I had to accept it, so I can live the little bit of life I have left in peace. I just…I just want to enjoy this time with my family and friends…that's why I'm here."

"Well, you do what you want," Dane offered coolly. "I'm trusting in God, Josh. It isn't over until it's over. You didn't believe you'd ever get the job you have now—you got it. You didn't believe Margie would agree to marry you—she did. You didn't think your sister would survive that car accident, but she did. I don't know what it's like to be in your shoes and I don't pretend to know, but I do know that God heals and I believe that with all my being. God believes in *you*, even when you have all but given up, and when God has faith in us, then that is enough."

Josh gave a weak smile and nodded as he picked at his plate full of creamy mashed potatoes, steamed broccoli and grilled lime chicken. Dane cast him a reassuring glance, then bowed his head and prayed over their food. He finished the prayer, but kept his eyes closed for a few moments as he deliberated about what had transpired. He could feel Josh watching him. He knew the man probably hadn't prayed in weeks and had all but waved the white flag on his life having nothing else to say to God, except a certain four letter word.

Josh, you may have given up, but I haven't. I can't lose you. God wouldn't let that happen right now. It's not your time to go. Margie just had another baby...you got promoted. You're my best friend, the only person besides my family who didn't treat me like a freak when I became a priest. The only person who I could tell anything to, the only one who truly understands me. No, this is far from over. I need you, bro...

CHAPTER FOUR

Two weeks later...

T HE DUCKS FLUFFED their downy black feathers, making
  sudden ripples in the placid lake surface, disturbing the
green moss around them. Tiny white fish swam below them,
searching for the perfect meal. Blues and pinks streaked across
the sky, blending together like flowing home-spun salt water
taffy. The air smelled of summer, teasing his senses with the
pending season, giving a preview of what was to come. Dane
looked over to his right, smiling at an elderly couple holding
hands, their slow bodies moving as one. Wrapped in a ribbed,
long white sweater, her thin, shoulder length silver hair
blowing freely in the breeze, the woman held on to her aging
husband's arm, smiling faintly out at the flowing freshwater.
Her face embodied peace, and an appreciation for every
moment they had together. Such a beautiful sight, like a
painting on Nature's wall that fit seamlessly into the gorgeous
day. Dane needed the reprieve, and he loved Mies Park, which

was the picture-perfect setting to unwind and release.

The huge area boasted scenic sights, long picturesque bike trails, discrete picnic areas and plenty of space for children and lovers to play. Sometimes he'd come, sit on his favorite bench under an old oak tree and read his Bible or write out his sermon. Other times, he'd just daydream. Every day here he found something extraordinary, beautiful or whimsical to sink one or more of his five senses into—something that moved his soul and spirit, making them slow dance to the natural music of the gifted day. Today, he came to escape his own worries.

Josh had been admitted into the hospital and was sliding further down into a dark chasm, which caused grief to all that loved him. Since their dinner, Dane had kept in constant contact with his ill friend on a daily basis, trying to not become a nuisance, but he was driven to hear the man's voice. The more time passed, the weaker Josh seemed. Dane tried to offer words of encouragement, refusing to admit that he, too, sometimes felt angry with God about the recent turn of events. He hung on to his optimism, hoping that this was truly one of those moments when things grew increasingly gloomier before bursting like a star storm of energy and bestowing a blessing in the nick of time.

Dane sat back on the bench, legs slightly parted, and crossed his arms over his chest as he drifted into his memories. He was briefly distracted when one of the priests from his parish walked past in the near distance.

"Hi, Dane!" Fr. Sinclair called out, waving.

"Hey, Stewart!" Dane waved and forced a grin, though he wasn't in a smiling mood, and the man kept on his way.

Dane could see Josh clearly in his mind—the two of them cutting across the high-school field, laughing and goofing off during football practice, only to be reprimanded again and again. They were bad influences on each other, but couldn't help themselves and were hitched at the hip. Twin souls, the best of friends, more like brothers. It started in the third grade, and never stopped. You couldn't find one without the other; their lives were intertwined and they'd experienced so much together.

He remembered how devastated Josh had been after his parents divorced but soon after, a new exciting chapter arrived in his life, saving him from his own hopelessness. His first love, Marilyn Lopez blew the lid off of the seemingly quiet, suburban life the two young men had grown accustomed to. The gorgeous Latina siren from Massachusetts moved to Lavonia from Canada with her father. She, too, was a product of divorced parents and lent Josh an ear, as well as her heart.

The new girl with waist length jet black hair, alluring green eyes and a Spanish accent made the boys' toes curl. All the junior guys wanted a chance at her, and Dane and Josh played a bit of rivalry to get her attention, but Dane could see that Josh *really* dug her, so he stepped back and let it all play out. After a while, they both had steady girlfriends and were living it up—football, dates, parties. Life was a blast. But then, Marilyn was gone, just as quickly as she'd arrived. She moved away after less than a year, when her father was transferred to managerial job in New Mexico.

Josh had tried to play it cool, but inside the poor guy was fading. Despite Dane's support, he did what anyone would do for a guy that was dumped by the girl he'd lost his virginity to—drown him in a bottle of illegally acquired booze. Dane quickly obtained a fake I.D. and purchased them both some beers to get them both completely plastered the night she pulled out of her driveway for the final time. He nonchalantly told him to forget about her, that she wasn't worth it, but they were just words, something to pacify the deep crater inside his best friend's fractured heart.

Josh had been there for Dane, too. Though Dane's childhood had been by all outward appearances good—damn near great—with a mom at all her children's games and events, a father who showed up to open houses and PTA meetings and played ball with his boys in the backyard. Yet, there were still *things*, feelings...those deep, dark nightmares he'd suppressed and hadn't told a soul about...except for Josh. The ones that caused him to sneak and drink in back of the bleachers, nursing his woes away until the morning, after which he'd feel a sense of shame that paled in comparison to his throbbing hangover. He wrestled with the newfound alcohol addiction, fought it whenever the ugliness came to the light. He did eventually win that daunting battle, stopped altogether, but the nasty, sticky crap that clogged his heart was still there in the morning, and the morning after that...

It ate at him so badly, he'd lock himself in his room, pretending to be doing homework when in fact he was writing angry words across his math class notebook and listening to Black Sabbath on his old portable CD player, the headphones blasting so loudly that if the entire house collapsed, he wouldn't have heard it or gave a damn. His mother discovered the CDs, worn and scratched with repeated wear, and threw them out, but the twisted lyrics still danced in his sordid, tortured mind for months, even years later. He couldn't talk to her, to the woman with unfaltering faith who insisted that nothing unpleasant be discussed in her home, despite her role in the whole ordeal.

Ugly emotions? Who had them? Surely not her sons and daughter and especially not Dane, her coveted 'human heirloom' child that was the spitting image of his grandfather. The man was even too good for a golden pedestal; she'd declared him a saint.

Dane was the only one of his siblings to have a widow's peak. He was also the only one to have dark sable hair that glowed in shades of gold, russet and tawny under bright light—an unusual shade, which many women seemed to take notice of with him, as with his grandfather. It was one of the things he recalled—the women and his mother going on and on about his mysteriously romantic looks…and his eyes—so blue, they said, you could swim in their vastness and declare them ocean-rich. And those peepers told stories, said so much, crystal clear, forcing him to at times, not look life in the eye. Then, there was the matter of his tan; people were certain he'd been going to the tanning booth, baking himself to an ochre crisp. Jokes from even his closest associates never ceased. But no, it was all due to the strong Southern Italian blood surging through his veins.

All in all, his mother said he appeared honest, and had actor good looks—but an even more attractive heart. She wanted him to be a person of moral character, an example of discipline, just like her very own father—a man held in high regard who, according to her, had run a strict but loving Catholic home.

Dane's thoughts drifted back to the here and now. Family was important, yet in the face of disease, illness and frailty, what did it matter? Fate showed neither allegiance nor concern in either direction and laughed at pity, turning away in disgust from the emotional display. Josh had a family—a wife, two twin daughters, Isabella and Abigail, and a newborn son, Leo—and now they all suffered from the cruelty of their father's failing body and spirit's lost resolve.

Dane gripped his jacket and pulled it closed as the breeze picked up, giving him a chill. Sighing, he leaned forward, rocking his body, and stared down at the grass beneath his white and navy Reeboks. In the distance, a child laughed, and intelligible words floated on the air.

Two men jogged past, their feet pounding the pavement as they each clutched their cellphone. After a few more moments, he convinced himself to stand, walk back to his hail beaten black Nissan Altima, go get a bite to eat, then head back to the rectory. As he made his slow steps toward the parked vehicle, still drowning in isolated, painful thoughts of his ailing friend, he caught an image out of the corner of his eye. Stopping, he watched the woman bend slightly as she stretched. Her elegant swanlike neck arched as she moved gently in the breeze, her form kissed by rays of sunlight. It seemed almost as if the sun had slowed down from setting, just to get a few more seconds with her. She'd wrapped her hair in thickly wound black fabric, and suddenly he wanted to know what those tresses looked like. Wearing a black leotard, she moved with grace, like poetry in motion.

As if aware of his presence, she slowly turned toward him, her arms outstretched as if she were a ballerina frozen in time. Their eyes locked. Caught, he simply offered a smile and gentle wave. She smiled back, then continued with her calisthenics. He sighed, shoved his hands in his pockets and proceeded on his way, hoping he could shake the nasty mood he was in—but seeing the loving, elderly couple and the beautiful woman had at least given his heart a break from the recent emotional stab wounds that refused to heal...

CHAPTER FIVE

"WELL, THAT IS just unbelievable." Daisy scoffed as she crossed her long, skinny, legs and blew her reddened nose. She shot an angry sky blue glare at her brother, Dane, causing him to grimace and turn away from her before he said something he may regret. Everyone sat or stood huddled close together in the stifling lawyer's office. Attorney Dawson licked his finger tip and nonchalantly turned the next page in the stack of papers, peering at the Caruso family from over his thin-framed dark glasses.

"Now." The older man with graying temples cleared his throat as the stuffy dust-filled place made Dane's nose itch. "Mr. Rossi made it plain as day about this. He left the bulk of his money to his grandson, Fr. Dane Caruso, in hopes that it would be used for the church." Coughing, he glanced around then turned back to the papers.

"Why are we just now hearing about this? The man has been dead for almost two years," Daisy asked, her tone pockmarked with jealousy and a dollop of animosity. She looked around the room, more than likely searching for support. Her gaze settled on Dane, who, however, couldn't humor her.

He was still in shock himself, unable to utter so much as a word. But his heart swelled with warmth as he contemplated what the church could do with dough like that…

$4,237,374.78

My God!

Fact of the matter was, Grandpa Rossi was miserly. According to family rumor and speculation, the man always claimed to be destitute, especially after his wife, Angelina, Dane's grandmother, had passed away long before he'd been born. The money was locked away in Italy, away from curious eyes and greedy hands, to ensure that the nursing home didn't get their claws on it and no fights would be had. A devout Catholic, he proved to be an astute yet slightly paranoid businessman that owned several dry cleaning stores, large plots of land for building real estate in prestigious suburban areas across the country, a grand rental house in Italy and two thriving foreign luxury pre-owned car dealerships, which he always pretended were on their way under. In reality, he'd made money while others went broke and had become a self-made millionaire, without anyone being the wiser. When his grandson had entered the seminary, the man accused of rarely showing a grin, smiled so much it may have hurt.

Dane had an agreeable relationship with his grandfather, but nothing, in his mind that warranted such a gift. Matter of fact, they rarely spoke apart from sharing pleasantries. Despite him being a spitting image of the man, they seemed to share little in common. As the shock mounted, he began to plan out things in his mind…

I can get Josh the best treatments in the world now! I'll fly him wherever he needs to go, get the best doctors and medicines around! Someone will cure him; someone out there knows how to stop this!

The church can really use this money. It's too small to accommodate everyone that attends now. The food pantries, my charities…what a blessing! We can add on, without worry of the financial burden, and build the daycare center. And, I can help other churches, too, Catholic churches all around the country…around the world.

Daisy does need money for the kids. Her husband's job doesn't pay enough. I'll help…no need for the children to suffer because they keep making bad choices…

Time to pay off Mom and Dad's loans…the medical bills and the house refinancing, get that all out of the way…I can get a new car, mine is always in the shop. There are so many people I can help with this…

"So, you see, he did let me know about the money, but it took this long for me to find the correct paperwork and get permission to have access to the corroborating documents and accounts. He had not provided it all before it was too late. He left the money to Dane, your son here, Mrs. Caruso, versus directly to the Church, because he wanted his grandson to actually manage it, to ensure it was utilized in the proper manner. I've been hassling with two banks in Europe—Rome was the worst." Attorney Dawson sighed and shook his long head. "And I finally have the information as well as the check."

Attorney Dawson cleared his throat again and shuffled through an envelope. He stood from behind his desk and handed a cut check to Dane. Daisy's glare hit the passing piece of pale yellow paper like a ton of bricks and she made no attempt to hide her review of the dollars and cents. Dane frowned at her, and snatched it past her, his patience running thin. Settling back in his seat, he smiled and shook his head in disbelief.

"Wow...this is...this is just amazing." He stared at the check, then looked over his shoulder at his parents, noting the smiles on their faces and a sheen over his mother's eyes. His two brothers, Joseph and Anthony sat straight-faced, devoid of much outward emotion. Dane got along pretty well with all of his siblings overall; regardless, he expected everyone to behave just as they were, after receiving such an announcement. Joseph, the eldest, was quiet and not easily ruffled though inside he knew a least at small smattering of suspicion swarmed. Still, Joseph wouldn't make a fuss. He was the eldest, had sometimes acted like a surrogate father to them. Like Dane, he tended to bury his emotions, and this was one of those times when he'd never allow his true thoughts to color his words.

Anthony, on the other hand, was a real card. Shorter than Joseph and Dane, and stocky, he looked like a stunted version of their father and behaved in a similar fashion—trivial, a bit immature, but with a heart of gold. Although only ten months older than Dane, he acted like the youngest of the quartet. Then there was Dane, the youngest son, nicknamed 'The rebel with a conscience', as well as, 'Old Soul'. Then, finally, the true baby of the family, Daisy, who'd been spoiled rotten since birth and never grew out of a sense of entitlement. Nevertheless, her heart was good under the icy exterior; she didn't wish ill will toward others, so Dane oftentimes dismissed her silly antics.

"Do any of you have questions?" the lawyer asked, his

bottom lip slightly poked out as he pivoted in his squeaky leather seat, his hands steepled.

"Well, this is, hmm…" Dane's father stood behind his eldest son's chair, gripping the headrest. "We actually suspected this, you know, money squirreled away somewhere, so to me and Maria, it really was no surprise. I am a little shocked about it being left to Dane, seeing as my father-in-law never—"

"Joseph." Maria shot him a look, a *begging* look, asking him to stop in his tracks. Everyone knew any unkind words spoken about her deceased, glorified father would render the one who articulated the ghastly words a scarlet letter and when mom was angry, well, one may as well pack one's bags and move on.

"Yes, mmmm," Dane's dad rubbed his chin. "Her father was a good man and…I'm sure that he had respectable reasons for doing what he has done. It…it is just a bit surprising is all." And that was how the now wise man, better known as 'Dad', left it.

"Well," Maria offered, brandishing a stiff smile after a long sigh as she cast a glance toward Dane. "My father was very pleased when Dane became a priest. My father's first love was the church…it makes *perfect* sense to me." Ending on a chipper tone, her gaze taut and unyielding, she looked around the room at her startled children.

No one said another word; they all just rolled in their respective elation, envy, confusion or turmoil as the heavy seconds passed, turning into minutes until they went their separate ways. Dane, of course, headed straight to the bank asking to speak to the branch manager and to immediately hire a financial advisor…

DANE LIT THREE more candles, thanking God for answering his prayers.

In the last couple of weeks, he'd effectively paid off all of his parents' outstanding bills, as well as given them spending money, upon the condition that they finally take the Caribbean cruise that they'd dreamed of since he and his siblings were children. Then, he wrote Joseph a nice, big check and mailed it privately, certain the man would refuse it if he handed the cash in person. Dane understood those unpaid medical student loans from years past would not pay themselves back, and they were mounting with staggering interest.

Joseph was a dentist, but struggling financially due to many of his patients losing their homes in recent years. And surely, the homeless are less inclined to get their six month cleanings, crowns, braces or root canals when they are simply trying to find a place to lay their head. He had a wife and children to take care of as well, but Joseph struggled with pride, always trying to be the beholden big brother who never had any struggles or worries.

For his part, Anthony was comfortable, but he too had dreams. Dane slid him some cash in hopes he'd spend it wisely, but didn't have high expectations. Anthony was a bit reckless and a dreamer, but at least he'd be happy for the time being. Then there was Daisy, smiling sweetly in her little yellow 1960's style dress with the tailored, cinched waist, like a doll perched on a shelf, only she was sitting in a plush, snow white chair, her hand out and her blue eyes lit up with emerald greed. Dane looked down at her, his lips twisting as he minced his words. The woman had a way of testing him, but he never let her see him sweat. He'd fought telling her a thing or two almost every day of their existence, and sometimes, he would succumb and simply let her have it—but she was his baby sister, and he knew she sometimes couldn't help herself.

He'd called her to stop by their parents' house for her share. In what seemed like moments, she was there, glammed up, as if she were going to receive a much anticipated Grammy for her leading role as 'Queen Pain in the Rear.' Regardless, the money was going for much needed repairs for her home, and for a better quality of life for his nieces and nephews—all worth it in Dane's book.

Plans to speak to a contractor regarding expanding the church were now underway, and the last piece of the financial windfall puzzle needed to be laid. The most important, the most crucial, but Josh repeatedly refused to be flown any-where, to be seen by anyone new, or to receive any additional treatment. Dane had planned to take things into his own hands, and requested two weeks off from the parish, which was promptly granted by Fr. Kirkpatrick after the recent events.

He'd fly to San Diego, and even if he had to drag Josh kicking and screaming, the deed would be done. He'd get that man in front of one of the best medical oncologists in the entire nation, and the doctor's highly skilled team. He'd already spoken extensively to one of the top pulmonologists and lung surgeons in the world, and though Josh's prognosis was still grim, they wanted a look at him, to possibly extend his life and give him more comfort. He was sure the money didn't hurt, made them more resolved to helping the ailing Josh, but he didn't care what the motivation was—this way, he could save the world, at least *his* world, thus, save himself. Full of optimism, he finally had an emotional moment's rest. He couldn't thank God enough for opening this door for him and he planned to walk right on through, with his chin up and pep in his step…

Several weeks later…

"I'LL DO AS I please." Josh flicked the hot amber ashes in the ashtray and crossed thin, pale ankles on the black ottoman, his hospital gown exposing part of his leg. Dane snatched the cigarette from his grasp.

"Hey!" Josh cracked a smile and rolled his eyes, then let his head fall back onto the chair as they waited for the doctor to come back into the small, stark white room. Dane was running on pure adrenaline. After three weeks of testing, Josh's health had further declined, yet he seemed to have peace about him. Dane had called Fr. Kirkpatrick, explaining he needed more time, and it was granted. He offered apologies to his parishioners via email and to a few that had depended on him for council via phone and Zoom meetings, but this simply couldn't wait. He crossed his arms and paced, still offering a smile, but inside, his stomach turned, flipped and kicked as his nerves tried to wrestle his resolve, twiddle it down to the nub. Meanwhile, Josh sat there peacefully, seeming fully relaxed, as the time ticked away.

"Would you be still, please?" Josh smiled, shooting him a lazy glance. "Geesh Dane, you're making me nervous with all that prancing and dancing around."

Just then, the door swung open and the doctor entered, holding a small tablet and a folder. He closed the door behind him and observed the computerized information before approaching his patient. He looked up at Dane, his eyes telling him what his mouth hadn't yet.

"I'm going to be frank, Mr. Leonard, you—"

"I'd prefer you to be Dr. Abraham. Don't care much for Frank," Josh joked, causing a stiff smile from the doctor and a stern grimace from Dane.

"You're supposed to be the best!" Dane yelled, losing control, as if he were having an out of body experience. He made a threatening step toward the doctor, exploding into a million fragments of his former self.

"Fr. Caruso, please calm down. I do thank you for—"

"No!"

"Dane, stop it." Josh waved his hand at him, causing Dane to stop in his tracks. Slumping down in a chair beside Josh, he stared at the wall—the blank wall where nothing began and nothing ended.

"I'm afraid, Mr. Leonard, there isn't much we can do. I agree with the original diagnosis of your doctor, uh," he scrolled through his tablet, "Dr. Turner in San Diego. I believe, based on the aggressive progression, you have approximately three months. I am very sorry."

"You're sorry! That's all you can say? You're sorry?!"

"Dane!" Josh called out, holding his chest.

"You're damn right you're sorry!" Dane snatched his jacket and, bumping the doctor aggressively in the shoulder; he stormed out of the room and paddled up the long hall, passing people in a blur. He ran away as far as he could but the emotions kept chasing him, harassing him, taunting him, no matter which way he turned. Soon, he found himself in a waiting room, in an area of the huge hospital he'd never seen before. He wasn't even sure how'd he arrived there. Gripping his hair with both fists, he turned in circles, round and around, his gut knotted like rope. He wanted to cuss, he wanted to scream, and he wanted to pound something into oblivion. He wouldn't mind a drink, or four, probably more.

He wouldn't mind cracking Heaven open, shoving his head through the damned clouds and demanding an explanation— in his fury, he no longer held back. Eyes blurred with hot tears, he raced out of the waiting room, bypassed the elevator and hot tailed it down seven flights of steps, as if competing in the Olympics. Soon he burst through the doors into the open air, tumbling forward, and landing on his knees in a praying position. The irony…

He looked around. To his right were several parked ambulances and to his left was a man smoking a cigarette, the guy's eyes shifty and his body motionless. Getting to his feet, Dane headed around a side area toward two benches sitting near an overstuffed, rancid trashcan filled to the brim, spilling fourth with rotting fast food, crushed aluminum soda cans and sandwich wrappers. He stood there, uncertain, trying to catch his breath—the little he had left.

"You alright there, buddy?" the man finally asked as he blew copious smoke out the side of his crooked mouth.

"Put that crap out…it'll kill you," was all Dane could muster as the tears flowed and his heart gave out.

The man offered a slight smile. "I know…" He took another drag and disappeared, leaving Dane to his own devices, more than likely not in the mood for a judgmental, holier-than-thou conversation.

But Dane didn't feel holy at all; he felt like raising hell. However, as soon as he came back to his senses, he finally realized his place was back by his friend's side. Summoning some form of control, he re-entered the hospital and made his way back to Josh.

Josh looked eerily calm while a male nurse explained his discharge instructions and handed him a pain medication prescription. He offered Dane a smile, one brimming with sincerity. A special smile that offered condolences on his pending death, gave Dane his deepest sympathies, as if Dane were the one dying, not he. For Dane was the one who was struggling, having problems letting go. He grappled reality to the ground and expecting that when they both rose from the dust, a brand new 'truth' would greet him with a promise to be different, to be better, and create 'make-believe' just this once. Just as Josh had told him over dinner, and numerous times over the phone, he'd accepted his destiny and now Dane knew without a shadow of a doubt, his best friend truly meant it.

Nothing else was left now but for Dane to accept it, too...

CHAPTER SIX

"HELLO, HENRY!" DANE waved to a priest in his parish. Fr. Daniel nodded and waved back as he made his trek across a small clearing through the freshly cut grass.

He'd seen quite a few of his fellow priests lately while sitting and relaxing, jogging or daydreaming on the lawn with a book and packed lunch. He reckoned they'd been around the entire time, but he had always considered the park his special place, to be guarded from the world. Now that it was getting warmer, people were coming out of the confines of their dwellings to enjoy nature and decompress. He leisurely walked on the bike trail he'd crossed a hundred times before, taking in his surroundings and feeling a sense of tranquility.

"What is that?"

Dane stopped dead in his tracks trying to figure out the source of the humming that seemed louder as the moments passed. The musical, feminine lilt warmed his heart. So low, soothing, earthy, and real. Soon, the hum turned into words, lyrics floating past his ears and tantalizing him with a rhythm that resonated inside of his heart. Somehow, it seemed familiar, like when one hears the very end of a song on the radio, but in other ways, it seemed brand new to his ears. People began to walk briskly as the rain started to fall, but he was stuck, still searching for her who kept singing as if the sun still shone and there wasn't a cloud in the sky. He gripped his gray sweatshirt hoodie, covering his hair as it came down even harder—then there she was, her back turned. She sang louder, her hair again wrapped up, high to the sky like Erykah Badu's, circa 2000.

"Jesus…what a beautiful voice," he said, caught in a trance as she slowly glided back and forth, as if reaching for angels. "She sure sings like one…" A lump formed suddenly in his throat, and he rubbed his swollen eyes. He hadn't slept in days, but he strained with all of his might to focus on her as she exercised, and her tune soon turned back into a low hum. She seemed unmoved by the rain, moving, twirling and prancing about playfully. She owned the space, she was the queen of serenity, she was the wife of 'not a care in the world'—she had papers on it. He wanted to know what it felt like again. He wanted a taste of the power and peace she had…

RHAPSODY GLANCED AT the clock above her living room television, not believing the time. She blinked, rubbed her eyes and struggled amongst the overstuffed throw pillows on the couch, trying to free herself from the cocoon of their softness that surrounded her form. It was two in the morning, and she'd fallen asleep there yet once again. The television DVR buzzed as her favorite television programs were taped, reminding her she needed some down-time. She had been too busy and tired as of late, but she promised herself she'd indulge in a 'stay-cation' as soon as possible. Rhapsody got to her feet. She stood and stretched her stiff body in need of the comforts of her Queen sized bed, not the broken-in-couch she'd made into a cot one time too many. Yawning loudly, she made her way out of the room, down the short hall and into her bedroom. As she slid under the sheets, she closed her eyes, but not for long.

That's right!

She popped back up, flinging the sheets off of her in haste. Grabbing a pen and paper out of her nightstand drawer, she jotted down song lyrics that had been dancing in her head for weeks. She felt inspired, and she'd dreamed of kelly green blades of grass, chirping birds and storm clouds that threatened to ruin it all. The lyrics kept coming, all streaming from her recent trysts at Mies Park. She reminisced as the words continued to take over, pouring onto the paper.

The people watching in the park while she exercised her body and vocal chords proved to be quite entertaining, but more than anything, she had some new eye candy and she was more than happy to take an indulgent nibble or two. What began as a secret glance here and there, escalated into curiosity. The man was alluring. He had a quiet strength about him, yet, he seemed troubled, regardless of the kind smile that would crease his face when she'd glance his way. Poems, song lyrics, thoughts and ideas raced inside of her based on her fleeting interactions with the guy. They'd never spoken a word, but she felt as if they'd been communicating for weeks…

She hated to admit it to herself as her pen moved hastily across the dark blue line in her binder, scribbling verses with nimble fingers, but he'd caught her attention alright.

Hell, if he is my muse for a new song, so be it...

She grinned as she continued to write, wondering where it would all end, but one thing was for certain before the end of that summer, she wanted the man to say *something* to her. Anything.

Yes, she'd sworn off men, but hey, this was innocent. She saw nothing wrong with admiring the scenery. Besides, just because she wasn't buying didn't mean she couldn't window shop and from her vantage point, he showcased an award-winning display of charismatic bling that she simply couldn't resist...

Three weeks later...

BEFORE HE'D EVEN had a moment to catch up and distract himself with overdue duties, Dane found himself in the midst of troubled waters, standing in the church that he and Josh's family attended when they were mere children. Where their families sat together, interwoven like carpet fibers, on the pews. Only this time, they weren't altar boys anymore...but Dane was standing at the altar nevertheless. He attempted to feel nothing, so he could get through the day...the day that had a sun and a moon, but he felt neither familiarity nor peace with this basic fact.

He put on a strong face and even stronger performance, in typical Dane fashion. Patting backs, smiling, offering hugs and kind words. He simply went through the motions. Margie dabbed at her eyes with an ivory, balled up Kleenex as the priest spoke, her children huddled around her and the church filled to the brim with family, co-workers and friends as the celebration of the Eucharist continued around the altar table. Josh knew so many people, and they'd all gathered to pay their respects and say one final good-bye to him.

Dane knew when he'd left Josh in his home, before returning several weeks prior after the bad news, that it would be the last time. He'd talked to him the morning he died. The man could barely speak, but he offered one sentence to Dane that was now embedded in his mind:

"Remember, it is better to have loved and lost, than never have loved at all, and I had that, buddy…my family, friends, everyone. Thank you."

Dane clasped his hands together, his white robe with gold embroidery flowing over his arms. He heard bits and pieces of the priest's words through the fog in his mind. Litanies and tiny tidbits as the Priest spoke the prayers and all-too-familiar words…

"…Jesus redeems us…the body and blood of Christ…The blessed mother Mary and her divine son…"

He crawled in his own skin, itching to say something, to protest. Such a strange sensation. He felt out of control. He glanced momentarily out of a large stained glass window, a colorful scene of the Virgin Mary holding her newborn son, Jesus Christ. The rainbow light filtered through, distorting passing cars, while he felt imprisoned inside of his own heart. He wanted to escape, to get away from Josh's casket so he could scream in private, but he kept it all in, bottled like wine to age perfectly, along with all of his other feelings from years gone past that had fermented.

The funeral waged on, each moment drawn out like damnation, an unwelcome eternity—and they moved outside to the cemetery.

"O God, by whose mercy the souls of the faithful find rest;

mercifully grant forgiveness of their sins to Thy servants and handmaids, and to all here and elsewhere who rest in Christ: that being freed from all sins, they may rejoice with Thee for evermore. Through the same our Lord," Dane said as Josh's casket was lowered into the ground.

He spoke in subdued tones, pleasant and calm, as though giving a five-day weather forecast. He'd attended and presided over thousands of funerals and prayed for all involved. Now, he needed some alone time but instead he was bombarded with family and old high-school friends, crying, hugging and clinging to one another, sometimes falling to pieces in his arms. He provided comfort for hours on end, for everyone but himself. In fact, no one even asked him how he was holding up. He didn't realize it until right at that moment. Afterall, everyone knew that he and Josh were best friends.

God, please…I need to get away. I need you to give me some solace, some peace. I've been begging you… Tell me where to go, where I can regroup and speak to you and get through this. Most of all, tell me how I can forgive you for taking him away from me—my very best friend?

THE DUSK HAD given birth to willowy purple streaks stretched across the Michigan sky while the mellow orange sunset disappeared behind slow moving cottony clouds. Dane leaned back on the park bench and sighed, his eyes closing momentarily as he gathered his thoughts. There were no ducks on the lake today, only light undulations from the wind.

He missed the ducks. They were a nice focal point when the pressure became too much. Every now and again, he'd see a swan or two, but he hadn't seen, except for the occasional solo one, in weeks. They were alone, just like him.

He'd jogged, worked out so much at the gym he almost passed out, threw himself into his work—even making over two-hundred sandwiches singlehandedly to take to the homeless shelter the night before. But it still didn't completely quiet the nagging voices, the hidden secrets and the resentment. The heavy chain-wrapped bitterness that he admitted in prayer remained deep inside of him, festering, growing stronger instead of waning as time promised to do. All of those ugly enigmas from the past died with Josh. Dane, exposed them, dug them up from the dank soil he'd buried them in so long ago. Perhaps they refused to stay in the grave with the man and clawed their way out, scrounging and fighting, kicking up freshly unearthed mud. They made themselves known, these secrets. Yes…secrets.

The ones that caused him to do things that he said he was ashamed of after he'd accepted his calling into the priesthood. Josh was there, picking up the pieces, making it right. He'd discarded the empty wine and beer bottles, cleared away the marijuana debris and chocked the pills. Dane had held on to the lie: that he'd hurt himself during a football scrimmage and needed help because his back was a twisted wreck. He soon discovered that alcohol and uppers made a surprisingly interesting cocktail, one that promised sweet relief from the incubuses that at times kept him up at night.

These were complicated feelings, a thorny place to dwell. Dane knew full well what his problem was. It wasn't only that he'd lost his best friend and sounding board—he'd lost his own *personal* priest—the man he'd confessed it *all* to, the things that Josh hadn't been privy to, but Dane purged all the same. He did it right before he was blessed by the bishop—he'd confessed his sins and prayed the dirt away, the guilt that tortured him so.

When he conducted his homilies, he often pulled from personal experiences, riveting the crowd as they held onto his every syllable from the pews. He was often told how 'entertaining' he was, how 'up to date', 'hip' and 'contemporary' his sermons were by the young and elderly alike. It was no coincidence. That familiar torment he turned around and used to help others, but no one knew why he sounded so authentic, why he seemed to truly understand their pain. The reason was the liquor, the pills, the guilt, the vicious cycle; though he never let these seduce him thoroughly, and had let God pull him out just in time.

Dane only gave a piece of himself, never unwrapped his full past for their public eyes and mental consumption. It wasn't that he cared what someone would think, or even that others would know, but because he understood that if he lost any of the respect of the devoted congregations, he'd be alienated at the parish and that would bring undesirable attention to the church, especially since he now dined once again with the enemy…

No, it had reared its ugly head from time to time during periods of extreme upheaval and stress. Josh knew all about it, and he kept him sane. He figured Josh wasn't aware he'd relapsed, though he told his best friend that very fact in his dreams. Secrets…more and more piled up like stinking trash. As a youth, keeping it away from home was daunting; explaining to a college professor why he wobbled into class was a chore, but like many addicts, he'd manipulated his way through. Now, who wouldn't trust an almost straight A, good Catholic boy?

Dane looked to his left then to his right. The coast was

clear. He slid the pint-sized bottle of Smirnoff Vodka out of his pocket, unscrewed the top and sucked down the final drops, hoping that they'd chase the demons away. He immediately rejoiced in the warmth, the soothing heat that coated his throat and relaxed his woes and tense muscles. He'd been isolated, suffering from depression due to it, and the liquid lady had been his friend, though he knew her assistance always came with a price.

In the past, especially while he was out of the country, in places like Haiti where disaster was so prevalent, he felt at times helpless and missed his family…but *she* was always there. He pitied himself a time or two, then pushed the pain away as he always had, off to the side like rubble or putrid debris falling down into a sewer drain. He'd prided himself on stopping—months, sometimes years rolled past when he stayed clean, but now that Josh was gone, the liquid lady sat by his side again, hugging him tight, making all the 'bad' inside him melt, and disappear into the bottomless depths of the lifeless lake…

RHAPSODY HATED THAT she was in love with the cold grass. Her allergies didn't appreciate the love fest. The ongoing love affair had been relentless, tugging at her need for nature, for weeks. Every spring, the fling would begin, then before she knew it, she was hightailing it away from her occupational obligations, and stretching her body to the beautiful limit— what she called, 'yogamatized'. It was a bit too cool to wear a leotard this early evening, so she settled for navy blue leggings and an oversized T-shirt. It messed up her mojo, but it still got the job done. Bending and stretching, she kept her eye on her surroundings. Children hand in hand with their parents, couples with barking pets that were better cared for than the average U.S. adult, and then, there was *him*...

On and off, she'd see the smiling man on the chipped paint wooden bench.

You've become a song, thank you and you know what? You look kinda familiar...

It was always the same bench, and if she didn't know any better, she'd swear at times he wasn't even breathing. He blended in like shrubbery—no, like a statue—but his eyes caught the glimmer of the sun and on cloudy days, they darkened with something she couldn't describe. He intrigued her, perplexed her, and called to her. From one angle, he'd look harmless. From another, something mischievous and possibly dangerous brewed. Nevertheless, he had a peace about him—yet, still, he also looked like the entire world was on his shoulders.

In short, he was an enigma. Someone that could both go unnoticed and command attention. Sometimes, he'd meet her glance, and give an acknowledging nod. Other times, he'd stare off into space, as if uninterested in his very own existence. Today was different, though.

While she lay on her back and brought her legs up, the fluffy clouds rolled by showing her all the soft pictures they could make. Yet, when she turned to the side, they were gone and all that was left was the man slipping what appeared to be a bottle of clear liquor into his jacket pocket. Worse of all, he had a nasty look of guilt about him after it was all said and done. She *knew* that look, she'd had it before—only her addiction wasn't a bottle, but a leeching ex-lover she'd allowed back into her life one time too many. Nonetheless, she was honest with herself and from that honesty came some pain, some harsh truth. Honesty was her teacher.

Sometimes, she just didn't want to be alone; it had nothing to do with heartbreak or love anymore. She wanted a warm body beside her, that was why she'd let him back, and when it was over, she didn't mourn him or the relationship any longer, only the familiarity. At last though, she'd had enough. He was wearing on her, getting on her nerves. She'd thrust herself back into her exercise routine a few months after she gave him his *true* walking papers, and never looked back.

The park was an awesome escape, a healing zone. People watching was epic. Plentiful animals, wild and domestic, to observe during their daily routines, and the perfect scene to stretch and simply appreciate the new opportunities coming her way. Yeah, she was in a good place, but her voyeuristic nature compelled her—her biggest downfall. In her enjoyment of nosey surveillance, she'd make up stories in her head about what people were doing and thinking. She'd even make up songs, but the one about him was far more serious. She paused, singing the lyrics inside of her head…

Thaaaa man, doesn't stand….he sits, bent like bows, under the tree limbs….

He flees inside himself, carrying a heeeeavy load,
The wind, will carry his sorrows away…on some empty road…

There was just one problem now. She didn't want to guess anymore. She wanted to *really* know what his deal was. It was killing her. Her inquisitiveness was on a rampage and some-where deep within, she demanded answers. He appeared aloof, but not cold. His smile at times was warm, at other times obviously manufactured as a simple courtesy. And good Lord, he was a handsome son of a gun—and conversant, from how she'd seen him interact with some people. She hated it. She prided herself on her memory, and something tugged at those strings, but she couldn't figure out what.

Where do I know that face?

Rhapsody surmised he was about six-two, maybe six-three and definitely in good shape—not that that was important to her; not that she was looking for a boyfriend or anything, of course.

She smiled at her own thoughts.

His brown hair was streaked with honey and blonde high-lights and went darker to a rich brown, almost black, closer to his nape, blending into his short dark sideburns. Almost *too* perfect hair—unnerving, as if he had an expensive colorist taking care of those strands, and something mystical kept every strand in place, like the damned wind would go straight to hell if it dared to blow that coif out of place. Yet, it didn't look hard or stiff, just obeyed his command. His light blue eyes popped against his tanned skin in a classically handsome face with a keen nose, fleshy lips that appeared soft, dark eyebrows and an undeniable boyish charm. She was certain he looked younger than he actually was. He had wisdom about him…

She'd occasionally watch him glide his fingers over his hair as he appeared to be in deep thought. She rose from the ground, huffed and gripped her water bottle. Removing the cap, she took a big chug, and smirked. He was staring at her now, and this time, he didn't look away or offer a nod. He just…well, he just glared.

He might be a drunk… Nah, I doubt it. How would I know? But he is sneaking sips from a damn liquor bottle. What's wrong with him? Hmmm… It's none of my business, I don't know him…or do I?

She grinned mischievously.

I'm a little tired today, but I did think of you inappropriately, sir. Well hell, you can't blame me. I'm only human.

She gave free rein to the thoughts in her head, let them roam freely, and relished in her silliness.

Why do you keep coming to this park, sitting in that same spot, looking the same way? Why do you smile at me more times than not? If I didn't know any better, I'd think you were looking for me. It could be just wishful thinking… That's just what I need, to get a crush on an unemployed drunk.

She turned away from him and returned to the grass, stretching her arms high above her head. She closed her eyes, mediating, enjoying the sounds of the water and people going past. In her mind, it was just her, all by her lonesome. Today was her 'staycation' that she'd promised herself. She planned the type of dinner she'd make that evening, and what she'd watch on television, and the new song she'd practice, and the calls she needed to make…oh yes, and the emails! *Don't forget the emails.*

But then, he touched her…

Before she even had the chance to fix her face and look casually over her shoulder, she felt his fingertips run smoothly across her shoulder blade. She knew it was him before she even looked up, and their eyes met. She squinted in the sunlight, and used her hand as a visor. He stood there for a moment, looking down at her, smiling so beautifully. She offered her own smile, hoping it wasn't too big or too small. No, this needed to be like Goldilocks…fit just right.

"Hi." He grinned. "I come here all the time and I see you," he shrugged, "and it's just rude for me to not say anything. I also have a confession, but before I get into that, I want you to know that the goofy guy that sits on that bench," he pointed to the area behind him, causing her to lightly laugh, "is named Dane Caruso."

The breeze caught his scent, and she got to know him even better.

He smells like laundry soap, fresh dry cleaning and incense…

"Well, it is nice to meet you, Dane Caruso." She extended her hand upward, feeling the warmth of his palm as he wrapped his hand gently around hers. They held each other's gaze, and she wasn't for certain what to make of it. Up closer now, she could see amazing details in his features—a small beauty mark by his earlobe, a probable chicken pock scar near his cheek. He had a well-trimmed beard that suited him just fine, and she liked how the light filtered through his facial hair, making it almost look like spun gold. Upon even closer inspection, she saw a small hole in his earlobe, must've been the remnants of a piercing. He bent a little lower, as if he were trying to figure out something, read her mind. This brought her attention to his unbelievably thick, dark brown lashes that curled at the ends, almost as if they'd been dipped in mascara.

The man is not just good-looking, he is kinda pretty…and definitely sexy. Now I'm even more certain I've seen this guy before. But where?

Before she could ask the question, he did it for her. "You look familiar." He smiled. "That's not a line, I'm serious. May I ask what your name is?"

"My name is Rhapsody Blue."

His brows furrowed and he looked confused. Then, his expression eased and he grinned. "What high school did you go to?"

"Stevenson High, home of the Spartans!" she said with pride.

Dane shook his finger at her. "That's where I've seen you before! What year did you graduate?"

"Class of 2012," she offered, slightly unnerved that she didn't remember him from there. She thought it may have been from a dream or just out and about.

"Okay, I was 2009; you were a freshman when I was a senior more than likely. Big school, but I knew you looked familiar." His eyes hooded. "Rhapsody Blue, huh? Interesting name."

"I would love to hear this confession of yours," she said.

He helped her to her feet. After patting off the grass from her knees and calves, she stood straight and crossed her arms. She was prepared to hear his pick-up line, to render it silly and meaningless, but give him a C for effort. Yes, he was pre-graded.

"My confession is." He clasped his hands together and gave her a lopsided smile. That mischievous expression she'd seen a time or two flashed across his face, but only for a moment. "I eavesdropped on you. I heard you singing one day here and you have a beautiful voice."

Taken off guard, Rhapsody hesitated. She did hum and sing words from time to time, but she didn't remember seeing him during her park concerts and serenades.

"Well, thank you."

As he slid his left hand into his jean pocket, the wedding band glimmered and she winced. But hey, the man hadn't asked her out, or done anything inappropriate...*yet.*

Settle down. No need to jump on his case but what a damn bummer. Married...

"It was a couple weeks ago or so." He cleared his throat. "I don't know the name of the song. I just heard you singing, well, humming, then you sang. It was raining."

"You were there? Did you have your head covered with a hood, possibly?"

"Yeah," he answered sheepishly, "I'm not a stalker or anything." He laughed lightly as he rocked back on his heels. She enjoyed watching him squirm. She remained silent, stretching it out.

I may as well get something out of this. He is already taken. At least a laugh can be enjoyed.

"Um, well." He looked around, looking embarrassed.

Okay, I'll be nice.

"Thank you so much, I love to sing. I'm a singer actually, and I teach the piano."

He smiled. "Wow, like, at a school? Elementary or high school?"

"No, I actually teach at Davenport University, part time. I give singing lessons, too, provide vocal coaching, and do gigs all over the country."

"Well, that explains it!" He laughed, showcasing nice, natural white teeth. "I know how to play the piano, but it's like 'Mary Had a Little Lamb' level."

She burst out laughing.

I'm sure it isn't that bad.

"I won't keep you, but I keep seeing you and, well, I thought it was time that I say hello and introduce myself. Now I know we are alumni from the same alma mater. I almost feel like I know you at this point." He extended his hand and shook hers gently, lingering a wee bit too long. She pulled back, feeling uncomfortable.

"Well, it was nice to meet you. See you again, Mr. Caruso." She forced a smile before turning away, her signal that he was now free to leave.

Mr. Married Man, flirting like the asshole that you are. I wonder how your wife would feel about this. What nerve, I gave you a chance…holding my hand like that…looking at me like that. I am so glad I am done with dating right now, anyway. Men! I swear. This is another example as to why!

She rolled her eyes.

"You can just call me Dane, or if you insist on being formal," she shot him a look from over her shoulder, her lips twisted in a frown—warning him ever so subtly to be on his way, "Fr. Caruso will suffice."

Then he backed away from her with a wave and disappeared toward the walking trail, leaving her blushing, embarrassed and soon after, laughing out loud at her own misguided assumptions…

CHAPTER SEVEN

"SO HOW MUCH is left?" Daisy pushed her hands into Dane's chest, shoving him against the kitchen counter. "I wouldn't ask if we didn't need it, Dane. I mean, that was a lot of money…surely the church and you didn't burn through it that fast."

Dane walked around her and entered their parents' dining room. He looked down at the neatly laid flatware and the matching tumbler glasses. Mom was always so particular about the settings. The smell of baked chicken permeated the house, making his stomach loop with hunger pains. Daisy gently grabbed his arm, throwing a faux grin at him like beads during Mardi Gras. Only he wasn't catching.

"I have put the money away, Daisy and will distribute it as needed. I have no idea how you and your husband could go through twenty thousand dollars in this short period of time but I am not giving you another red cent right now."

He jerked away from her, leaving her seething, he was

certain. He'd heard her urgent voicemails over the past few days. She'd even put their father up to calling a couple of times and he knew what had happened. She'd given her husband most of the money, and he'd gambled it away. Dane was rather surprised as he hadn't realized that Rob's gambling problem was this extensive, but it all made sense now—the second and third mortgages on their home, the repairs not being done. Of course, he'd been laid off and out of work for a few weeks, taking handy-man employment, but even before that, financial trouble had brewed and Daisy was a sucker for the man. He was a charming liar, shiftless and lazy, and this was the final straw. Dane turned to tell Daisy a thing or two but caught himself...

Who am I to judge that man when I've sunken to an all-time low?

He'd been drinking again, nipping here and there, but making sure to never get intoxicated. He even made excuses for the behavior, just like in years past. What started the whole tangled, dirty ball of dependency rolling again was when Josh had told him he had cancer. Dane hadn't touched a bottle in years. Even when offered beer at the festivals, he always declined, though at times, it had been tempting. This last event, however, had sent him over the edge and he was having a hell of a time controlling it. The first time this happened, he'd got off the sauce cold turkey. Other types of liquor were much easier to get away from because he didn't like them as much, and they didn't give him the feeling he was looking for.

Back in college, he'd first started to try and cope, but then he started liking it, *really* liking it. It got to the point that he'd wake up thinking about it. The drinking replaced football, his girlfriend and even, to some degree, Josh. It definitely replaced family—he'd retreat, withdraw and alienate.

Now he needed to stop again—he could do it. He needed to get dry and he had to address it as soon as possible before it got further out of control.

"Look, Daisy." He sighed. "I know you love Rob, I understand that, but can't you see what's happened here? If you need any more money, Rob first needs to get some help for his gambling addiction, and then, and *only* then, we can talk about money."

In response, she glowered, her eyes becoming blue slits. She was no longer Daisy, but hatred in a pretty dress.

Just like Mom—defend wrong-doing to the death if it makes you feel uncomfortable. Yes, today I am disagreeable.

He shook his head and took a seat, waiting for the rest of the family—kids, brothers, brother-in-law and parents to join them. All throughout the dinner, Dane made small talk and laughed with the rest of them, playing it cool while inside, he felt raw with worry for his predicament. He was craving his lady… Occasionally, he'd catch Daisy cutting a sinister stare his way, but she finally stopped once he looked back at her and gave her a non-verbal warning to cut it out. Shaking his head, he cast a glance at Rob who sat in his chair, his back slumped, his expression one of sheer defeat.

No, I am not bailing you out, again. It would be a disservice. Rob figured he could just piss it away, and then come right back to me to ask for more, like nothing had happened. Like I'm some ATM. I am nipping this in the bud tonight.

He'd already seen what had happened. They'd whispered to each other all night; he wanted to know if she was getting the money and once she delivered the unexpected answer, he, too, started aiming pitiful looks at Dane. After Dane and Anthony helped their mother clear the table, it was time to leave. At the front door, Dane felt a hand on his shoulder.

"Dane, I need to speak to you." His mother's soft voice cut through the quiet like a small pebble rolling across the hardwood floor. Suddenly, he heard piano music playing...someone had put on a CD. He listened closer, trying to identify the familiar tune.

"Dane?"

"Uh, yes, Mom, what is it?"

She sighed and ran her hands along her apron. "Daisy really needs that money. Rob has gotten them into an awful mess and they may lose their house now," she pleaded with every fiber of her being. He knew what she was *really* saying.

"Dane, you have the chance to keep everything peaceful and perfect...please help us keep this charade going. Please help us keep the dollhouse intact."

The music grew louder, "Chopin... fantasie impromptu..."

"Excuse me?" his mother asked, her brows slightly furrowed.

"That's what's playing...that's the song that's playing." He pointed toward the CD player.

His mother grinned. "I never took you for a classic music lover. I just turned on the radio is all. I have a mountain of housework and you know how I like to listen to music as I do my chores. It makes it go by faster."

"I'd forgotten all about this song. I remember in high school the orchestra playing it over and over for practice. They were going on a trip to Paris, and wanted to get it right. My locker was right by the music room, and it drove me crazy, but I knew this song all right, chord for chord." He shook his head as the memory filled him with calm warmth.

High school…

"Yes, well, back to what I was saying. You see," she began again. Dane couldn't hear her as he listened intently to each note. The rhythm reminded him of Rhapsody's singing that rainy day in the park…as if she were singing to that very piece of music, the tempo similar. Something stirred in his chest, but his mother kept pulling him into reality.

"Mom, look." Gripping her arm, he bent down to meet the five-six woman almost eye to eye. "I know what you want, and usually, I'd do a lot of things to make you feel okay, to make it better, but I can't do that anymore, Mom. I'm a hypocrite right now, but I still know right from wrong and I—"

"Dane, what are you talking about? Now listen to me, this is serious. You must!"

"Mom, I'm sorry, but you're wrong. I won't enable her anymore. What I *need* to do is not keep throwing money to cover Daisy and Rob's problems. And if I give them the money that is what I'd be doing. They'd just be back next week, and the week after that. When would it stop, Mom? When?"

She got ready to protest in Daisy's and her son-in-law's defense, then her shoulders slumped in resignation.

"That was just a small amount, Mom, compared to what I *was* going to do. I was planning to give her more, but I first needed to see if they could be responsible, to do the right thing with *that*, before going any further. And look what they've done! I have no idea what bookie or casino now has the twenty grand—but it's gone, and though that was a small fraction of what I received, it still was a lot of money that grandpa worked hard for, and they blew it. I bet the kids didn't see a dime of it. I don't want to see anyone suffer, Mom, especially my own family, but we have to learn from our mistakes. We have to love ourselves enough to understand what went wrong, and change. How can we appreciate the need for radical evaluation and the reward of sunshine if we never endure a cloudy day?"

And with that, he kissed the top of his mother's head, left her house, and got into his car, mixed emotions swirling deep inside of him. He'd never told his mother 'No' before, at least not in that manner, and he was certain she stood there in a whirlwind of confusion—probably exactly where he'd left her in the foyer, the music still playing. A part of it stung; he hated doing it, but he had no regrets.

After a while of driving, his thoughts dancing all over the place, he pulled over to a curb by a city trashcan. He popped the trunk, got out of his car, and, without hesitation, removed the two six packs, slick with condensation, that he'd purchased earlier in the day. Gripping the brown, crumpled bags, the long green bottles inside clinking—his special lady—he made his way toward the can and dumped them.

The street was dark and desolate, sprinkled with a few lit storefronts. Everywhere it seemed businesses was closed and the occasional low drone of a car broke up the stillness. He got back inside his car and drove home toward the parish. The evening would be hard, but an evening he had to have. Tonight, for the first time since Josh had passed away, he was going to be completely sober. Grief overwhelmed him, with Josh on his mind more times than not.

The acting out, wanting to fit in and praying his mother would notice him as a child—to really *see* him for who he was—and not simply what she wanted him to be, a replica of her father—had poisoned him. He needed to find a way to process it and make it right for himself, so he could begin to heal, this time, for good. It was hard to be mad at a lady who loved you so much; she'd give her life, no matter how twisted her thinking was, but he was going to have to try to find a way to forgive everyone, including himself. Time to accept everything, from start to finish. He hadn't gotten this way overnight, and it would take longer than he'd cared to admit to work his way through it, but what was the alternative? He owed it to himself; he owed it to Josh and he owed it to God. He wanted his life back, once and for all...

"HOW RIDICULOUS." MELODY, Rhapsody's sister rolled her inky eyes and hugged the warm yellow mug of cocoa to her chest as she leaned lazily against their mother's kitchen counter. "I mean, really, Rhapsody? When are you going to stop this music stuff, and do something else, something more? Something that lets you live more than from just pay check to pay check?" She shook her head, judgment dripping off her downturned lips.

Screw you...

"Excuse me?" Rhapsody said coolly. "Uh, my bills are paid and I can get most of the things I actually want, and more importantly, I love what I do. Worry about your own shit."

"Don't get mad at me because I told your butt the truth! Your singing is just *aiight*," she sighed melodramatically, "you *aren't* all that, and besides, it can't be a full time career."

"Mama made a career of it. She travelled all around the world singing with Stephanie Mills, Gladys Knight and Patti LaBelle." Rhapsody looked into the pot of boiling pasta, adding a sprinkling of salt and pepper, teasing her wayward imagination into the thought of throwing the potful of steaming water right in Melody's face.

I wish they were grits, like what happened to Al Green. Now that is some singing to remember!

"You ain't Mama," Melody muttered under her breath.

"And you aren't worth a damn, how 'bout that?!"

"You two at it again?" their mother asked wearily as she entered, her light pink robe wrapped around her securely. "I haven't been feeling well, this cold is at it again. Gonna sit down here for a sec and please," she slumped in the wooden kitchen chair and closed her eyes, rubbing her head, "no screaming and yelling. You two never stop and I got a splitting headache."

"Hmmmph," Melody took a sip from her cup, turned her back toward Rhapsody and joined her mother at the table. "Do you need something, Mama?" she asked in an overly sweet voice, cutting her eyes at Rhapsody who now looked at her demented sister and shook her head in disbelief at the ridiculously fake display.

"Peace and quiet, girls…that's what I need," their mother answered wearily.

The two sisters shot each other menacing looks.

"Mama, the pasta is almost ready," Rhapsody offered as she bent to retrieve a large ceramic white bowl from a cabinet.

She placed it on the counter and looked back over at her sister. They favored quite a bit—same toasty brown complexion, same open, dark eyes that curved exotically upward at the ends and the same supple lips, shaped like hearts. Their noses were a bit different, Melody's was more like their father's, rounded and somewhat turned up. Rhapsody's bridge was longer, her nostrils slightly flared, like their mother's. Her jawline was stronger, giving her a slightly athletic appearance that blended smoothly with her otherwise distinct African American features. They both were a decent height—Rhapsody stood five-eight while her sister stood five-nine—as well as long legs and small waists. And they could share a C-cup bra. Rhapsody loved her body, liked how it felt under clothing, but most of all, she cherished her voice and talking to people from all walks of life. A woman in love with life, period. And when she looked at her sister, she saw her polar opposite—a burning pit, a black hole, a wretched soul with an axe to grind. But she loved the woman. Where had they gone wrong?

Several weeks later…

HE TOLD HER.

She caught him at a weak moment, came upon him on that bench, and now that he was feeling his pain to the utmost capacity, no longer courting the liquid lady, he was a bundle of raw nerves. She'd walked past casually, gave a slight wave at first, then double backed. Without a word or explanation, she took a seat by him, and then it just poured out. From the moment he was told about the cancer, to right then and there, he let loose. When he'd finished, he could see the sympathy in her dark, glossy eyes. Eyes that he wanted to swim in. He was sitting so close to her, he could see the slight sheen on her bottom lip was more lustrous than the upper one, and her eyeliner drew his attention, swinging up into a slight black cat-eye. A medium brown, her skin was perfect, smooth and taut. Oh yes, he studied her—the whites of her eyes gleamed bright like freshly fallen snow and she reminded him of the illustrations of Nefertiti, especially with the head wrap she customarily wore. No, it wasn't a golden crown with rubies, but still, definitely a sight to behold, giving her the look of royalty.

Her voice—airy, cool and smooth. He loved that sound, the low pitch, a voice that haunted the soul and left a pleasant aftertaste in his thoughts. But still trouble brewed and bubbled inside him. He was thinking about her frequently—too frequently. She enveloped his mind as he stayed locked away in his quarters just to spend time with her in his imagination. She caused smiles to appear on his face out of nowhere, and before he'd have to explain it, he'd tuck the grin away before anyone saw and asked for the source of such an expression. He'd find himself distracted, in the middle of a kind word, and his thoughts would drift. This alluring woman featured so clearly in his mind, and what had been initially pleasant became uncomfortable. He tried to stick to the facts, to concentrate on things that didn't dance around her eccentric beauty.

Over the past few days, he'd tried to put pieces of the puzzle together, trying to recall images of her from years gone past. In small doses, his wish was granted. His sober nights were now filled with colorful memories of a girl who'd once walked past him each and every day. He'd see her come through the school's front door, meander down the hall, sometimes with friends and sometimes alone, then disappear inside the music room by his locker...

The music room. She was in there for choir practice...the room with a dog-eared green flyer for the orchestra going to Paris...Yes, Paris...I love France.

She was skinnier then, less filled out, and a beautiful face, but even more so now. She never paid me any mind, but I noticed her, with her baggy jeans and tight, colorful tops. Straight hair, yes, jet black and pulled tight into a pony tail. Real cool, quiet—until she entered that classroom. Then, the magic would unfold.

He remembered one day being late for class, standing there peeking into the tiny window of the vast room with cellos, drums in the corner and cathedral seats, listening to the songbird do her thing while the teacher's fingers ran across the piano keys. The teacher had been the crotchety Mrs. Tucker, the music instructor with the high, flat behind, who always wore a charcoal gray skirt with lint balls along the hem and thick stockings. She had a quivering bottom lip when irritated, and embarrassed him one day when she angrily stormed over to the door and swung it open before he'd had a chance to break from his hypnotic trance and beat it down the hall.

"Can I help you, Mr. Caruso? You slept in class all week, why would you want to loiter around now? This isn't the pep rally!"

Her performance caused the entire room to rock with laughter. He'd looked over at Rhapsody, who'd smirked, but didn't make eye contact with him. But he wanted her to, he wanted her to notice him, like all the other girls did, but she paid him no mind, no mind at all…

She broke the trance of his memories, bringing him back to present day as they sat together on his favorite bench.

"Fr. Caruso, I am so sorry about your loss."

"…Dane."

She smiled ever so slightly. "Dane, now that you've explained your relationship in more depth, I completely understand. It clarifies so much. So, that is what brought you back here, huh?"

"Well, I'd been coming to this park for years, to think and just have personal time. I love this park, but, I started coming more after he got sick and passed because," he shrugged, "he and I had a lot of great conversations here, some of the best."

This is where I told him what was in my heart…and all the crap I did…and he supported me anyway.

"Sorry for dumping this in your lap. You're practically a stranger and here I am chatting away and—"

"No," she put her hand up and shook her head, "I'm glad you told me. You obviously needed to get it out, it's fine," she assured. They paused for a while.

"Well, thanks. I didn't expect for me to blurt it out like that. Some days are easier than others."

"Of course they are."

"So, that's what happened. I come here to think." He looked away from her, out toward the lake. "It just feels right, you know? I really don't know how I thought I was going to react when it was all said and done—when he passed, but my imagination didn't fathom this sort of emptiness. He has lived in California for years now, so we had distance between us and didn't talk every day anymore. But at least I always knew he was there." He briefly looked down into his lap, "And now he isn't. I feel guilty for not calling more…flying out to see him more. I should've known better." He looked away, up into the sky.

"You can't do that to yourself. Just because you don't speak to someone every day doesn't mean you don't love them. Bill collectors can talk to you every day…doesn't mean they give a damn about you or care!" She covered her mouth, as if to take back the curse word and muffle her laughter.

"You're fine," he reassured and, without thinking, patted her hand. Just a simple pat, a gesture he'd offered many times, but the feel of her skin under his fingertips, the smoothness, the slightly raised vein he'd swept past with his fingernail—he'd enjoyed it a bit too much.

He was not telling her the complete truth, and he simply couldn't.

Let me just enjoy this time, the ability to talk to a stranger and purge…someone that doesn't know me…that can't judge me. I'll say it in my mind, confess it, and then, it'll be done. Here it goes: I also started coming more, Rhapsody, after I first saw you here. I wanted to run into you again. You are like a haven, and your smile, well; I needed to see it again. For when you smiled at me, I thought you could possibly be my new friend. I need new friends, Rhapsody…someone I can trust. Is that you?

But he kept the thoughts to himself, where they were safe and sound.

THE THIN ORANGE pamphlets for the teen Sunday school had arrived. Dane gathered the bundled heap; the odor of the freshly printed dark blue ink on the pages wafted passed his nostrils as he toted them to a small room. The space was filled with shiny wooden desks, a large window and a guitar leaning against the side of the doorway. He sighed and put his hand on his hip as he looked around, trying to find a place to put them so that Fr. Daniel would see them. The man had a habit of becoming spastic, hunting Dane down in customary fashion, asking frantically where they were right before he was to teach class.

I'll set them right here.

Dane glanced at the cluttered front desk and decided against it, but beside it was an empty chair. Surely Fr. Daniel wouldn't miss them right there. As he set them down, he took notice of the cover. Right there on the front was an illustration of a young woman holding hands with a young man. He chuckled at the 1960s' type illustration.

Why don't they draw these in a more modern style so the kids can relate a bit better?

He removed one from the rubber banded pile, and flipped casually through it. On page five, he found the illustration again, this one laid out as a timeline. It featured the same couple, then another drawing of them leaving a church with big smiles on their faces and people throwing rice. The next illustration had them in front of a house holding a baby and in the next, they looked older with teenage children. The final picture was of them as an older couple, holding hands on a church pew. What was meant to encourage family unity, and God's plan for husband and wife, had placed a bitter seed inside of him. Suddenly, he felt hot with resentment. It began as a slow build-up as he perused each drawing, taking his time at the continuum. Something so innocent was driving him to madness. A wave of jealous rage crashed through him at that very instant, tearing a hole in his being. Throwing the darn thing down, he stormed out of the room, slamming the door behind him...

CHAPTER EIGHT

R HAPSODY COULDN'T HELP but laugh. The man was
hilarious, and what was a priest doing saying such things?
She couldn't believe she'd thought he'd been flirting with her
the first time they spoke, when he was just being friendly. All
these days, all these weeks of interactions, of wonderful,
intricately constructed morsels of conversations, usually lasting
no more than twenty minutes—she cherished them. They
were always way too short...

And she did remember him from school now.

Their discussions sometimes went back there, and they
recalled certain instances, old gossip, and what ever happened
to so and so? She'd kept some parts to herself however, like...

Why does that boy keep looking at me? And... *I like the way he
looks at me when I go into class...*

She started wearing shirts that would push her breasts
together, make them pop, to gather his attention with her little
sneaky, woven basket of feminine tricks, but the star athlete

never said a word, he only stared…

Ho hum, and damn, he was so sexy back then…and he still is.

This is wrong for you to be thinking about how sexy this priest is, she chastised herself.

That didn't stop her from thinking about the previous evening when she got home and it didn't stop the song lyrics that continued to dance inside of her head about him, maybe even *for* him. Now, he'd shared heartbreaking words regarding the death of his friend, and her mind drew back to the bottle of alcohol—it all made sense now. She could see how one could be driven to drink after such a trauma. Catching his laughter, she turned her attention back toward the conversation.

"It's true!" he laughed as he crossed his ankles and leaned back. She caught a whiff of him; he smelled like chamomile tea and pine trees.

"I kid you not; I do listen to it all!" He counted off his fingers—"Country, rap, rock…I like…uh, what's her name? The full figured pretty poetic lady with the beautiful smile. She's an actress, too…Jill Scott, yes, that's her name!"

Rhapsody looked at him closer. Such an endearing man. They'd been 'running into each other' and the delightful conversations and sweet pleasantries were becoming addictive. Over the past few days, he came to the park more and more, or maybe, it was her that was coming more and more, and he'd been just there all along—with or without her.

'Easy going' described him well. His laugh, soothing and relaxing; she couldn't help being drawn to him. She found it astounding that he never discussed his religion with her, nor did he ever wear a collar. Had he not made the admission, she wouldn't even know he was a man of the cloth. She'd catch herself before cursing or saying something crude, and he'd smile at her, as if knowing what she was *going* to say.

But today, the man with the calm exterior was sinking low. He'd been in a happy mood, and she blamed herself a bit for bringing him down, but she wanted him to get everything off his chest, just in case he had no one else to talk to. Rhapsody never took herself as much of a counselor, but there was just something about him. Clearly, he needed her listening ear, and he was a great conversationalist. She'd dragged him down the rabbit hole, bringing up his friend, not to hurt him, but she knew how it felt to lose someone, and others did not quite understand the pain endured, the vast emptiness it left.

He drew quiet as she uttered Josh's name. Though she never saw a tear, his voice shook a time or two as he recalled memory after memory of his best friend. This purging would help him heal and it was no coincidence that they ended up on this bench, sharing these words. The right place, the right time—this man deserved some peace and in this moment, she could give it to him.

She caught him several times looking at her head wrap. Today, she'd worn the white one and large silver hoop earrings.

Why did I dress up for this man? Like he is checking for me. Rhapsody, you are so ridiculous, girl...

She didn't understand her continued attraction to him, and she didn't understand why in the hell she didn't resist it.

Sometimes, I tell myself, 'Just act like you don't see him.' But I do, and he knows it, and he walks over with that easy going smile and stance, and he says something amusing, or kind...or just, ordinary. But the tone, the way he says it, is just as wonderful as the actual words.

Well, I suppose I will be able to tell my future kids one day that I had a crush on a priest—it can go in my memoires. She grinned and shook her head.

"What?" he asked gently. "What are you thinking about?"

His voice sounded like velvet…smooth and silky. She hated that about him. Not only was he like a relaxation tape, but his damn voice was actually sexy, too, not just comforting. It was deep, and he pronounced words so smoothly. The man conducted mass, spoke over people who were dying, yet, he was so alluring.

You need to stop it, Rhapsody, this is just silly.

So glad he can't read my thoughts.

"Oh nothing, just thinking about what you said is all… Yeah, I love neo-soul, too. It is my favorite music, actually."

He nodded. "Hey, I wanted to know, and I hope this isn't too presumptuous, but maybe I could hear you play one day? You said you sometimes perform in public, outside of the classroom. You know, when we spoke the other day, I was thinking about that. I love listening to piano; it is like the most perfect instrument. Wait, I take that back! The drums, electric guitar, then the piano." He laughed, that friendly smile that warmed her throughout. The wind rustled his hair, exposing part of his scalp and darker roots.

"Of course you can hear me play. Matter of fact, at the end of the month, the last Friday night, I'll be helping a buddy out. I am filling in at a jazz club, Envy's, over on Kercheval. Their regular pianist will be out of town."

"I think I know where that is. Either way, I'll find it, I'll be there." He narrowed his eyes, flexed his fingers and rested his arms along the top of the bench while speaking so matter-of-factly, so effortlessly. Her heart skipped a beat; such beautiful eyes…

"Do you dye your hair? It's like three different colors…gorgeous, actually." Rhapsody asked before reaching out
to touch the windblown tresses. Just then, she caught herself.

Can't believe I did that.

His smile softened, then slowly faded. Yet, he didn't look
angry. Maybe perplexed?

"No." His smile returned and he tapped on the bench.
"It's always been this way. I used to get asked that a lot."

They shared silence as the sounds of birds became their
music. Rhapsody felt her heart flip again, and she didn't
understand why. He kept staring at her with those damn blue
eyes looking deep inside of her. Preacher men, priests and
rabbis; their presence was sometimes hair-raising. They had a
way of looking at people, and you'd swear they knew your
entire life story. What if he could really see inside of her? What
would he find? Would she try to hide old hurts and secrets, or
lay them all out for him to see, take him on a hand-held tour
of her bad choices, failed relationships and free-living outlook
on life? She was just fine with her mistakes; they made her
who she was. Rhapsody liked herself, no, she *loved* herself and
rules were not something she followed, especially in matters of
the heart, although she did practice the *golden* rule—that one
she kept near and dear.

"May I ask why you wear that hair wrap?" He pointed to
her head. "Since we are speaking about hair. I like it actually."
She watched him study the fabric, as if mesmerized. "How in
the world did you even get it like that? That is just amazing
and more so, you work out in it and it doesn't fall!" He
crossed his arms over his chest, as if pulling an invisible armor
over himself. His gold wedding band gleamed under the
afternoon sunlight.

"I do it so often," she grinned, "I don't even think about it anymore. I wear it to protect my hair, plus, I just like how it looks."

He smiled at her, a smile of appreciation, and warmth. "And, is your name really Rhapsody? Or am I going too far? Delving too deep? I never spoke to you in high school; I never knew your name."

She shook her head and looked briefly away. "Yes, my name is *really* Rhapsody, but my last name is not Blue. I just use that for my performances. My real last name is Thomason."

"I'll call you Rhapsody Blue…it suits you."

"Thank you, Dane." And there it was again, that sparkle in his eyes. She found herself holding back a smile.

He accepted her answers, nodding, but she couldn't shake the nagging feeling that, from his expression, he had more questions. However, like all other days before this, they stopped, said their goodbyes and went their separate ways. Next time, they may pick up the conversation where they last left off, and other times, they'd start clean—just like the brand-new day they'd been given…

DANE SAT IN the nursing home lobby gripping his leather-bound, worn black Bible. He'd finished his rounds, and usually, even with them being so close to death and him losing people he'd befriended, he was in a good mood after seeing a smile or two on his favorite elderly patients' faces. Mrs. White would slowly creep past him, her smiling dark brown eyes twinkling under the harsh ceiling lights. Unable to speak, she'd gently tap his knee as she walked past. Mr. Harris always greeted him with a toothy grin, his thick rimmed glasses sliding down the long bridge of his freckled nose. The man was an inspiration; in terrible pain and a double leg amputee, he kept in good spirits and became a good friend.

Regardless, Dane felt heavy uneasiness and he wasn't sure how to rid himself of the emotions. He wanted to discard them, throw them away in some invisible receptacle in the sky, but instead, they grew by the minute, festering. He continued to have times like this as he struggled with what the future held, but today, something happened that caused him alarm, something he hadn't anticipated, and it tore at him in ways that left him emotionally exhausted. Nevertheless, he wanted to gather his thoughts and get himself together before he drove back home, and the best way for him to do it was to think about how he felt and why, and try to get through the ordeal, ask the important questions. He traced his steps in his mind.

When he'd arrived at the nursing home, he'd felt perfectly fine. He did his usual tour of duty, walking from room to room, talking with various people, and stopping to say hello to the staff that seemed to truly appreciate his visits. He'd also left the usual bouquet of yellow roses for Ms. Ivy, a woman who held a special place in his heart and was soon to be moved to hospice in the next day or two. Then, he walked into the cafeteria to get a glass of water before heading out for the day. Just then, he spotted a man he'd never seen before sitting at a small, round table, isolated, all alone with his thick salt and pepper eyebrows bunched, hovering over two sullen, cloudy blue eyes.

Dane walked up to him and extended his hand. The man's body straightened from his previously slumped position and his gaze slowly drifted upward. The two men locked eyes but the gentleman's look of disdain didn't lessen. Instead, he grunted and clung tighter to the edge of his chair. Dane looked at the table; the man's food seemed untouched and a balled up napkin lay next to his plate, as if he'd taken all of his aggression out on the poor thing.

"Hello. My name is Fr. Caruso. I come here every week and—"

"Oh, here we go." The man glowered, disgust in his tone. "I'm not Catholic and I don't care." He huffed, turning away and looking toward nothing in particular.

"Well, it is nice to meet you all the same." Dane kept his smile and a small part of him was tickled at the man's response. He'd seen it many times before, and considered the man now a much welcomed challenge. "Do you mind if I have a seat?" He pointed to the chair across from him.

The man looked at him, rolled his eyes, but remained silent.

Dane sat down and clasped his hands together. "This is a nice day for a walk. Would you like me to walk with you? We can go into the garden, or just hang around."

"What the hell for? I don't wanna walk. What's the purpose of that?" He looked away as he continued to rant. "I'm in the Forest Grove Nursing Home! I'm old, but I know where I am. No one gives a damn about me, and you're not different from anyone else. Just go away," he wheezed and waved Dane away, as if shooing a mangy dog that had wandered in from the outside.

Dane grinned and cocked his head to the side. "You know, I'm a good listener. You seem upset. What's bothering you?"

"I just told ya! What are you, hard of hearing? Ya deaf?!" the man hollered, spit shooting out of his mouth. Dane was unmoved and kept his same expression. "Damn it, I'm in this nursing home. I don't have anybody to take care of me, no one! I don't wanna talk, I don't wanna walk, I don't wanna eat!" The old man gave his tray a hard shove, causing the contents to tumble in various directions. The open container of milk saturated the napkin, making it soppy.

"That's fine." Dane said calmly. "You don't have to do anything you don't want to, but being alone is a choice."

"Like hell it is! You can be in a room full of people and still be alone. I've been alone my whole life, after all the service I did. I am a Vietnam Vet!" The man sat straighter and proudly poked his chest with the tip of his finger. "I paid my dues, and this is the damn thanks I get...sitting here with bland undercooked food, no one speaking to me for days on end unless it is to force me to take a pill. And here comes a chipper, know-it-all priest boy with a smug smile on his face trying to uplift me in my time of need!" he sneered, sarcasm dripping off the words. "I served my country, no one gives a shit about me. I'm useless now. Old and can't keep hold of my own piss!"

Dane's smile and resolve slowly began to melt. The words hit him in the gut—they hit him harder than bricks—and resonated deep within his core as he now felt a heaviness in his heart. He repeated what the man said in his mind, *You can be in a room full of people, and still be alone...*

He quickly gathered himself. "Well, talking may help and you aren't alone right *now*. I'm with you."

The man exhaled loudly and slapped the table, a cheerless grin across his wrinkled face.

"You just don't get it, do ya?" he sighed as they both observed another old man moseying past, his hands trembling as he carried a tray passed them. "I don't know you and I don't want to know you. You aren't my friend, my brother, nothin'.

These bastards in here, like that guy that just walked by, he shits on himself, but at least his son and grandkids come to visit. When a guy likes you comes around, it means the person is dyin', at heaven's gate. You're the damn grim reaper!" He laughed, tears welling in his eyes. "I've been here two weeks; no one has come to see me. Notta one!"

"Well, maybe I can help you contact your family so we can arrange that. I can speak with them and we can get some things settled."

"Call who?! I ain't got a wife, never had one! No kids, no grandkids, parents been dead since I was thirteen and my sisters and brother are clear across the country in their own state of falling apart! Who needs it!"

"You are angry, and I understand it. In times like these, we have to trust God and—"

"Ha! What a joke! I wish you all would just let me die in peace. Where was God when I had bullets flyin' past my head and saw my cousin get his brains blown out, huh? Where was God when I had to throw several of my comrades' body parts in a home-made grave I dug with my bare hands so that their bodies wouldn't be desecrated by those bastards? I came back to Michigan and people threw food and beer at me. Americans! Home of the brave! Told me I was a killer and the war was bogus! I was gone, living in hell, fightin' for their freedom and they spit at me! You and your God can kiss my white, wrinkled ass! You're a priest. That's funny!" The man ended with a maniacal chuckle.

Dane leaned back in his seat and studied the man. He was a stranger, he didn't know his name, yet he seemed so familiar in that moment, as if they'd had this conversation before. It had a hint of déjà vu, and he found it unnerving.

"Why is that funny? Nothing you've shared is funny. It is

heartbreaking. That doesn't make God any less real though. You have to rise above this, you're better than this."

"Oh, it's *plenty* funny," the man continued to laugh, "because you're no better off than me. If I had to do it all over again, I'd choose differently, that's for damn sure. You are going to end up just like me. Just you wait and see." He vigorously shook his head, a smirk on his face. "Look how young you are? Living in nursing homes. And I ain't queer, but you're good lookin', too. You're just wasting away. If I had to do it all over again, I sure as hell wouldn't be wastin' my life away like you, goin' to prisons, hospitals and walkin' around watching people die. You got your whole life ahead of ya! I don't understand your religion. I don't understand your God that you keep defending. Bunch of kooks! Forcing young boys to give their whole lives away, and for what? The army did the same thing to me. The army takes young boys and makes 'em choose and then throws 'em away! You are in the same fight and you don't even know it."

"How so?" Dane fought his emotions, and continued to engage the man; he was driven to do so.

"You'll get old and still be in the same spot you are right now, *alone*. No family, no one carin' about you. They only care about cha when you're useful. Once people get done usin' ya, they'll throw ya away like some old dishrag. After that happens, then you can come talk to me about this great God you serve. I bet you'll be singing a different tune!"

And with that, the man hobbled to his feet. His chair abruptly hit the floor as he stomped away, leaving Dane alone, stewing in his own thoughts. After a while, Dane got up and picked up the man's tray of scattered food. He placed it in the trash receptacle and headed toward the front of the building. Normally, he'd get in his car and drive away, but instead, he sat down on a bench in the lobby and held that Bible so tight, it twisted in his grip. He now understood why he felt so out of sorts.

It wasn't the interaction within itself, or even what the man had said. He'd heard things like that before, and you had to have a tough skin when dealing with the public. It was something much worse, something that dug deep inside of him and brought up the recent struggles he'd been tormented by, night after night—for he couldn't shake away the thought that that man was his *future*. Looking at him had been like looking at himself, fifty years down the line, and this haunted him. He could feel the forthcoming nightmares being sewn together and he hadn't even closed his eyes. That stranger was no stranger at all. It was as if he'd looked into a mirror of what was to come.

Dane was on the frontline of a spiritual war, assisting the people, a faithful servant to the Church. There was honor in that, and he'd paid his dues. But after it had all been said and done, and he'd sacrificed it all, then what? Would he be okay with giving more of himself than he could afford? Would he look back and wonder about all the 'what ifs' and 'could've beens'? Would he be filled with horrible regrets after decades of faithful provision? He knew it was possible. At that moment, the fear birthed inside of him, real and all encompassing, no longer a shadow of itself, looming here and there. He now knew, despite the differences, there were too many similarities to the old man's story and his own worries and concerns, things he hadn't dared utter, but troubled him nonetheless. That man was no stranger at all. That angry soul who'd knocked over a tray of food was him…

CHAPTER NINE

R HAPSODY SAT AT the edge of her bed, a candied orange slice dangling out the side of her mouth as she peered down at the sheet music. She'd been fussing with a new song and it had her by the throat. Slightly raw from the morning's practice, she chewed the candy, tossed the paper aside and gulped her warm lemon tea.

Mmmm, that's better...

Her doctor had warned her to give her throat a rest for at least a week, and she'd promised, knowing full well as soon as she left his office with her prescription in hand, she'd be right back in front of that piano singing a tune. She couldn't help herself—what he'd asked of her was like expecting a child to stay away from a grand birthday cake. She did manage to take the rest of the day off. No exercise, no classes, no park. What she was left with were swarthy thoughts of a man that she had no business obsessing about. Yet here she was, once again. Her mind had turned into a ball of bizarre contemplations, and she bounced ideas around, strange ones, with whimsical twists.

What if there is something going on between us? You are crazy, of course there isn't…

Taking out her cellphone, she searched for the recent photos she'd taken of the man. They were just playing around, and she decided she'd snap some shots. Truth of the matter, she wanted something to look at when he wasn't in her presence. She hated admitting that the park visits didn't seem to be enough anymore.

Ahhh, there he is…

She grinned as she gripped her phone, smiling wider and wider until her teeth were exposed.

Damn he is fine… Dane, my God, what a waste. I shouldn't say that, but shit, that's how I feel…

She jumped, startled by the phone ringing. She burst out laughing, closed her eyes and clutched the fabric of her shirt before placing the phone to her ear.

"Hello…"

"Hey lady, it's Tyra. What are you up to? Lauren said you were sick."

"Yeah." Rhapsody sighed in resignation. "My throat has been bothering me the past few days. I am much better now though. Thanks."

Tyra was Rhapsody's friend from the Thursday night class she taught. The woman, only a year Rhapsody's junior, had some pipes on her that Rhapsody couldn't believe. With just a little training, she knew Tyra was destined for greatness. They hit it off immediately, their relationship graduating from teacher and student, to the best of buddies.

"Well, that's good. I missed you in class today, but you have to take care of yourself. We can't have our favorite teacher being speechless," she joked.

"Like that would ever happen. When have you known me to mince words or not be able to say anything at all to you guys?" Rhapsody laughed as she leaned back on the bed, looking up at her ceiling.

"True! So, do you want me to stop by or anything? I make some superb chicken noodle soup, straight from the can. No one knows their way around a microwave like I do." This caused a painful burst of laughter. Rhapsody rubbed her sore throat.

"That is nice of you, but you just enjoy your evening. I'll see you in a couple of days. Promise."

"Okay, that's a deal. Make sure you get plenty of water and rest."

"I will, thanks… Hey, before you go, can I ask you something, Tyra?"

"Of course, what's going on?"

Rhapsody sat back up and swallowed. All she could think about was how she needed someone to talk to, someone she could trust to utter the words that were growing in her heart.

"Have you ever had a crush on someone, that you shouldn't have?"

"Hmmm, what do you mean exactly?"

"Like…a guy that maybe had a girlfriend, or he lived in another country and you both knew neither would be moving, so it made things difficult."

"Oh yes!" Tyra laughed on the other end. "It has happened more times than I'd like to admit, but yes I have. Why? Are you feeling someone?" Rhapsody could hear a smile in the woman's voice.

"Well, a little bit. It's complicated, but yeah."

"I knew you were hiding something, Rhapsody. Even though I've only known you a little over a year, I feel like I know you pretty well. You're good people."

"Awww, thanks Tyra. I feel the same way about you, too."

"Before, you'd hang around with us after class, but now, you rush off, like you have plans but you never say what they are. I suspected you had a boyfriend." She giggled. "So, why is this complicated?"

"Well," Rhapsody bit her nail, gnawing the thing to bits as she rocked on her bed, "he isn't really…actually *allowed* to date. We are only friends."

"What do you mean he isn't *allowed* to date? Is he a minor?" Tyra joked. "Jail bait, girl!"

"No, no," Rhapsody grinned, "Nothing like that. I'm saying, we are only friends and it can't go any further than that. He isn't with anyone else or anything like that, but, it just…" She sighed. "He can't date me and I don't know," she said, huffing, "all of this might just be in my mind. I mean, we are only friends and I might be making this into something that it's not. Tomorrow, I could feel totally different."

"Well, then, it sounds just like an innocent crush to me, if you think you could feel differently that fast. There's nothing wrong with finding a friend charming. So, how long have you known him?"

"Well, that's another piece of the puzzle. I've actually known him for years—well, knew *of* him. He went to my high school and then we ran into each other again and have been speaking ever since."

"You know what?"

"What?"

"Those are the best kinds of love affairs, Rhapsody."

"You're making me edgy, don't call it that!" Rhapsody laughed nervously. "We're just friends…"

"Yeah, well, when you have known someone for years and

then you run into them again, that is a good way to make some sparks fly. It's like…destiny," Tyra said, with vivacity in her tone. "The longest and best relationship I ever had, Rhapsody, was with my ex-boyfriend, Jonas. That's what happened to us. We went to high school, never dated, then met up again after college and were together for five years. The only reason it ended was because his son's mother kept interfering and he was afraid to lose visitation…vindictive, horrible woman. I didn't want him to have choose between me and his child. But anyway, those are the best ones…"

Rhapsody rolled over in her mind what Tyra said. The words *did* ring true.

"Well, thanks, Tyra. I believe I'm just thinking too much. He is a great friend, and I'm fine with that. I'm sure my little crush will wane, just like the one I had on L.L. Cool J when I was a little girl."

"I need looooove!" Tyra crooned the hook of one of L.L.'s songs. "Okay girl," Tyra added, laughing." If you need to talk again, let me know, okay?"

"Thanks Tyra, I will. Good night." She disconnected the call.

Rhapsody took another sip of her tea. Her entire body trembled. She was unnerved, because she'd just swallowed a lie. She tried to claim the damned thing as true—the false words she'd said—but she knew they weren't. This crush wasn't going anywhere, anytime soon. The man was doing something to her and Tyra was right—she'd been rushing away from class, butterflies in her stomach as she'd pulled up to the park, praying he was there. She felt out of control, but she hadn't done anything inappropriate, although the whole ordeal was always so tempting. She imagined them kissing, wanted to hold him, feel his heartbeat next to hers.

You always do this…chase after men who are emotionally unavailable.

She chastised herself, guilt now consuming her.

It's like you want your life to implode over and over again. I thought you said you learned from your past? She continued to speak to herself in third person. *What is wrong with you? Look, he is going through a hard time right now. He doesn't need this shit and the last thing you need to do is ruin something perfectly sweet by getting all horny, hot and heavy. You know better than this. The man lost his friend, has been depressed, and this is what you try to go and pull?*

Begrudgingly, she searched through her phone for his photos and deleted both of them, hoping, with all of her might, that that small gesture would somehow help cool her heated jets. It didn't.

When she went to sleep that evening, Dane swirled in her mind, enticing a dust storm of lust. But even more disturbing to Rhapsody was the allure and the sweetness…and the purity of it all. It began as a flesh feast, and ended with her heart pounding, reaching out to him, completely in love—and in those sweet images from her colorful imagination, one more facet entered the picture. She was presented with what had evaded her in real life: a simple kiss. Not just *any* kiss, but a kiss from *him*. It was so real, so enchanting, she'd sworn it was genuine when she awoke and found herself wide awake, her fingertips dancing along her lower lip…

DANE CROSSED HIS arms over his chest, closed his eyes and shook his head in disbelief. That morning, after breakfast with the priests, he told himself that he was not going to the park. He *promised* himself that he would not go, that he would put some space between him and Rhapsody, and not create a situation he'd find he could no longer control. But of course, that would in turn mean admitting that there was a situation to begin with, or even worse, one that needed monitoring and honing in. Honesty was the best policy, especially with oneself. He thought about their last encounter at the park...

She'd bent over and plucked a wild daisy from the grass, placed it behind her ear and continued to walk in one single bound as if she were one with nature. The way that simple gesture moved him, and the feelings that swelled within from the sight, let him know without a doubt that he in fact had a situation on his hands: he was strongly attracted to her. There was no way to deny the magnetism at this point. While he walked beside her, he felt his heartbeat increase and his palms grew moist as his nerves warned him of what was happening within him. He was lost. Still, he felt terrible for how he'd abruptly left, making up an excuse that he was running late, waving goodbye and promising to see her soon. He knew it looked odd to her, but what could he do?

One moment, the woman was sauntering by his side, telling him about her new student, a young nine year old boy, a musical prodigy, then the next, he was practically flying down the walking path, barreling toward his car as if a fire alarm had gone off. He got in his vehicle and drove and drove and drove, his mind in a daze as he gripped the steering wheel and fought himself at each and every turn. But the next day, it was like nothing had happened. He was right back at Mies Park. He'd lied to himself, broken his promise...

He was there anyhow, waiting for her—hoping she'd come and hoping she wouldn't. But she did, and he sighed with relief, and then with worry. They had their usual small talk, and occasionally, their hands would brush up against one another as they walked so close together. The mere touch of her finger across his sent him into spells of euphoria. Then, they'd part ways, and he'd go back to the rectory, filled with anxiety, yet simultaneously anxious to see her again.

It's just a phase...

This was what he told himself as he re-opened his eyes and moved away from his apartment door, settling on his couch. He could still smell the scent of grass on his clothing from when he sat down with her on a blanket by the water. He'd failed...

Running his hands up and down his face, he sighed, completely exasperated. Finally, he dropped to his knees, and knelt over his bed. It was becoming too much, the temptation too great to control. This made alcohol feel like the easiest thing to kick. But Rhapsody, well, that was an entirely different matter altogether.

"Father, please help me. I don't know what I'm doing, what I'm thinking or feeling anymore. I've met someone, and I was already confused..." He swallowed. "And now, I don't know what's happening. I don't want to do the wrong thing and disappoint you. I need people around me though. It feels good to be around her. I can be myself, but, I feel like...like I'm doing something wrong. I'm afraid to talk to her now, afraid to see her, but I'm more scared of letting her go and not seeing her at all. Please help me; please show me what to do."

He got to his feet and sat back down on the bed, trying desperately to push away the fleeting images of recent sources of resentment—the passing of Josh, the Sunday School pamphlets, the old man at the nursing home, all of it was eating away at him, festering, making him fight his own self on a daily basis. He just wanted to be happy...

CHAPTER TEN

Two weeks later...

S HE PUMPED HER legs, and a squeal of childish delight had escaped from between her plush lips. Dane relished the sight, felt alive just by looking at her, but that in itself gave him pause. He couldn't help drawing inward, in his own thoughts. Despite his repeated prayers, he once again continued to find himself at the park. For the second time, he'd found a way to suddenly excuse himself, and this time, when he returned to the rectory, he stayed in his room the entire evening, praying for forgiveness. Attraction and lust had merged, causing emotions and fantasies that he found reprehensible. *The erection... I had to quickly hide it. God, how embarrassing!* Nevertheless, he couldn't stop the pull, and went there again, searching for her.

Upon his return, he noticed Rhapsody was a bit standoffish. He promptly apologized for his abrupt departure, blaming it on an engagement he'd completely forgotten about. That was a half-truth. He did in fact have to get back to the parish for a meeting, and time had escaped him, but he couldn't admit that he was running away from her, he simply couldn't. After more prayer, he'd convinced himself that she was simply a friend, and the fact that she was attractive to him should have no bearing on that.

He relished the here and now, their friendship building and building. He surmised that she was healthy for him. It was natural for his body to respond to her beauty, he was flesh and blood, and a heterosexual man, but he was fully in control of himself. It was fine. It had to be because God hadn't taken her away. God hadn't made her less beautiful, nor did his need to be around her become any less strong or tantalizing after many days and nights of prayer. In some way, he felt that he had permission, and it gave him a slight sense of a peace, though deep inside he suspected it would be short-lived and he'd have to battle his own conscious once again.

"Ahhhh!"

She giggled, swinging high up in the air. He swung to her left, ignoring her half-hearted requests for him to slow down as they enjoyed a bit of playful competition. "Dane, Father Dane, Dane of Wrath!" she teased, screaming at the top of her lungs. "I thought you were a nice man?!"

Then she winded down, swinging slower and slower when he sat up from his swing, unable to wipe the smirk off his face. Like two children, they'd swung from the steel monkey bars, glided down the short, stiff slide that was entirely too small for either of them and made a mess in the sandbox. She'd complained that she hadn't gotten her work-out in ages, and he'd complained that he needed to get back to the gym—but neither of them budged. The sun was beaming, the morning was beautiful, and the park hadn't yet filled up with the weekend crowd.

Such a perfect day, but still he couldn't erase the deep bruise on his heart, from a nightmare he'd had the evening before. Josh was screaming for help, and Dane had woken up in a cold sweat, his striped pajama top stuck to his chest and his hair plastered to his face as if he'd been dumped in a vat of water. He'd let Fr. Kirkpatrick know that he may need to seek a grief counselor. Despite his ability to demonstrate empathy to others, Dane rarely extended himself the same courtesy. He wrestled with his inability to fully cope with Josh's death, seeing it as a sign of weakness. He'd even said it in his prayers...

'Lord, you owe me no explanations as to why he is gone, and I humbly apologize for questioning you.'

But he still hurt and although it got a little better, some anger remained.

He walked backwards, wrapping his arms around himself as he tried to muster a smile, and move out of the sudden returning funk, but it was too late. She was now swinging at a slow crawl, her eyes keenly upon him and her lips slightly parted.

She got up and took him by surprise when she ran her hand down his shoulder and arm. Her look of concern stirred him from head to toe, and her touch made his nerve endings sing. They stood so close. He could make out all the details of her face—a blemish here, a beauty spot there...

She makes me feel free. Why'd she have to be so pretty? I wish....

Then, he stopped himself.

"I'm not going to ask you what's wrong. Just let me tell you what I know, and then you can decide if you want to talk to me about it. Do we have a deal?" She cocked her head to the side and kept her hand on his arm—a touch meant for comfort.

He swallowed hard and nodded in agreement.

"For the past couple of days, just like when I first saw you, you looked sad, Dane. That is actually what caught my attention about you. I saw this nice-lookin' guy… no offense."

He couldn't help but smile.

"I'm a priest, not a robot. I can take a compliment," he joked, causing her to laugh.

"I know, I know." She rolled her eyes. "But, as I was saying—I noticed you, but you had this sadness about you and, I'll just let you know," she lowered her voice as if she were going to divulge a juicy bit of gossip, "I saw you drinking…"

Dane sighed and turned away from her when embarrassment took over, making him feel like a damn fool.

"Yeah, uh…about that. I don't do that anymore," he assured. "It has been an unfortunate vice of mine, and I've stopped. I'm actually back to going to AA meetings again." At her stunned expression, he added, "I've used alcohol to help get through some rough times. I guess I am one of those you'd call a functional drinker…doesn't make it any better, just means I am one shot glass away from full-fledged addict. I don't kid myself."

She nodded in understanding.

"I'm one of those people that's not in denial about it. I have a problem. I understood what was going on. I fell off, but I have no need for it anymore, and no need for any more excuses about it, either." He sighed.

"Look, I'm not here to judge you, Dane," she finally uttered, her expression relaxing. "I don't know what was going on with all of that, the drinking – you don't have to explain it, but thanks for telling me."

He nodded.

"I know you're used to being the counselor and giving support to others, but you know, it helps to talk sometimes so that is why I keep asking you about your friend, how you are grieving. I know you probably thought, 'Why does she keep bringing this up?' but that's why. I wished someone would have asked me to talk about it when I'd lost someone, you know? I felt like I was getting on people's nerves, but it helps. It really does."

"Thanks Rhapsody, you did make me talk about it more than I ever would without your inquiries. I've had family members pass before, but I took Josh's death much worse and I am starting to understand why."

"Well good. Maybe if you think back to some of your golden years with him it would help. Maybe focus on the good times, instead of the last few months you had with him. The guy standing by his locker, being late for class while he loitered around the hallways—some of him has to still be in there, somewhere." She pointed to his chest. "What's going on, Dane?" She stepped a little closer to him, so he felt the warmth of her breath heat his neck and jaw. "Are you upset that this grieving process is taking longer than you expected? You actually seem angry with yourself that you are still sad about it." Her brows furrowed.

"It's more than that. What has happened is that his death has caused me to think about other things in my life even more so than I was previously, stuff I'd been grappling with for a year or so now, but yeah, I'm having some problems." He admitted. "I go back and forth with it; one day, I give it up and I am in a good mood and then the next, well… I mean, really," he said in exasperation, "how long is this supposed to go on? I don't know what's going on with me, but it is awakening all sorts of difficulties I had in the past—doors I thought were closed." They began to walk slowly, side by side, with her arm wrapped around his. He looked down briefly at her hand on him.

We look like a couple.

"Everyone has trouble every now and again. Some of it is self-imposed, I suppose. I guess its ego." He shook his head in frustration. "But, his death and just…life in general. I feel really confused right now, Rhapsody. I am going through some things. It's not just his death anymore, it's…it's what it means. It's making me think about things in an entirely brand new way, not sure if that is good or bad yet." He gave a choppy chuckle. "I have a lot of questions, and only a few answers. I don't like that," he said with a more serious tone.

"Why do you think you have to understand everything? Why can't some things just *be*?"

He stopped walking and looked at her. The simple words made him pause and reflect.

"That's a good question, and I honestly don't know."

They started to walk again.

"I mean, you're a priest now. You live on faith, right?"

"*By* faith," he corrected.

"Yeah, well, you accept things you can't see, believe in things many people don't, and you talk to someone who doesn't verbally respond. You believe in stories about virgin women giving birth." She laughed lightly. "Surely, you can trust that this part of life—death—sometimes doesn't have the resolution that we want? It's death…the death of a life on

Earth, not the death of love. Your love for him will remain the same, maybe even grow. You still have a relationship with him, regardless of him not being here, Dane, just like you have a relationship with Christ, the son of God that you can't see or hear. And, sometimes, in death, though we hurt, there is a lesson for us, a lesson about love and friendship. I have never believed that God takes something away from us without giving us something back in return," she shrugged, "but that's just me."

He could feel her words moving throughout his heart, awakening a new understanding.

She has faith. She wouldn't know these things if she didn't. She's a believer, too.

"You're not allowing yourself to just *be*. To simply exist and feel, and now the feelings have caught up with you. You have to allow yourself to feel the pain before you can heal, Dane." She stopped walking and gently put her hand on the side of his face.

So soft...so right...she's so right...

"Thank you for those words, Rhapsody."

"You're welcome." She patted his arm and released it. They continued to stroll in silence for a few moments. The faint sound of water splashing increased in volume. They both looked to their left, at the lake. Three small row boats bobbed about with people inside them wearing orange life preserver jackets.

"They've got the boats out already?" He stopped walking and faced the lake head on, smiling. "I guess it is about that time."

"Yup, looks like fun." She shot him a look.

He smiled at her. "What's that about? You want to get on

one?" He pointed to the people on the boats. "I dunno," he grinned and shook his head, "you may try to do some of that yoga on it and make us fall overboard." He laughed louder when she stuck her tongue out at him.

"Okay. Let's do it, let's go." Grabbing her wrist, he took off, pulling her to a small white shingle covered booth. A ruddy-faced teenager took a five dollar bill from Dane, and before long, they were on a small red canoe with flaky paint. Dane rowed while Rhapsody leaned back and looked up at the sky as if she were some actress being filmed for a 1950s blockbuster.

"You're going to let me do all the work, aren't ya? There is a heck of a current here!"

"A big strong man like you?" she teased. "I figured you had this all taken care of." She cast a lazy gaze his way, her dark eyes hooded. "You're funny, you know that?" A lopsided smile budded across her face.

"Am I?" he laughed. "I like to think I can make people laugh from time to time."

"Tell me a joke. I could use it."

He studied her for a moment, "Okay, sure. Two peanuts were walking down the street in a bad neighborhood. One was a salted."

He was met with silence, could almost hear crickets chirping, and then she burst out laughing.

"That was corny but funny!" she managed in between chuckles.

"Okay, I got another one. What do you get when you cross an elephant with a rhino?"

"Um, I don't know…"

"El-if-i-no."

FORGIVE ME FATHER, FOR I HAVE LOVED

"What!" She laughed harder. "Did you just cuss in a roundabout way, Fr. Dane?" She looked so beautiful when she laughed; it stirred him in unexpected ways.

He felt his groin stiffen, causing him a slight bit of anxiety. He'd been working out at the gym extra hard the past few weeks. It was great for the body, and helped during times like this. But he was stuck. There was no elliptical or weights to lift to ease the strain. He cleared his throat, and decided to focus on something, *anything* but her…just for a few seconds. Out the corner of his eye, he could see her undoing the wrap on her head.

Oh God…no…

He swallowed again, pretending not to see. A light wind blew her wild, jet black locks around. No way he could get away from that sight, so he just stared at her hair falling like inky sunrays, each coil gleaming and healthy.

So much hair…and soft. It's not straight anymore, how it was in high school.

…And he wanted to touch it.

Shoving her headscarf in her bag, she leaned back, her back arched and breasts pointing to the sun. Laughter escaped her—deep, throaty, seductive and free. Through the thinness of the fabric of her taupe leotard top, he made out the details of her torso as she moved. Her lean stomach disappeared into a pair of dark gray yoga pants. He studied her thighs, flexing as she extended her right leg and stretched her black Mary Jane slipper covered feet.

She's so alive. I wonder what that feels like?

In that instant, he desired to live vicariously through her, even if just for a few moments.

After a while, she sat up and looked at him, a broad smile

on her face while the wind picked up a bit, moving her wild hair to and fro.

"You know what?"

"What?" He turned away from her again, trying to ignore his growing attraction for her.

"This is the most peaceful I've been in a long ass time, I mean…" She shook her head, clasping her hands to her face in embarrassment. "First," she counted off her fingers, still laughing, "I befriend a priest I used to go to high school with, and tell him he is hot, and then I keep cursing in front of him. Just like my mother told me, sometimes it's like I don't have any home trainin', I'm sorry." Her laughter tapered, but the smile was still on her face.

She'd said the words, but she wasn't sincere. She wasn't sorry one bit; she just felt it was the right thing to say, regardless of her true feelings. The woman simply wasn't politically or religiously correct, but she tried.

"I told you it's fine. I mean that. Just be yourself." That was all he really wanted anyway—Rhapsody in her natural form, because she seemed to be at her best that way.

She nodded. "Well, I've made you tell me in full detail what's been going on with you, and you said you came to the park for some peace, to think. I want to say, you're not the only one."

His eyebrow shot up inquisitively.

"I've been dealing with a lot of mess and I started coming to the park again to clear my mind. I came during the winter, happy no one was here. I had gone through a breakup. Breakups are horrible in the winter, Dane." She shook her head and looked away into the water.

"I'd imagine they are, especially a Detroit winter." He

smiled.

She says it like I've never had a love life...like I came out of the womb as a priest. Well, I can't blame her; she doesn't really know that part of me...yet.

"Yup." She sighed, clasping her hands together and sitting straighter as waves made their boat bob a bit more aggressively. "The breakup was a mess, but it was long overdue. And, there is constant tension between my sister and I." She glanced at him, a bit hesitant, as if gauging his reaction. "Can I use you as a sounding board? I would like your input on this—someone impartial."

"By all means."

"I was actually a little jealous when you described your relationship with Josh at first."

"Really? Why is that?"

"He was more like a brother. I can see why you'd have a hard time letting go, Dane. That was a *really* special relationship and I'm sure I don't even know the half of it."

Again, she reads me like a book.

"I like how you seem to know me so well, Rhapsody." He allowed the thoughts to finally leave his mind and let her know just how he felt. "You understand me, you fill in the words, the puzzle. It feels good talking to you."

I'm giving you permission, Rhapsody...come inside.

They just stared at one another for what felt like an eternity, until she looked shyly away. He found it absolutely adorable.

"Tell me about your sister, what seems to be the issue?" he encouraged.

She exhaled loudly. "She acts like I think I'm the best, or some mess." She grimaced, shaking her head in confusion.

"Like I'm Ms. IT! Whatever... Her name is Melody, and when we were little, we were super close." She linked her fingers tight, locking them like a licorice vine.

"Then, I don't know what happened." She looked back out into the water. "She told me I think I'm better than her, and she makes fun of me, like we are ten years old! I'm talking really silly, snide, sometimes cruel remarks, Dane. Like, for instance, she says I'm strange and sit around with candles, dancing and meditating all day. Just stupid shi...stupid mess." She shook her head.

"Well, do you?" He grinned, forcing her to laugh, to let the pain glide down smoother.

Regardless of her nonchalant behavior, he could tell that the ugly words said by her sister really hurt Rhapsody. She tried to act as if it was just annoying, but it was so much more.

We have more in common than she'd like to admit. She tries to be too strong, too.

"Now, normally," Rhapsody twisted her lips and put her hand on her hip, "I wouldn't give one iota about what someone thinks of me, but my sister? My mom, yeah, I care!" She looked straight at him. "Their opinion means the world to me but, you know," she shrugged, "what can you do? You just have to get over it."

"But you're *not* over it. What she says, it hurts your feelings. It's okay to admit that, you know." He smiled at her as he continued to gently row the oars through the dark blue water.

She looked at him for the longest. He wondered what was going on in her mind, but he remained quiet, loath to disturb the moment just yet.

"I know, and you're right. It just seems a little silly. I mean, I am twenty-seven damn years old, Dane! My sister just turned thirty. We are better than this, or so I thought."

"I had no idea you had a sister in our high school, you know that?"

She must've been in at least one of my classes.

"You didn't know anything about me in high school, so it makes sense."

But I wanted to.

He didn't dare say it, lady liquor would have given him the courage but he was done with her, he had to rely on his own scruples now, no beer bravado allowed.

"So anyway, she called me last night—left a voicemail about our mother having some party for her friends and wanted me to swing by and say hello. My mother had called me before, and I told her I'd try to make it. I didn't need Melody calling right behind her, telling me how important it was!"

Dane almost felt as if *he* were Melody as Rhapsody cut evil glares his way. She became more animated, unleashing her burden. If he couldn't hug her the way he wanted, he'd settle for second place, giving her a comforting word.

Dane offered an encouraging smile, urging her to get it all off her chest.

"And another thing," she said, "she has never, not once," she pursed her lips, "*never* has that woman come to a show of mine, Dane. I have invited her to countless performances. Let her be having a sorority party, then she wants me to come but gets mad if I sing. For example, usually one of her friends will ask me to, and her sorority sisters she graduated from college with, will tell me how nice I sounded. She only invites me to try to show me up, to show them how much better she is than me, but then she accuses me of acting that way and it backfires!"

Dane was convinced that Rhapsody barely spoke to anyone about this problem. It felt too fresh, unrehearsed and raw, and he'd heard enough confessions over the years to be able to properly diagnose a complaining personality versus a person who was purging emotional trauma for the very first time.

"I mean, I'll be the first to admit," she continued. "She and I are like night and day. I am this person that just goes and does stuff. Yes, I can admit it. I know exactly who I am and what I am about. I need to look before I leap more, but I'm just not wired that way, although I'm learning, indeed I am." Her eyes narrowed. "But she sits around wanting to impress people 24/7." Pointing at herself, she added, "Me? I don't want to impress, I want to *move* and stir people. I want the inside of the person to grow, the outside will take care of itself, it will follow. That is what music does in my book…it moves people to action."

"It does. It is a universal language."

"Exactly! People all over the world embrace music, no matter their language, ethnicity and religion. We all react to rhythm. Life *is* rhythm. The seasons, our relationships, everything alive moves, even if you can't see it. Everything breathing has a pulse, a beat it follows."

Dane nodded in agreement. She was passionate about her vocation, about the crumbling sibling relationship; and her way of describing music, he wholeheartedly agreed with. He resolved to not speak for a while. She was like a patient on his imaginary couch, and he wanted her to keep purging, keep talking, until after a while, there was nothing left to do BUT listen.

She is rather poetic even in her anger. How beautiful.

"Our spirit is where it's at! She's superficial and silly, and doesn't care about her fellow man…like, she could look at you sittin' there on that bench, the way you were that day, and act like you didn't even exist."

But this isn't about me right now, Rhapsody. Stay on track.

"She does that with everyone but she wants all the sympathy in the world when she breaks a nail or her day didn't go quite right," she continued. "Melody is a bitch!" The words came out steeped in immense hurt and dripping in hatred. This time, she didn't apologize for the profanity. She said it. She meant it. The end. He watched her tense; the once calm and collected Rhapsody was emotionally injured—a wreck. This reaction caused him to wonder what else lay under the surface.

What about the relationship that died right in the dead of winter? What did it *do* to her? Was she turned inside out? Did she shrug that off and run away from the emotions, and now they came boiling out of her heart, frothing over the edge, bubbling, and catching fire—burning her up with the scorch of the truth? He surmised she'd been in love, but possibly convinced herself otherwise toward the end, just to get over the heartbreak. She was a 'Braveheart', but it was time to stop equating hidden emotions to strength. Strength is not in what you do or say, and what tears you do not shed. Strength knows that you must purge, because you are a creation of love. She had his same ailment—cure the sick and distressed, but the healer gets no aid or care.

"Sometimes I wish I could just beat the living shit out of her!" Rhapsody's voice echoed.

Well this surely escalated fast.

He stifled a smile, knowing it was highly inappropriate for

him to appear slightly amused by her last confession.

"Let me offer you something." He continued to row, smooth and even, turning them around ever so gently.

"Yes," she said meekly, as if aware that she'd become too excited, her emotions roused and raw. He watched her chest rise up and down then slowly begin to calm but the unease on her face increased as she looked down onto her lap, nervously rubbing her palms together.

"From what you've described, and from what I know of you, it seems to me that you wish you had a more productive and healthy relationship with your sister. Despite your demonstrative flare-up, I can see through that."

Her lip twitched, but she kept her eyes lowered.

"But Rhapsody, it takes two people to have a relationship. They have to be on the same page. Not necessarily in the same state of growth, but their goal has to be compatible, and that is to fortify the relationship, make it strong. Relationships are built on trust, and you have to be willing to be vulnerable with one another. This goes with *any* type of relationship. Whether it is a marriage, mine with the church, and yours with your students and even your audience when you perform. When someone doesn't trust, accept or appreciate the other person, and can't be free to be honest, then the relationship is off balance."

She slowly looked up at him, taking an obvious interest in the words he'd uttered. A faint smile tugged at her lips.

"You are trying to equalize a mountain and an ant hill, make them weigh the same…place one on each side of a seesaw and force them to even out. It simply can't be. Once you let go of the idea of what you *want* your sister to be, and how you wish for her to receive you, you won't feel as strongly about this. The only expectation we should have is to expect nothing and that change, whether good, bad or indifferent, is inevitable. Now, sure," he shrugged, "you may always wish the relationship were better, healthier, but you won't lament over it or become so angry about it anymore. It's okay to care, Rhapsody. It's great to want better, and to want things to improve, but *you* are the only one you can control. Nevertheless, I'm glad you had a chance to get this off your chest. You clearly needed to. It's good to hash this stuff out. You taught me that as well."

"Well, I think you about summed that up!" She chuckled and gently slapped her knee, causing him to laugh back.

"I hope I helped you, like you helped me."

Silence.

"You did and you're right. I knew that, you know?" She shrugged. "Everything you've said I knew, but when you are in the moment—"

"Or not accepting the situation in here," he looked down at his chest as he continued to row the boat, "in your heart, then you'll keep fighting. I know all about that." His thoughts drifted to him racing around the country speaking to different doctors about Josh's condition. "This may not even be much about you, Rhapsody. This may be a problem that Melody is having and it doesn't have anything to do with you."

She clapped her hands. "Amen to that! I agree." A few moments passed.

"I feel better…I really do. Thanks."

"Awesome. Mission accomplished." He held her gaze as they neared the dock, then, took her hand and helped her off the boat. Her legs wobbled, and he instinctively grabbed her around her waist. Conflict raged inside of him.

Do I remove my hand and let go now?

He slowly released her, and she did him a favor by not looking in his direction, ignoring the smoldering build-up. Let off the hook, he allowed her to move ahead of him, walking on the uneven earth until they were both settled on grassy higher ground.

After a few awkward moments, they walked to the parking lot, exchanging inconsequential tidbits.

"…Yeah, the New York cheesecake is better," she said.

"What about their key lime pie?"

"I've never tried it."

"It's delicious. Maybe one day we can go to Detroit's Cheesecake Bistro for lunch."

She sighed and leaned up against her car. Instead of unlocking her black Corolla, she just stayed there, as if she were waiting for something or someone.

"Hey Dane, let me ask you somethin'." She drummed her fingers against the roof of the car.

"Sure."

"How did a football jock like you end up becoming a priest?"

He laughed and ran his fingers through his hair. "I get asked that all the time. I was called. That is the simplest, most concise answer I can give you."

She nodded, seemingly deliberating over her next words. "You seem to be into philosophy."

"I am. I studied it in college, it is customary, and at the time, I didn't know for sure I was going into the priesthood but it has served me well. I take it that statement is going somewhere? Another question?"

"Why have you taken an interest in me? Hmmm?"

He detected a slight annoyance.

"I'm not Catholic," she said. "I'm not interested in con-verting. I want you to tell me why after all these weeks, we are talking and getting to know one another. Hell, I'd even say you are a friend of mine at this point!"

"I'd say the same…"

"You now know more about me, well, about how I *feel*, than anyone else. I don't trust easily, not anymore," she rolled her eyes, "I *barely* trust myself nowadays so…why are you here, talking to me?"

Her suspicions began to choke them, but he wouldn't stay in her aim of fire. He knew where she was driving— destination paranoia, he'd become a suspect.

"I could ask you the same exact thing," he replied, then stepped a little closer to her, resting his hand on the roof of her car.

She nodded and smiled, "True, but you haven't answered the question. Why is a priest, that being *you*, just so we're clear here…" *Sarcastic and suspicious. Nice…*"…talking to me like this? I enjoy you; don't get me wrong, it just strikes me as, well, a bit strange to tell you the truth. We're spending time together now. I actually schedule my work-outs around my conversations with *you*."

"You know," he scratched his head and looked briefly around the parking lot, at the people mulling about, "I've asked myself the same thing. I think we meet people when we are supposed to meet them, just like you said to me when I was telling you how messed up I am about Josh's passing. You've already answered your question to me, with an answer *you* gave to me."

She nodded and crossed her arms over her chest.

"I've just accepted that I needed a new friend, and maybe you're her. Who am I to question that?" He smiled widely. "And for the record, priests can be friends with anyone they like. Am I supposed to only be around Catholics? How does that help anyone? Isn't that, as they say, 'preaching to the choir'?" The wind carried the scent of her perfume past him, causing him a mixture of sensual excitement and worry.

"Oh." Her eyebrow shot up and she put her hand on her hip, a slight smirk across her face, "So, you're trying to save me, hmmm?"

"You know better than that." He grinned. "But if you grow from our conversations, then that is fine with me."

Truth of the matter, he wasn't concerned about saving Rhapsody from anything. She seemed to be doing just fine on her own and he was extremely intrigued with her spiritual beliefs, at least the ones she'd communicated. She had been baptized. She appeared to have a general understanding of the bible that aided in their small discussions concerning it as of late and she was able to present her own ideas in a clear manner. He couldn't argue with that. The woman, though different than he in this regard, could hold her own.

They shared another brief silence.

"And just so you know." She slicked her tongue slowly across her bottom lip, "I like your personality. I find you intriguing. That is why I talk to you. I have questions."

"And I have answers...and questions, too."

"Well then, the communication will never stop." She looked him up and down, her eyes hooding, her hips swaying ever so slightly.

"I pray not."

Don't ever stop...

"Can I call you?" he added after she gave a light chuckle and got into her car. He leaned in the window after she rolled it down. She moved back a bit, looking surprised at his question.

"Yeah, I suppose. I think conversations on the phone *and* in person would be great."

She stared straight ahead, running her fingers along the steering wheel. Then, as if she came to a decision, she took out her phone and typed in his name.

They exchanged numbers, and soon, she drove away. He didn't dare take his eyes off of her car until he could no longer see her, and she was but a distant visual memory...

CHAPTER ELEVEN

"IS THIS A problem? I was just in the area." Her voice trailed as she pointed to the open church door. All around, parishioners spoke quietly amongst themselves and spilled out onto the street. She crossed her ankles as she stood before him, a sight to behold.

"No, of course not." Dane tried to hide his surprise, his shock…his exuberance.

She looks beautiful.

There she stood in a long, flowing floral print skirt and black fitted top. Her hair was wrapped differently; he paid close attention to the black loose strands cascading down the sides of her elegant neck. Her large, silver hoop earrings sparkled under the high ceiling lights. People moved around, some making their way to the altar, while some walked to the exit. Mass had just ended and during service, Rhapsody had admitted to sitting in the back and listening. He swallowed and looked around, seeing Fr. Kirkpatrick nod in his direction before turning away.

"I don't work too far from here actually." She looked around in awe at the high pillars, frescoed ceilings, grandiose stain glass windows, large organs and intricately laid out alter table. "I had no idea St. Michael was less than twenty minutes away. I had to um, go to the post office, and I got a bite to eat out this way. Sunday is my one day to relax, do whatever I want to do. I remembered you were over here so...I..."

He held up his hand. "You don't need to keep explaining. It's great to see you, I'm so glad you came. Hey, would you like a tour? Let me get changed, and then I can take you around. Stay right here, I'll be right back."

Before she could respond, the man was gone and back in a flash. He gently took her by the wrist and led her to the new daycare center area that was being built per his generous donation.

"Oh my goodness, this is so nice! It's so modern and big." He watched her eyes widen as she looked around the bright, cheery room and noticed the silver tool boxes lying about, blueprints and construction debris.

"Yes, it should be ready in about a month. We've already hired two teachers and four teacher aids. It's a very exciting project. This church is over two hundred years old, and though some renovations over the years have been done, not nearly as many as needed. Due to a financial blessing, that has all changed. The modifications and updates were definitely needed."

He led her to two side by side kitchens with double ovens—the area was spotless. Many of the parishioners had volunteered to clean it in months past, but now, they had enough revenue to splurge and have a cleaning crew come in twice a week. Dane made sure they were people who needed a second chance, a company started by an ex-con that offered janitorial services. They'd done the best job he'd ever seen. The entire place sparkled.

"And where do you and the other priests stay?" She clasped her hands together, her purse swinging over her shoulder as she looked to and fro, as if expecting to see a few cots laid out nearby.

"Right, through there, down that hall." He pointed down a long hallway with brick walls and dull, recessed ceiling lights. There were large wooden doors on either side. "This entire area is being renovated as well. Our apartments look really nice now. We all have our own space, equipped with small kitchenettes, full private bathrooms and the like, and we furnish and decorate them as we see fit. They aren't anything to brag about probably by most standards, but they are comfortable and I like my studio."

"Can I see it?"

"Oh, I don't know about that, Rhapsody," he grimaced and shook his head. "We really aren't supposed to take anyone back to our private quarters."

Disappointment etched her face. He sighed and looked around, taking note that no one was close by.

"I tell you what; lucky for you, my door is the second one on the right, so we don't have to go too far down the hallway and possibly disturb anyone. I will let you peak inside, but you can't go in, do you understand?" he smiled, one tinted with a bit of a warning. "I understand that you're curious what it looks like. I get that."

"Oh, thank you and yes, I totally understand and won't step foot inside." She laughed giddily. "This is all new to me, so you'll have to excuse my ignorance. I wasn't raised in the church but when I did attend, it definitely wasn't a cathedral."

He nodded in understanding. "Well, Rhapsody, come along, let's make this quick though."

Dane knew this was against the rules. Regardless, her child-like curiosity was innocent, and it propelled him forward. Inside of him he believed it was an opportunity to teach, to expand her horizons. For reasons still unknown, he wanted her to know everything about his beliefs, his life, his world. It would draw her closer to him, of this, he was sure.

"I will open the door and remember, stay right where you are at." He removed his key from his pocket, and got a whiff of her sweet perfume as she leaned in closer. The honeyed scent reminded him of a mixture of cherries and sage, and he found it delightful. He opened the door slowly, allowing her to take in an eyeful, but not without checking over his shoulder a time or two.

Music sounded from somewhere beyond, while she studied the hand-woven floor rug, neatly hung photos and elaborate painting of the Virgin Mother. Rhapsody appeared to be taking it all in, stretching as far as her neck would allow. She glanced past neatly stacked periodicals and books on the coffee table, then tried to see better inside the half opened door of his bedroom. He grinned as he briefly looked down at his shoes.

She thinks she is really smooth about it. You won't be able to see anything, Rhapsody.

The music continued, and she turned away from her view of his digs, back up the hall, her eyes searching for the source of the exquisite sound.

"They sound...surreal." She cupped her ear and smiled,

swaying a bit, as if mesmerized by the compellingly beautiful voices. "That's a *real* choir, isn't it? Those are actual men, not a recording?"

Dane crossed his arms. "Yes, it's the Men's Choir. They are singing 'Dies Irae', which means, 'Day of Wrath.' What you're hearing is their rendition of the 13th century Latin Catholic hymn."

"What are they saying, what's it about?"

"The second coming of Christ…judgment day, Rhapsody."

They shared a moment of silence and just listened. He'd heard it so many times, it no longer had the effect on him that it apparently had on her, but he was glad to see it—a mystical change right before his very eyes. He loved seeing the light in her shine, her spirit moved. Regardless of her not understanding the words or the feelings behind the hymn, she clearly burned with spiritual passion with the intensity imprinted on her face, as if she were being led astray by an invisible entity that had completely brainwashed her, stolen her heart away and made her soul dance. Seeing how mesmerized she was, he led her back to the front of the church, and they sat side by side, listening as the choir continued to practice. He watched her out the corner of his eye. She was in a trance, completely captivated.

I will make her a tape, a copy of this.

He resisted the urge to speak to her, to engage her further, to give her additional information. He probably couldn't distract her, even he'd wanted to. She had no idea how she was making him feel, simply by sitting there, with him, feeling what he felt as a child. He now took the music for granted, but she was a newborn to the life the song gave, and he delighted in her response. There he sat, next to her, feeling all sorts of things. As she continued to listen, his thoughts drifted. When she'd first walked up to him after service, making her way through the thick crowd of parishioners, she'd scanned him from head to toe in his vestments. He stood there in his purple and gold chasuble that covered his alb and stole. This was who he was, and it pleased him that, notwithstanding, she could still relate to him…she *still* wanted to be there.

After the choir had finished the song, Rhapsody sighed and stood. She hooked her purse back over her shoulder.

"I had to resist the urge to clap," she said. "That was amazing, Dane. Thanks for letting me sit here and listen, and thank you for showing me where you live. I know it was asking a lot, and I appreciate it. Well, I better let you get back to—"

"No." He stood, gently touching her hand. "Won't you stay and have lunch with me out back, in our courtyard? I know you said you already ate but we have lots of refreshments and we can just talk."

She seemed taken aback, but nodded.

He lightly ran his fingers over his shirt sleeve, his footsteps echoed loudly as they trekked toward the garden. Occasionally, he glanced over his shoulder to ensure she was still close behind. He could feel her burning gaze on the back of his head, and wished he could have just sixty seconds inside her brain, to see what she *really* thought, what she *really* felt that she may not have shared.

They sat, just the two of them, amongst tall, pious stone statues, cobblestoned enclosures, a white water fountain of two birds with their mouths open and new landscaping that made the area pop with bursts of color. Beautiful, lush greenery surrounded the enclosed area and the rock picnic table felt cool under his fingertips as he took his seat, and ran his hand leisurely along it.

He cleared his throat as he looked across at her, locking his fingers together.

"It's pretty out here…you said this church is two hundred years old, right?"

"Actually, I cheated you out of the complete history," he offered as he tilted his head ever so slightly. "The land had service, a very small chapel, almost three hundred years ago. This building, however, that you see behind you," he pointed over her shoulder, "has been here for a little over two hundred years. It is one of the oldest Catholic churches in the entire area."

Just then, they heard faint singing once again.

She turned back to him, smiling. "That's another Gregorian Chant," he offered. "It was originally sung by monks." He stopped, not wanting to go too far or overwhelm her, but his desire to teach her, to feed her curious mind, was almost irresistible. It fed his daydreams, the ridiculous ones that he knew he shouldn't be giving any sort of 'bread and water' to. The ones he drifted in and out of while he studied in his bed. The ones that said:

What if she were Catholic, too? Would it then be easier for me somehow? What if she loved God as much as I do? Maybe she does, we are just different faiths. I have no way of knowing that as of yet. I want to know, it's important to me. What if one day I—

…And before he ever let the thoughts mature, the ones that involved more than he was willing to contemplate, he'd turn away from them, feeling guilty for even delving there.

Dane, you're just hurting…clinging onto someone. That's all this is.

And just like that, he'd push the feelings aside.

Leaving her alone for some moments, he returned with two large glasses of water, chopped salads with sliced strawberries and mandarin oranges and a small loaf of warm, fresh baked wheat bread. He set a plate down in front of her, placing her fork and knife alongside it. He felt her slightly tremble as his arm brushed against her's. He assumed it was due to the occasional breeze. The knife was slightly crooked, so he reached over her shoulder and corrected its placement. Her scent entered his nostrils, intoxicating him with her femininity. He swallowed and rushed back to his seat.

As time passed, they spoke, laughed and ate, and the mood felt relaxed. Out the corner of his eye, he noticed a white curtain being pulled back from a window. Only one office was located in that wing. He looked upward and saw Father Kirkpatrick staring down at him.

Dane would normally have not been concerned; however, the look on Father Kirkpatrick's face made him pause; even from the distance he could make out the downturned lips and sour expression. He'd never seen the old man like that before—not toward *him*, at least. It seemed to be some sort of warning, as if the revered priest was well aware of what was going on in Dane's hidden thoughts and cloaked heart. This wasn't his first time having lunch with a woman; typically, it was done during or immediately following a counseling session. He'd prayed with women, heard their confessions, and they even told him their issues regarding their married lives, to which he gave prayer and advice. He didn't shy away from it, and it was not forbidden and that wasn't how he was raised or led to believe. He'd never acted inappropriately toward any of the female parishioners or nuns. It was rumored that several women had crushes on him, but that was never discussed in depth and he never paid the gossip any attention. He made sure his conduct was acceptable, regardless.

No one seemed to bat an eye about this sort of recreation, and he had an exemplary record for his years of service with the church. Thus, it unnerved him how Fr. Kirkpatrick continued to stare down at him. A part of him, his flesh, wanted to react, to take Rhapsody by the arm and lead her somewhere out of his view, but the other part of him understood he must stay. He was innocent, so there was no need to run away as if this were the scene of a crime. Finally, the old man turned away from the window. The curtain fell back down. Dane sighed, and picked up the woven bread basket.

"Would you like some?" he offered.

"Yes, I would like a slice. It smells really good."

He handed her the basket, along with a small plate with pats of warm butter. "Hey, I gotta joke for ya."

"I hope this is better than the one you told me the other day about the rhino!" She laughed heartily. "So silly!"

"You laughed, you know it was funny." He loved her smile.

"I was slightly amused." She winked.

He shrugged and grinned guiltily. "Yeah, well, here is one, and I promise you won't be shocked that a priest said it. I've told it to little kids, so it's rated G. Us sitting here eating reminded me about it."

"Okay, shoot." She took a bite of her bread.

"There was a Catholic school. The children were lined up in the cafeteria for lunch. At the head of the lunch counter was a huge tray of slices of bread, like wheat, rye, and the whole nine. Because of people taking more than they needed, the head nun put up a sign that said, "Take only one slice. God is watching you."

He watched her chew, her mouth full of fruit.

"So, in the end of the line …"

"The other end of the counter." She laughed, her mouth partially full as she interjected.

"Yes, thank you." He smiled back, ignoring the warmth growing in his stomach as he stared into her eyes. "There was this big plate of Oreo cookies."

"Mmmm, Oreos!" Rhapsody encouraged, still grinning as she took a swallow of her water.

"Yes, they are good, aren't they? Well, one of the children whispered in the ear of the kid beside him, and said, 'Take all the cookies you want, you're safe. God is watching the bread.'"

Rhapsody looked at him quietly, then burst out laughing.

"That was cute! Yeah…now *that* joke is one I'd expect you to say, but I liked them both."

He grinned and nodded, taking a swallow of his water before playing with his salad.

"Got anymore?" she asked, sucking her bottom lip.

"Jokes? Oh man, we'd be here all day!"

"Well entertain me, I'm ready for it."

He laughed, and rested his hands on the bench. On one side of him in the garden was the statue of Saint Patrick, and on the other, Saint Valentine. He felt their stony regard, and was filled with encouragement.

"A rabbi, a priest and a minister walk into a bar…"

CHAPTER TWELVE

Several days later…

"I'M SO GLAD you came," Margie said as her shaky hands gripped two antique white tea cups with blue swirls from the dining room table.

"Let me help you." Dane stood, removing the dishes from her unstable grip, set them back on the table and helped her back into her seat. Then, he took the cups in the kitchen and returned, sitting close to her. He placed his hand over hers.

"When you told me there were some things Josh had for me here, I hesitated, I'll be honest about that, Margie. I have had a hard time with his death, but I'm making it through. I'm getting better and I want the same for you, though I know it will take time. More importantly, I am glad that you and the children are taking it day by day. That is the most that can be expected."

She nodded, lowering her pale face toward the mahogany table, the ivory, lace liner bunching under her small, grasping palm.

"He said you were the strong one." She looked up at Dane and smiled—a sad smile, one that more than likely took all the strength she had in her to muster. "And he said you were an inspiration to him, and so many other people."

Dane swallowed, grappling with his emotions. He wished he could have said so much more to Josh.

"He really saw you like a brother, Dane. That is why he waited so long to tell you. He was…he was afraid you wouldn't treat him the same. He knew you'd dote on him; he wanted to enjoy what you two were, you know? Have a little more fun with you."

Dane nodded and looked away.

"So," she sat up a little straighter and pointed to the card-board box at the end of the table, "those are the items he wanted you to have. I have no idea what's in there. I could've just mailed them but—"

"It's fine," he offered, patting her hand. "I'm glad to be here. And, thank you for cooking dinner. That was very sweet of you."

"I am surprised you came all this way, but I understand it. Sometimes a trip like this can help with closure."

Dane nodded. That in fact was part of the plan. He'd opened himself further up to healing and moving forward with his life. He needed to allow the emotions to come, as well as to seek an exit during his grieving process, but one filled with peace. When Margie called him and said Josh had some things for him, he immediately booked a flight. He wanted to be inside the man's home, go where he'd gone during happier times. He was ready to forgive. Rhapsody was right. He couldn't have gotten to this point without allowing himself permission to feel the pain. He did just that, and though it was debilitating at times, it sped up the process, and now, he could finally move about without the heaviness on his shoulders from heartache.

"You're more than welcome to stay here in the guest room." She pointed up the stairway. He looked toward it, remembering all too well that, just ten months ago, they were having renovations done to their home. Josh had told him all about it. His promotion afforded them the ability and he'd re-painted the stairwell himself. Dane gulped as he looked at the nearly-fresh paint on the wall.

Josh did that…ran around to three hardware stores, trying to find light mustard with a touch of cream. He smiled as he recalled the conversation.

Margie slowly slid her hand away from his and stood. She ran her fingers over her burnt orange dress and tilted her head, smiling faintly at first, then more with heart.

"You know, Josh was supportive of you when you became a priest, but…"

She hesitated.

"But what?"

"No." She laughed nervously and turned away. "I probably shouldn't say it. It's not like he is here to defend himself." She began to walk toward the kitchen.

Dane called out to her, needing to hear the words. Anything that Josh had said, he was hanging onto by a thread. Somehow, the thought gave him another free second with his best friend. "No, Margie, what is it? It will be okay. What did he say?"

She stopped and turned around, looking uncertainly. Her dark brown eyes glowed as she stood directly by a corner lamp.

"He said…Dane, please just forget I even said anything. I don't feel comfortable about it. It was no big deal, but I don't feel I have the right." She twisted in discomfort.

"Margie, okay," Dane conceded. "I suppose that it can just stay with him. Don't worry about it." He let it go, seeing how terribly uncomfortable she'd become with whatever it was she was now hiding on her deceased husband's behalf.

"Thank you, I'm sorry. Uh, is there anything else I can get you?" She smiled nervously. "There's plenty of food left. I'm sorry, Dane. I started speaking and…I should have just kept my mouth shut. I'm not thinking clearly."

"No, no it's fine, Margie. Everything is okay, really," Dane offered sincerely. His gut churned, although a part of him desperately wanted to beg her to reveal the revelation. He'd had no idea that Josh was keeping a secret from him and he was now curious as to why. It didn't make sense. What could it be? This made no sense, and he felt unnerved by the mystery but was determined to not show it. They shared everything, why would he not tell him such a thing? He'd kept his true feelings under lock and key. *More secrets…*

After a while, he prepared to leave and gave Margie a big hug. In the living room, he kissed the twin girls and his new godson goodbye, then he left with the sealed cardboard box, back to his hotel room to sleep off the strange conversation that only gave birth to discomfort and questions left unanswered. In the morning, he packed and made his way to the airport, in anticipation of seeing his new muse, once again…

RHAPSODY'S BROWN HANDS were covered in warm, frothy

white suds. She sung high up into the heavens as she washed up her mother's piled up dishes from the evening before.

"Birds, flying hiiiiigh! You know, how I feel! Sun, in the skkkkky! You know, how I feel!" she sang.

"Breeze drifting on byyyy! You know how I feel!" her mother crooned, joining her daughter in the tune as she entered the kitchen with a taupe jogging suit on and her short, salt and pepper wavy hair combed to perfection.

Rhapsody spun around toward her mother, her smile wide as they continued to duet together.

"It's a neeew dawn! It's a new daaay! It's a new life, for meee! And I'm feel-liiing, good!"

"Whew!" Her mother clasped her hands together and sat down at the small table. "Nina Simone, honey! No one can do a Nina Simone song like you, Rhapsody." She nodded approvingly as she crossed her small ankles.

Rhapsody tilted her head and smiled at her mother, a woman she revered and owed her natural born gift to.

"Come here and sit down, talk to me." Her mother patted the table, her dark eyes smiling right along with her plush lips, covered in neutral matte lipstick.

"Let me just finish these dishes and then—"

"No, no, now." The older woman shook her head and looked down at the table, "You come on over here right this instant. I don't need maid service, honey. I'll get to 'em, but thank you, just the same."

Rhapsody quickly dried off her hands and made her way to the table, sitting directly across from the woman she adored.

"Rhapsody, I want to tell you how proud I am of you," she said, crossing her hands.

"You tell me that all the time, Mama." Rhapsody blushed.

"But thank you."

"But," her mother shook her finger at her, "it is never too much. A mother can never compliment her children enough. I know it has not always been easy for you and Melody…with your father dying while you two were so young." She paused and looked down, as if filled with deep regret. "Many times, I wasn't home and you were left with my mother. I was—"

"On the road, working. We were proud of you, Mama. I didn't want for anything! And you always came home and—"

"But there is no excuse. I think if I had put my dream off, deferred it, you and Melody would get along better and things, in general, would be better."

"Mama." Rhapsody sighed. "You can't accept responsibility for Melody's mess! The woman has it in for me!" She laughed angrily. "It has nothing to do with you, she's just crazy. It isn't your fault."

"No." her mother shook her head. "Rhapsody, that's where you're wrong. Melody told me that I treated you differently after I had to retire from singing. She told me that I tried to live my dreams through you, pushing you out for rehearsals and left her in the wind. If I did, it wasn't intentional, but I can't argue with the girl. She is entitled to feel how she feels." The woman shrugged sadly, her shoulders slumped. "I saw you had a gift, everyone did. I wanted you to have your chance, you know? Melody is gifted, too. She's great at planning events, she is great at her job, she just can't sing." She laughed heartily as she tapped the table with her fingertips.

Rhapsody offered a sympathetic smile. She knew better than to toot her own horn or overdose on her mother's compliments. Mama was coming for her; she could just feel it…

They shared a brief silence.

"So, how are you doing, Rhapsody? We haven't had any girl chat for a while."

...And she was right.

"I am doing good, Mama."

"You smile a lot more lately...you've got your pep in your step back. I like that." Her mother grinned as she ran her hand along the dog-eared plastic placemat. "You been keeping any new company?" she asked, eyebrow lifting.

A chill went up and down Rhapsody's spine.

Do I make up something or tell the truth? Shit. I know the answer...

The dreaded conversation had reared its ugly head. She hadn't shared the information with anyone but Tyra, and even in that conversation, she kept the details under lock and key. She surely wasn't going to confide in Melody, but she'd been wrestling the last few days with the realization that she was developing stronger feelings for the man... Surely, Mama would not approve and Melody would have a field day with the information if she ever got wind of it.

"It's nothing romantic, just a friend. He is really nice."

"I see..." Her mother paused, licked her upper lip, an all-knowing smile forcing Rhapsody to suddenly turn away, as if the clandestine key to reveal her shrouded contemplations had been presented.

"You can't fool me, girl." Her mother cackled. "If it *isn't* romantic, then you want it to be." She sighed. "I'm just glad what's his name is gone," she said, shaking her head, her lips twisting in disgust.

Raul. Mr. Lovah Man...Scumbag.

"Yes, we don't need to say his name." Rhapsody looked

absently out the window. "But believe you me, that is loooong over with."

They shared another brief silence.

"What is it? Is he married?" her mother didn't look directly at her, but Rhapsody's throat caught a lump. She ran her fingers up and down her neck, alarmed, not sure how to answer. To say 'Yes' wasn't exactly true, and to say 'No' wasn't either. But Rhapsody would never date an actually married man…she found the notion repugnant and it was against her beliefs. After all, when she initially thought he did have a wife, she was seething, and immediately removed her wayward thoughts only to realize his 'wife' was a building with people inside milling about taking communion…

"Why'd you ask me that?" Rhapsody's said as a mixture of defensiveness and alarm swarmed within her…as well as a need to buy an additional second or two.

"Because you are being secretive. I'm just grasping at straws here, but it would have to be something like that for you to keep this from me. You always tell me about your love life…*always*." Her mother smiled at her and winked. "You're grown, Rhapsody. I can't tell you what to do. Now, if you ask for my advice, then," she shrugged, "that is a different matter altogether." She continued to stare at her, as if waiting for Rhapsody to take the bait.

"Would you like something to drink?" Rhapsody offered finally, trying to buy even *more* time but to also help her mom.

"There is some sweet tea in there." Her mother pointed to the refrigerator.

"Sounds good, I'll pour us both a glass." Rhapsody opened one of the tall white kitchen cabinets and removed two red cups, wishing her mother had something strong she could mix in it. Rarely a drinker, she thought however she may need the extra edge to confide completely to the woman. In all honestly, her mother was her best friend, and she only kept things from her, if she felt somehow her actions wouldn't be understood. She tried to make good choices, and typically she did, but when it came to men, Rhapsody was the first to admit sometimes her judgment was lacking. One thing was clear, however—she would never again accept the likes of someone like Raul and she remained optimistic about finding 'the one' someday, although that expectation no longer ruled her. She never chased love or a boyfriend; it would simply happen and she'd welcome it, sometimes not checking out the merchandise deep within before making her final purchase.

"Tell me about him." Her mother cut through her wayward thoughts as they sat together, their cool glasses in hand.

"He's a priest." Rhapsody tried to wipe the smile off her face, but couldn't. It sounded so funny coming out, so ridiculous, she couldn't help it and before long, she was cracking up. Her eyes squinted and tears welled in them. She cast her sight back toward her mother who was slowly shaking her head and tapping the table with her French manicured gel tips.

"Rhapsody," her mother laughed, "I don't know about you sometimes, girl…"

"Mama, I told you it wasn't romantic, see?" She continued to laugh, so much she had to set her glass down as the contents threatened to spill.

"How'd you meet a priest, Rhapsody? Are you Catholic now?" she joked, knowing full well Rhapsody was somewhat against organized religion.

"Guess what? I actually went to high school with him. I'll

admit it. I thought he was attractive back then, but we never spoke, not even once. I never even knew his name." Rhapsody filled in the story, bit by bit, telling her how she'd came across Dane in the park. "And he lost his best friend. We struck up a conversation and have been talking almost daily now. It really was just that simple."

"You saw a priest sitting on a bench drinking a pint of liquor?" her mother back tracked, her finger pointed directly at her daughter's face.

Rhapsody lowered her head and chuckled. "Yup, and I haven't seen him drink since…said he was depressed. His friend had died, Mom. I understand it. He was open with me once we talked about it more."

She looked at her mother. The older woman seemed to be rolling the information around, weaving thoughts beneath her furrowed brows, sizing it up, stretching it out and dissecting it like a biology guinea pig. She looked toward the kitchen window, a smile on her face as she obviously deliberated. A part of Rhapsody wanted to hear what dear ol' Mom had to say about the whole situation. It was so gray, nebulous, so unclear, but another part didn't want to hear one word at all. Her mother never really showed disappointment in her, and she feared, she just may this time. She'd made it clear nothing had happened with the man, but she wasn't going to lie to the woman and say her heart didn't skip a beat or two when her eyes met his…

"Well," her mother looked back at her casually, "you two seem to need each other." She watched her mother slowly stand to her feet, and swallow the last bit of her sweet tea. "That's what it looks like to me."

"Oh, but I'm fine," Rhapsody offered. "I mean, he was

helpful to talk to, you know. I did speak to him about Melody and me but—"

"You're *not* fine, Rhapsody." Her mother smiled and nodded at her, a smile filled with wisdom and understanding. "You *pretend* to be fine, and from what you've shared, he did the same. You hide your truest concerns, hate feeling as if you don't have control over a situation. It is the one aspect of your life that contradicts your personality, and you struggle with it."

Rhapsody felt a chill in the room. She wasn't sure if it was real or self-imposed. For one of the first times in her life, she felt uncomfortable in her mother's home. The woman was too close, hitting a nerve, a place that Rhapsody hadn't travelled yet. She did have some resentment and pain, the loss of her father at such a young age, the emotional turmoil she endured with Raul, and now…now she had romantic feelings for a priest, for God's sake. Melody was just one of many wrinkles in her life fabric, and she decided to place the tightly rolled material atop her head, open her mouth, and let it all burst forth in the form of a song…

So many songs she'd written, standing at the sidelines of her own life, giving herself therapy from a distance with a chorus and funky drum solo but once the music stopped, all that was left was her raw voice—out there in the air, lingering, shining, golden expressions begging to be heard.

But when was she going to sit down and actually listen to it?

CHAPTER THIRTEEN

H E COILED THE phone chord in between his fingers as he leaned back on the headrest. While his cellphone charged, he'd resorted to his landline, enjoying the rustic feel of the experience. This conversation helped bring back moments from his childhood, and his cheeks were already sore from all the laughter, so much so, he'd shoot a look at his apartment door, reminding himself to 'tone it down.'

"So what happened next?" he asked.

"He told her she must have a lot of her mind, because her head was super big so it must've just rolled on out."

He burst out laughing again, rolling to his side and facing his bedroom window. Oh, it felt so good. The silly conversation was just what the doctor ordered. Boy did he miss her. He was so happy to be back home.

"Hey, can I ask you a religion question?" she asked, after his laughter subsided.

"Of course." he immediately sat up, prepared to listen to

every word.

"Why aren't priests allowed to marry? I never understood that. I mean, it isn't in the Bible, is it? I don't think it is."

"Well, you're right, it isn't in the Bible. The reason for that Rhapsody is because our attention needs to be focused on the Church and the work of God. That is our mission. Married men are divided. Marriage is good, but we believe that priests should not enter marriage, because then our attention would be focused on our wives and subsequent children from that union."

"Hmmm, I see. That doesn't seem quite fair, still…you know, I believe Jesus was married. I really do."

"Yes, I've heard that theory before. It's an interesting one. It grew in popularity due to the buzz regarding the Di Vinci Code."

"Did you see the movie?" He detected a faint laugh, ever so slight.

"In fact, I did."

"Really? I'd think you'd be against that."

"Why?"

"Because well, it criticized the Catholic church to some degree."

"It's art—in art lie truth and lies, or shall I say, perception and interpretation. I take it as such."

"So, you think it is a lie that the church is corrupt and Jesus was married?"

"Well, as far as Jesus being married, I don't believe so, no, but if he were, it still wouldn't negate his teachings."

"Right, he still was effective, so why would priests be forced into celibacy if Jesus could marry? God never told Jesus he couldn't marry, so why would that be expected of priests?

That doesn't make sense to me."

Dane grinned and clutched the phone a bit tighter, enjoying the conversation. For some, it may have unnerved them the way Rhapsody kept digging and searching, grabbing clumsily at controversy, but landing her points never the same. But, for him it proved his suspicions that she *did* understand his religion to some degree, and found it interesting.

"Let me ask you, Rhapsody, what are your beliefs before we continue with this conversation? I'll address everything else you said. I just want to know."

"Well," she hesitated, "I believe that there is a God and I believe in Jesus. So, I suppose that makes me a Christian by definition but I think the Bible is all messed up, though. I think it has been tampered with and used to control people, to get people to fall in line with the laws of the land. I just live by the golden rule, you know? I don't complicate my life with religion. It is messy. If we all just treated each other with respect, then it wouldn't even be an issue. I don't need a bunch of rules. I respect other people's beliefs though."

"I can understand that perspective, I really can," he said earnestly. Instead of moving forward as he was tempted to, he kept to his promise and answered the rest of her earlier queries.

"Now, as far as Church corruption, every manmade entity is flawed, Rhapsody. We are men first, and that appears to be the most forgotten fact when an offense takes place that reaches media attention. We aren't puppets or flying on auto-pilot. Priests, ministers…we feel the same way you do. We have the same needs and desires; we are just to handle them differently."

"Yeah…and what you just said brings me to something

else. Can I ask you a personal question, Dane?"

"You can ask, but I may refuse to answer," he said candidly.

"Fair enough. I'll try my hand at it anyway. I don't mean to intrude, but how long have you been celibate? Have you *ever* been with a woman? At *all*?"

He felt himself becoming warm. He should've suspected this type of question would be asked. Rhapsody was outspoken and at times childlike in regards to her curiosity. Very much an adult and in tune with herself, but she was also a bit untamed, running free like a pack of wild horses. She said things that would make someone blush or hide away like a turtle in their shell, and she did it with the sort of honesty that people lost along the way after being educated about social mores or taught, 'It is impolite to be so brash. Start lying, that is better.' She always delivered the question or news with a pleasant smile, but her handling of it was raw and unvarnished, all the same.

The funny thing about Rhapsody was that she could turn it off, but with him, she simply chose not to. This was her. Honest. Blunt. He noticed that about her soon after their first exchanged words. He had no desire to discuss sexual matters with the woman, not because he found it embarrassing, but because these conversations meant he'd have to think about them…with *her*…hearing her voice…he alone in his bedroom…talking about sexuality and physical intimacy, or lack thereof. He ran his fingers through his hair and cast his gaze out the window toward the darkened sky, the moon shining brightly, smiling down on him as if she, too, were in on the joke.

"Sorry…" she finally offered, after the silence continued to weave like a spider web in the air, leaving him just as un-nerved.

He took a deep breath and sighed. "Before we go there, with this type of questioning and answering session, may I ask why you are curious about it?"

"Well, it is just strange to me, I guess. Like I said earlier, in some ways, religion seems to be created to control people. In some ways, I think religion is beautiful, you know? But these self-imposed rules, to prove how holy you are, are just silly. Now, that's just my opinion but I am open to hearing what you have to say about it. Matter of fact, I want to hear your views on it, Dane."

"How else does one show they are dedicated, Rhapsody? It takes great strength, self-control and resolve. We all can't live our lives doing what we want, when we want, because it feels good or right. Life is bigger than that."

He was met with silence and now regretted the words, because she may have felt that his defensive stance was a dig at her, her free-loving nature and in a way, it was, though not intentionally. His sense of self-protection came from recent events that were no fault of her own. And now, his physical attraction to her was manifesting, growing rapidly, a passion reignited after years of distance, and he began to worry. But his need to speak to her was stronger than his desire to stop cold, dead in his tracks. He continued to pray about it, and felt he was never given a sign to cease. Never the less, It was becoming an internal battle. The woman had been his saving grace, keeping him from going overboard with grief. He hadn't touched any more alcohol, stayed away from the dark thoughts, and kept busy and positive. All he had to do was think of *her*...and it made it all better...

He started when she cleared her throat. "Rhapsody…"

"Yes?"

"To answer your question, *yes,* I've been sexually intimate with a woman before. I had a girlfriend in high school, we were exclusive. I lost my virginity with her. She was my first but I dated quite a bit in college, too, and more times than not, was intimate with those women as well. I definitely have had my share of sexual experiences with multiple women in the past. I am not proud of it, but it happened and I've been celibate for almost eight years now."

He could almost hear the wheels in her head spinning.

"And that does include self-pleasure." he added.

He wanted to cover all bases, so that she understood. She wanted to learn, she wanted to be taught, and regardless of her questions causing him concern, they were an opportunity for him to help her, to be a shepherd and to establish more trust.

"I wasn't aware that you couldn't masturbate, either. I guess you think this conversation is inappropriate, right?" she asked, taking a deep sigh, and then lightly laughed.

"It has the potential to be," he answered, feeling a bit more relaxed at this adult dialogue. "But at this point, I'm just figuring you want answers, and there is nothing more to it. No hidden motivations or objectives."

"I don't have any hidden agenda, but I do find you attractive. I told you that, but it's no biggie."

You noticed me in high school, too, didn't you?

"I just see no reason to keep secrets. I want to be open, show you that you can trust me. I like you, Dane." He heard her sigh again, and he felt his body warm once more.

"Well, maybe we need to stop discussing it then, okay? But I hope I answered your questions." He cleared his throat and tried to find a focal point in his dimly lit bedroom. He landed upon a neatly folded towel. That didn't help. It reminded him of her intricately spun hair wrapped tightly in the colors of the rainbow.

"You haven't answered everything I want to know, but I understand. Let's talk about something else." The conversation then became stiff and unyielding, the fun zapped out of it.

He had no idea what else to say—well, he *did*, but he knew better than to utter the words.

I find you attractive too, Rhapsody. I have feelings for you, and they are growing...

"You know what? I'd like to invite you over for dinner, Fr. Dane." Her laughter, light and airy, moved him, but the words had come out of the blue and hit him in the gut. Here, he thought the conversation would taper and wane; they'd run into each other at the park again and continue to talk about this and the other, with a gradual build-up to more fruitful conversations. Instead, things had escalated. He was amazed at his surprise and he should have expected it from a woman who didn't follow predictable conversational cues. He shook his head at his own foolishness.

At your house?!

"Uh…"

"What? You can't do dinner? Priests don't eat after five P.M.?" She giggled.

"No, well, yes, but I don't think it would be—"

"Appropriate to come to my house? Why is that? We're only friends."

A brief silence.

"I hate to keep questioning you, asking so many questions, but why are you inviting me, Rhapsody?" He sighed and ran his hand over his face, growing tired, concerned and wary.

"What? To eat. To show off my skills!" She laughed. "Look, if it makes you feel uncomfortable, just scratch it. Forget I said it. I meant nothing by it, it was just an invitation. Hey, in other news, I wondered if—"

"I'd love to come."

He could envision her dancing in her seat, doing a fist pump.

"Okay, great, but before you come, what are you concerned about? Let's get it worked out," she said, her tone serious.

"It's just...I mean, look at this. We just finished discussing my past sex life, you tell me you're attracted to me, and then invite me to dinner. Rhapsody," he chuckled lightly and looked back toward the window, his thoughts like mud, "it just, I dunno...I have to walk a fine line, here."

"Well, regardless of my own beliefs, Dane, I still respect yours. It wouldn't matter if I find you appealing or not, especially if it isn't mutual. Everyone knows priests can't date." She gave a light-hearted laugh. "You'd see it as harmless, because it *is*."

But I'm still a man, as I keep telling you.

"Well look, I don't want you to feel pressured," she offered. "Let's put it on ice, mull it over and talk about it later." And just like that, she changed the topic, allowing him to sigh with relief, but it would be short-lived.

Later that evening, he envisioned sitting at her dining room table with her, over candlelight, their hands touching and caressing, and he loved every daydreamy, forbidden moment of it...

CHAPTER FOURTEEN

Several days later…

"**O**KAY, JUST ONE more!"

Rhapsody sighed and made a silly face, using her hands to squish all of her features together. Her eyes slumped sleepily and her lips resembled a duck's. Dane stepped back, shaking his head as he lowered the camera to his waist.

"Now come on, this was your idea!" he chastised.

"I know, I know. They need a photo of me for the concert brochure and I'm resistant. I hate pictures." She turned away from him, as if she were trying to get her thoughts together.

But you're beautiful…

Her backdrop was a setting fit for a painting. The slightly rippled lake housed multi-colored ducks vying for smidgens of bread being tossed their way by a man and a girl, probably his daughter. A few white long necked swans and other marine life floated and swam about as a slight wind caught the hem of her forest green sundress, making it sway to and fro, catching ever so gently around her bare ankle. The sun was setting and Dane glanced down at his watch, knowing he needed to return to the rectory soon. They were having a special program and he was on duty for the confessional later that evening as well.

"Are you ready?" His voice cut through the silence. She eyed him discerningly from over her shoulder, her lips poked out before turning into a wide grin, then, she casually looked down at her cuticles, running her finger across them contemplatively.

"Yeah," she finally uttered, jetting her leg out ever so slightly. Placing her hand leisurely on her hip, she lowered her chin and looked at him out the corner of her eye.

"Almost perfect…give me a big smile. Lift your jaw a bit more." He snapped the camera; the flash brightened the area in an instant, then disappeared. "Oh come on, you can give me a bigger smile than this. Let's try again." And then it hit him. "Okay, I've got a joke for you. A new nun goes to her first confession."

"Oh no, a nun joke!" Rhapsody smiled.

"I promise it won't end the way you think. So, she goes to her first confession and tells the priest she has an embarrassing confession. He assures her that he has heard everything under the sun, and for her to proceed. So she says, 'Father, I don't wear panties under my habit.' So the priest says, 'That's not so bad. Say five Hail Marys and five Our Fathers and then do five cartwheels on your way to the altar.'"

Rhapsody's sudden loud laughter caused birds to suddenly fly from the fresh cut grass into the sky. Dane got the shot he desired as she came undone.

"I hope you didn't catch me blinking. That flash was super bright."

Dane flipped through the images. "Ahhh, many of these are quite nice. I took so many, surely you can find one that suits your tastes." he handed her the camera back, taking notice that she didn't preview them.

"You really should look at them before I go." He zipped his jacket up and glanced back down at his watch. "You know, just in case you don't like any of them at all, I could take a couple more to be on the safe side."

"No, no. I'm sure they're fine."

She carefully placed the camera in her bag and rummaged through it for a while until she dug out a tiny white pill and popped it in her mouth. She swallowed, then dug into her purse again, riffling for a while until she brandished a worn tissue and gently glided it along her nostrils, sniffed and returned it to her bag.

"Allergies," she mumbled as she shifted her weight from one foot to the other while snapping her hobo bag closed.

"So," he glanced out at the water behind her and looked back into her eyes, "I've had some time to think. I'd like to set up that dinner. Maybe we could play a board game, too?"

That sounded stupid…

"Oh, great." She seemed surprised, taken aback, but pleasantly so. "I'd love that. So, you just let me know when, then, okay?" She crossed her arms over her chest, smiling.

"Well, I know now, actually. I looked at my schedule and next Thursday would work. I'm not sure how your work is scheduled for that day, but—"

"Yeah, I think that will be fine." She smiled as she dug into her bag again and retrieved her cellphone. He waited as she scrolled quickly down what he presumed was her calendar.

"I have to do a private piano lesson at two, and I teach

class right after that, but that will only be an hour. So, let me give you my address."

Moments later, he had the information in his own phone, and they said their usual goodbyes. After that, he sat in his car and, once again, watched her drive away until he could see her no more…

THEIR STEPS SOUNDED in unison, soft against the shiny floor of the bustling shopping area. Fr. Kirkpatrick rarely came out into these sorts of public places anymore, but after asking about Dane's plans for the day, he'd invited himself to stroll around with Fr. Caruso in the mall. They talked, shared familiar pleasantries, caught up on current events. Regardless, Dane was on full alert. He knew exactly what this was leading to. As soon as he saw the elder approach him in the rectory, he hung his head, grinned and waited. Once Dane had been seen sitting in the garden with Rhapsody weeks earlier, he knew that this moment would come. The boiling, predictable situation quietly crept into his day like mice scurrying across a cloud.

The old man sighed and slumped down onto a glossy tan mall bench. Across from them was a cluttered store specializing in women's shoes and accessories, packed with teenagers and women vying for their size and favorite styles. Big red signs marked, 'Clearance' and 'Sale' dotted the storefronts. The two men sat side by side, in uncomfortable silence for a while.

"Dane." The old man chewed on his inner jaw, his expression tight as he briefly glanced at him, then back away at the crowds. "I need to discuss some things with you." He clasped his heavy, age-spot covered hands, one over the other, across his robe covered lap. Every now and again, someone would glance their way. People, after all of these centuries, were still fascinated with seeing priests in their vestments. Neither of them had bothered to change from their black robes after service and since Dane had been stopped from going into his apartment, he decided to stay dressed as he was.

"Yes, of course." Dane tried to keep his cool, reminding himself to not become defensive.

"Since your friend passed away, you've been under a dark cloud. Well, you actually seem much better now, but, I noted the change at the time. I offer you my condolences once again."

Dane smiled, and offered a quiet "Thank you."

"I knew you and the young man, Josh, right?"

"Yes, his name was Josh."

"You were quite close, he'd spend hours with you during his visits, and you spoke of him so highly. We all could see the friendship. You both seemed to look up to one another and I could see where you got some of your sense of humor from."

Dane cleared his throat, and nodded in agreement.

"Sometimes, when we lose someone we love, we doubt God's love for us because, well, He took someone from us, someone we weren't prepared to let go of. We hurt so deeply. Our lives are sometimes not easy. We work for God, we are here for the Church, that is our first priority, and sometimes, that lends way to loneliness. You lost your grandfather a couple years ago, then Josh and you became close to many patients at the hospital. Many have passed away. I know it had been difficult."

He paused.

"I also know you've been spending quite a bit of time by

yourself, and that sometimes is helpful, other times, maybe not." He shrugged. "You said you'd been in prayer, and trying to sort some things out, and I respected that. You needed it, we understood."

Dane was comforted by the older priest's sensitive, caring tone, despite the ball that was about to hit his wall.

Wait for it...

"In that alone time, sometimes things we struggle with become even worse and it is a fight that becomes harder instead of easier. It can make us question ourselves and our beliefs all the more." He took a deep breath, looking out into the sea of people. Gearing up. Dane braced himself.

"Do you recall my story, Dane?" He turned to him. Dane's eyes met his dark brown ones, soulful and rich, riddled with crow's feet and love.

"Yes, Fr. Kirkpatrick, I do."

"Well, then, you recall that before I became a priest, I was married, correct?" The man turned away from him again. He seemed a little breathless.

"Yes, Father, I do."

"And she passed away." He pulled a Kleenex out of his side pocket and blew into it. Dane's stomach churned as he waited for the hammer to drop.

Just say it. We know where this is going.

"That was the worst day of my life, the day my Ingrid passed. She'd been sick, but it was painful, all the same. I accepted my calling into the priesthood after that. I knew I had been called, even before I married her, and I felt like, in some way, this was my second chance. It was far less common at that time for a priest to have ever been married. Then, of course, the sex abuse scandal hit, and the church scoured for people…for new priests," he said with a faraway look. "I want to tell you that I once was in love, and I know what it looks like, Dane. I know what it feels like…I recognize it."

The men exchanged glances.

"Once you know it, you never forget it, but I've transferred that devotion to the Church, and you vowed to do the same. When you entered the seminary, you were very young, only a senior in college. In that time, however, I got to know you." He looked at Dane, his eyes earnest—almost pleading. "We talked quite candidly and after you spent four years at St. Agnes, you came to our parish. You've been here for almost two and a half years…and in that time, I've started to see you like a grandson, and got to know you even further." Fr. Kirkpatrick smiled.

"Thank you."

"I remember the things we discussed, and I knew you had a promising future ahead of you at St. Michaels, and anywhere else you'd go to. I also know that we are human, Dane, we are just men, and things happen sometimes that get us off track when we don't keep the temptations in check…like a pretty woman."

A thick layer of tension grew and choked the air, strangling the oxygen, making Dane's throat tighten. He rubbed the side of his jaw, his back slumped a bit as he leaned forward in his seat.

"…A pretty woman that goes to the park…and you go, too…*hoping* to see her there, day after day."

Fr. Daniels and Fr. Sinclair! Nosey jerks! Spreading gossip! Dane fisted his hands, but tried to remain outwardly calm.

He'd seen them several times a week; sometimes they'd stop at a water fountain, other times approach him while he was sitting with Rhapsody. They smiled and laughed, engaging in small talk, never alerting him of any concerns they had regarding his private life. He grinded his teeth, wanting nothing more than to give them a piece of his mind when he returned to the parish.

"From what I understand," Fr. Kirkpatrick gave a slight grin, "she moves like an angel caught in the rapture." The man's eyes twinkled as he spoke. "I could see how that may be exciting. It makes you react in a carnal fashion, especially those of us that have had the pleasure of a woman in an intimate manner before. You'd fornicated repeatedly, in high school and college, by your own admission."

Dane shot him a glance, vexed.

"This isn't a judgment from me to you, Son," he said sincerely. "Please calm down. You've already been forgiven for those sins. It is just me explaining to you that it may be even *harder* for you, because you have experienced sexual intimacy before and all those old feelings could be riled up, causing a great temptation. That's all I'm saying. It's a test." He patted Dane's leg. "You are a nice looking young man. You will draw female attention almost anywhere you step from that fact alone. You already do. If you haven't noticed, the church attendance grew after you started working at St. Michael's, and many of the new parishioners are single women. We all knew it was because of you," the old man chuckled. "I've heard the whispers about you over the years. You're quite the eye candy to the ladies. You are a great speaker as well, so it was a two for two deal, I suppose."

Dane smiled, but it was wrought with anxiety.

"Dane, women, you will discover if you haven't already, have some misplaced attraction to men like us, which may make it even harder. Some see us as a challenge, to try and see if they can break a priest, make him sin."

Dane felt his body warm with slowly simmering anger. He ran his hands ruggedly along his knees and swallowed.

"But you are holy, you serve God and the Church. You cannot serve two masters, Dane. You cannot drift down this path because," he looked at him, worry deep in his expression, "it won't end well. You are vulnerable right now, you've suffered a great loss, and I strongly suggest you stay with us, in the rectory, far away from the woman that you met at the park, until you get this situation under control."

Dane was at a loss for words. He knew that the topic was coming up, but he never expected it to be quite this way. He was sure Fr. Kirkpatrick was going to yell at him, and he'd more than likely yell back, defending himself, denying the accusations. But, as it was laid out, he was tongue tied.

"And before you ask," Fr. Kirkpatrick offered, "I know about her, because some of the others have seen you out and about, speaking with her. No one paid it any mind initially, from what I gather, but after a while you seemed distracted and when she came to the church, well," the old man shook his head, a frown budding across his wrinkled face as he surveyed the bustling crowd full of shoppers, "I saw how you looked at her, Dane." He removed his glasses, wiped off a speck of dust, and put them back on. "You're falling, hard and fast. She's very attractive, and seems nice. I understand why you are drawn to her, but you must resist. You're going to bite off more than you can chew if you keep this up."

Dane cleared his throat, trying desperately to figure out what to say. Still, nothing came; at least nothing that he felt was suitable.

"You're too quiet. Tell me what's on your mind, Son." The old man turned toward him, his tone serious, demanding a response, something that would put his mind at ease.

"Fr. Kirkpatrick, she is just a friend. Nothing has transpired that would be deemed inappropriate. She has been helpful regarding my grief, I'll admit to that, and she is a good person."

Another brief pause.

"I see…" It was apparent Fr. Kirkpatrick wasn't pleased with his response, but seemed to expect it.

"I believe you, Dane, but you and I both know that's how it starts. You already know this in your heart, that this is how it begins. You feel that way today, but may not feel that way next week."

"She is not trying to get me to do anything." Dane tried to not sound as if he were upset, but he was and he knew Fr. Kirkpatrick knew it, too. "We just talk about music, school, movies, and books. It's nothing serious. I just needed the companionship, someone from outside of the parish—a fresh face. It's not what you think."

"I repeat, I understand that right *now* it isn't." The words, dipped in red hot warning, hung in the air. "And she doesn't have to try to tempt you," he added, "you will crave her even more as each day turns into a week, and a week into a month. That is how love works, Dane. It starts small, then grows if you water it. You're holding a canister and allowing the rain to gush. The same love you felt for the Church when you first began, you will have for *her*. It will be just as exhilarating, and you will have the same zest and passion. There is nothing at this point that she needs to do or say. Her mere presence in your life is the issue. For her to just be herself, just sitting there, is enough."

"With all due respect, Fr. Kirkpatrick, I disagree. You make it seem as if she is a Jezebel, or a wanton temptress. She is just—" He looked down at his lap then back up. "She is a person that has a warm, good heart and she has helped me greatly. I believe she was sent to me by God, to be my friend."

"I'm not making her into a devil." The old man chuckled. "I'm eighty-seven years old. I've been around, Dane. I've seen men like you and me fall apart from loneliness, depression. I've also seen us fall in love, and then regret it, wishing we'd never opened the Pandora's box. You've been a priest long enough to have heard the stories, too. It happens, and the sap it happens to always says, 'No, it won't be me'."

Dane turned away, wishing he were with her right that moment, instead of sitting there with the scent of popcorn and cinnamon buns floating in the air. The smiling faces of children, knotted expressions of crying babies and vacant stares of husbands holding purses became a blur. None provided any comfort...but *she* did. He was taken aback by his own wayward thoughts, but not enough to stop contemplating them.

"She is a lovely, single woman, and you are a grief-stricken, unwed man in your prime. If you like her, you will eventually love her, and it will be as more than a friend. *Something* is happening between you two, and it's not platonic. Whether you two are admitting it to one another or not is beside the point. From the sound of things," he shot Dane a look, raised white eyebrow and all, "you honestly *believe* what you are saying to me because, right *now,* it is accurate in your mind, yet your heart tells a different tale."

Dane swallowed and folded his hands together. He wasn't

sure what was going on, actually—and because of that, he didn't feel he could argue in either direction with the man. He simply began to shut down. Fr. Kirkpatrick looked at him, waiting for a response once again. He received none.

Dane didn't wish to move forward with the discussion. He teetered the line of trying to remain respectful, demand that his private life be just that, private—and wanting to stand up and walk away, leaving the elder sitting right there on that bench, all alone. He knew the man meant well, but right now, Dane couldn't stomach it any longer.

What did Fr. Kirkpatrick know? It was a new day and age. Men and women could be friends without it turning into more, regardless of a mutual physical attraction. So what? There were lots of pretty single women who attended church. He'd never even thought of crossing the line. He and Rhapsody were adults and could practice self-control. He'd already proven that he could in other areas of his priesthood. Didn't the old man know that?

"I know you think you have this all under control, Dane. You believe you can find her exciting and intriguing, beautiful too, and keep yourself untainted."

Just great. So now he is reading my mind.

"Please heed my warning. You are playing with fire, son. Your soul is on the line. Less importantly, your future, too." The old man wobbled, rising to his feet. Dane immediately stood and helped him, cupping the man's elbow.

Yes, finally, let's go.

Fr. Kirkpatrick's turned his thin, tall frame toward him, his garb flowing. "Dane, I hate to keep hammering at this, but from your expression and lack of response, I feel compelled. I care for you, that is why I must bring it to your attention. Are you dismissing this, what I'm saying?"

"I'm not. I simply don't believe you understand the situation in the manner that you believe you do, but I respect your opinion and thank you for sharing your insight with me." He'd sounded cold and stiff, the words snappish with faux gratitude.

Fr. Kirkpatrick frowned. "You're being stubborn. If you don't reel this in, we will be talking about this *again*, under *much* different circumstances. Unfortunate ones, no doubt." The man pointed in Dane's face, his lips twisted and a threatening scowl on his face. "I cannot forbid you to see her, I do not have that sort of power over you, but I highly advice it. It is apparent that she is simply too tempting for you to resist. I had to bring it to your attention, Dane. It's a slippery slope, and you are trying to climb it uphill with butter on your feet."

"But Fr. Kirkpatrick—"

The man closed his eyes and held up his hand, asking for silence. "You're attracted to her, Dane. I am old, but far from senile or stupid! There is no way around this. It's impossible for the two of you to just be friends due to the fascination with one another. You want her, you're just in denial. I could see it on your face! Please do not feel ashamed to be truthful with yourself. You are not the first to deal with such a temptation. Many priests have and it can be crippling. That's why it's important to be proactive. Please stop this relationship at once before it goes any further. It's for the best."

Pain flashed in the old man's eyes.

After a few moments, the man softened, coming back into the here and now after a visit down a road Dane hadn't seen him travel before. He patted Dane's back, and they made their way past the storefronts, lively with busy people eager to go further in debt and collect the latest gadgets. Dane had all but forgotten that he'd wanted to go to the mall to pick up a new light blue shirt. Now, he just wanted to go home and be alone.

Not another word was spoken until they arrived back at the church. Fr. Kirkpatrick stopped before walking down the hall to enter his private sanctuary and took Dane gently by the arm. Dane resisted, wanting the conversation to be over and done with.

Not again. Please just stop it.

He felt violated, with his fellow associates spying on him and running to tell the 'big boss.' He was mad at himself, too, for not being more discreet. He should've known his activities were being scrutinized, but he didn't feel he was doing anything wrong. Thus, there was nothing to hide and keep under cover.

"Dane." The old man sighed. "Please, don't be angry. Just remember what we discussed. Don't forget what you were called to do, you have responsibilities. People depend on you. You are gifted, the Lord uses you in special ways. It would be a great loss, for everyone." Then, he released his arm and wandered down the hallway until he'd disappeared into his quarters...

CHAPTER FIFTEEN

R HAPSODY WAS SICKENED by Melody's continuous smacking. She turned to her sister, watched her chew the bread until she gulped the remaining crumbs in a final swallow. Thoughts of smacking that smug face with all of her might reeled in her head.

"So, Mama said you have a new boyfriend." Melody's perfectly arched eyebrow shot upward, the one she took fifteen minutes to draw on, the one that looked as if it had been stenciled on and airbrushed and then set out on display in a Sephora makeup catalog.

"Mama didn't tell you that," Rhapsody dismissed her as she continued to drive, anxious to drop off the prying heffa as soon as possible. She gripped her steering wheel and put a little more gas behind it, eager to get rid of the dead weight.

"I asked 'er if you were seeing anyone, you've been acting weird. You always act weird when you get a new man."

Rhapsody knew better; it was a trap to get information.

Melody was in a long-term relationship with a man named Adonis, and boy did he live up to that name. He had been born in Greece, an army brat, and his mother came from a family drowning in money. Besides that, the man was absolutely gorgeous, Rhapsody couldn't take that away from him— six feet of smooth, imported chocolate, and his body would mold into a suit like nobody's business. He was a sportscaster, and his suave, silky voice would melt the panties off Frosty the Snowman's wife, while atop a glacier at the apex of the North Pole. Despite having the gorgeous trophy fiancé of almost eight years by her side, Melody still made her rounds to delve into her sister's love life. Rhapsody was sure it was so Melody could feast off a buffet served in her sister's room at the heartbreak hotel. Regardless, Rhapsody knew their mother quite well regarding these matters. She wouldn't have given away her secret, and for *certain,* she didn't tell Melody's gloating, nosey ass a damn thing.

"We are only a few blocks from your house, better get your key out," Rhapsody said flatly.

Melody laughed, loud and obnoxious, forced like a strained bowel movement. Reaching into her burgundy purse, she removed her door keys. They clanked about as Rhapsody shot her a look, hoping that just this one time in history, a look could kill.

"Fine, don't tell me, but I'll get it out of you." Melody said as the car slowed. Rhapsody was tired of picking her sister up from her job. The woman's car, her beloved canary yellow convertible, was back in the shop and Adonis was conveniently out of town, unable to lend his damsel in distress any aid.

He is out screwing someone else, no doubt, and she sits here all complacent. Keep on top of your own love life; you don't have time to investigate mine.

Instead of getting a rental, Melody immediately called Rhapsody stating, "Your schedule is all over the place so I'm sure you can arrange to pick me up for like three or four days. It won't last forever. They are fixing Fiona." Yes, she'd named the Buick Lesabre convertible, too. At first, Rhapsody was going to tell her where to go, how fast and how high, but then she recalled the night she kicked Raul out for good, how her sister called and was actually sweet and loving as she poured out her heart to the woman.

They'd talked all night; it had been one of those conversations that caused her to remember why she hated that they were no longer close, and it had happened purely out of the blue. Her sister was there for her, but after the interpersonal crisis was over, she went right back to her hateful, despicable ways.

Rhapsody had figured it out soon enough. Melody only wanted her around when she was miserable and falling apart, a fraction of her true, vibrant self. When Rhapsody felt good about life and her placement in it, which was the majority of the time, she grated on Melody's nerves. Yes, Melody dined off of her sibling's sadness, and when it was gone, so was she, her bib hitting the floor as she exited stage left like the big baby that she was.

"I don't have a boyfriend, so you can drop it," Rhapsody called out as she watched her sister walk up her short walkway to the front door of her faux château home.

The insufferable woman stopped and turned. "Like I said, I'll get it out of you. Oh! And don't forget about—"

"I know." Rhapsody waved her off as she started her engine to drive away. "Be here early tomorrow...you have a meeting."

"Thank you!" her sister said with a huge, obnoxious grin, pivoting back around. "Love you." she added before swiftly disappearing inside of her house.

Rhapsody looked at the closed door for a while. She hadn't heard Melody say those words to her in eons and couldn't help but smile even though she knew it was simply being used as fertilizer to dig further into her garden of personal business later. Truth of the matter, Rhapsody felt sadness as she continued to stare at that closed door. Melody was inside, alone in the beautifully furnished, expensive condominium once again. She was in there, fighting with herself, hiding behind designer purses and ridiculously expensive shoes she'd yet to wear anywhere but in the confines of her lavish walk-in-closet.

She tried her damnedest to be more than she portrayed and have the life she pretended to paint for the world to see. Adonis hadn't married the woman after all this time, people at her job often got on her last nerve, and she put up with so much, but she stayed in the relationship, because he was too damn good looking and had a job in the spotlight. She remained at her job because it paid well and it was prestigious. Her decisions were based on garnering the approval and attention of others, never for her own wellbeing and happiness. Melody, being all about appearances, seemed to fail to realize one simple thing, however—she was the Empress with invisible clothes. Everyone could see she was naked as the day she was born, but she clung to the dream of being fully dressed head to toe, her unseen tiara sparkling brightly, and her heart filled with dark pearls of hatred, strangling her as she bought into her own hype…

THIS ISN'T A big deal. Don't turn it into one. Besides, she is helping you even though she may not realize it. Just a visit between friends. Fr. Kirkpatrick has me all over the place, confused, putting doubts in my mind. Like, what if she does only see me as a challenge? See, that can't be. Rhapsody isn't like that.

Dane warred with himself until he became an anxious mess. Sliding black slacks up his legs, he glanced back down at the button down, white Polo shirt lying across the bed, the one he'd spent an hour picking out from his small closet. He was tempting fate. Some would say he shouldn't be alone with her in the first place considering the circumstances.

But we aren't alone…we are always out in the public, and tonight is no different. I'm just going to go see my new associate perform, is all. That's it. I've had plenty of female friends over the years.

And he had, but he was never attracted to them, at least not in the way he was to Rhapsody. Those weren't physical attractions; they never made him uncomfortable, nor had he had the urge to make excuses for the contact and interaction. Dane was quite self-aware, regardless of sometimes being put on a pedestal by others, which risked a possibly inflated ego. He knew that he liked looking at her a bit too long, and he thought about her in ways that a man thinks about a woman— a *special* woman. Yet, it didn't stop him from paving a way, so that he could do what he felt he needed to survive this traumatic, confusing time in his life. As he continued to dress, he let his thoughts drift back to the day he finally got up his nerve to speak to her in the park.

He walked up to her after an afternoon of drinking. He had the courage then. Not because he was afraid of speaking to a lovely woman, but because he knew what he was and what that oath stood for and despite it all, he was drawn to her. He simply wanted to say 'hello', and that was God's honest truth. He realized later he wanted something from her though. What that was, he wasn't sure at that point, but he needed to find out. Yeah, he hurt, and he needed someone to talk to.

Nevertheless, it was awkward for him. He hadn't initiated a conversation like that since college. The ladies in church, and the nuns were the women that he'd laugh and talk with. Not beautiful black women doing yoga and singing harmonies in the middle of grassy parks…

He'd tried earnestly to busy himself as she consumed more and more real estate in his thoughts. Additional visits to the nursing homes seemed to initially do the trick. He loved sitting with the elderly, they were testaments of long life lived, and it would work for a while, help feed the crater inside of him, until he had to stop daydreaming and the reality of the situation returned.

The inability to control his heart proved disturbing. Some days were a battle. Some days he fought wanting to go find a release, a coping mechanism to tune out the old tapes that kept playing in his head, running and running and going absolutely nowhere. Other days, he was still so angry with God that he barely spoke to him. And the remainder of the days, he dealt with them more diplomatically—accepting that this was a process and that if he was truly going to heal, he had to take it step by step, not try to run a marathon when he was only equipped to crawl. As long as he was moving, then he was progressing, and that was the hardest to accept—that he had little to no control over so many aspects of his life right then and there.

He kept a brave face, and played his role, but for the first time in a while, Dane wanted to be someone else…something *more*, possibly? Life was opening up, presenting different scenarios.

Was he destined for more? He wasn't sure, but he felt compelled to dig a bit deeper to find out…

RHAPSODY SNUCK A look from behind the silky, deep red curtain as the band gathered, getting into position. The lights slowly dimmed and people moved about the stage, conducting a quick and final sound check. She'd been asked to sing a song that evening at Club Envy, a spectacular nightclub with an eclectic crowd that appreciated soulful sounds. She had been prepared to play the piano, tune after tune, but later found out that the demanding patrons would also request her to sing a ditty. Happy to oblige, she asked for a few moments to warm up her vocal chords before they started their next jam session. After quick deliberation, she took a chance, as she was known to do. She was going to sing a song no one had ever heard before. That within itself was risky, but she didn't mind…until she peered out at the audience.

She hadn't spotted him, but something told her he was there…

She'd written the song—that within itself was unnerving, for she wasn't certain how'd it be perceived, but excitement filled her with the desire to take the plunge.

Well, here goes nothing…

She listened to the MC make some preliminary statements, and the small crowd erupted in applause. She checked her reflection in a nearby backstage mirror. The shimmery light blue dress clung to her delicate curves just right and her curl strands were picked out, high and wide, a lovely soft coif with a sparkling light blue flower that matched her outfit to azure perfection.

Heels…

She looked down at her feet, hoping she didn't fall on her face, and smiled at the thought. Even *that* unfortunate possibility she'd find a way to embrace because tonight was the evening she'd sing in front of some of her adult pupils, friends, business associates and strangers who'd come there just to hear her play.

She took a long, deep breath, exhaled, then stepped forward. When she emerged from the curtain, the place went silent, the only noise being her footsteps across the stage, tip tapping until she reached the piano bench and took her seat. She slowly closed her eyes, straightened her back and took another deep breath, then, looking out toward the audience, she spoke softly into the microphone.

"Good evening, everyone. We are now going to start our second set. So glad you all are spending the evening with me and these wonderful musicians."

She waited for the loud round of applause to die down.

"For those of you that may have just come in, my name is Rhapsody Blue, and we are going to have one hell of an evening. I want to thank this band, 'The Vice'," she gave a slight of hand, causing the room to erupt in another appreciative wave of applause, "for allowing me to fill in for Sydney this fine full moon. It is an honor. I've done it a couple times before for them, but I was never asked to sing so…I hope you all enjoy it and if you don't, don't say a word." She put a finger up to her plush lips and giggled, causing the roomful of people to laugh in turn. "'Cause like Ms. Erykah Badu said, I'm sensitive about my shit." The audience laughed and whistled, encouraging her, making her feel okay to become one with them that night, to make love to the music, right in front of their very eyes.

She turned away from the crowd and looked at the band. They gave their 'We're ready' nod—Tony on base, Pete on drums and Andrea at the keyboard. Before she began, Rhapsody looked out at the audience once more and her heart pivoted, turning slowly, making Father Time stop and listen. There he was, he'd come…front row and center. Just like in the park when they'd first laid eyes on one another. Dane gave a gentle wave and tossed a sentimental gaze her way, making her feel as if she was the only person in the entire world he'd ever seen, or cared to envision.

Wow, he really came…

ABSOLUTELY STUNNING. SHE could not look any better.

Dane leaned back leisurely in his seat, taking a sip of his seltzer water. He stood in the back of the room during the first set, hardly able to view the woman who played the piano so splendidly. Once the crowd thinned, he raced down to the front during the intermission as if he were on fire, making himself comfy while others refreshed their drinks and took time to stand outside and make cellphone calls. He nodded at her and winked, and at first she held his gaze, then shyly turned away.

She knows I'm here now. I wonder if she expected me or remembered I'd planned to come? I can't wait to hear this.

He'd dreamt about that supreme voice, that God-given expression that made his spirit and loins want to have conversations behind his back. It seduced him, never letting go. He'd come to hear her play the ebony and ivory, not expecting to be treated to this as well. He clasped his hands together, an empty glass by his side, and thin trails of smoke drifting past him. He was in a room full of music lovers, and they'd come to see this lovely lady. The crowd had lit up at the mention of her name from the MC. She had a gift, they knew it, so he watched them work themselves into frenzy, chanting in unison that she deliver a song, and they waited to collect. He desperately wanted to see her…needed to hear them again, the sweet melodies dripping in Rhapsody vocal wine. She was a living, breathing cure to all that ailed the world.

He watched her sigh, smile and gently place her fingers on the keys. As she leaned ever so slightly toward the piano, she let the first chord hit.

"Thaaaa man, doesn't stand…"

There it is…that voice. Jesus…so pretty…

Dane closed his eyes briefly then returned his gaze to that beautiful sight, and listened carefully…

"…But inside, he is ten feet tall…

On the outside…the thin shell, well,"

She looked out absently at the audience, smiling ever so slightly.

"He's got it all…

He sits under swaying branch-es, bent like saddened bows, the tree limbs…become home…

he is stuck…rooted in the fear of the unknown…

He flees."

She closed her eyes, turning back toward the piano, her forehead etched with lines as her eyebrows furrowed.

"…inside himself, what a fight, he haaaas….

Better daaaays, My God…I promisssse, better daaaaays…

Are to be had…"

The audience sat quiet, swaying to her deep, rich, velvety voice wrapped around the painful yet beautiful lyrics. Dane tensed, feeling a bit violated and annoyed, yet, simultaneously, he felt honored and renewed. His ego screamed in his ear—*"You know this is about you, right?"*

While his brain said, *"Yeah…it really is."*

He leaned on the armrest, resting his chin on his hand as he looked up at her, concentrating, deeply entrenched, wanting to say so much but forced to remain silent.

Hmmm, she thinks she knows me. She does, actually. In all of this time, have I opened up a lot? Enough for her to see inside? Yes, I have I suppose…and now, she sings about it. About me. She must've known I meant what I said, that I was coming. She believed it. Would she have sung it if I weren't here?

He continued to listen, rocking to the music, but trying hard to remain impassive, while grappling with his emotions. He was used to being the one identifying issues, problems and struggles with his words, offering a prescription in the form of prayer and Hail Mary's. Now, he was on the other side of the fence. She'd heard his confessions, even though they'd mostly only resided in his head.

The woman made him stir. She knew him all right, and he hadn't said a word about all the sordid mess, some of which he still couldn't articulate into tangible sentiments, built from his own reflections and struggles, brick by brick. The structure was weak, and she helped him tear it down…

CHAPTER SIXTEEN

RHAPSODY STOOD, BEAMING, taking a fluid bow as the clapping blended in with the final guitar chord strums. Wisps of spiraled smoke drifted past her under the dim lights. She averted his eye contact for a while, but not for long because she had to see what she'd stirred, what she'd pro- voked. And she saw in his eyes the shades of melancholy, before another wave of smoke drifted past his frame. She wasn't sure what Fr. Caruso—*Dane*—would say or do about her performance, and now she felt slight regret as she enjoyed the audience's reaction. Still, she kept a brave face.

His expression darkened and then he stood to his feet— not a smile in sight. He began to slowly clap, then it picked up momentum. She watched his large hands coming together over and over, faster and faster, forcing others to join, once again, in the applause.

He looks mad as hell.

I thought he might like it. Maybe it is too soon. I rewrote it, changing and tweaking the lyrics so many times. I mean, I wrote the song before I even had spoken to him but…

A loud whistle from someone in the audience pulled her out of her own mind, as if she were being chased with a broom. She regrouped and refocused. Time to start the next song. Leisurely taking her seat, she began to play an instrumental ballet, accompanied by the other band members…

DANE WATCHED HER slender, brown fingers move over the smooth keys, fascinated by her agility as they worked the long black and white rectangles that bended to her every musical whim. Her elegance and earthiness mixed with a dollop of uncouth truth lured him into a delightfully tempting snare he never wished to escape. Yeah, he was a bit disconcerted, but more pleased than pissed. He had never discussed his internal battles with depression with her, the unhappy years as a teenager, pretending to be on top of the world so that his family could continue to play their perfect roles. Yet, in her lyrics, the ones spoken and unspoken, he felt she somehow knew. As she continued to play, he thought about the two of them in the park.

When she spoke, the light from the sun would hit the side her profile just so, illuminating her succulent lips. He'd find himself staring at them, half hearing her describe her day. And then he'd look into her eyes, and they'd both get quiet until one would turn away, breaking the eye lock, dismissing what was going on beneath the surface. They never got too heavy—the conversations stayed pretty safe, minus when he divulged his feelings about the death of his best friend and her recent telephone inquisition regarding his past intimacy. That was simply offered as an explanation, an excuse for his continued park presence. It was a half-

truth, and now, he felt she may have known it was a lie dressed in melancholy colored clothing as soon as it left his mouth. He feared but loved that in some way, he'd ended up emotionally naked in front of her, and there wasn't a damn thing he could do about it...

He clapped after each song, falling more under her spell as she owned the notes. Each note became her lover, and she loved them all the same. She bore their children and gave them to the world as gifts, and everyone greedily accepted them, screaming out, encouraging her with striking profanity in the aim of letting her know—she was bad...gifted...and beautiful...

"Girl, play that shit!"

"Do it, Rhapsody! You fuckin' up my bad mood, baby!"

And Dane would smile at the crude words coming from all directions, and they didn't faze him for they came from a good place, and he just wanted her to be herself. He didn't want her to alter her behavior because he was before her or sitting next to her on a bench. He wanted her to keep her hand where it rested when he'd brush up against it. He wanted her to lay her head on his shoulder and he wanted to lie down beside her in the grass, stretch with her to the moon and back. He wanted to go wherever she was going, because wherever it was, it offered something he needed, something like perfect peace and golden days. With her. He wanted to bask in her glow.

He glanced back up at her on the stage, while his heart swelled with something new.

I forget about it all when I'm with her. But why is that so bad?

He shook his head and ran trembling fingers through his hair. The smell of a freshly lit cigarette stung his nostrils.

She lets me be me, without having to get into the gory detail. That's why I want to be next to her. There is no performance needed, no expectations. Rhapsody, I believe you entered my life for a reason that goes beyond a lending ear, and I want to find out what it is. I gotta find out what it is and a part of me is concerned because...I think I already know...

SHE WATCHED A fluffy ball of dust float past as the back door opened, ushering in warm night air. He'd stayed for each song, even as the crowd thinned out through the evening, and the drinks flowed less, yet, he was still there. The room became smaller and smaller and then it got to the point, where it felt like it was just the two of them, until finally, it was.

She sat at the piano, continuing to play songs for him. They hadn't spoken; he just sat there, with that mischievous grin and perfect hair. His shirt was buttoned up too high and his pants too straight, and that made him even more endearing to her. She had no idea why after she knew he was a priest, she'd remained intrigued and even invested into forging *something* with him. What that something was, she still wasn't sure, but they had a connection. No doubt about it.

He made her feel free and buoyant. He appeared so cool and relaxed, never seeming to break a sweat, even when she broached him regarding topics possibly deemed controversial. The opposite of what she imagined a priest to be, not at all like the arrogant jock she envisioned him being back in high school. And she realized now, that wasn't fair. She didn't know the guy at all back then; he could have been exactly how she knew him now, and maybe, if she'd paid less attention to enjoying him squirm as he'd stare at her too-tight shirts, she would have approached him, said something, any ice breaker at all. Just *maybe*, if she would have, things would be different right now…

Rhapsody continued to stroke the keys, thinking of Dane—thinking of him in so many ways.

She'd occasionally glance down at the crucifix around his neck and that golden wedding band. She smiled as she reminisced about her investigation. Just to make sure he wasn't full of crap, she'd looked him up online to confirm his butt *really* wasn't married after their initial meeting at the park. She found out he truly was a priest after all, and in that same instance, relief and sorrow filled her heart. Incense smoke had wafted past her while she focused on her laptop screen, reading his name and seeing his profile photos.

Fr. Dane Caruso.

There he was – on the screen, his bio so perfect and clean-cut and even the most discerning eye wouldn't suspect the man was fighting a demon. Tortured souls had a way of identifying one another. He felt like a twin flame. Dane seemed to want to be free from confines, and she wanted discipline. She knew, deep down, they'd find it in each other.

Now, they stood outside, the lone two cars left in the patron section of the parking lot—one parked across the lot, the other, right up front, her new golden Prius she'd gotten herself as a token of her own appreciation. A street light shined down on it, making it sparkle like a piece of favorite costume jewelry.

"So," she turned toward him, "thanks again for coming, Dane."

"I wouldn't have missed it." He offered no smile as he slid his hands into his pockets, keeping his eyes on the parking lot. His words trailed at the end, as if he were trying to figure out what to say…or maybe he thought he had slipped and fallen into a dream.

"That...that song?" He turned toward her suddenly as he scratched his temple, his lips curved upwards. She looked up into his eyes—the blue eyes that seemed brighter right about now. "It seemed familiar to me."

She swallowed.

Don't back out now, girl. You were big and bold enough to sing the shit, even after you saw him there. You did this, now pony up.

"Okay." She looked at the ground then back at him, offering a soft smile. "Well, you'd be right about that, about it seeming familiar. So I take it you that you know what was going on?" She laughed lightly.

"Yeah, it was about *me*, right?"

"Yes."

He looked away, at the street lights, scratching his beard covered chin. It was almost three in the morning. For her part, she felt feverish with desire to touch that dear face. She leaned against the building, and he followed suit, mirroring her actions. She crossed her arms, he crossed his. He looked away, she did, too...

He looked back at her, and their eyes met.

"Rhapsody." He licked his bottom lip and turned away again, then turned back, his eyes hooded. "I like you...a lot," he finally said.

His voice sounded so deep, it made her throat vibrate. She could see he was shopping for words, trying to purchase the best that subtle money could buy. He swallowed. "Are you uncomfortable with my vocation? I want you to feel comfortable around me."

"I'm not, I mean," she laughed, "I'm not uncomfortable with you being a priest."

He nodded.

"Are you uncomfortable with me being, well... *me?*" He touched his chest, his fingers spread across it.

"No."

"I don't know all the specifics of your beliefs. I just know what mine are." He pointed to his heart. "But, I know God brings everyone into our life for a reason and I think...I think I'm supposed to learn something from you and not only that, I'll be honest, your song was good, but more importantly, it was true, and that's okay. That's good, actually."

"Thank you...I..."

"It was beautiful. Your voice..." he shook his head in disbelief, "it just amazes me. The way you play, you're so gifted."

He's getting closer...

He leaned toward her, their bodies almost touching. And there it was—he smelled of incense, second hand cigarette smoke and leather...and she liked it.

"Thank you..."

"Don't thank me, I just am telling you what you know is right. You have the gift of musical ministry, Rhapsody."

Taken aback, she rolled her eyes and crossed her arms over her chest, wincing.

"Is this the part where you try to convert me? You heard me singing and think you have a new choir director now? It all makes sense." She laughed huskily, a part of her really believing that may now be the motivation. As she stiffened, she felt him gently run his hand over her arm, and gasped when his fingers intertwined with hers.

"No, not at all." His voice deepened as he looked so intensely into her eyes, she barely had room the breathe.

Oh my God...what is he doing?!

She watched him cock his head slightly to the right and stare down at her lips. They were so close, the tip of his nose brushed against hers.

Please…don't…please…don't…you'll regret it, Dane…Please… don't…

Warm air from his nostrils tickle her upper lip and his breathing accelerated as he gently pushed her back against the wall. Keeping his fingers linked with hers, only a bit tighter, he stood with her, simply quiet. Time and space had frozen while his gaze fixed on her, his lips parted—the gaze of a lover just before kissing his woman.

His Adam's apple bobbed as he swallowed deeply. After a while, the tension subsided and he relaxed his fingers around hers, lessening the grip, although he didn't seem to want to. Taking a half step back, he stood in front of her. She saw the want in his smoldering blue eyes, now with twinkles of silver. He hadn't done it, but his intention was clear and she felt warm as she studied him, for he didn't look guilty at all. Not with the smile he was just giving her.

She smiled and shook her head slowly, placing her hand on her hip.

"Are you sure you're a priest?" she joked, causing them both to laugh. "Damn," she said under her breath.

He put his hands on his hips and looked toward the street as if he were waiting for someone—or something—to save him from himself.

"Yes, I'm sure. Look," he sighed as he turned back toward her, "I don't know all the dynamics of what is going on between us right now." He ruffled his hair with a rough hand, but didn't seem to care. Avoiding her gaze, he seemed to be processing his thoughts into words. "I think I need to be honest and admit to you that I'm wrestling with a lot of stuff right now."

I know.

"And obviously, based on the song, you already knew that but…I'm attracted to you, too, Rhapsody." He now looked squarely at her. Her body relaxed but her heart beat faster. "I've always been, ever since high school. Not just physically, okay? I'm feeling things for you…feelings I've never felt before, well, not in many, many years." He laughed. "My original thought, once I confirmed it this evening was—"

"This evening?"

"Yes, I suspected my feelings were changing for you, but I guess I was still making excuses for it, for *me*." He pointed to his chest. "Making excuses for what was happening inside of *me*, but not anymore." He paused. "So here is what's going on. I'm a priest," he said, pressing his palm against his chest.

"Yes, we've established that." They both laughed.

"But I am still Dane. I have feelings, I get lonely, I notice women, but this is different, like I told you. I haven't succumbed to any temptations, and honestly, I say to you with a straight face, I've *never* been tempted this way before since I took my vows."

"I'm a temptation?" She crossed her legs and rocked from side to side, trying to stifle a grin.

He rolled his eyes at her and sucked his teeth. "You *know* that you are." Taking a deep breath, he went on, "So, I have some choices to make, and so do you. We can try to see what happens or go our separate ways. But, before you make your choice, let me make this clear," his voice dropped lower as his eyes narrowed in on her, "I *want* you. I want…I want someone to go to dinner with, but not just *anyone*. It has to be you,

Rhapsody. I want to hold your hand at the movies." He huffed in frustration, turning in a circle as he rubbed his forehead, before facing her again. "Not just sit there and laugh and wave good-bye afterwards. I can't keep doing this neighborly stuff. I want to be *more* than just your friend."

Lonely, like me. He has all those people around him, people that are obsessed with him, no doubt…people that think he is a saint…but he is still so very lonely. Rhapsody, you've got a priest baring his soul to you. Mama always told you that you were trouble.

This man was falling to pieces in front of her…

"I want to take you out, on *real* dates, to concerts, just like the ones we talked about, the singers that inspired you. I want be right next to you, right by your side. Rhapsody, I," he turned in exasperation, "I don't want to be Fr. Dane to you, I want to *just* be *Dane*. I live in a parish. I have dinner with men almost every single night, men that I love and see like fathers, grandfathers, brothers and uncles…but, I don't know…" He raised his hands in frustration. "I've honestly, Rhapsody, never felt compelled to seek the private companionship of a woman until you came into my life. I was already frustrated before I'd ever laid eyes on you. You came along when I needed you most, and it made things so much clearer."

It took all of her to keep her budding smile at bay.

"I am saying it again, because I feel you need to hear it, to understand. I've *never*, since being a priest, thought I might be missing out on something until this year. Something about you," he shook his head and briefly turned away, "I just need to find out more. This isn't a mistake. It's a miracle."

Rhapsody, do the right thing. You want him, you do, but this isn't right…

"Well, in all honestly, Dane, that's heavy and I don't—"

She turned away trying to find a focal point, anything but those damned, intense blue eyes as he drilled double holes inside of her soul. "I don't want to be the cause of you having any trouble or guilt, okay? I don't have the same religious beliefs as you, let's just get that out the gate." She gave a nervous chuckle. "Not only that, I don't go to church regularly and don't want to. I have to be honest. I don't see how you can accept me like this? Not believing as you do, as strongly as you do."

He cupped his chin, listening intently. He didn't appear the least bit upset; matter of fact, he looked more connected and confident as each millisecond passed. His expression made her stomach jump.

"I mean, I find you attractive," she offered. "I already admitted that. I'm not trying to be responsible, though, for bringing a damn priest to his knees, excuse my language."

"There's nothing to excuse," he said, looking at the ground.

"Dane, look." She took a step toward him, placed her hand on his shoulder. "I know you're lonely, but...I'm not the answer." It took everything inside of her to utter the lie. She knew she was falling for him, but she couldn't let him do this. The golden cross across his chest kept glimmering under the street lights, reminding her who the man worked for when those damned blue eyes had almost hypnotized her into a world of amnesia.

"You think this is just about loneliness? Really?!" He turned away from her and gave a sarcastic laugh, then threw her a glare, looking so mad it sent a shiver up her spine.

Oh shit.

"I am fully aware that we don't have the same beliefs. I

knew that the moment after we had our first conversation. We are different, I get it. I could see the dissimilarities the first time I noticed you in the park, Rhapsody. You wear Egyptian and African adornments, sing out loud like a one-woman concert, have a contagious laugh, and you don't care who hears you. You're a mover and a shaker, daring to be you. I'm not an idiot, give me some credit here! Just like you know who I am, based on that little number you pulled tonight, I know who *you are* as well."

Dane had managed to do the unthinkable. Render Rhapsody speechless.

"There are many things different about us. Some of those differences are obvious, some, not so much." His eyes narrowed. "But we have *far* more in common and an ability to help one another. The best relationships are built on friendship, and just that, *differences*, just enough so that each person can learn from one another and grow. I don't want a carbon copy of me! I'm not even," he said, his voice escalating— frustrated. "I'm not even sure what the hell is going on here! But I do know one thing," he held his index finger up toward the sky, "I am certain about *you*, about how I feel. There are only two people that matter right now, me and *you*."

They rolled in the pause, taking their time as they both seemed to drift away in thought.

"I've done some really dumb stuff, Dane. I let my heart lead the way instead of my mind, too many times in the past when I knew better. And I can't keep messing up," she explained. "What if I want to get married one day? Maybe have a child or two?" She shrugged. "I don't know...but I want the option, and I can't do that with a priest, Dane."

"You want children?" his voice was low as he turned on a

dime, looking her squarely in the eye. His question caught her off guard.

"Well, yes…I believe so…" she shook her head in confusion, "Look Dane, I—"

"I want children, too. I think about that a lot now. Maybe I am the man that is supposed to be the father of your children. Not just father of a church." She felt her belly knot. He looked her up and down, and stopped at her stomach, as if he were trying to visually plant a child inside of her right that very second.

She smiled nervously, trying to offer comfort and bring him back into reality. "I said it doesn't bother me that you're a priest, and it doesn't, and I could even still be your friend, but now that I know you're attracted to me too, well," she swallowed hard, "that is just playing with fire." She looked up into his eyes, watched them darken with an emotion she couldn't describe or latch completely onto. "We can't do this…I can only offer friendship," she said halfheartedly.

This hurts like hell, but I have to. I can't let him throw his career away. What type of woman would I be? Oh my God…

She looked away and shielded her face, feeling the burn of her words right through to her soul.

"I don't believe you. Matter of fact, I *know* that isn't the truth. You just lied to a priest. Tsk, tsk," he taunted, pushing her words aside as if he wasn't the least bit fazed. He stepped closer to her, crowding her personal space, and when she saw the way he looked at her, she placed her hands on his chest, both palms flat against it.

Oh shit. Damn. The man is built…Jesus. Don't move your hands, Rhapsody. Keep them right there. Don't move them…

And then she felt his hard pecs jump from beneath his

FORGIVE ME FATHER, FOR I HAVE LOVED

clothing.

This is torture!

She swallowed hard, again.

That's right, he works out, like, all the time. He is in even better shape than I thought. Lord, I don't call on you often but I need some help if you want me to leave this man alone. Sweet Jesus I need to leave this man alone but I don't know if I can!

Her emotions boiled, so she did what she knew—tried to temper them with internal humor. Tried to laugh the feelings away, but how was that possible? A lump stuck in her throat as he cupped her chin, raising her eyes to his.

Dane, don't kiss me...don't! I won't stop you...but I want to want to stop you...

"Rhapsody..." He said her name low and slowly as he brought his lips to her temple then let them trail down her face in a gentle caress. Soft, lingering, dragging along her skin. "I *need* to see how this feels. I need you to be by my side. No worries. I won't let you bring me down to my knees. And besides, I've already fallen. Fallen so helplessly in love with you."

He pulled back and looked into her eyes.

"I just felt you deserved honestly at this point. I needed you to know what was going on in my mind, my heart, and yeah, I took a risk. See what's happening? You're scared, but I'm not. I can't believe this, but I'm not."

"I'm not scared," she said, avoiding his eyes. A chill invaded her, though she knew it wasn't cold outside.

"Okay, you are concerned about my well-being," he corrected. He pushed against her, leaving no room to breathe, no room to move. "If I was so *well*, Rhapsody, I wouldn't be here, now would I? You're a hospital, and I'm sick. I need to find out what this is between us, Rhapsody, and I believe a part of you needs me as well and wants to find out, too. We're in love. No regrets."

And before she could respond, his lips brushed against her cheek again, and he kissed it…soft, enduring, sweet. Then, just like that, he abruptly turned away and walked to his car. No 'goodbye', no 'we'll talk about this later.' Nothing. Apparently, he'd had his say, and he was now done discussing it with her.

Her stomach caved as butterflies released. He climbed in the car, started it and drove away. He hadn't said anything but she knew she'd see him soon in the park, and tonight would just mark the beginning of something strangely wonderful…something she half-heartedly resisted because she needed to be able to say, *"I tried."*

Even though her heart said, "Like hell you did…"

Dane wanted to have her in his life, and she accepted it, proud that he put his foot down. Yet, in some strange way, though he clearly made his feelings known despite her protests, he still did it beautifully—as if he'd done it on bended knee…

CHAPTER SEVENTEEN

The following week…

RHAPSODY SWAYED TO Ariana Grande, as the songstress belted out, 'We Can't Be Friends'. *Oh, the irony.* She glanced at the clock, and knowing Dane, he'd be right on time. Although she tried to pretend she wasn't nervous, her stomach told another story. Since the man had laid his cards out on the table, they'd shared quiet, strange moments together in the park and on the telephone. He'd hold her hand for a few seconds, release it after a gentle squeeze, and not speak, just look out into the lake. She waited, wanting him to unload whatever guns he had, but instead, he'd refocus, caress the side of her face and ask her about the tiny details of her day. She turned her attentions back to her task. The kitchen filled with intoxicating aromas from the dressing she'd made for the arugula salad.

"A little bit of lemon juice, just a drizzle of evoo….dash of salt and pepper…steak done in ten minutes!" She smiled as she peeked in the oven at the potatoes covered in garlic, chives and sage. A few moments later, the doorbell rang. She froze. With a nervous laugh, she walked to the door, then hesitated, noticing that the red apron printed with, 'Kiss the Chef' was still wrapped around her and to make matters worse, she'd stained her chic, form-fitting black shirt and denim leggings. Sighing, she slowly opened the door to find Dane.

There Dane stood, holding a bottle wrapped beautifully, with a silver bow on top. A giggle escaped her when he stared at her a little self-consciously, as though they were young and green high school students all over again.

"This is a nice street. Beautiful trees." he sighed and grinned wider. "I like it, you know? But, uh, I was hoping at some given point in time, you'd invite me inside."

"Oh!" She laughed, and opened the door wider. "I'm so sorry, Dane. Please come in." She stood out of the way as he leisurely entered and scanned the living room. "Uh, excuse my appearance. I looked much better an hour ago. I think I'm a good cook, but I'm also messy." She locked the door and fretfully ran her hands together.

Turning back to her, he handed her the bag with the pretty bow. "It's white grape juice."

They both burst out laughing.

"Thank you, that was very thoughtful. You should've gotten red grape juice, though."

"Why? We're having beef?"

"Yes!"

They both burst out laughing again, then she moved toward the kitchen. Without invitation, he trailed behind her.

"This is a nice house, Rhapsody," he said sincerely as he leaned up against the counter, crossing his ankles while she slowly opened the oven door to peer inside.

"Thank you. I've been here for about four years, my first major purchase. I couldn't miss out on it. The real estate market had plummeted and it was an opportunity for me to be a home owner. The mortgage was cheaper than my rent; it was a no-brainer."

He nodded in understanding and casually crossed his arms over his chest.

"I even mow my own lawn." When she closed the oven door, the mouthwatering smell of steak lingered in the air.

Dane nodded and smiled, remaining strangely quiet. A few moments passed when she continued to check on the food. Her back toward him, she had a strange sensation. She looked over her shoulder and realized he was staring at her. His light eyes sparkled under the small but modern kitchen's recessed lighting. And he looked good, *damn* good. Dressed in a dark gray, long sleeve shirt that slightly clung to his muscular arms and wearing casual, dark, slightly faded jeans, she enjoyed taking in his image. His hair was less perfect, a bit messy as if a dollop of gel had been applied, or perhaps he'd run his fingers through it. She loved it and briefly imagined her fingertips moving through the shades of amber, warm brown, and sparse blond and black tresses. She kept looking at it—just as mesmerized as she'd been the first day she saw him at the park. It was truly one of his best physical features but those eyes…well, they won first dibs.

She swallowed and tried to concentrate on the tasks at hand. At the park, they would be among nature and the many passersby. But here, in her home, they were all alone. In that moment, she began to feel the gravity of the situation. He remained calm, as if they met here, like this, all the time. How surprising! Typically, she was the one running head first into unchartered territory. Hell, this had even been *her* idea, but now, here he was, and she was the one sweating bullets.

She'd asked him to dinner innocently enough, but now, *she* even questioned her motives. He held the handle to sanity, while she slipped down the slope of surrealism. For a brief moment, she thought she may be imagining the entire scenario, as if, for instance, he was never at the club, listening to her sing a song about his fractured heart. The whole thing felt dreamlike, and then, reality snatched her back into the present as she felt his lips run along her cheek.

Oh God...

He stepped back again. She hadn't even seen him approach.

"Uh, let me get these steaks out. Please," she pointed out into the living room, "have a seat out there, relax, make yourself at home. I will get dinner on the table."

"I would prefer to help you," he offered as he removed two fluted glasses from an open cabinet and held one in each hand, his blue eyes hooded and lips curved in a smile. Such a seductive smile, too!

"I'm sure you would, but you are the guest, so mosey on along." She playfully turned him around as if they were about to play a game of 'Pin the Tail on the Donkey', and gave a gentle push forward, ushering him away. He obliged, not looking back. After setting the glasses on the table, he sat down on her over-stuffed tan couch and studied her small, antique piano, the pitiful thing, and then looked around the arched room at her art, mostly consisting of West and East African paintings and masks.

She continued to toil in the kitchen, flitting about here and there, but not nearly as much as her nerves, which were rattled like a salt shaker and worn down to a bare nub.

"Have you ever been?" he suddenly called out.

She paused, setting the old green and white checkered oven mitt on the counter.

"Ever been where?"

"To Guinea? That is where that mask is from." He pointed across the room toward one of her prized possessions—a long, wooden hand-carved mask with a slightly sinister face and beautiful red and white paint around the hollowed eyes.

How'd he know that?

"No, I haven't. I purchased that at an art show. It just drew me in, you know. Have you been there?" she asked as she opened the refrigerator door, removed a large glass bowl full of freshly tossed salad and placed it on the counter.

"Yes, I recognize the symbols on it, the painting."

"Really?" she asked, impressed that he'd said 'Yes'.

"Mmmm hmmm, I've been to many countries, and several in Africa. Guinea's continued fighting with Liberia—well, it appears Liberia keeps in one way or another bringing their problems *there*—caused some tension while we were visiting. The political climate felt a bit unstable. Their economy is weak; that is why we were there actually, to lend a hand. They have so many refugees from other neighboring areas, the country is overwhelmed, not nearly enough resources. Regardless, I completely enjoyed my conversations with many of the school teachers and officials there."

"You weren't there to try and convert, were you? Like a missionary?" Rhapsody half-heartedly teased as she gave the salad another toss with two long, white spoons.

He shook his head. "We always talk about God, and we

hold public prayer. We offered advice based on our own beliefs, but we were there to serve, first and foremost."

Rhapsody nodded as she made her way into the dining room, setting the salad bowl down.

"I'm going to grab the bread, and then we can get started." She grinned at him, perhaps a little too over-the-top, and before she could turn to the kitchen, their eyes locked. They simply stared at one another, neither willing to turn away. Time stopped. Forcing herself to move, she returned to the kitchen and opened the hot stove, causing the delicious scents to billow out and kiss her cheeks with heated culinary love... *love?*

From behind her, she felt his glare on her, and she toyed with the notion of swaying her hips a bit, to entice, then decided against it. There was so much she wanted to say to him, so much she wanted to ask. She'd been anticipating this evening, wanting to crack him open like a piñata and dive deep inside of him. Not only emotionally, but also physically. To touch him, feel him—it would be heaven. Shoving those thoughts to the side, she took a deep breath and walked back out of the aromatic kitchen with a hot pan of buttery rolls.

She looked across at him, and he kept his focus on her décor, his eyes bouncing from object to object. The blended living and dining area allowed her to double-task, keep her keen eye on the mysterious, handsome fellow with a golden crucifix handing from around his neck, as well as finish setting the table. She smiled and turned away, placing silverware and saucers at each setting. Before it was all complete, her hard work displayed in artistic fashion, she smelled woodsy cologne and the all too familiar incense from St. Michael's Rectory.

He is behind me...

She briefly closed her eyes and swallowed, then looked down at the perfect place setting and took in the sight of his large hand next to the saucer she'd just set down. His warm breath caressed her ear as his hand slowly slid over hers, his wedding band glowing bright, as if it were on fire.

It's going to be a long ass night...

DANE HAD SPENT the evening and morning praying... and praying...and praying a wee bit more. He prayed as he drove to Rhapsody's house and he struggled with the fact that not a bone in him screamed warning, cautionary alerts or swayed red flags while some invisible ghost boo'ed and hissed. Nor did any alarm sound, 'Mayday!'

His sixth sense had never failed him, and yet here he was, willingly driving to a woman's home—the very same woman that Fr. Kirkpatrick had warned him about. A woman that had caused him to have two wet dreams, much to his dismay and a woman who he'd pictured in ways that he knew for a fact were inappropriate. Fr. Kirkpatrick had urged him to keep his distance from the temptress and, though he'd denied she was anything like that—indeed she was. No need to mince words.

A temptress is someone who tempts you to do something out of the ordinary, someone who entices you. Whether they mean to or not is irrelevant. Nevertheless, it wasn't her fault. She was cursed with good looks, a beautiful face and body, and natural bohemian charm. She spoke the truth when it was needed most. She was brave and intelligent. Gifted. She was his muse, and he chased her, even in his dreams.

Temptation resistance is the truest test of character, they say. I don't know about that.

He craved the scent of her silky, smooth skin and wanted to hear her laugh, speak…that voice. She entertained him by her mere presence, helped him see the world in an entirely different way. At this point, he simply asked for understanding—asked the Lord to help reveal to him each step he should take.

He stood behind her, fighting the urge to kiss the back of her exposed neck. Her tightly coiled hair was partially braided in a beautiful updo, and it smelled of honey, cinnamon and vanilla.

What type of shampoo does she use?

"Dane?" she called out, seeming to struggle to turn around as his arm blocked her pass. He looked down at his hand over hers, and dug his nose deeper into her tresses until she called his name again. Falling out of his own thoughts as if he were cast from the sky, hurled back down toward Earth, he blinked and looked around, for a brief moment, forgetting where he was. Her shoulder blade pushed into the pit of his arm as she continued to strain against him, to turn in the circle of his physical blockade. Her lips parted, glistening with what appeared to be freshly applied russet lipstick. When she smiled, they framed her teeth, making the already white beam appear even brighter. He could smell her sweet breath as she repeated his name.

Fresh mint and celery…

"Dane…" she repeated, for now the third time.

"Hmmm?"

"You are in another world," she said, shaking her head. "You have me so boxed in here, I can't…" her voice trailed at the end.

"Oh," he immediately took a step back, "my apologies. I

was just coming over to help." The pitter patter of rain started against the windows. The drops tap danced along the sides of the house, creating an orchestra concert just for the two of them.

He exhaled and watched as she squirmed away, down to the other end of the table, removing her apron and placing it on a nearby chair.

"Everything looks beautiful." He rubbed his hands together anxiously.

"Thank you, have a seat," she offered without looking his way.

He stood there, a bit longer and took notice of the long, wall length chocolate curtains on the emporium windows. The modest, delightful house had trey ceilings. Well built, with no detail left unnoticed in the great craftsmanship, as well as her eclectic, avant-garde tastes. Each item told him a bit more about her. One wall was a bluish gray, while the others, much more vibrant. A deep, muted orange, the walls complimented the beige area rug with pale tangerine swirls. In the center of the dining table was a simple yet elegant plant in a sterling silver bowl. His eyes roamed back to her. He walked to her and their bodies brushed against one another. Her hand teetered and shook as she poured a glass of iced water.

"Ahhh," she gasped, her voice deep and throaty as a playful smile took over her beautiful face once more. "What are you doing?"

"Pulling out your chair." He gripped the back of the chair beside her with both hands and quickly scooted it back, waiting for her to take her seat.

"Thank you." She sat down slowly, but not before he noticed her dark shirt with a floury handprint over her left breast.

He smirked and made his way back to the opposite side of the room, taking a seat.

"Well, you look really nice," she offered as she took a sip of her water.

"Thank you, so do you." He gripped his glass, raised it in a toast, then took a sip and placed it back down.

"Did you have any problems finding me?"

Yes, but not in the way you mean. Now that I've rediscovered you, everything is fine.

"No, it was a piece of cake. Thanks." He bent his head down and clasped his hands to say a prayer. "Dear Heavenly Father, thank you for this dinner that you've given me and my friend, Rhapsody. Thank you for using her hands and culinary skills to make such a wonderful feast for the sustenance of our bodies and minds. May we enjoy this fellowship. Amen."

Without a glance in her direction, he picked up his fork and pierced the crisp lettuce that she'd placed in a small, wooden salad bowl before him.

"Amen," she said softly, drawing his focus to her. He zoomed in on her lips, then her eyes. Oh how they sparkled and gleamed, even in the dimly lit room. The place was romantic, all on it's on. Food aromas floated about, mixed in with a natural earthy scent and a certain sweetness, reminiscent of nutmeg.

Oh yes, that reminds me.

"Rhapsody, I have a really silly question to ask you."

"The perfect kind!" She laughed as she stabbed her salad with her fork, looking up at him every so often between tight chews.

"What type of shampoo do you use? When I'm close to you, I can smell it, it's really nice."

"Why? You wanna use it?" She smirked.

"Maybe."

I'd like to wash your hair for you, Rhapsody…run my fingers through it…

"You wouldn't believe me if I told you."

"Try me."

"I use raw honey with a dash of cinnamon and a drop of vanilla extract. You'd think I was baking a cake."

He took a big bite of his salad, rolled around a cherry tomato and nodded with a sly grin.

"That's amazing, well, your hair looks beautiful and smells delicious…I could almost eat it up."

She laughed and moved her fork faster through the roughage, as if trying to find her own tomato buried beneath the arugula leaves. He wasn't positive, but if he were a betting man, he'd put money down on this little observation: the woman appeared to be blushing.

The meal continued with small talk about the day's events, even a bit of pop culture to soften edges of uncertainty. All the while—exchanging glances, peeks, and many unsaid words until finally, they spoke at the exact same time, their words tumbling over one another's, which caused them both to erupt in laughter.

"Okay, you go first," Dane offered as he began to slice into his tender steak, exposing a perfectly cooked medium well sliver.

"No, you go."

She took a small bite from her dinner roll. He watched her work the soft bread in her mouth, fascinated.

"Okay. I just want to tell you that I'm not going to play games with you. I meant what I said the night I came to hear you play."

"Yes." She lifted her glass of water to her lips. "We hadn't discussed that night in depth since it happened. But, the way you left it," she cocked her head to the side, smiled and placed the glass back down before folding her hands together, "I figured you were the wrong person to second guess."

They shared a brief silence. He mulled over his words briefly before he continued.

"I want…" He paused, looked at her seriously and he placed his fork quietly down next to his plate. "I want to know everything about you. I want to know the things, I should've known had I not been such a bonehead in high school."

He watched her eyes widen as she sank back into her chair. He had trouble gauging her reaction, yet, his best grasp on the situation was that she was surprised at his revelation.

"I should have said something to you back then, Rhapsody. That way, I wouldn't be playing catch up now," he further explained. "Anyway," he wiped the side of his mouth with his ivory napkin and drummed his fingers on the table, "the food is delicious. Thank you." He looked at her, and she still wore that strange expression. "You are looking at me like something is wrong."

"Well, I'm just surprised to hear that is all."

"Hear what?"

He knew what; he just wanted to hear her say it.

She shrugged, looked down at her dinner and moved the food around on her plate as if she were trying to corral it into one lump sum. "Hear you admitting you wanted to talk to me in high school."

"Why wouldn't I? We were kids then, I'm a man now. I can own up to it."

She placed her fork down and looked at him. The right corner of her mouth lifted slightly…possibly a smile.

A brief silence ensued.

"Okay," she picked up her fork again, and showed incredible interest in the meat on her plate. "You've said quite a few things lately and I haven't really addressed them."

"Yes, and we need to talk about them, but before you do," he took another swallow of his water, "I want you to feel comfortable talking to me, calling me. I feel that so many times, we both want—"

"To say more." they said in unison, laughing at the irony once again.

"Yeah, to say more." He nodded seriously as he stared at her from across the table. She seemed so far away, he wanted nothing more than to lessen the distance between them.

"You've given me courage to tackle some issues I've been wrestling with."

That admission clearly piqued her interest as her eyes expanded and she stopped playing with her food.

"I know Josh's death was hard. I'm glad that I was able to help you cope a bit better."

"No, not just that."

She folded her hands on the table, graceful hands…*pianist hands* with long fingers. Sitting straight, she assumed a near regal appearance.

"Look." He sighed, running his hand over his face as he sat back in his seat. "I was struggling with some things right before Josh's death, Rhapsody. I found it cruel, how everything came to be, like I was being given some test I could never pass. I feel like you are supposed to know this, and I pray to God that what I'm about to say, doesn't scare you away, or make you hold back." He paused and gauged her, but she remained calm and seemingly at peace with his declaration.

"I...I have never once questioned being a priest. I believe that I was called to do this, as I told you, but I also believe that I was running from some things. I'm almost afraid to tell you, Rhapsody. No one but Josh knew."

"No," she said curtly, shaking her head, her eyes closed as if she were trying to stop a storm from rolling through with a mere hush from her mouth.

"No, what?"

"If you are going to tell me something that you will regret telling me later, then don't tell me. Don't force it. You'll know when the time is right." She smiled at him, a warm, sympathetic smile laced with a diluted but protective warning. "I don't want you to have any regrets with me, Dane. Those are the rules." She swallowed and looked at him sternly. "I refuse to be anything you wish *hadn't* happened."

He could sense the claws around her heart sinking deeper, reflected in the words. Her spirit spoke to him, stepping ahead of her as her lawyer and representative and announcing over the sky airwaves to expect a turbulent conversation. Yes, it was a rough conversation, despite the smiles and admissions. This was all cards on the table time, and she fought him, completely taking him off guard. Regardless, her reasoning was genuine and lest he admit, it made sense.

"Up until this point, we've been honest with one another, but safe." She nodded thoughtfully. "Nothing has happened that you will have to say Hail Mary's for." She laughed, but she was obviously not tickled.

"Don't tell me anything, Dane." She pointed at him, her finger far away, but the look on her face made him believe it would push into his forehead at any moment. "Nothing that you will later think, 'Damn! why did I say that?' I don't want it, I don't need it, and you don't, either." She picked up her fork and drove it through the meat as if the steak were butter. He watched her chew, then reach for her glass, taking a confident gulp.

"Okay. But, this isn't over. Eventually, you will have to let it happen." He placed his napkin across his lap. "But you want to stay in the 'safe zone'", he said, putting his fingers up like quotation marks. He'd already had time to think about this, and though the memories were upsetting, he wanted to go into this right. Nevertheless, she wasn't ready, and he couldn't force it. Timing truly was everything.

"Safe zone?" She smiled and rolled her eyes.

"Yes, 'safe zone'. You don't want me to make this more complicated than this already is."

"Are you a murderer?" she asked.

"No."

"Did you molest some children?"

"What in the world? No!"

"What about grown women, or grown men?" He detected the attitude in her tone, mixed with a bit of sarcasm.

"Of course not."

"Then I don't need to know. Pass the pepper."

"You are something else, Ms. Thomason. Pardon me, Ms. Blue." He took a bite of his steak, and grunted at her expression and his eyes rolled in the back of his head, making her laugh.

"Please! It's good, but it isn't *that* good. Thanks though." She giggled as she placed a French cut string bean in her mouth.

"It is *that* good. You are an exceptional cook."

"Thank you kindly, sir." She winked at him. "You told me a while ago you know how to play the piano. All this time we've discussed *me* and my career, but I've yet to hear you play." She pointed behind him to the rustic instrument that had certainly seen better days, but was surely her pride and joy. "You are going to play for me tonight."

"Like hell I am."

She burst out laughing, practically falling out of her chair. He felt his face redden as she delighted in his impromptu response. Her curls came undone and cascaded onto her shoulders.

"Look what you did? You made me laugh so hard that my damn hair has unraveled." she mock chided, scooting back in her chair.

"Look," Dane laughed as he pointed at her, "that is like a master artist asking a three-year-old to sketch a doodle. I'm not playing that piano in front of you. You won't embarrass me like that, I won't have it."

"Oh, are you scared?" she taunted. "That isn't very masculine, Dane!"

"That won't work, Rhapsody. I'm one hundred percent man. My actions show it, not my words."

His words, cloaked as an anecdote, hung in the air—their heaviness more than apparent.

Did I just say that?

Pseudo-flirtation was not something he ever entertained, but this woman did something to him. Brought out the "man" in him, kicked the "priest" to the wayside. He should feel guilty. He should leave. Not in a million years did he want to leave this woman. Something slipped into place then, like a mechanism engaged within him, and he knew at that moment—his life was about to change. *Everything* was about to change. Including all that he was, all that he'd represented in the world until now.

And he wanted this. Yes, he'd brave anything to have his Rhapsody, for nothing would be more of a sin than losing her...

CHAPTER EIGHTEEN

IT WAS TIME to make things a bit clearer, to be candid, sincere. To no longer walk the fine line between one world and another—Dane's world in the Church and the outside world where Rhapsody lived.

He ran a hand through his hair. "Look, once I realized I wanted to see where this thing between us would go, I felt at ease," he said gravely. "Crazy as that sounds, I was at peace with the possibilities."

He chanced a glance at her and caught her pleading eyes. "Don't," they said, but he refused to let her back him into a wall. She needed the words, and he would no longer appease her, at least not this time.

"I don't think you know how much you mean to me," he finally said.

"I've heard that before," she mumbled, then forced a smile—a smile that he had no doubt was meant to cover hidden pain. That was how she operated, by covering hurts with humor and witty comebacks. He was determined to confront and sooth that pain within her once and for all.

"You don't trust yourself." He smiled at her and clasped his hands together after pushing his empty plate aside. "You think you're making a mistake, in some way, by even dealing with me, but you wouldn't be true to yourself if you ran away from this. You've been struggling this entire time, haven't you? We are *both* fighting. Just two different battles."

"What if I told you I think I'm afraid of true commitment, so I subconsciously find men I know are not available for long term relationships? What if I told you that I accept that about myself?" She crossed her arms over her chest, her face placid.

Dane cocked his head to the side and deliberated. "Some of that may be true, some of that may be," he shrugged, "you are trying to figure out if I'm even worth the effort. Do you *really* think you are afraid of commitment?"

Her expression turned shy and she shifted in her seat. "I wonder sometimes." She sniffed, rubbed her nose and contemplated her half empty plate. "I sure know how to pick 'em, that's for sure. I thought…I thought I had finally learned."

"Rhapsody, did you ever stop to think that it would take someone like you, someone open-minded and willing to even consider such a possibility, for me to be comfortable enough to even be sitting here with you tonight? You *did* learn. Only this time, something in you trusted that I was worth taking a chance on. You believe I am different, somewhere deep inside. You bet on the underdog, only this time, it *will* be worth it. The odds are clearly in your favor."

She immediately looked away, as if someone had rang the doorbell. The woman was squirming in her seat and he was certain her blood pressure had went up, based on her reddened complexion and silence.

"I know though, that that comment is more than just about *me*."

He cleared his throat, leaned back in his seat and raised his arms, crossing them behind his head. He wanted to get it out of her, wanted her to purge, to cleanse, to confess.

"Tell me about him."

She ran her fingers slowly over the table cloth, smoothing out a slight wrinkle.

"His name was Raul. He was liar and a cheat. End of story."

"Nah," He shook his head. "That's just the beginning. If we are going to do this, let's *do* this, Rhapsody. Come on, be *all* in. This is discovery time. Now, I let you off the hook when you didn't want me to just let it all hang out, but I personally don't feel that way. You rejected my offer, but that doesn't go both ways since you opted out. No way. I need full disclosure. Not to cause you pain, but to truly understand the woman I am with."

He could see on her face that she was taken aback by his candor.

"I bought the lie and accepted the cheat that was in him the entire time of our relationship, until I couldn't any longer. There is something," she swallowed, "demeaning and belittling about recognizing that you've played the fool for love. It is shameful." She looked at him then—directly, intently—as if searching for his very soul. She poked her chest aggressively as her voice rose, "Shameful to know that someone such as myself was someone else's sucker. I'm not stupid, but I sure as hell felt like it. Smart women don't fall for players, right?

Strong women don't stay with them. Oh, well. It wasn't the first time, but it was the *worst* time."

He nodded, painting a picture of her inside his head, weaving thoughts of comfort to offer at the right time.

"I had taken a break from love before him. Focused on *me*. I thought I was ready."

"You *were* ready. It was he that was not."

"You know what, Dane? I really don't think I want to talk about this." She threw her napkin off her lap and abruptly stood. "That man had enough of my damn time." She laughed, turning her back to him, hiding something, something she refused to show or relinquish. "Let's talk about something else, okay?" She glanced at him from over her shoulder then got up and walked into the kitchen, returning moments later with the sparkling juice bottle he'd brought.

I won't push her anymore. She will tell me soon, give her some breathing room. Just back off a bit.

Wearing a manufactured grin fit for a factory baby doll, she gasped as he snatched the bottle from her grip, slammed it onto the table and grabbed her roughly around her waist. His fingers trailed up her stomach; he felt the fabric from her shirt bunching as he stood from his chair, turned her toward him and placed his lips gently on hers.

Impulsive, compelling—a kiss he couldn't avoid. How did he ever think to continue this charade, to keep on controlling himself? To stay away from her? Would he go to Hell for this? No, God is forgiving. God is love.

And love was what he felt for Rhapsody.

The kiss was soft, warm, her full, moist lips against his. He cupped the back of her head as his need for her became more determined and aggressive. The heat from her body against his stirred him, pushed him to leave all the shadows behind. What felt so odd to him was that it didn't feel like their first kiss at all. He'd experienced all this in his dreams already. A hundred times over.

After a while, she pushed softly against his chest, the palms of her hands digging into his pecs.

"Whew," she said, a little breathless. "Uh, okay." She pulled back, laughing nervously and running her hand across her brow. "Wasn't expecting that!" She tried to look away but he gripped her chin and turned her back toward him for another kiss, this time tracing her bottom lip with his tongue. He felt her hesitation, then, slowly, she relinquished, opening herself up to him, allowing him to explore her fully. He moved his hands to the small of her back and pulled her toward him, embracing her tighter as he deepened the kiss.

Yes, he was going to hell, but at least, now he knew. From now on, he was no longer a priest, and he wouldn't live as a hypocrite.

With a groan, he fell deeper in a spell that had him entrapped in a mystical entanglement for two. After a while, with reluctance, he ended the kiss, holding gently onto her elbows as he took a step back, while still savoring the flavor of her sweet mouth.

They exchanged a look of awe, of surprise, as though a great discovery had been made. Rhapsody tried to break free from his embrace, but he couldn't let her go, not completely. He pulled her back, close to him.

"Dane, oh my God!" she said.

"What?" He smiled into her hair, his chin buried in the soft mass.

"Don't play with me," she murmured, her face pressed to

his shirt. He could hear the smile in her words. "You kissed me. You kiss good, too." She laughed.

He smiled. "It's been a while. I guess you never forget really, kind of like riding a bike."

Finally, she pulled away, taking his hand, she led him back to the living room. The sun was setting, and the room drew darker, casting strange glows and blanketing them with perfect ambiance. He took a seat, while she lit several candles on the coffee table next to a woven elephant mask with colorful mosaic tile ears. More interesting pieces caught his eye. They fit oddly in the room, in some ways, perhaps, matching Rhapsody's personality. Something he wanted to find out. He leaned forward in his seat, gearing up.

Is this really happening?

"So," he said, finally after a pregnant silence. "Now, here's the thing... You laid out some rules regarding saying things I might regret, and I do have some rules, too."

"This is a list I am sure to not follow." She smirked and crossed her legs, swaying them back and forth. Long, gorgeous legs, which he couldn't help appreciating.

"You will follow them," he said, surprised at his boldness. He was putting everything on the line for this...for her, for *them*.

"How can you be so sure?"

"Because you want me as much as I want you. Your kiss told on you." There, he said it.

She bit her bottom lip and turned away, blushing. Feeling more confident, he leaned back in his chair.

"Now, we are going to be honest with one another. I am not going to put you in any precarious situations, okay?"

She nodded and stopped swinging her legs. "Is this a prelude to get me to talk about *him*, again?"

"I want to see you, as much as possible. I want to be open with you, and I want you to tell me what makes you, *you*. That includes your ex."

"Why are you so obsessed with hearing about him?" She grimaced.

"Because I want to make sure I do the exact opposite of what he did. I want to know what he did, how he did it, and I want to make sure that I never cause you a moment of distress or hurt. In many ways, this is brand new for me, Rhapsody. I am a much different person now than I was eight years ago, so I can't apply my old ideologies on dating and women to you. I need some help from you here. I don't want to make you do or say anything out of your comfort zone, okay? That is not what is going on," he reassured. "I just want to know how he affected you, so I can understand what I'm up against. You can tell me now or later, but I will continue to ask."

She laughed—though it was evident by her twisted facial expression, she was insulted.

"Look, Dane." She rolled her eyes and huffed, exasperated. "There is nothing to compare or discuss. Just be you, and it will take care of itself."

"No, it won't. You opened up to me when we were at the park that day, on the boat. I've never seen you that vulnerable since. It was like, you had to be in the middle of nowhere to completely let loose. The man affected you, he took something from you and I, I need to know what he did to *my* heart, so I can figure out how to help mend it."

He could tell she was struck by what he said. She needed the reassurance that he wouldn't judge her, and the words came out naturally, unplanned, from his gut. Real, concrete, earnest. This woman *was* his heart. She got his blood pumping in the morning, and nothing less than "love" could describe the feelings boiling inside of him.

"Your heart?" she repeated, seeming to stumble and choke on the word.

"Yes…my heart. I'm in love with you. I told you that weeks ago, I've said it several times since. I mean that."

At that, she closed her eyes and let her head fall back. She gripped the arms of her chair and looked up at the ceiling. A slight sheen appeared just below her eyelashes. Standing, he got on one knee beside her and took her hand, but she kept her eyes closed, as if afraid to look at him. That was okay, he'd be brave for both of them.

He ran his fingers along hers, admiring the softness of her hands.

"Do you ever wish you had a second chance to meet somebody again for the first time?"

Lifting her head from the chair, she finally looked at him, her eyes brimming with deep things, things that had been hidden and stuffed away, things that she poured forth in song. But songs were a curtain—she could blame it on her mood, the tune or the rain; she never had to fully claim her true feelings if she kept them under the guise of a rhyme, or pegged them as inspiration from an exterior source. The song was her get-a-way car, driving fast, and going nowhere.

She nodded, but kept silent, as though she couldn't speak.

"Well, Rhapsody," he squeezed her hand, not taking his eyes off of her, "this is our second chance."

"But—"

"No, Rhapsody," he interrupted. "If you think that you are the beginning of this fight inside of me, you are mistaken. You

are simply the one that reminded me it needed to be addressed, and you are worth that consideration. You, Josh, all
of it reminded me of that. I was called, Rhapsody, but there
was never anything written that I wouldn't have a new calling
later down the line. It's confusing." He rubbed his head. "It's a
lot for me to process, too, but God uses people in some ways
we may not understand, and sometimes, we just can't question
it, even when everyone else is."

Rhapsody looked away, her expression hard to read.

"Don't you think I know what I'm up against? This has the
potential of getting ugly. I have to get it figured out. I don't
have all the answers, I am just kind of floating along here. But
I promise you, you will have no—"

She looked away from him, and put her hand up to make
him stop.

"What?"

Her mouth parted and she shook her head in disbelief.
"Don't say that to me. You can't promise me anything."

"You don't expect much? You should."

Her face looked like that of an innocent little child—
terrified, out of her depth. "I thought you were safe, Dane.
You're a priest... Now here my behind is involved with you,
and kissing you." She sighed. "Falling in love with you. How
do I get myself into this stuff?!" A nervous laugh escaped her.

And now she admits it. She loves me as much as I love her...

"This time you saw in me what *I* needed to find on my
own the entire time."

He caressed the side of her face and pulled her down onto
the floor with him. Her eyes gleamed in the candlelight.
Moving her hair out of her face, he kissed her, a mere peck,
then again, and again, until passion took over and they clung

to one another, two bodies molded into one. Lying on their sides, they kissed and stared at one another, moments of silence stretching between them, filling in the gaps where words didn't.

"This is difficult, complicated." She ran her finger down the bridge of his nose, making him smile and lean into her touch. "I didn't expect this, I'm serious," she whispered. He could see concern on her face; she was finally letting her guard down, exposing her raw vulnerability.

"It is complicated but we'll get it figured out." He caressed her shoulder.

More time passed until the sun was all but gone, and the room was only lit by the slowly melting Yankee mulberry candles.

"You know what? You're right. You deserve to know what happened. It's not like I'm still pining for him, I just feel like a fool when I talk about it." She sighed, "I'm going to answer your question," she offered quietly.

The shadows and lights played on her face, while they remained intertwined on the soft carpet.

"About your ex? Don't feel that way. Well, I can't tell you how to feel, just know that we all make mistakes but please believe me when I tell you that I consider myself quite objective. I'm listening."

She nodded. After a brief hesitation, she began. "I met him while at a really great point in my life. Like I told you, I thought I was ready to date again, thought I had my crap together finally." Her dark eyes met his, filled with so much sorrow and sadness, he felt a lump in his throat, hurting for her. "The man promised me the world and delivered a pile of drama instead. He moved in with me, then fast forward, the jerk was using my money to take other women out."

"Oh man. I'm sorry, Rhapsody."

"Now you see why I felt like a fool. I hate that feeling. Admitting this, admits stupidity as far as I'm concerned."

"Rhapsody, you are not the only person in the world that has been used and lied to by someone. Sometimes," he shrugged, "we have lapses in judgment but the person that hurt us is still the culprit. Blame the cheater, not the one that was cheated on."

"I know, but I have to accept my responsibility in the whole mess, too. I don't profess to have a crystal ball, but I think I'm a pretty good judge of character, or so I thought. That relationship put everything on the line as far as me trusting myself. To make matters worse, he wouldn't move out of my house, so I had to go to court and get an eviction notice. I was embarrassed, Dane," she paused. "I felt like an idiot. This man had taken me for a ride. He kept lying, saying he'd changed, and I am going to be honest with you, you can judge me until the cows come home but I—"

"I'm not going to judge you, Rhapsody. I told you that and I meant it."

"Well, I took him back a couple times after that. That is the real kicker. That is the part I can't forgive myself for, Dane. It was just plain stupid. I was so angry about that relationship. Not just because of what he did to me, but because I *let* him do it to me! Don't you see? That is why I don't trust myself anymore." She shook her head. "I tried to convince myself it was because he was a beast in bed. Actually, he was good, but I'd had better."

Dane grinned, a light laugh escaping his mouth as he listened to her, and watched her become more and more animated. This was what he loved about the woman—her realness. She wasn't crude, but she shot from the hip and her beauty radiated from the inside to the outside. Every time she opened her mouth, she forced him to fall deeper in love with her. And now he understood her even more. She couldn't afford to feel as if once again, she'd given her heart to another, only to have it shattered by her own lapses in judgment, not seeing a person as they truly were. The woman was in love with him, but paralyzed with fear. He knew this now without a shadow of a doubt. How could he blame her? She made sense, and yet in still, here he sat.

"Is that it? Because I can promise you that's over. I would never hurt you like that. You never have to speak of him again, I just needed to know what happened." He ran his thumb slowly over her lips, feeling the soft plushness that made his heart race.

She nodded. "Yeah, that's it as far as him…nothing earth shattering, but it was bad enough."

"What was your home life like?" He moved his thumb to her chin, slowly caressing it.

"Is this an interview?"

"Sorta." He smiled wider at her.

She rolled her eyes and grinned, readjusting her position to move a bit closer to him.

"My father died when I was very young. I barely remember him… He was an assistant football coach for Michigan State."

"Get outta town!" Dane exclaimed, prompting a laugh from Rhapsody.

"I should've known that would be right up your alley."

"What was his name?"

"Kenneth Thomason." It rolled off her lips, and she

smiled, a hopeful yet sad expression encompassing her features, softening them even further by the warm, flickering glow.

"Hmmm, doesn't ring a bell but I'll have to look him up now."

"Well, after he passed my mother had me and my sister all by herself. She is a singer, a very good one, Dane. She sang professionally. I don't touch the surface compared to her."

"I highly doubt that, but it is nice that you revere her gift the way you do. Apparently, it was inherited."

"I believe it was." She paused. "So, we spent a lot of time with my grandmother because of my mother's career. She travelled a lot. I had a pretty good childhood, our needs were taken care of, as well as many of our wants." She shrugged. "My mother has some guilt about not being there as much, but I never gave her a hard time about it. She and I are extremely close. She was my first teacher and has been my best fan." She grinned wide, showing shiny white teeth.

So beautiful.

The sight of that smile seemed to light up the entire room. He needed to touch her, feel her once more. Reaching out, he traced her face as though she were a delicate sculpture. And she was.

"What did you think of me when you first saw me back in high school?" she asked, her voice cracking a little.

Wrapping his arm around her back, he brought her nearer, so close, he could feel the softness of her breasts compressed against him. He ran his nose along hers.

"I thought, 'Wow, she is hot!'"

She laughed.

"Seriously, I did, but I remember your singing the most,

Rhapsody. I was so impressed with your voice, even way back then." He scanned her face, and right there, with her being so close to him, he now noticed how one of her eyes looked slightly lighter than the other. He blamed it on the flickering candlelight. "I'd be at my locker, and I was late to class so many time because I had to wait until you all got settled for—"

"…Third bell…"

"I can't believe you remember that. You noticed me too?" He hooked onto her words, a part of him hoping she also had seen him how he'd seen her.

"I did, and I thought you were cute, but…I kept to myself back then," she said, biting on her bottom lip. "I never thought it would go anywhere, but I did notice you staring at me sometimes. I didn't even know your name, I just knew you were on the football team. Sometimes you had on your varsity jacket and girls were always around you and your friends during lunch."

"I don't remember it that way." He grinned.

"Yeah right!" She snickered. "Now that I think about it," she tapped her bottom lip with her finger, "I think I remember Josh, too. You two played football together, right?"

"Yes. I was outside linebacker, and he was cornerback, sometimes safety."

He watched as she continued to deliberate, her eyes shifting, "Yeah, I *do* think I remember him… A smidge taller than you? You both were tall…yes," she laughed, "I do remember him, I believe. He had a goofy laugh!"

"Yes! That was him. Everyone knew Josh's laugh." Happy memories flooded him, and he delighted in the fact that she, too, had his best friend dwelling in the deep recesses of her high school memory bank.

"You know, you were one of my secrets that I told him while I was in college."

They both sat up then, their legs crossed over each other's. He leaned in close and rested his hands on her upper thighs.

"Secrets?"

"Yeah… One night, after I had been drinking and got accepted into the seminary, I—"

"Now see," she shook her finger at him and laughed lightly, "Dane, that didn't even sound right."

Grinning, he looked down into his lap then back at her, a little self-conscious. "I know…but it was my way of celebrating, having my last hooray. I told him some things, he told me some things."

"Batta bing, batta boom!" Rhapsody taunted, causing him to shake his head at her, his heart light.

"We talked about everything, and soon enough, the discussion switched—we were discussing women."

"Da da da doooooooom!"

"Would you stop it?!" Dane laughed.

"Okay, I'm sorry," she said, "I just thought you needed a musical soundtrack for this."

Smiling, he continued, "Well, he teased me that if I became a priest, the sex was over with and I told him I was fine with that, I knew that was part of it. The conversation got a little seedy, so I don't really want to get into details but—"

"No," she shook her finger at him, "tell me."

He sighed and took a deep breath. "We were talking about all the girls, *women* actually, we wished we would have gone out with, or had sex with, and we were naming people from high school and college. I rattled off some, he rattled off some…and I didn't know your name, just like you didn't know mine…so," he shrugged, "I only described you and told him there was this girl I wish I would have asked out."

She kept staring at him, clearly wanting to hear more.

"I told him there was this songbird that would fly into the classroom right by my locker." She sucked in a breath. "I told my best friend that her voice was like an angel's…and it was soulful, and rich." He swallowed, feeling emotion well up inside him. "And she and the voice matched, because, the vessel that the song came out of was a perfectly divine, Godly creation. I said that God couldn't have made a woman more beautiful."

Rhapsody shifted her weight and brought her knees to her chin as she listened, smiling ever so slightly as if it were story time and she were a six-year-old girl hearing the tale of 'Hansel and Gretel'.

"I said it differently than that, but that is what I meant." They both burst out laughing. "You know, guy-talk. I refuse to give you the play by play, it would be disrespectful, but I *definitely* remembered you."

"That's funny how we recalled different things about one another. You look different, but I can still see that it was you, you know? You actually look better."

He felt his face warm with a blush. "Thank you."

"So you really did recognize me, at the park. It wasn't just something to say to break the ice." she said, her head slightly tilted.

"You know, you looked familiar to me, but you are even prettier now than you were back then, as if that were even possible."

"Now you're just putting me on, Dane."

"I am not!" he protested, but unable to wipe the smile off

his face.

"You have such beautiful eyes," she said dreamily, then looked away shyly.

"Thank you. So do you."

She turned back toward him and ran her hand over his. "Now, what about that duet?"

"The duet?"

She stood and stretched, then looked at her watch. "Oh my God, Dane. Look what time it is! We've been talking for hours. You need to get back, don't you?"

He laughed and slowly stood from the floor.

"It's not a prison, Rhapsody," he teased. "I can come and go as I wish. I do have some work in the morning, but I can stay a bit longer. So, you want to hear my horrible music, huh?" He laughed and made his way over to the piano, felt the cool keys beneath his fingers.

"I know she doesn't look like much, but my father had bought her for my mother. Their house flooded and she got the bad end of the stick, but was still playable. So, she means something to me and she plays beautifully, actually."

"What a nice story," he said, pointing to the bench. "May I take a seat here?"

"Of course." She bounced over toward him, gleefully sitting beside him. "Now, what are you going to play for me?"

"I thought you said we were doing a duet?"

"Hmmm, maybe, maybe not. Let me hear you first." Her eyebrow shot up and a mischievous grin creased her expression.

"I don't get a warm up?" he protested.

"You don't have time for a warm up. Besides, you never forget."

Like a kiss...

He took a deep breath and put his fingers over the keys.

Soon, he was playing the Charlie Brown Piano cover, causing a crackling, loud roar of laughter from Rhapsody. She stood and began to clap to the rhythm as he beat the keys with his nimble fingers, then she disappeared suddenly, like a ghost that had evaporated. He wondered where she had run off to, but continued to play. Seconds later, she emerged holding maracas and shaking them to the beat, making the song come alive. It sounded just as it did on television, and she wowed him once again. He continued to play, no longer looking at the keys. He couldn't take his eyes off of her.

Once the song was over, the last note stayed in the air, until it was gone, forcing them to dance with their own silence until she broke the hush like an arrow through the air.

"You actually aren't that bad, I think you were being modest. Honestly, Dane? It was pretty good. That isn't an easy song to play."

He nodded in appreciation of the compliment, then watched her glide toward him and place the maracas on top of the piano. Scooting over, he gave her room to sit. She gently touched the keys, and closed her eyes. His pulse started to race when he heard the first few notes of the 'Moonlight Sonata' by Beethoven.

"Oh my goodness," he said aloud as he watched her work the keys and the haunting song vibrated through his body. He then realized what it was. Rhapsody didn't play the piano...the piano became a part of her body, a limb, and she simply twirled with it, dancing, moving inside each beat as her feet worked the pedals and her fingers turned into ebony and ivory keys.

When the song ended, she gently tugged at his shirt collar, ushering him closer to place her lips on his. Too soon, she pulled away with an assessing smile, as if to gauge his reaction, then did it again. A few moments later, they were holding hands, their fingers wrapped around one another's on top of the black and white keys.

"Five questions before you go," she said, glancing back at him out the corner of her eye.

"Shoot."

"Your favorite band, favorite song, biggest mistake, happiest childhood memory and place you want to go that you've never been before, and make it fast, damn it. If you stall or take too long I'll think you're lying."

"Led Zeppelin, their song 'All of My Love'."

"Okay! Good one!" She gave him a high five.

"You said fast, you interrupted me. Now I can't remember the third question." He laughed and bumped his shoulder into hers.

"Biggest mistake and—"

"Okay, let's see…"

"Well, hurry up."

"I will!" He wrapped his arm around her waist and pulled her close before looking down at her. She swallowed when he grazed the side of her hip with his fingertips. "I don't know what my biggest mistake is; I'll have to live longer to find out. Happiest childhood memory was waking up and having the black Schwinn bike that I wanted in the driveway for my thirteenth birthday, and place I want to go, that I've never been before?"

"You're stalling."

"I'm not! I'm thinking…Greece. I'd love to go to Greece."

"Well done!" She applauded him as he stood and took a capricious bow.

Moments later, he was standing by her front door, trying to collect seconds and turn them into additional minutes. Anything to drag the night out, to make the wonderful time never end. It had been a simple dinner, but he knew in his heart, before he'd arrived, that he was there to settle a score. Not with her, but with himself. As she spoke, he bent down and quieted her with a kiss—hard, passionate. In that, he poured all his fiery desire. Then, he took a few steps back from her and opened her front door.

She gaped at him. Speechless. Then, with a laugh, he practically leapt off her front steps toward his car.

"Call me, let me know you got in okay," she called out as she waved in his direction.

He turned and blew her a kiss, relishing in the delight of her smiling face. Getting in his car, he started up the engine and drove away, his heart pounding with excitement, marveling in the lack of fear. But after a while, dark thoughts crept in…

What am I going to do? I can't just pretend this didn't happen. I'm in love, I'm in a relationship now. Fr. Kirkpatrick was right about that, but I need to think this through, figure it out…

The parish…my family…my brothers…they will all have something to say if word of this gets out.

A dead weight filled his heart, despite his happiness at finding Rhapsody. In his case, love came with a hefty price. He didn't have any remorse for going to her house because he needed answers. To find out whether his feelings were real— once and for all.

Oh my God, I've been waiting for her my entire life.

As he thought of her dear face, the weight lifted, replaced with raw emotion. Perhaps he was kidding himself, for a difficult road lay ahead of him. But if God had sent Rhapsody to him, surely, it was meant to be.

She has awakened something in me. Father, please forgive me, but I can't help myself. I'm in love. I'm really in love…

CHAPTER NINETEEN

S WEAT TRICKLED DOWN her face as she pounded the pavement. The early evening jog felt wonderful, allowing Rhapsody to process better the tapestries of ideas, dilemmas and nuisances that crowded her mind. She'd just finished teaching her class, and all she could think about were the past day's events. The distractions proved unnerving. Several of the college music students had to repeat their questions as she kept drifting into another world during class.

Oh what a pickle you've gotten yourself into, woman…

She rounded the corner, feeling free in her black spandex leggings. She looked down and took notice of her untied Nike sneaker. Sighing, she came to a halt, bent down retied the rebel shoelace. Since the dinner, she and Dane had spoken at least twice a day, and he typically ended the call with, "I love you."

Those words kept rolling around in her mind. Words meant something to Rhapsody; she used them to tell the world of things that mattered to her. Married to music, words created miniature realms that she dove into on a daily basis. She'd made a conscious decision, however, to either move forward or jump ship—no more of this back and forth mess.

But, she was struggling.

How does one explain that they've fallen in love with a priest?

How does one explain that he loves her, too?

And we kiss...and hold hands...and go out together...to bookstores, restaurants and movies...and the way he looks at me...Oh God...

The way the man would rest his eyes on her oftentimes sent shivers up her spine. His blue eyes would slightly darken as his brows gathered, and he had a habit of rubbing his jaw before he drew closer to her to embrace, almost as if he were touching himself, to ensure that the situation was real. His body was hard and strong and she'd feel herself tremble and throb as thoughts of their naked bodies lying together, touching, exploring, began to take over her mind.

What would it be like to make love to him?

She struggled sometimes with answering his calls, then other times, she wished he'd call more or resisted the urge to tell him she just wanted to hear his voice. She wondered if it was the long time he'd endured from extending affection to a woman, or just his natural inclination, but the man was brimming with passion—and when he'd pressed his lips against hers, almost making her jump out of her skin with shock and delight, her nerve endings went on fire.

His gentle yet assertive touch, the way lights hit his hair and eyes, the nicely cut and shaped beard, the lean, taut muscles, hidden beneath his clothing, the wonderful clean smell of his skin, mixed with a bit of incense residue—all of it would send her over the edge. Dane lit so many candles and incense during prayers, the smell had infused itself in almost everything he wore, a proof of his journey, of his spirituality, and she found it delightful. He had an amazing sense of humor – a treasure trove of corny, insightful and witty jokes, many of which he thought up himself. He was simply naturally funny. Good hearted, too. And, she had to admit it. The bad girl in her got some sort of sick kick out of knowing the man hadn't been laid in a while. She wanted to see what was simmering underneath, liking to think he'd been saving himself just for her.

She replayed his words about seeing her in school, over and over, like the last record on Earth. They'd grown stronger, the relationship deeper, as each day passed. They shared of themselves, delving into topics that would have been previously seen as taboo. They even discussed religion more now and she soon came to realize, they agreed on many of the same things. He was a bit more liberal than she'd imagined, and she followed more rules than he'd initially surmised. Together, they could learn a lot from one another, and in that, she had a newfound respect for their differences, which made the situation harder to resist.

One of the more recent conversations stuck out in her mind:

"No, I don't feel that way," Dane replied. "I think there is room for many thoughts and ideas. I respect that you don't agree with everything that I do. That reminds me, one of the most beautiful relationships I've ever seen was between a Muslim woman and a Hindu man. They were very much in love, and they spoke two different languages. They barely understood each other. They had a cultural, religious and verbal barrier, so do you know what they did?"

"Dane, is this a set up for one of your jokes?"

"No!" He laughed on the other end of the line. "You suspect me all the time now."

"Because you play too much!"

"Well, I'm not playing now, this is true. This is serious."

She drew quiet.

"They started to draw things, tiny sketches, while they were trying to communicate to one another. Their only choice. They were both refugees during political upheaval. Every morning, he'd come into the mess hall, and he'd have a drawing of what he wanted. She'd match it with her picture until soon, they were sitting together, drawing places they'd been, people they knew, and all that time, they were falling in love and didn't even know how to say, 'I Love You' in each other's language.

Soon, they learned how to speak to one another, but their hearts did the translations initially. So I tell you that story, a true story, Rhapsody, because I met them. They are in their eighties now. They had nine children and a slew of beautiful grandchildren. This is to let you know that just because we don't speak the exact same language doesn't mean this can't or won't work. I will never try to make you convert. If you wanted to, of course, I would encourage and teach you, but I would not dare try to make you do something you were staunchly against."

Rhapsody took a few deep breaths and deliberated.

"What about the kids? What happened to the children of that couple? Did they raise them Buddhist or Hindu?"

"From what I could tell, they let them decide. Now, If I were to ever have children, I'm not going to pretend like I wouldn't want them raised Catholic. I do, but there comes a time when you have to let your child once they become old enough, regardless of our own personal spiritual beliefs, make their own spiritual choices. I would take them to church, but if they wanted to attend another church of a different faith as well, then, I would have to accept that. When you mix two different religions, of course these things come up."

"That had to have been hard for the couple you just described, especially for her because a Muslim could be murdered for that."

"You're right, she could have been and more than likely would have been killed if she were still living in her native country, but she was brave, and needed out of the area. The world was larger than she realized; from her new standpoint, she saw that there were all sorts of people in it, and they weren't evil because they didn't believe as she did. No one man had treated her with that much respect and love, ever. Her husband wooed her with his heart. He'd won her over...and he didn't even have to say one word."

Damn that man!

Rhapsody played back the conversation so many times in her head; it now seemed to be on auto-replay, looping over and over. She didn't think Dane really understood how powerful those words were, or maybe he did, she wasn't certain, but one thing she did know—it was just what she needed to hear to put her mind more at ease. The man was open and willing, and if that Muslim and Hindu couple could do it, with death looming over their heads, surely she could give it a try as well...

DANE STARED AT the brown box from Josh. It still sat there unopened. One side had been crushed a little by a gym bag he'd placed atop it, as if to try to hide it from his sight. He'd been dreading delving into it, and today was no exception. He'd tried a couple times to speak with Rhapsody, the way he'd done with Josh, but realized she simply wasn't ready. He surmised she was afraid whatever his confessions were, would bring their courtship to a halt. The woman admitted now several times she was falling for him as well after all; she had a dog in the fight. He was ready to come clean, but he knew he couldn't rush these things. Everything had its season.

Pushing the box to the far side of his desk, he paced his apartment, biding time until he made his trip to the hospital to pray over the sick and hospice patients. After a few minutes, he walked back toward the box, ran his hand over the top of it, the thick layers of double tape smooth under his touch. He stepped away once more, shoving his hands in his pockets as he just stared at it. The months had gotten easier, but a part of him dreaded what may lie just beneath the corrugated surface, possibly starting a fire storm that he'd burn up in—heated memories that would take him down, down, down.

He'd been upbeat and in good spirits; he didn't want anything to wreck his mood.

Looking at the time, he sat on his bed and passed sweating hands roughly through his freshly brushed hair.

You may as well get it over with.

He walked back toward the box, resigned to tear the damn thing open, but paused when his cell phone rang. He sighed, slightly relieved, and looked at the caller ID.

"Hi Mom," he answered, then walked to his bedroom window to look out and watch the cars moving up and down the street during lunch hour traffic. He sniffed, feeling the beginning stages of a cold coming on. Looking to his far right, he saw a car almost rear-end another, one of them honking. His thoughts drifted as she began to speak.

"Hi, Dane," she said, full of chipper. Her mood, warm and comforting, cut his daydreaming short, dragging him gently by the arm into the here and now. He could almost envision her wrapped in her apron with the tiny sunflowers all over it, and her brown flats that made her diminutive feet look even smaller than they naturally were.

"What are you up to? I haven't heard from you in a few days," she asked.

He heard what seemed to be pots and pans lightly banging together, and running water.

"Oh, just been busy is all. How are you doing?" He forced a smile, knowing it would reflect in his tone and hopefully appease her.

"Just washing up some dishes. I made your father and me a wonderful stew. You should come over and have some! It had fresh carrots from the farmer's market, they really do make a difference," she said proudly.

"I bet it was delicious, Mom. How is the old man?" he teased.

"His ankle has been bothering him again." She sighed. "I told him to not to try to move the couch by himself but you know how that goes."

"Yeah, you know Dad though. He thinks he is He-Man." Dane slipped a hand in his pocket and casually scratched above his brow as he continued to gaze at the passing vehicles. "Next time, have him call me before he decides to be a one-man moving crew." He laughed lightly. "I could have helped, all of us could have helped. He could have called Joseph or Anthony if I wasn't available."

"I know, but you know how your father is, stubborn to his core. To him, admitting he needs help means he isn't man enough to handle it by himself."

Yeah, and sometimes I have the same affliction. I guess I got it honest.

Dane nodded as they shared a brief silence.

"Dane," the cheer was clearly out of her tone as her voice

deepened, "I was thinking…I know, all of these years, you've had a lot on your shoulders, and I want to just tell you, thank you, you know, for being a listening ear to me. I just…"

Dane closed his eyes and suppressed a groan. She was doing it again. He couldn't take it. On one hand, he wanted her to simply let sleeping dogs lie; on the other, he was grateful she was acknowledging the past trauma but then, his gut twisted. Alarm bells struck and he opened his eyes.

Why is she saying this to me right now?

"Is something wrong?" he blurted. "Is this about what I think it is? If so, we talked about this right after it happened, and you told me you didn't want to discuss it ever again."

"Well," she hesitated, "no, nothing is wrong per se, just, well, I suppose you are owed the truth," she said solemnly. He heard the water turn off and her light footsteps across the kitchen floor. A chair slid across a floor, and he assumed she'd sat in it. "After you received the money from my father, it brought up some old memories. It has been a tough few months."

Dane cradled the phone in the crevice of his neck as he continued to stare out the window, now leaning slightly against the frame.

"I know it seemed strange to everyone, Mom, that he didn't leave it to you—you being his only living child and all." He sighed. "I didn't know what to say … I couldn't offer an explanation."

Dane briefly reflected over his deceased Uncle Luigi's funeral, which had left his mother an only child at the age of forty at the time. At the time, Dane was just a thirteen-year-old boy, fascinated and mesmerized with the church and life in the parish. His cousins, he'd never laid eyes on some, lined the back of the church with dark, worn leather jackets over their crisp black suits. They were the epitome of the stereotypical 'tough east coast guys' he'd read about, and they were *'la famiglia'*.

This was *his* family, a rough bunch who were taught just like his mother to act like a man and swallow your pain as if it were chocolate cake. And whatever you do, you don't say one word to let your oppressor know he'd found a weakness. Just obey. Say the rosary in the morning, curse out some punks late in the afternoon, and head back home to wash the blood off before supper.

He'd tried in earnest to live that way, to stand in the crammed chapel in Manhattan, New York, while they had given reverence to the Italian war veteran and big brother and protector of Maria Caruso. He recalled looking up at his mother, not understanding that her tears were shed that day for a myriad of reasons he was far too young to yet understand but later, he most certainly did.

"Of course you couldn't." She laughed, one chock full of sorrow. "It reinforced what I always suspected."

"Which was?"

"That my father knew what had happened. If he did, he never forgave me…"

Dane was quiet for a moment as he deliberated over her words. "Well, if that is true, Mom, it is not Grandpa that had to forgive you, but God, and yourself."

After a few moments, he heard his mother's soft cries. He dropped his head and stared down at his feet. The outside traffic seemed to be growing louder and louder, as if he were in the midst of downtown Detroit versus the corner of Hope and Understanding. Everything around him felt tight, overpowering and devouring. All of these years, he'd tried to bury the past, repress it, as he became further and further weighed down with the secrets of others—and the worst one of all was his mother's, a woman he adored, loved and respected. And yes, resented. He understood *what* she was, however. A woman who was incapable of facing her true self and the real world, the ugliness that lay just beneath the polished surface. She'd tried to clean away the memories with a smile. The stickiness, the crud, just set there, taunting her no doubt, no matter how much she denied it. She'd soon discover the muck would return time and again to mar her present, all the way from a childhood that caused her shame. For, simply and truly, one cannot erase the past, and the past is what it is.

"Mom, don't cry," he said. "It's over, okay? You have to stop beating yourself up about this. God gave you a second chance; it's called today, and tomorrow."

But the sobs kept coming, muffled, probably trying not to not alert his father. She seldom cried, and it always unnerved him to see the outwardly sweet woman come undone at the seams.

"Sorry to bother you. I will let you go." She sniffed. He heard her blow into a tissue as she regained her composure. "I just needed to get that out I suppose," she said with forced cheerfulness.

"I hope you feel better, Mom. And I love you."

"I love you, too, Dane. So very much. Don't forget about that stew. Come by and have a taste."

"Okay, I will, Mom. Thanks... Bye." He ended the call, placed his phone on the nightstand, and tucked his hands under his arms as he looked back out the window. These were the moments that made him want to dive tongue first into a pint of warm, soothing liquor—preferably Jack Daniels. He debated calling his AA sponsor but felt okay after a few moments. It wasn't as much of a struggle now—the urge simply lingered in the air during times like this and he always declined, refusing to step one foot back into his old ways of coping. He turned back toward the window and prayed. After he was finished, he grabbed his jacket and car keys to head to the hospital. At least this time it wasn't him that was in need of intervention…

CHAPTER TWENTY

One week later...

"I BAPTIZE YOU in the name of the Father and the Son and the Holy Spirit." Dane sprinkled the head of the infant baby girl, her ruby cheeks bathed in streams of colorful light filtering through the stained glass. The droplets fell away from her head, his fingertips moist from the Holy Water, while her parents grinned from ear to ear as they turned toward the congregation, chock full of pride. Their extended family began to gather and he stood and watched. For now at the least the third time in his priesthood, he burned with resentment. Once again, his heart ached with jealousy. He was nursing a new secret, the one that involved the woman that he was madly in love with—the one that he'd just spoken to an hour prior—and now he stood here, in his robe and a forced smile, looking at something he could never have in his position.

And, he was faced with the question—*"But why?"*

What he was taught had made perfect sense to him at one

point. He listened to the men he looked up to explain to him that he couldn't have two masters; you can never be married to two at once. You have to serve with all of your heart, free from distraction.

You can't serve the church as a priest, Son, and have a family. You'd be torn in two directions...

You can't have sex, because fornication is a sin, and since you can't get married, it in fact would be fornication. And you can't get married, because you already have a wife...The church.

And so the vicious cycle of reasons continued. Dane drowned in a sea of thoughts and reflections, combing through all of the things that upset him. Old wounds became fresh, raw and sensitive. He thought about so many things related to his life, his relationship, his family and the Church. He thought about the sex abuse scandals that had hit like a storm, a scarlet letter on the Church, which was now under scrutiny—even the innocent appeared guilty. All of the secrets, lies and deception.

At the time, he was outraged, not just with the Church, but with the judgments from non-Catholics that looked at him with suspicion, as if he, too, were in some way a sexual deviant simply because he was a priest. It became tiresome...the questions:

"Did you know that priest that did that? He spoke at your parish before..."

"My friend's brother was one of the victims of Fr. so and so, what are you all going to do about it?"

And so on, and so forth. So many things had gone wrong; the real issues weren't being touched upon, only the symptoms. The Church was treating the illness with pseudo-prescription medicines, instead of spiritual lifestyle changes. No, you can't turn a person into a pedophile—either it is in them to do such a deviant deed, or it is not, but the entire culture that he was knee deep in caused him to have complete awareness of his religious surroundings. How could something be so beautiful and so vile, all at once?

Over the last few days, Dane studied his Bible, the same Bible he had practically memorized, knowing his search would be fruitless. But he had to. He was trying to find something, *anything,* that would explain to him why God would not want him to have a relationship and marry. He read the passages with a discerning eye, with new logic, and was hit with the deep desire to dismiss them. He loved being a priest and he knew he was good at it. He believed he could do both, but how? They'd never allow it. The Church would wash their hands of him if he didn't break it off with Rhapsody, at once. Probably transfer him to some other parish, far, far away—or worse, in a foreign country to help with one of their missions. Some place, far from Rhapsody.

The very thought terrified him.

Every now and again, he'd hear about one of his own leaving the priesthood because he'd fallen in love, and he honestly never understood it. He didn't believe it would happen to him, just as Fr. Kirkpatrick had warned: *"They always think it will be someone else."*

But he should have known. All the signs were there. It just took someone special, a woman that his heart couldn't deny, to bring it forward and make him take note, for once and for all. For a time being, he'd fooled himself into believing he could barrel through it, that he was simply being tested. So he played with the hand he was dealt, not willing to believe that those cards were really for him. They were for him, alright, and the worse part of it, the part that stung the most, was that he asked to play the game.

Then, Josh died, and his world crumbled. That was the final straw, when he torpedoed into depression. He wanted to self-medicate, and he did, though he fought it along the way. As he'd slid that drink out of his pocket on that park bench, uncaring, he finally took a good look at himself and he hated what he saw. He'd been grasping at straws, trying to make it right, cure himself of the afflictions. Then he saw *her*.

Yes, new company would help. A fresh face…someone that doesn't know me…

But she *did* know him, at least in a sense, and instead of running, or being unnerved, he found it somehow refreshing and comforting. He'd even reported himself to the parish, letting them know he was having trouble coping for being in denial wouldn't give him any semblance of peace. They understood, allowing him to go to his AA meetings whenever he needed, to get himself together again but he didn't need AA anymore. The drinking actually wasn't the problem, and frankly, Dane didn't even care for the strong taste of it. Regardless, it would keep coming back into his life until he dealt with the root cause, the reason it had been there all along—and now, he was ready. This was his rock bottom.

It began with being forced to be the gatekeeper for domestic secrets, always the family protector—help your father with *this*, help your mother with *that*. Daisy and her wayward husband needing his help once again. It wasn't the first or tenth financial handout, he'd been giving them money out of his meager earnings, unbeknownst to his mother. But now, he'd had to put his foot down. Joseph also had a drinking problem, only his wasn't being addressed and was neatly pushed under the rug so that everything in the Caruso home remained nice and tidy. Finally, Anthony was unreliable—the forever 'kid' who needed his brothers to be his father, too, while he ran wild. And now it all came crashing down. It all ended with the realization that Dane was all alone in the world and though the Lord was his brother, and God his *true* Father, he wanted his own *Eve…and her new name was Rhapsody…*

And Adam wanted her *now…*

DANE TENSED. ALTHOUGH he tried to tamp down his irritation and rage, he wasn't successful. Standing in a black tank top, dirt-stained loose jeans and tan work boots, he looked exactly how he felt—a hot mess, ready to tear the Earth apart. His father sat on the stoop, staring into space.

"So, you helped your mother plant the mums," the older man said, ignoring what had come out of his son's mouth.

"Did you hear me, Dad? I'm leaving the priesthood."

"You did a good job on the flowers."

"Listen to me, damn it!" Dane threw down the soil covered garden hoe and rake, then the grubby gloves as his voice shook the air around them. His father looked at him in alarm, as if he were shrinking right into a crack on the concrete step he sat on—away from his son, away from the world. The man recoiled, as if he couldn't stomach Dane's words.

Exhausted, Dane was running on empty, sick of everyone not being able to handle their problems like adults, all for the sake of appearances, and not caring about the toll it had taken on the family unit. He wasn't born an ostrich, but was encouraged to follow their lead. Head in the sand, to keep the peace, follow along. For years, it had torn him up, destroyed him from the inside out, and he was going to deal with it once and for all. He'd called his mother, asking to speak to her just an hour previously. She cheerfully invited him over, and when he pulled up to the house, she was digging into the soil, unearthing daddy long legs, dandelions and denial.

He bent down and helped her, sliding on his father's garden gloves that lay over the side of her favorite yellow work pail. Meanwhile, he listened to her rattle on about the weather and how Daisy had bought the most adorable dress for her daughter. At that point, he'd had it. She knew he needed to speak to her about something important, he'd said so, and he saw the realization on her face when she looked up at him, partially blinded by the sun as she put her hand over her eyes. He could sense the panic just below the surface, sense that she didn't want to face this—and she'd fight him if he brought truth to her feet.

He didn't give an introduction, no prologue, just blurted it out. Then, he watched her continue to smile as she straightened and disappeared into the house. He contemplated rushing after her, but instead, waited there to see if she was going to, for once in her life, face the world. He wasn't surprised when she didn't. The house swallowed her whole, and spit out someone else. Instead, his father came out to her rescue, her fixer-upper—the man that helped keep things keenly dysfunctional.

"You can't be serious, Dane," he simply said, the judgment in his voice thick like phlegm. "Do you understand how horribly you will affect others?"

The gall.

"I am *very* serious. I need to talk to you both, so I'm glad you're out here."

"I refuse to discuss this with you." His father waved him off. "You are clearly under a lot of stress. Take some time to think about this, Son. Go on vacation, get some air."

"You think this is some whim or crazy notion that I just concocted this morning while scrambling eggs? You think I just woke up today and after service thought, 'Wow! Today is a good day to throw my career away and let down the parishioners and make my family angry!' You haven't even heard *why*, don't you care what the reason is?"

And with that, his father said nothing further. He changed the topic, turned into an ostrich, leaving Dane reeling, grinding his teeth in frustration. He hadn't even noticed he'd balled his fist until his fingernails cut painfully into his palm, giving a warning signal.

Dane began to storm off, then stopped in his tracks and marched back to his father, up the porch steps.

Shoving his finger in his face, he spoke low, between clenched teeth, "Let me tell you something, Dad. I am sick and tired of living for everyone else around here! It's done and over with. I'm finished being Dane, the great gatekeeper! No one gives a damn about my well-being, only what I can *do* for them. It's a wrap. I had to be the man you never were!"

Finally, his father had the guts to look up at him, anger on his face. Still, he didn't say a word, more than likely surprised at his son's raised voice and angry demeanor.

Dane counted off his fingers: "When you lost your job, you left us at home for months on end. I had to go out and get a job to help support the family. Then you came back home like nothing happened, like what you did was alright! You ran! I had to make up a lie to my coach and teachers as to why I was falling asleep in class and coming in late, and almost passed out in practice. I wasn't getting enough sleep due to working at that hell hole of a restaurant and I was stressed out. You were the head of this household! When in the hell are you going to act like it?!"

His father shot up from his seated position, the older man's lip quivered with rage.

"Don't you ever speak to me that way! I am still your father!"

"Yes you are, and what a shame that is!" Once the words left his mouth, the older Caruso stiffened in shock for he surely knew, once and for all, the chickens had come home to roost.

"I was out trying to find work! No one told you to go and get a job. You did that, Dane, and I told you 'thank you' but you—"

Dane shoved his finger into the man's chest, shocked at his own reaction as he burned with fury. "On what days, Dad? When, out of all those days gone, were you looking for work? Was it before or after you left that woman's motel room, hmmm?"

He watched the color drain from his father's face.

"I know all about Ms. Kathleen Mitchell, Dad." Dane seethed, feeling as if he may accidentally bite his tongue in two as the feelings from yesteryear resurfaced. "You had an affair! Went out into the world, feeling sorry for yourself, and ran off with your mistress!"

"Keep your voice down!" His father looked back at the house, a mixture of shock and sorrow on his weathered face.

"I never told Mom, and have no intentions of doing it, so don't worry, you can keep playing games here. Keep playing pretend in the dollhouse." He pointed to the house. "You and everyone else can keep painting pictures that don't exist. I am done being your stuntman! Taking the heat and the bumps and bruises while the rest of you live on easy street." His father stumbled backwards, almost as if he were about to fall. "Mom has always been so worried about your opinion of her, and she had no idea it was her opinion of *you* that would be challenged!"

Caruso, Sr. got his balance and simply stared at him. No words came out of his mouth for he finally had to face the fact that since Dane was sixteen years of age, he'd known about an affair that he thought, for sure, no one was the wiser to.

Dane had set out looking for his missing father when he had to deal with night after night of their mother worrying, yet trying to keep a brave face. She insisted the man had been looking for work, when Dane and Joseph knew full well she hadn't a clue as to where he really was. The bills were piling up; he had to do what he had to do, so he and Joseph got jobs—pizza deliveries after school and part time fast food joints. In that time, he'd looked everywhere for his father, week after week, month after month, until finally, he'd gotten word he was living only thirty minutes away, in a run-down motel. He staked out the place and saw the man coming and going, with a woman on his arm. Then he'd gone back home and never spoke of the instance. Two weeks later, his father returned, smiling and telling everyone he'd found a new job. Business as usual.

Finally, his father found his tongue. His eyes glistening, he put his hand on Dane's shoulder and whispered, "Can we talk about this, alone, please?!" He looked over his shoulder again, ensuring no one was around.

Dane began to walk to his brand new car, a snow white Toyota Rav4, his father hot on his trail. Both men got inside. Closing their respective doors, neither dared to look at the other. The confines were filled with the scent of new leather that did nothing to soften the mood. Dane gripped the steering wheel and thumped it impatiently with his fingers.

"Dane," his father said softly, turning to him. "I really did go out to look for work. I told your mother that and then, well, I made a mistake. I was so down in the dumps, I just felt like a failure." His voice quivered.

"Where'd you meet her at?" Dane asked; ice cold steel in his voice as he kept his gaze straight ahead.

"Does any of that matter now?"

Yes. Where'd you meet her?" he repeated.

"I met her at a bar. She...she had a room, so," he shrugged, "that's how it started. I told her what happened and she was a listening ear. I felt so ashamed afterward, Dane. You have to believe me. I *never* cheated on your mother before or after."

Dane exhaled loudly and then returned his father's gaze, feeling nothing but disgust and sadness. He knew the man was probably on the up and up, now that he was on the hot seat, but it didn't shake Dane's disappointment in him.

"It all makes sense now." His father looked away and rubbed his forehead. "You were acting so strange after I returned. Everyone else was happy, but after that..." He shook his head. "It seemed it took forever for you to trust me again. I'm sorry, Dane."

A trembling hand touched Dane's arm.

"Dad, I'm sure you are sorry, I believe that, but, you just caused us so much unnecessary pain." A few moments passed.

"I came over here to talk to you and Mom about what is going on with me, my pending preparation to leave the priesthood, and what do I get in return?" He glared at his father. "I get Mom running into the house, yelling and screaming to you that I've lost my mind. I heard her tell you I'd shame the family, and you running out acting as if I've threatened her life. It's always about everyone else. When is anyone going to wonder about *my* life and what *I* need?!"

His father swallowed and pulled his hand away.

"Dane I just want you to be happy. I thought you were happy being a priest."

"I am."

"But that doesn't make sense. Why would you want to leave then?"

Dane took a deep breath and let his head fall back on the seat. He looked up at the ceiling of the car and pondered just how to phrase the words, to make it all make sense.

"Was it Josh? You really haven't been your typical self since his passing. Son, grief is hard, but I promise you that—"

"No, it's not Josh." He looked at his father earnestly. "Dad, I've fallen in love…"

CHAPTER TWENTY-ONE

R HAPSODY CROSSED AND uncrossed her legs as she sat on Dane's favorite park bench. But Dane was nowhere in sight. She began to worry as the clouds drifted in a dark gray backdrop, the sure sign of a storm brewing. He hadn't returned her phone call that she'd made to his cellphone during that hour; it had gone straight to voice mail. They'd agreed to meet there and then grab a bite to eat. He *had* been acting a bit strange the past few days.

This isn't like him...

She looked out at the water and watched the Indian summer breeze blowing it into rippled waves. Peaceful. Beautiful. Sublime. Leaning forward, she let herself drown in her own thoughts.

Maybe this is a sign?

She shook her head. After a while, she stood from the bench and made her way to her parked car, resolved to go to lunch by herself. She turned on her playlist and moved her thumb over the buttons of her phone. Hitting the shuffle function, she pulled out of her spot, past the trees on the winding park road. She smiled when Maze with Frankie Beverly's song, 'When You Love Someone', blared out. She swayed to the soothing '80s R&B song. The lyrics spoke to her, about their special situation, and it seemed right on time. Chancing a look at her phone, she noted she hadn't missed any calls and sighed.

I hope you are okay, Dane…

She turned the corner and began to sing along with the lyrics, *"…You can't tell me it ain't right, when you love someone…"*

DANE SAT QUIETLY in his parents' living room. The only sound that could be heard was the bubbling of the nearby aquarium, filled with assorted tropical fish swimming about, a tranquil scene during a distilling emotional storm. Heidi panted as she made her way toward her former master. Dane had always been her favorite and the old canine seemed to be wearing a smile, her mouth spread wide and the long, pink tongue hanging lazily out of the side of her mouth. Pushing her golden head into his hand, she let it hang over the arm of the dusky blue lazy boy chair.

He looked across the way at his parents, studying them in the deafening silence as he played with the crucifix around his neck. His mother remained despondent as she looked down into her lap. She had built an invisible wall, a fortress, but he could still feel her discomfort, the emotions bubbling underneath as she tried to keep her cool.

She was so angry, she was rendered speechless from his announcement in the garden. Knowing his parents well, he'd expected this reaction after thinking about this scenario a million and one times. Still, that didn't make him any happier. Sometimes, knowing the truth doesn't dissolve the lump in your throat when you know you're about to break someone's heart. Regardless, he wasn't completely shaken by it, but he was going to have his say, and then be on his way.

"Mom," he paused and gathered his words, "I know that you're shocked about what I said to you while we were outside. If you don't mind, I'd like to speak to you privately."

He looked at his father. Their eyes locked. Dane felt calmer, although his father's tense body gave his mood away. The man's hazel eyes tinted, concern filling them—no doubt fearing that Dane would let the old, dead cat out of the bag. He shook his head as if saying 'No' to his father, in an effort to offer reassurance, then watched the man sigh and slowly rise from his seat, soon disappearing up the steps.

Dane sat for a moment, frowning, his large hands clasped. Bracing himself, he looked at her, but her head was still down, just as it had been five minutes previously, and five minutes before that.

"I know that you were very proud that I became a priest, and I understood why, Mom. I'm sorry that you're upset about this, I'd expect you to be, but I refuse to make my decisions according to other people's expectations anymore, Mom."

She finally raised he head, her eyes narrowed as she seemed to tussle with mixed emotions.

"Dane." Her voice shook. "You told me that you wanted to be a priest while in college, remember?"

"Of course I remember. I was excited to tell you that I had been accepted into the seminary, too."

"I supported you, even told you to stay in college, to make

sure! You said, 'Okay.' Yes, I was very proud of you. It was a serious decision. You knew the gravity of it...I just," she shook her head angrily, "don't understand this." She ran her fingers through her dark brown, shoulder length hair.

Dane threw his arms up in the air. "I have a feeling that nothing I say to you will change anything right now, but you needed to be told. It is a matter of—"

"Have you told anyone else?" she asked, her eyes pitiful and glossy.

He knew what that overwhelmed look was all about. She wanted time to talk him out of it, to stop the rocket of shame from blaring through space before it crashed and burned. She wanted to make it all right, fix the mess he was about to ignite. She had hung tightly onto her proud father's hand on his dying bed and the words he said regarding Dane being a priest. Even on his death bed, he wanted to give glory to God, and to his grandson, whom he told everyone who would listen, was a priest, preaching the word of their Lord and Savior. It gave her joy that the man showed that type of exhilaration, though he didn't show her a kind word once she reached her mid-teens. She'd only received affection from a distance, through her son. Dane also came to realize something more, he was his grandfather's favorites, but for all the wrong reasons.

"No, you are the first to know."

She sighed with relief. "Please don't tell Bishop Thayer or Fr. Kirkpatrick right now. Dane, you need to think about this; this is very serious. You are being too rash, you're...you're confused!" Her voice trembled, her hands flew to her face as though she could hide from the cruel world.

"Mom," he said on a sigh, trying to be as gentle as possible. "I am going to tell you some more things you will not like.

I'm not confused. I'm tired." He sighed heavily, angst tearing him up inside as he slumped in the chair. After a while, he rose and sat beside her, taking her hand, but she kept her eyes averted. "It's time for everything about me to be out in the open, for me to come clean, and *this* time, you are going to listen to me."

She lifted her head and stared at him, and he let his frustration show.

"Do you even know who I am? Do you know who Joseph is, Mom? Antonio? Daisy? Do you actually *really* know your children?'

"Dane, how dare you." She snatched her hand away and rubbed her palms nervously up and down her thighs. "Of course I know my own children!"

"I don't think so, Mom. I don't think you or Dad do, quite honestly. You live in this…bubble," he said, gesturing with the words. "It keeps all the stuff out that you don't want, all the debris. But the funny thing about that is that it doesn't really keep it out, but only delays it from showing. Dirt is still on the floor, whether we see it with our own eyes or not."

"No, I don't want to hear this nonsense." His mother put her hand up and shot up from her seat as if she were on fire.

Dane sat back, prepared for this, as well. He watched her move about, pacing, nerved up and twitching with anxiety. "Dane, I don't know what has gotten into you, but I suggest—"

"What? That I bury it all…ignore it and start drinking again?!" He was coming undone.

A look of bewilderment crossed her face. Her brows dipped.

Dane leaned forward, his eyes on her as he clasped his hands together. He cleared his throat and smirked. He didn't mean to, but he was at the end of his rope and he couldn't take this anymore.

"Yes, Mom." He nodded, his tone calm, cool and collected. "Your third son, Dane Giovanni Caruso, is a functional recovering alcoholic. You are going to hear this whether you like it or not. You need to know the truth, once and for all. I've had a sponsor in AA since I was twenty years old. Sometimes I'd have to drink a bit in the car to even walk through this front door. I hid bottles of booze under my bed and some were not hidden at all. You did my laundry, I'm sure you saw something a time or two."

At that, she gasped and covered her mouth. He stood, took her gently by the arm and helped her sit back down.

"Dane," her voice trembled as her eyes watered, "you can get help. You don't have to leave the priesthood over this. I didn't know." She shook her head, her face a mask of grief. "I thought you were, maybe, just experimenting. I never saw you drunk and you never got into any trouble."

"But I *was* in trouble, Mom. Deep trouble. Just because I appeared fine, doesn't mean that I was. You of all people should understand that," he shook his head, "But Mom, that's not the problem anymore. I haven't touched any alcohol in months, and don't plan to again. I mean that. I can't drink. I can't trust myself to indulge every now and again to take the edge off because when something is bothering me, I use it to escape. I know what my triggers are, but around the time Josh passed I had my final relapse."

"Relapse?"

"Yes. I'd stop cold turkey. A year or two would go by—my longest stint was four years—and then it would happen again. This was my secret. The only reason why I am so sure it won't happen again is because *now* I know why I was doing it, and that cause will be eliminated, because I am sitting here with you right now, and the running has to stop."

She stiffened, as if bracing herself for a swift kick in the gut.

"I am sitting here in front of you, no longer ashamed. You need to hear what I've been doing, going through and hiding. I didn't tell you, not because of fear of your reaction but because I didn't believe, Mom, you were strong enough to deal with it. I was protecting you, like I always do."

She lowered her head, and tears fell down her cheeks. He leaned forward and lovingly brushed them away.

"On the outside, you appear resilient." He swallowed and looked down at the floor, Heidi's tail wagged back and forth as she lay indolently, looking up at the pair. "On the inside, you're fragile."

"I…I can't believe this," she mumbled tearfully.

"Oh, I think you can, Mom. I think a part of you deep down knew something was wrong, but then, that would…never mind." He shook his head, wanting to keep on track, stick to the task and not start an argument. "Look, this is who I am. I am a human being who has made mistakes."

"And you think becoming a priest was one of them? No, Dane, it wasn't. I've seen you flourish. Do you realize how much people love you at St. Michael? Everywhere, actually. Let me get the articles, all of them, the local ones and the national ones, written about you and your work."

As if renewed with new life, she shot up again from her seat to go gather all the periodicals detailing his wondrous deeds, the ones she kept stowed away to remind herself that she was a decent person, because she had a decent son to prove it. Dane patiently shook his head and gripped her wrist.

"Mom, I can't do this anymore, okay? Not because I want to stop being a priest, but I want something, or shall I say *someone*, much more."

"What? It's…a woman?" Her voice trailed as she looked down at him. "You've met someone? But how could that be?"

Had he gone too far? Was it too much shocking information all at once? Soon, she relaxed and regained her composure and sat back down, the small area rug bunching under her shuffling feet. Suddenly, she turned toward him, the tears still flowing. She grasped his hands tightly between her own.

"Dane, I knew something was going on with you," she said, after a silence during which she just stared at him, with the emotional torment etched on her face. "I knew for a while, and that is why, the other day, I told you thank you about—"

"Are you sure you want to do this?" he interrupted, still in protection mode from years of training, for fear of his father overhearing. He didn't feel it was his duty to unload the old man's secrets. That was his parents' responsibility, and he prayed they'd handle it before leaving the Earth.

"I need to know." She trembled. "I need to know…if you drank…because of…"

"Mom, that was only a small part of it." He looked over his shoulder out into the hall, checking the way. "But, it wasn't your fault. I was the one who chose to drink, I made that choice, and now, I am making a new one." He rose from the couch, took her by the arm, and led her out the front doors. They sat on the front steps of the wrap-around porch, listening to the birds on this beautiful day—the sky so blue after the afternoon showers. It looked as if it were painted by a master artist, and he knew it in fact had been. The clouds slowly meandered by, collecting and passing like dreamscapes, shifting into teddy bears, ice cream cones and men with bags over their shoulders. They told stories, they told lies, and they promised another day was to come.

The two looked straight out, watching slow moving cars go by every now and again causing a sloshing sound from the freshly laid puddles. The sweet scent of the recently planted flowers mixed with the earthiness of overturned soil tickled his senses. Purple and yellow tulips waved to and fro in the light breeze, offering a focal point as he cleared his throat and geared up for the final leg of his honesty tour that day.

She looked at him and gripped his hand hard. She was afraid, but he appreciated her earnest attempts at gallantry.

All the things we didn't talk about, mom, we'll do it now.

CHAPTER TWENTY-TWO

D ANE SMILED AT mom, and she smiled back through eyes still brimming with moisture. As he looked back out into the quiet suburban street, he reflected back on the day that started the downward spiral…

One week before Christmas, festive music blared throughout the heavily decorated house, decked out in crimson, gold and cheer. It was his mother's favorite time of year, and the humongous tree blazed bright with antique holiday ornaments, strewn colorful lights and thick, silver tinsel on the real pine tree their father had brought home. A mere sixteen, his birthday had just passed. Dane was taller than most of his peers, so as he ascended the attic steps at his mother's request to find a missing box of decorations, he bumped his head, causing a headache and swollen temple. Muttering a string of curses, he paused to rub his head, while moving about the cluttered, stuffy attic. Meanwhile, his parents, brothers and sister moved about the house on the relaxed Saturday afternoon.

"She said it was marked, 'Luigi'," he murmured as he continued to pilfer through grimy piles of memories, some dirty, worn, or sealed in

yellowed envelopes and brown tape. He looked through all manner of old boxes, plastic cartons, discarded moth bitten clothing and the occasional creepy doll, with one eye permanently open and the other shut, giving him the willies.

"Everything okay up there?" his mother called from down below, no doubt passing by with her hands full of more items to hang around the home.

"Yeah...still lookin', Mom!" he called back. "Damn it!" He'd walked smack dab into a cobweb and fought the ropey, gray matter that wrapped around his face, even consuming bits of the old, nasty thing. Spitting, he ran his hands feverishly over his lips, aggravated, but then laughed at his own misfortune. In a deep, recessed corner, under the alcove by a small window, lay a water-stained box with shiny silver duct tape along the edges. He pushed old lamps and chairs as he made his way through until he stooped over it. With his bare hands, he tore the tape up, exposing the contents.

Finally...

He stared down at assorted ornaments, wreaths, more tinsel and a few hard bound books, most of which looked to be from the 1960s. He picked up one after the other, brushing them off as the sunlight pilfered in, exposing dust particles that looked almost magical as they landed on gold streams of exposed holiday yarn. She'd mentioned three wooden soldiers her brother Luigi had had as a child that would be lying inside. She'd packed it herself once she cleared out the old house many years ago. They were toy nut cracker soldiers, and she wanted them on full display, atop the fireplace hearth, in honor of her big brother, her protector, who no longer walked the Earth. After a few glances, he placed the items back inside, then lifted the box in his arms, taken aback when the bottom fell out.

Cursing some more under his breath, he chased a silver ball here, a red painted bell there, until he had them all collected and back inside, and peered around the attic trying to spot a temporary replacement container.

Oh screw it…I'll just take a few down, grab a bag, then get the others.

He rummaged through, picking and prodding, until he came upon a small black book with a ballet shoe etched on it. He'd missed it on his first go-round. Setting the ornaments and musty soldiers aside, he sat closer to the window, leaning in, hearing the occasional car go slowly past on the ice covered road. He opened it, with its yellowed pages and the edges sticking to one another. Gently prying them apart, he started to read, delighting in his mother's description of a crush she'd had in her young days.

He was sure he had the goods on her now, and planned to tease her mercilessly about that, but then he continued on, and his heart stopped… Yeah, he died a little…

There wasn't much written in it, as it appeared to have only been used for a few months according to the diary dates, but what he read was enough to turn his stomach into hot, volcanic soup. Feeling woozy, he barely managed to get to his feet, then fell back, almost crashing into a pile of artificial plants. The book slipped from his hands. Then, he gathered his composure and ran his hands along the filthy floor until he felt it, and had the book in his grip.

"Dane!" his mother called, laughter chasing her voice. "What is taking so long, sweetheart?"

He dropped it once more when her voice rang out, making his mind spin. Grabbing one of the soldiers and the book, he made his way down the rickety ladder steps until he stood face to face with her. She looked at the sad wooden soldier, the Nutcracker, his nose splintered and his mouth, agape, full of wooden teeth…and then at the diary. Her eyes stayed on it until seconds had turned into a minute, maybe longer. He thought he may have to catch her as her eyes suddenly fluttered and she haphazardly stepped back. Instead, he followed her back into her bedroom, and waited while she closed and locked the door behind them.

She crossed her arms, her face a mixture of anger and desperation.

"So, you read it…"

He looked away, and nodded, then sank onto the bed. The room smelled of sweet floral perfume and baby powder. It sickened him more— the strange contrast of the alluring, fragrant bouquet didn't match the sentiments that grew inside of their hearts. Instead, the odor of hot, rotten trash should have been present. Isn't that what dashed dreams and horrible tragedies smell like?

They said nothing, but he knew what was coming…a promise to keep to his death.

"Don't tell your father, please!"

It was all there, written in faded black ink in the diary.

At the age of fifteen, his mother, Maria, had run off with the neighbor boy, snuck away as sometimes lovers do. She knew her father didn't approve of him, as he came from a Protestant family, and to make matters worse, he was bad news. Grandpa had called them trash that had acquired a little money and set up shop right next door. It seemed the boy, originally from a rough borough in Philadelphia, appeared tough and rugged with his leather jacket and slick black hair, and rode a motorcycle. He was a greaser, and he had a standoffish way, the kind that women adore. Yes, the girls loved him, but he chose the pretty wallflower—the sweet, shy Maria…

One night, under the stars, he took the one thing from her that she prized above all else. A thing a girl would never admit she'd given away, not even to her own self. And it happened a time or two more, but she believed she was in love. It didn't take long before the rendezvous and fantasy teen romance burned out like a fire in the woods after a torrential storm. Soon, her clothing began to fit tighter and she was filled with insurmountable fear and humiliation. To make matters worse, when she told Ronnie of the news, he disappeared, like a shadow once a bright light is shined upon it.

One moment he was scorching the night air with his rough elegance, next, he left a smoldering, shameful stench and only a whisper of his name. She was stuck, her virtue gone, and indignity fell upon her. She'd been Daddy's little girl…and she was sure that status was in jeopardy. And she was all alone, for no one else was there to help in her time of need. Her own mother had died when she was only ten. She struggled to hide the hideous ways in which her body was changing, telling on her, as her stomach swelled a bit more each passing week. Meanwhile, she wondered about the retired doctor from Sweden that lived in Flint and gave cold, garage abortions. She'd heard the rumors of the bad girls seeking him out, but no, she was too afraid. Yet, she had to. Who could she trust? Who could she run to?

Another month past, and most her clothing no longer fit. Luigi looked at her suspiciously over dinner one evening while their father read the paper and smoked his pipe, completely oblivious as the radio played low in the background. A lanky, auburn haired boy with quiet mannerisms, quick wit and a loving nature, Luigi took his little sister by the arm to a far corner of the house, and made her confess her sins. She did so tearfully, terrified, in explicit detail from the morning sickness, the missing father who'd run off after the news reached him, and no man from Sweden to be found.

Luigi kissed his little sister on the top of her head and assured her that he'd find someone to help. If their father found out, he'd kill her, and the threat of that was quite real and almost scarier than the pregnancy itself. Their old man had only remarked playfully that she'd had plenty of cakes—never suspecting that it was a different baking bun altogether…

No, not his little girl…she'd never do anything so vile.

A week later, Luigi shoved a wad of cash into the old doctor's hand and waited in an old kitchen while she screamed in pain in the adjoining room. After a while, her brother carried her out of there, put her in his car and drove her shivering, traumatized self back home. He took care of her, telling their father she'd come down with an awful cold, and had to miss school. While their old man toiled away at his company, brother and sister sat together, making sure she didn't bleed to death. Finally, the blood had stopped, the pain was gone, and she could walk with ease once more. Though the words were never spoken, she believed her beloved father treated her differently after that horrid ordeal. She'd never whispered a word to him, and knew her brother would never betray her in such a manner, but the glow in his eyes when he'd look at her was gone…

A few years later, she met Tony, Dane's father, and pretended to be the virgin bride he'd assumed her to be. Surely not a young woman who'd become pregnant from a wayward street punk and did the unthinkable, the 'no-no' in Catholic law…snuff out the life of a child. Maria carried the guilt with her like a scarf around her neck, and it strangled her into submission. She walked around needing to make things right, to think that nothing bad would ever happen to her again. All she had to do was make certain that the world around her was safe by simply pretending that all was well.

Dane did her bidding, promised to never tell their father of what had occurred, even though he tried to assure her that Dad loved her so much, he would not hold this against her. She staunchly disagreed, and when he saw the trepidation in her eyes, he knew, he must never even insinuate that it should be addressed again. Ever. He promised to let sleeping dogs lie, but then, the following year, he saw his father and his mistress, and that, too, would have to be a secret, for Mom couldn't handle any more bad news, it would break her in two.

He tucked it all away, and before he could catch his breath, Joseph confessed to him in an inebriated stupor, after they'd played a liquor game with their father's beer stash, Playgirl magazines and a pack of old cigarettes, that he didn't have a part-time job to help with the bills while Dad was away. He stated that wasn't enough to keep them from all being out on the street, so instead, he was selling marijuana. The money had gotten good to him, and he thrived on his illicit business, still dealing long after Dad came back with the promise of a new job and a fresh start. Yeah, Joseph laughed and bragged about the gravy train that only got thicker and thicker until Dane had to bail him out of jail...another family secret he was sworn to keep to himself.

He poured the pain into Josh's ear after the final blow toppled him like a cinder block. The final aggressive hard hitting punch came from a woman named JoAnne, who knew her way around a Chrysler, as well as Daisy's heart.

That was it. Dane was then convinced that God was chasing him down, tormenting him, trying to make him do right, and bend left, so he ran straight into the Lord's arms, sober and certain he'd be finally delivered. Enough of the girls, parties, drinking and secrets all piled inside of him like rotting autumn leaves that molded, turning blacker and blacker until they died. He became a zombie, so he did what anyone in his predicament would do—he stopped running away, and instead, ran toward... He ran into the safe confines of the priesthood. Regardless of the haphazardly way it fell into place, he knew he was being called because that could be the only explanation for all that he had seen and endured. That one final straw had been life changing, the pivotal moment in which his entire world changed and he finally surrendered.

His dilapidated world came crumbling down the rest of the way, on a fine spring day. The day he'd visited his little sister in college and her girlfriend popped over to tell him the damn truth—that they were in love and planning to get married...

Daisy had lied, said the woman was only a friend and kidding, but Dane knew better. She'd tried to hide the relationship but the truth was, the woman who was madly in love with his little sister and refused to be hidden away like some filthy disease. She wasn't ashamed, and figured out Daisy's little hoax to keep her clean front before big brother came to pay a visit. Tired of being forced in the closet with her lover, she told on Daisy; let it all out with Dane. He'd stared at the woman as she confessed—her hair the same length as his, yet her features soft. He could see she loved his little pain in the butt sibling, and he respected that, regardless of his religious beliefs regarding the matter. She'd fallen hard for the petite head-turner, and wanted Dane and everyone else within earshot to know all about it. After it was over, JoAnne stormed away, angry and resentful of the stunt her lover had pulled.

With sad eyes, just like their mother's, Daisy begged him to keep it to himself. And then he got the same awful wails of despair from Joseph, when he called from behind the black, chipped paint of the jail bars with criminals willing to eat him alive. He needed to be bailed out and pleaded that nothing be said about his criminal activities then and forever. With the little money he had to his name, he made sure his big brother was released. Dane agreed to keep his secrets, even helping him find the right lawyer to get his record eventually expunged.

And now—the same haunted, hollow look he'd just seen from his father, after Dane confessed to him that he knew about him and his whore. The woman he went around town with, hand in hand, laughing their cares away while he and his brothers and sister were collecting foreclosure notices and burning them in the fireplace for heat.

Then, there was Anthony, who simply floated through life, detached from reality, just like their mother, but he was the sanest of them all, despite his four leaf clovers and grungy music. Nevertheless, he was a walking liability, and had no clue of the truth of the situation, nor a shared desire to be taught. The family was a stack of cards, and something from up above had blown the whole damn thing down.

All the lies became too much, and the occasional nipping turned into an all-out alcohol induced stupefied love affair. The bottle became his best friend, and he loved it so as the liquid fire slid down his parched throat, sometimes straight from the glass bottle. The alcohol promised to make all the secrets go away, to make the dark thoughts dissipate in his head—so he surrendered to it. Let it slowly destroy him.

Then his saving grace arrived, and he was saved. He owed God…God that loved him in spite of himself, and so, it was written— Bible passages, strange dreams, a willingness to let go and transcend the flesh, to become holy…

He could help others; pour some of that energy into something positive, wrap it in the soiled cloth that covered Jesus' beaten and bloodied body, nail it to the cross, sacrifice the pain and trade it in for something bigger, brighter and better. Oh yes, you could sell sins to the lowest bidder, you could sell the sins of others, take on their pain, let it ride on your broad back until it broke you down into nothing but ashes, and not only on Wednesdays…

Shhhh….don't say a word, don't cry, don't scream…simply help. Help and help and help, until you can't help anymore, and then, help again, any ol' how. Every face that turned his way, needed him. A prayer, a kind word, a donation… Help us Fr. Caruso! Help us, please! The voices grew louder and louder until he'd scream and gnash his teeth, praying for God to wipe it out, like a memory that was never meant to be. But instead, it only got worse…

The loneliness crept in on its tippy toes, stole him away as if he were a rare jewel, stole him from his declaration, his promise. It had little to do with sex; it all had to do with love. For the past year, he'd kept it at bay, and then God drove the final nail in his hand—he took Josh away, his only slice of sanity, the one person he could depend on, the man that he'd emptied all of his pain into, confessed, and felt clean, whole and pure again. Did the secrets sleep with a corpse? No, they rose from the grave and came after Dane, telling him that he must take them back, let them live inside of his heart and consume him while his heart still beat. They'd returned for their pound of flesh, because he owed them. Yet, all of that did nothing but kill him inside, crush him under their weight.

Because in the end, no one was happy, still. However, it was also understood that if he let the secrets fly free, that everyone would be unhappy. How can you go from ten to one, when you are already at negative ground zero?

Shhhh….don't tell that Mom got rid of her baby, the oldest sibling of them all…

Shhh….don't tell that Joseph sold drugs and liked it…and he took a few too….

Shhh…don't tell anyone that you are an alcoholic, Dane…

Shhh….don't tell that Dad is screwing another woman and doesn't give a crap about his family of five nor his damn self.

Shhh….don't tell mom that Daisy is a lesbian and would rather be unhappy and live a lie than let anyone find out the hard, honest truth.

Shhh….don't tell, because you promised us, Dane. You promised to keep our secrets.

He was trying to keep alive a dying ogre, a demon that demanded he give it CPR, every morning, noon and night. He hated how it smelled and begged and threatened, but he'd promised…he promised to make it all right, to make it all better. So he slept with the beast, so that no one else would have to…

Dane was the protector, and that is what protectors do…but now, something had happened. He'd fallen in love, and he would be damned if he was going to continue to carry the burdens of others, leaving no room for Rhapsody in his heart. Things had gotten so crowded, he was suffocating. He wanted to offer her a mortgage there, deep inside him, and thus, he was prepared to swiftly issue an eviction to the demon that refused to budge. He picked up his crucifix and prepared to slay the ghastly vampire of secrets that had feasted on him for far too long, plunging it deeply into the heart of the creature. He heard the monster cry out, but its pain did nothing but please him as it fell helplessly, moaning, clawing on the disturbed ground of Calvary…

He held his mother's hand tightly as they sat there, emotions running high. The sun begun to set, giving one final show of lights. Streaming rays glimmered through the trees, casting shadows along the lawn, beaming in front of them politely, bowing her heavenly golden head before closing her eyes for the evening.

"So…who is she?" her voice broke the silence, but barely.

"A singer, musician. A beautiful person. Oh, and she knew nothing about my financial status, so, she's not after me for anything like that. Just want to make that clear."

A woman walked her dog down the street while Dane stared at the lady that gave birth to him, taking note of her laughter lines, and the beautiful eyes that were now swollen with tears.

She smiled. "So, you really love her?"

"Almost more than life itself."

A brief pause.

"Okay." His mother laughed nervously and slowly turned toward him. "Okay," she repeated, smiling wider, another fat tear rolling down her tanned cheek. "So, my son, the priest, has fallen in love." She shook her head, still obviously trying to process it all.

"I want you to be happy, Dane." Her voice quaked, but this time, Dane knew she meant the words. She grabbed him around the neck, bringing him close. She embraced him like she needed it for her very survival. Something changed then, an understanding between them.

The woman knew what it felt like to be in love—whether it was with a bad boy that lived next door, who was too young to handle the responsibility of being a new father, or falling in love with a blue-collar guy named Tony, who worshipped the ground she walked on. So much so, he took her father's abusive words throughout the years, that he was no good for his daughter. So when Dad failed as provider, he was afraid, and ran from mom, too—the one woman he'd tried to always protect. It didn't make sense, it hurt, but affairs of the heart are often not black and white. Things happen, people change. Mistakes are made, but Dane understood now that running from the past never made the present a gift or the future brighter.

He kissed his mother's cheek and lightly laughed. "We can close our eyes, Mom, to all the things we don't want to see, that *none of us* wanted to see, but we can't close our heart to the things we don't want to feel…"

CHAPTER TWENTY-THREE

Several hours later...

RHAPSODY KICKED HER feet up on the pillow she'd tossed at the bottom of the bed as she watched the small flat screen television in her bedroom. She pushed the bread pieces around on her saucer before casting it all to the side. She'd devoured the grilled cheese sandwich, but the half bowl of tomato soup had grown cold. The phone rang.

"I want to see you." His smooth voice came through the line, surprising her. She figured it wasn't him as she hadn't recognized the digits, and thought possibly it was a wrong number. Normally, she wouldn't have answered at all, but she was in a generous mood.

"Dane, you need to stop." She looked at the time. "It's a little late. Besides, you stood me up and didn't bother to call."

"I know. I had a bit of a family emergency. You know I wouldn't do that without good reason. I'm the one that is always early, you are the one running late." He laughed.

She grinned. He was right. "Hmmm, everything okay?"

"Not completely, but it will be. I need to talk to you." His breathing was deep and labored, as if he were trying to calm down and rest after a vigorous jog. Running her fingers along the spaghetti strap of her white nightgown, she thought about his proposal.

"I won't stay long," he assured.

"Oh." She sighed. "Okay. I have to go to work early tomorrow so…"

"I'll be in and out."

She fought the sexual thoughts that tried to twist his words into something she could chew on, and just smiled.

"Okay, see you in a bit."

DANE STEPPED OUT of the shower and pulled on a black shirt, followed by boxers and faded jeans. He trimmed up his beard and winced as he splashed on a little cologne along his cheeks. He looked at the clock—it *was* late. He didn't even bother to check after he'd spoken to his parents in detail regarding his vocational plans and called her from their house immediately afterward. The evening was tense, but it ended with a family embrace and an earnest attempt at understanding.

Before long, he was standing outside Rhapsody's door. He rang the bell and waited impatiently, his foot tapping and his hands on his waist.

What is taking so long?

A light turned on inside, and he saw movement through the front window. He walked closer to look inside, his nerves getting the best of him. The sheer curtains were layered, so he peered harder, cupping his hands around his eyes as he leaned into the window. A figure, long and lean, approached the door and he quickly stood at attention, pretending he'd not just been a peeping Tom. She opened the door and stood there, looking stunning, her thick black hair hanging about her shoulders and her prominent cheekbones glistening as if gold dust had settled upon her magnificent face. Her bottom lip, full and shiny, drew his gaze, made him long to kiss her. He smiled down at her, and she cracked a grin, then a laugh, as he presented her with a large bouquet of purple and white ombre orchids.

"Oh my goodness." She smelled the flowers, inhaling deep, pleasure on her face. "They are beautiful and smell so good. Come on in." As she moved out of the way, her silky white gown moved over the curves of her body. He walked in, shooting her long shapely legs a look out the corner of his eye. He sighed, rubbed his hands together and smiled at her, not even sure where to begin.

"Why do you seem ever taller now?" She laughed as she closed and locked the door behind them.

"Because you have on no shoes." He casually glanced down at her bare feet, then back up at her face, swallowing.

Such perfect feet.

She pointed to the couch. "Come on and have a seat."

Rather than take her cue, though, he took her into his arms and kissed her softly, quickly, then again, a lingering kiss—and again, soft kisses, over and over, until her breathing accelerated. Only then did he take her by the hand to a chair, where he sat and pulled her on his lap.

He leaned back and closed his eyes.

"Dane, what's wrong?" she asked after a few quiet seconds.

He slowly opened his eyes and ran his hand over his hair, messing it up, bringing it toward his face. It had been a long, emotionally exhausting day, but he needed to do this. The time was now.

"Baby, I need to talk to you about some things," he said, and felt her stiffen. "I've—"

"Well, the last few days, you've been acting strange." She slid off his lap, leaving him by his lonesome.

"Rhapsody, I know. I had a lot of things on my mind, and I was trying to sort it all out. Look, I need you to just listen to me for a moment," he said, "and once I'm finished, ask all the questions you want, okay? This is a discussion, but first, I need to get it all out."

She seemed to relax. He hated to admit it, but it pleased him that she, too, feared he could disappear, that the threat was very much real. Though she didn't say it, her eyes let him know. She'd played it so cool for so long, and all of that was finally over. Reaching out, he gently grabbed her and made her claim her original position on his lap.

"I'm leaving the priesthood."

Their eyes locked. Then, as if they were in some old, black and white horror movie with Vincent Price making a grand announcement, a strike of lightning lit up the room, and soon, soft rain began to hit the windows, just like earlier in the day. The rain was back. They looked at each other and laughed at the irony.

"Uh, when…" She stopped and cleared her throat. "When did you come to this decision?" she asked, her voice soft and low, as if she were afraid she may wake someone sleeping in the next room.

He ran his hand slowly up and down her back, resisting the

urge to kiss her again.

"When I realized I couldn't live without you… Since the church will make me choose, well," he looked away, a slight bit of sadness stabbing at his chest, "then I choose *you*."

He didn't miss the way her face brightened. Leaning a bit forward, she ran her hand along the bottom of her foot, massaging it gently.

"I am going to request a meeting. I already gave a written heads up, without saying what it entailed as I want to get my affairs in order first. So this will take a little while, but I let the bishop know I needed a moment with him."

Rhapsody remained quiet. He reached over and took her hand.

"Is your family okay?"

"Oh, the family emergency? That was me telling my parents about what I'm telling you *right* now. I told them first out of respect so they wouldn't hear about it from someone else later. It was a tense situation, but it needed to be done. My family has problems," he said thoughtfully, slowly releasing her hand. "I wanted to talk to you about this previously, but you were resistant to the idea. I believe I understand why, but it can't be put off any longer."

She ran her fingers lightly through his hair. "I'm sorry. I *did* want to know, I just didn't want you to have any remorse or anything, just like I said. That probably wasn't the best way to handle it. I thought I was helping you, alleviating some of the pressure. I'm sorry if I gave you that impression, Dane. Honestly, I just wanted you to feel comfortable, to not have any doubts. Please believe me when I tell you it was more about my love for you, than my own problems. I didn't know you felt that way, but regardless, I'm listening *now*. I'm ready to hear it, *all* of it." She sat straighter.

"You know how you saw me with that alcohol in the park?"

"Yes."

"I admitted to you that I had a drinking problem. I still have a sponsor and when you saw me, I was in the middle of another relapse. I know I told you that part, but I never told you why. I never addressed what triggered it."

"Okay," she said, keeping her expression neutral.

"Even though I attended meetings and prayed to keep myself on track, things had fallen apart. I had stopped going to meetings when Josh told me he was sick; that was part of the problem and I had no one to talk to."

"Dane." She frowned. "I'm sorry you felt so alone. There seem to be people around you all the time, I would've thought you had a lot of friends."

"Not any that I would feel comfortable sharing something like that with. Yes, the other priests knew I had a drinking problem from the past, but they didn't know I'd relapsed. If they had of known, I would have been sent away, and I wouldn't have wanted that. I knew what the problem was, like I said, I just couldn't address it, at least not right then."

"Well," she caressed the side of his face, "what are your triggers?"

"Trying to be everything to everybody. It had to stop and tonight, I took a big step towards closing that door."

She nodded in understanding, and intertwined her small fingers with his. He looked down at their linked hands, loving the skin tone contrast and the softness of her flesh against his. He was dropping a lot in her lap, but if he wanted her, he needed to offer full disclosure.

"I'm open to you." He pulled her closer, making her squeal. "You can ask me *anything* you want. I want you to, baby."

"Just do it," she said, smiling. "Dane, just tell me everything you want me to know, and I'll put on my big girl panties and listen to it all, and then I will tell you what I think."

"Okay, well, my family is really dysfunctional, Rhapsody."

"Who's isn't?" She laughed.

"Yeah, that's true, but this was...well..." He shook his head and leaned back as she slid off his lap, sat right beside him and locked her hand with his once more. "This was more than average. I am going to tell you everything that I told Josh. I am going to tell you when the drinking started, what the specific event was and then when I'm finished, after you kick me out on my butt...just remember I love you." He touched his forehead to hers.

"Just go ahead! It couldn't be all as bad as you make it out to be."

Twenty minutes later, Rhapsody was lying across his lap while he ran his fingertips slowly back and forth across her collar bone.

"Thanks for telling me," she said sincerely. She looked up at him, her mahogany eyes glowing. "No one family is perfect, and I already knew about the drinking; you were forthcoming with that, and I appreciate it. I knew you weren't drinking anymore. It was just instinct, I guess."

"No more secrets..."

"Dane, I've been around you long enough now where I can tell when you are having a good day, hiding something or upset. This definitely explains why you've seemed preoccupied as of late...distracted. I am so sorry you went through all of that, honey."

He swallowed and remained quiet, continuing to feel her silky skin, his body coming awake, screaming for closeness. He initially tried to fight it, push the thoughts away, but he didn't want to fight any more. He wanted her. Needed her. Had to have her. Pulling her closer, he brought his lips to hers, while she cupped the back of his neck. Without hesitation, he drove his tongue between her lips, inside her mouth, taking her off guard. She gasped, then wrapped her arms even tighter around his neck. Dane sighed, and his pulse accelerated. Sliding his hands to her back and under her knees, he stood and carried her to the bedroom.

"Dane," she traced his face, her sultry voice slightly cracking, "are you *sure*?"

Pushing the bedroom door open, he walked in, laid her down onto her partially unmade bed and covered her with his body, pushing her thighs apart.

There's your answer...

He felt so safe as their warmth embraced him close.

He lifted her arms above her head, linked their fingers and kissed her hard. His erection pushed into her stomach, flourishing, determined. Letting her hands go, he explored down her body, first her arm, then her waist and thigh through the silk of her gown. Reaching for the hem of the nightgown, he pulled it up until it was bunched around her hips. She sighed, pushing her face in the cool sheets, eyes closed in anticipation of pleasure as he let his hands trail up her inner thighs. He massaged the skin there, gently, as he kissed up and down her neck.

"Ahhh," she moaned. "Mmmm!" Louder, as she wrapped her legs around his waist and bit down on her bottom lip.

"Dane, just so you know, I'm on birth control."

He simply looked at her, not sure how to respond. He didn't want the mood ruined, or their encounter to turn into an after-school special. He was sure most men would have been relieved at such an announcement, but he wasn't most men.

Then, he pushed her words aside, and stayed on course.

Getting up off of her for a moment, he quickly removed his shirt, casting it haphazardly across the room, then undid his zipper. He watched her watching him, and it spurred him on. Now in only his underwear, he lay back down on top of her, kissing her cheek, taking in the sweetness of her flesh against his lips.

"Rhapsody…" he moaned in her ear.

"Yeah," she said dreamily.

"I love you so much."

"…I love you, too."

"You may need to cancel your plans tomorrow," he said, nibbling on her ear. "I want to stay the whole night." Closing his lips around the lobe, he sucked hard, and she took a sharp breath and arched her back.

"I dunno…I may have to make you earn that right." Her smile gleamed in the dim room.

"Oh, believe me, I'll earn it."

She laughed as he pushed her aggressively toward the headboard, his heavy hands grasping onto the sides of her hips, placing her just where he wanted her.

"You sure have a lot of confidence for someone that has been out of practice for so long," she joked, teasing him by slipping her nightgown strap off her shoulder and exposing part of her left breast.

"When you knew how to do something well, if you did it right, it doesn't matter if it was thirty seconds ago or thirty years…it's like riding a bike or playing the piano…"

Your body is my altar…

"Mmmm." She moaned as he pushed her legs apart and made himself comfortable, his erection now thicker, longer and stronger as he grinded against her panty covered entrance. The warmth of her lower lips against his engorged muscle sent his nerve endings into an abyss of pure pleasure. He kept rubbing against her, driven to go a bit harder and deeper at each rotation as they kissed so intensely, their breath hitched on each other's rhythmic tongue strokes.

"Mmmm, Dane…" Her head fell back but he pulled her back, and consumed her lips once more, without shame or remorse. Regret never crossed his mind. He simply went with the flow, following his heart, taking her in. He believed that this was where he belonged, where he was supposed to be, and what he was supposed to do. He admitted he was in a state of weakness, but he needed her body against his, her love in his heart, and he wanted them at the same exact time.

Leaving her lips, he rose on his hands and looked down at her partially covered breasts. Staring into her eyes, he slowly slid the nightgown straps down from her shoulders and arms, until her soft mounds were completely exposed. He smiled at the luscious sight. Bending down, he took a round, perky nipple in his mouth while massaging the other, his fingers pressing into the delicate, delectable softness causing her to utter things he'd never heard before. Sexy, dirty things that fueled his blood. The more he rubbed against her love, the more vocal she became about her pleasure. He slowly sped up his pace until he'd swelled painfully through the slit of his underwear and slid against her moistened lower lips, still covered in the panties, but soaking wet.

He transferred his mouth to the other breast, and softly wound several strands of her hair around his finger, feeling the curled texture against his digit. He smiled as he felt her growing even wetter, his now semi-exposed nature hard with desire.

"I want you so bad!" burst from his between his lips as he ran his hands roughly up and down her silken body.

Every fiber of his being was awakened and alert, as if he had been a dark, abandoned home, and then all the lights were switched on, blazing, and a party of epic proportions was taking place inside. He slid her gown the rest of the way off and had it join his clothing somewhere across the darkened room. Slowly, slowly, slowly…he kissed his way down her body, past her rib cage, then her navel, until his lips brushed against a small thatch of soft, dark hair. He felt her shake as he gently opened her legs wider and positioned himself between her warm inner thighs. He gingerly opened her lips with his thumbs, then closed his eyes. It had been so long, but this felt so right.

One tongue flick…across her clitoris, then another, until he had her spread wide open, and he licked, sucked, and devoured her garden, making her moan loudly, rise from the bed and buck against his lips. He quickly reached under her, grabbing her ass cheeks so hard, his fingers sank into the soft fleshy globes. All the while, he held her in place, so that she'd never leave his mouth again.

Murmuring intelligible things, she shook in his grip, while he tasted her, and he loved it, wanted more of it.

"Mmmm Dane! Oh! Shit…"

Delicious…

Her thighs tightened as she approached her orgasm, and he so desperately wanted to see and feel it. He loved that he was giving her pleasure, and though initially it was a bit awkward as he regained his bearings, moving about blindly in her womanly terrain, he soon fell right in line—knew exactly what to do, and how to do it. He was devoted to her, wanting only to bring her the maximum release.

The song Anne-Marie – 'YOU & I' featuring Khalid, played in the background, stirring him on, making the gifted musician's body bend and melt to her lover's every move, his mouth now her percussion. Windsong. He knew she'd been practicing the tune and playing it on her piano for a student, and he loved the song. The rhythm filled her bedroom, the baseline loud and commanding, the tempo reminiscent of a grand cowboy entrance.

Dane snaked his tongue inside of her, and she screamed so loud he thought the windows would shake. Her back arched over the green satin sheets, submitting to the sensations he gave her. Sliding his arms and hands underneath her and lifting her slightly above his chin, he continued to devour every single bit of her sweetness. The rhythm of their bodies echoed the music—strong, pounding, passionate. Looking up, he didn't miss the gleam of ecstasy in her eyes. He redirected himself, orally massaging her, tonguing down her clitoris, sucking it more vigorously, then ran his tongue quickly back and forth across it, and in jagged, hard circles. And at last, he felt her falling apart, her screams piercing as he gingerly lowered her back down onto the emerald sheets. Immediately, he slid a finger inside of her and continued to work her over, her juice coating his lips and chin.

"Mmmm!" He groaned as he tasted her honey and heard her body sing. Shivering uncontrollably, she screamed out his name, her hands running ruggedly through his hair. He went on and on, wanting to make sure he got every liquefied musical note out of her. She clawed at his bare back, writhing and wiggling until finally, she was still…quiet…and then, there it was… a light giggle, then another, until he too smiled and slowly ascended back up her body. He crawled over her like a tiger out of a thicket, and when he got where he wanted, he landed a gentle kiss on first her cheek, then her neck.

He grinned. "So even though it's been a while, and I'm out of practice, I take it I did okay."

She looked away shyly, and he loved that. His confident muse was now speechless, as an occasional lingering orgasmic twitch from her body made her jump beneath him. Bending down, he kissed her softly on the lips before rising back on his knees and sliding down his boxer shorts, casting them toward the bottom of the bed, devoured by the darkness, forever more. He burst out laughing as he watched her eyes widen and she cover her mouth with her hand.

"What? You thought I didn't have one anymore? Like we have to turn it in or something, like money and jewelry before being booked for jail," he teased.

"Dane, damn! You got it goin' on!" She crowed. "I mean, I felt it when we were grinding, I figured it was nice but…yeah…this is going to be good. … And that sounds so superficial, sorry."

Her laughter subsided when he glided back over her body, flesh to flesh, their naked temples sliding against one another.

"No, you aren't," he taunted, "but I'm glad it meets your expectations."

He was so hungry for her, and he wasn't sure he'd be able to last much longer. Before he knew it, she was feverishly reaching between their bodies, trying to reach his prized bodily possession. He followed her lead, and soon, he turned on his back as she slid down his body and hungrily eyed his manhood. With bated breath, he waited. He was ready to take her *there*, to heaven and back, but she had something else in mind.

Closing his eyes, he gave in to the sensation of her small warm hands around the base, and before long, her hot, wet mouth was on it, up and down, licking and sucking, turning him into a puddle of his former self.

"Mmmmm!" His legs stiffened, his body went wild as the long lost sexual healing took him over. The wet sounds of her tongue and mouth gripping and releasing him stoked the fire inside him. Gently gripping the back of her head, he lightly thrust, meeting her rhythm, falling into an abyss of extreme sexual pleasure.

"Rhapsody, ohhhhh baby, that feels so good!"

He groaned when she paused and took one his testicles into her hot mouth, slowly sucking then gliding the tip of her soft tongue over the sensitive, rounded flesh. Lifting himself up, he reached out, going out of his mind, then fell back against the bed. He sank his teeth into his bottom lip, stifling an orgasmic scream, pressing his eyes closed.

"Ahhhh....Oh God!" Fisting the sheets, he opened his eyes to look at her, through the shadows and traces of light— to look at his lover giving him due attention and delightful pleasure. Again, he rose on his elbows, about to lose complete control. She continued on, driving him completely insane. He gasped for air, fell back on the bed.

"Ahhh, you're killin' me." he groaned, smiling.

Heat surged through him, every muscle burned and tightened. At last, she released her prisoner, and he was free to have the final say. Reaching forward, he gripped her wrist and pulled her to him, roughly and possessively. She became tangled in the sheets, and they burst out laughing as he helped her escape the linen monster. But then he turned serious when he got her where he wanted, lying in the center of the bed, beneath him. They locked gazes, drowning in each other's eyes as he caught her hips in his grip.

I'm making love. We're making love and...I love her...so much...

And then, her legs wrapped lovingly around his body, cocooning him devotedly close to her slightly quaking form as he positioned himself just right. When she locked her hands behind his neck, the scent of her fragrance floated past, enticing him even further as they kissed one another, panting, heated air escaping their hungry mouths that freely roamed each other's lips and cheeks. The soft curls of her hair felt damp to the touch. He traced her skin with his fingertip, delicately going along the circumference of her face, while he kept his gaze on her eyes—her eyes like black star dust, glowing brightly in the night, sparkling with love.

She's got me...

And then, he was ready...

He pushed inside of her, she gasped, the utterance loud and seductive in his ear. Her natural reaction made him jerk uncontrollably and moan at the contact. Then, he moved inside her and she echoed his movements, both in harmony.

"Ahhhh, Mmmmm!" He gritted his teeth as her silky wetness enveloped him in a world that was all brand new and made, designed, refined just...for...him.

He rode her into the bed with each deep thrust, his hips

turning rhythmically as he found just the right groove. He'd pant and moan, and she'd follow, their love rhythm beating sincerely and deeply, one to the other, as they became one.

"Mmmmm, baby!" She dragged her fingers across his back, leaving heat in their wake.

"Ahhhhhh..." *God, give me strength.* He didn't want to cum too fast, but damn she felt so good.

The sounds of their desire got louder, more intense, blending together with each lunge. Dane felt himself sink deeper and deeper into her—and not just physically. This was love...

"I love you so much, Dane. Mmmm, it feels so good, baby!"

As if transported to a different world, she turned her head to and fro on the pillow, lost in the moment. Her walls clenched and relaxed around him, drawing him in, pulling him deeper inside, baptizing him right then and there. He loved how her body told on her—it revealed to him that she wanted him in her life as much as he wanted her, that she was head over heels in love with him, and that this act, this coming together, may be sin to many, but it was a blessing to *them.* They were now becoming one, joined together, sealing their love with a kiss from their mind, body and soul.

So he dared to challenge the principles of his Church, to make love to her, to make himself clear, to let her know where he stood. This had little to do with sex, and far more to do with the way his heart tormented him when she was not near. He learned, with Rhapsody, there could be no sin in loving, only in taking without giving back.

"I love you too, baby...so much...much more than you'll ever know." He pushed harder, faster, their bodies in tune with the rising and falling tempo of the music.

"Ahhh…Ahhh, Rhapsody…"

Burying his face in the cradle of her neck, he gripped her hips tight and took her, with all the strength inside him. He moved further down her body, his face between her breasts, his body taut like a guitar string, electrified—her moans, sighs and cries blending into the world of sensual music they were creating. He filled her, thrusting in and out of her,—making her his very own, once and for all. Although he had been out of the game for a while, he had not forgotten the moves.

The outside world bled in when the lights from a passing car filtered the room, settling briefly on them, on his gold crucifix and chain that dangled between them—the very thing that was supposed to divide them, made them as one. *Divine, God-given love…*

Pausing for a moment, he kissed her so tenderly, as if she were a fragile doll, running his fingers gently down her cheek, before he probed deeper, making her scream out his name.

"Dane! Ahhhh…"

"Mmmm!"

And then he felt her orgasm, her tight, wet spasms that squeezed him over and over and she trembled in his arms, carried away. He brought her lips to his, protecting her as her entire body shook while she fell apart. A sexual seizure that made his heart skip a beat. After she calmed, he resumed, going after his own gold, but not before sliding his thumb between them and circling her clit in tantalizing, skilled caresses.

He felt himself draw nearer, so he rose, away from her, balancing himself on his hands and looked down at his angel, at her glazed eyes and wondrous expression, as she kept coming apart beneath him in back-to-back orgasms. And then, he flew over the edge, joining her in the euphoria, moving faster, shaking the bed so hard, it banged into the wall with each thrust.

"Uhhh! Uhhh!" he cried, his body tensing, taking over.

"Mmmm, baby... Don't hold back," Rhapsody encouraged, rubbing her hands up and down his torso, playing delicious sexual games at this most pivotal moment, tracing his flesh slowly, licking her finger then returning it to the scene of the crime. He barrelled deep within her then retreated, the noise of their lovemaking, wet and echoing, causing him to lose his mind.

"Uhhh!....Uhhh! Oh God!" His climax gripped him, his butt cheeks tensed as he drove deeply within her, making her scream as his life force left his body and entered hers. He shivered and shook, never recalling love making feeling like that before. Out of his mind he flew, drowning in an ocean of ecstasy. The waves of orgasm came and came again until he fell down on her, a soaking wet. A lovely mess. He heard himself panting, but couldn't stop, calm down, and pretty it up. His heart pounded out of his chest and his lips curved when he felt her lightly finger his hair, so lovingly, so sweetly. She embraced him, making him fall further apart, as he kept his place, resting inside of her, their bodies entangled, her nipples brushing lightly against his chest.

Moments later, they kissed, eyes locked, then kissed again. He fastened his legs around hers, possessively holding her against him, never wanting to let her go. He finally felt at peace, at home. Everything was right; everything was just as he needed it to be. He wanted no further confirmation. She kissed him again, her soft lips brushed against the side of his face as he lazily rested against her.

Soon, though, he felt her touch on the head of his member, bringing it fast back to life, without the need of a second or third invitation. Leaning over onto his side, he gave her better access, and before long, he was on his back, with her falling upon him like syrup on a sundae, covering him in her sweet essence, forcing him back inside of her. He reached for her bouncing breasts, rubbing over them, teasing them, as she drove him once again over the edge.

That night, they made love two more times, until they were too exhausted for more. When he awoke three hours later, he was still inside of her, and she was fast asleep, with a big smile on her face. He delighted in knowing he was the reason for it.

He kissed her and gently ran his thumb along her chin—gently, so as not to disturb her—taking in the beautiful sight of the woman who had stolen his heart. He just wanted the quiet, to enjoy the beauty before him, to seal it in his mind, and never forget the moment that he gave himself away to a woman that he simply had to have, and could not envision his world without…

CHAPTER TWENTY-FOUR

R HAPSODY TURNED OVER on her side, straining to focus after the black-out type sleep. The type of rest that only comes after your body has been 'done well', by someone who adores you *simply* for existing. The tight, folds of the sheets wound around her long legs as she laughed and struggled to break free once again.

I am so clumsy lately! How did this even happen?

Sitting up in the bed, finally free from the sheets, she rubbed her eyes, realizing what had awakened her. The smell of eggs and fried bacon wafting in from the kitchen... She looked at the clock, seeing she'd overslept.

Oh damn!

Leaping out of the bed naked, she made her way into the classic jazz décor and trumpet wallpapered walls of her bathroom. The medicine cabinet was shaped like a clarinet, and various paintings of instruments were placed along the walls in perfect spacing. Not in the too far distance, she heard echoes coming from her kitchen—sizzling meat in a pan, the refrigerator door closing, a cabinet drawer opening and a light, low, masculine hum. She grinned, feeling joy and enthusiasm like a little girl as she ran her hands under cool water and washed up. Grabbing a towel, she dried herself off and left the bathroom. She just wanted to see him again…look into the eyes of the man who had made love to her body, heart and mind, all night long. She walked into the kitchen, catching his bare muscular, tanned back as he stood by the stove, shaking the frying pan, grease popping.

He stood there in only his jeans, and she felt her flower open, wanting another go round.

Damn…

His shoulder muscles shifted, his skin glistening while he moved slowly from side to side, his hair in beautiful messy contrasts against the sun peering into the small window—dark wheat, touches of auburn, but mostly rich mahogany with a kiss of blond that would go almost unnoticed. She continued to stare at his tresses; so intriguing to her even after all this time. Most people could be described as blond, redhead or brunette—but not Dane. Though most of it was a dark brown, the lighter portions weaved their magic, and that was what she'd first noticed about him in high school and coincidentally, also the first thing she'd noticed when she saw him again, after all those years.

That, and those eyes.

She walked further inside the small kitchen and wrapped her arms around his waist, laying her head on his back. With his free hand, he caressed her arm, as if he'd been expecting her. She peered over his shoulder as he kept his eye on the hot skillet, and ran her finger over the soft, downy hairs covering his arm.

"Don't you have to get back?" she asked sleepily.

"Yes, but I preferred to be with you right now," he answered, shooting her a small smile. "I know you have to get to work soon, we both do, but I thought I'd cook us something to eat before I left."

"So sweet of you, thank you." She rose on her tippy toes and kissed the side of his neck before leaving him to sit herself at the two-seater table with hand-painted strawberries bordering the circumference. She caught him glance her way a time or two, scanning her nude body.

Yeah, I'm still naked...

Smirking, she set her elbows on the table and tapped her finger playfully against her teeth, knowing full well the effect she was having on him. While she sat there, he kept looking back, raw desire blazing in his eyes. Bringing a leg up, she placed her foot on the edge of her chair and rested her head on her knee, staring at him like a tiny puppy wanting a good cuddle. He looked back, his eyes drifting toward her partially exposed sweet bits, then, with a regretful look, he turned back around and concentrated on the food preparation.

Taking out two blue plates from her cabinet, he placed the hot food on them, arranging it just so, with thick slices of strawberries and juicy, green grapes.

Rhapsody briefly looked away into the living room.

"It's still raining. I wonder how long this is going to last? I'll have to cut my grass sooner because of this. I hate mowing the lawn." She smiled and shook her head.

He walked up to her with a glass of juice and the loaded plate, and set them in front of her.

"I'll cut it for you," he offered.

Sitting across from her, he bowed his head and prayed.

This is crazy. He made love to me all night, tore my body up like he'd just been released from prison.

She grinned to herself at her thoughts.

Now, here he sits, praying, and getting ready to chow down. Serving me food, too. Truth is stranger than fiction. And I love this man. I love that he has these strong beliefs and is still going to do something about it. I love his beautiful blue eyes, that hair, that smile, those muscles…damn…and his…yeah, that too…

Picking up her fork, she tried to gander his attention as she worked her plate over. The only communication was their forks hitting the plate, the lifted glass being returned to the table and the audible chews. His face appeared tense, serious as he ate, as if drifting away from her in some way, then back toward her. She hoped it was simply paranoia, and debated asking to probe his mind. Instead, she rose from her seat, walked over to her computer—the old one she kept off to the side—and turned on one of her favorite songs by the songwriter, Freckles the Writer. "Uh Huh" came on first, filling the space with music.

That's better.

She returned to her seat, folding her leg under her, and ate. Occasionally, she looked in his direction, but he kept his head down, eating, living inside himself and closed off from her. She began to feel uncomfortable, like she wanted to put something on, like her robe, but she simply relied on the music to ease her woes as it always did. She began to sing the lyrics and bounce to the rhythm, popping the fork in and out of her mouth. At one point, his fork hit the plate a bit louder, and she looked at him. This time, he was staring at her.

"I've never heard this song before. I like it." He looked

back down and clasped his hands together.

"It's a really good song. The artist is also a song writer and has written music for some pretty big names…but," she shrugged as she picked with a slice of bacon, "she isn't as well-known as she should be. This food is really good by the way."

"Glad you're enjoying it. She?" his eyebrow rose. "Hmmm, thought it was a guy, great song. I'll have to download it."

Silence reigned again for a few moments.

Suddenly, he pushed his chair back, seized her and lifted her into his arms. Ignoring her shrieks, he carried her into the living room, over to the piano, and sat her bare behind roughly on the keys, pressing them down into a distorted, uneven groan. Kissing her so hard it knocked the breath out of her like oral armed robbery, he unzipped his pants and roughly entered her, thrusting in and out, letting the piano play out the distorted tunes of their lovemaking. Her butt rose and fell aggressively off the keys, while he gripped her tightly around her waist, making her come to him over and over again.

"Uhhh!"

He buried his head on her shoulder, his eyelashes tickling her skin, warm breath caressing the side of her neck as he continued to move expertly in and out of her, jabbing and moaning. "Ahhhh…" he whispered in her ear. Their bodies continued to make indistinct music, with her flesh moving in passion across the ebony and ivory. She gripped him tightly, feeling her own orgasm heightening and heightening until it burst forward, causing her to jerk against his hard body. He gripped the back of her head, the warmth of his hand heated her curls, giving comfort, and he didn't stop, he kept going, seeing her through her climax.

"Mmmm." She grew wetter, throbbing and pulsating

against him, and gripped him closer, his back now slick with sweat. "Uh!" He dove deep and downward, cupping her behind, fully immersed inside of her. All his generous length and thickness filling her up, the tightness paramount.

"Uhhh! Uh! Ahhh!" He thrust in short jabs and she felt him hasten, knowing he was close.

"I love you so much, Rhapsody…so much!" and then she felt the liquescent warmth shooting into her as her body twisted against his. After a while, he slowed, then lifted her into his arms and placed her down carefully on the couch, lying on top of her, their bodies, wet, vibrating and inter-twined. He smiled down at her and moved curly spirals of hair away from her face.

"This has been difficult," she blurted out, the emotions bursting forward. Her heart couldn't take it anymore. She'd tried to dance around this, just as he had—to pretend they were just friends when the entire time they'd been falling in love, and now that he'd been inside of her, everything came to a culmination and her spirit cried out. When he hadn't shown up at the park, she felt vulnerable. But instead of running away from the pain, she ran for help… For the first time in years, she'd done the unthinkable.

"Dane." She kissed his forehead as he rested on her breasts. "I prayed last night. It was the first time in years. I'm so in love with you. A part of me is so scared…so afraid you'll change your mind, or that in some way I have messed up things for you. But I can't deny my heart and how I feel. I just can't." Her eyes watered, she quickly wiped the moisture away, refused to lose complete control of the situation, although she needed to come clean. The man had confided his deepest thoughts and secrets, it was the least she could do.

He rose on his elbows and looked down at her, his expression thoughtful.

"Well, I've been praying about this a long time and at this point, Rhapsody, I just understand that I can't be expected to be the same man I was while in college, and have to stick by all of those choices. At the time, it was the right thing to do. I helped a lot of people, and that is the reason I was there." He said it so confidently, so matter-of-factly. It gave her peace that she could fully trust him, made her relax a bit more.

"We have to be real about this though. We made love, Dane." She shook her head, her body still so thankful for what they'd done.

"Yes, we made love," he said with tired eyes, as if the entire world were on his shoulders. "And I know according to my faith, because we aren't married, that was wrong, Rhapsody. I am not going to sit here with you and pretend like I don't remember what the Lord says about fornication, lovemaking outside of marriage. I knew when I came over here last night what may happen. But I needed you; I was at a point where I needed the physical contact. Real intimacy. I know that my love for you will come as a shock to so many... I never once complained to anyone about the priesthood. I never confessed that I was lonely. I should have, but I didn't. Heck, that may not have helped regardless. I imagine everyone would have just tried to talk me out of this, or tell me it'll pass. That the way I was feeling was only a phase. No one even knew until fairly recently that I *may* actually be in a situation, so to speak." He cupped her chin.

"Look, honey, when it is all said in done, I think I did the best job I could. By most accounts, I believe, people will say I was a good priest. I worked on my homilies for three to four hours per week. I heard confessions every day before daily Mass, and invited the congregation to share in my Holy Hour in the morning. During those Holy Hours, I would ask God to free me of love to my paramour, and freedom from my desires but only my removal from the parish was the answer to my prayer. I've known for a while that something was nagging at me, that it may be time to move forward. You coming into my life gave me the permission to do that—it was our friendship, before any hand holding, visits or kisses had transpired, that freed me. I just want to be with *you*, Rhapsody. I can't do this with them anymore. It's over. And in the last few months, I've had signs that I was holding onto to something that wasn't meant for me anymore. So many signs."

She ran her fingers through his hair and looked up at the ceiling. "Me? I was the sign?"

"Yes, and many others. You may or may not be aware of this, but priests don't make much money. I have my education from the seminary, and received my college degree as well, but I have no job training outside of it, which would make it extremely difficult for me to find a decent wage with a good company. That was one of my worries about leaving, before I'd met you. Then, as if out of the sky, Rhapsody, I came into some money and I've helped so many with it. Now, it may be time to do the same for myself."

He caressed her chin and kissed it, then leaned back on her breasts.

"That explains your new car." She laughed lightly. He laughed back and nodded.

"...And I love that you've told me you love me, knowing none of that, Rhapsody. You fell in love with *me,* for me, despite the possible issues we'd run into. You can't control this, *we* can't control this. We fell in love, and now," he shrugged, "I am ready to just move forward, in a positive direction. Back to the bedroom is a positive direction." He snickered as he felt her moving beneath him, stifling a laugh herself.

Oh Jesus…

He kissed between her breasts, let his hands explore her, sensually, hungrily. Finally, he raised his head to look into her eyes—his sparkling blues told her how much he wanted her. Again.

I thought he was kidding!

"I thought…I thought, ahhh…. we are going to be late for work!"

She grinded against him, unable to help herself, but he didn't stop. Her body ached, the way he kept taking her over and over, but she couldn't deny him. She knew what he wanted, what he needed. The pain was still so clear in his eyes and at the breakfast table, she realized, he wasn't distant. He was *closer,* much closer as he was busy formatting the worn disks in his mind, trying to get the disastrous situation under control. Scraping at his own soul, no doubt asking God to forgive him for each thrust he'd made inside of her body, each kiss planted upon her skin—and yes, he'd covered all areas from head to toe multiple times…

But more importantly, he would have asked God to forgive him for not wanting to stop, and for being completely in tune with her.

He entered her again and she relished it, met his thrusts, one by one. They were a silken skin liquid orchestra, a two person sensual band. He pushed forward, his chest pressed against her breasts; she responded, taking in his slow, sweet thrusts. He looked down at her intensely, making her heart break, freeze and heat all at once.

She caressed his lips with her own, cupped his ears, kept his face near, so close.

"Are you getting what you need, baby?" she whispered.

"Yes." He pushed a bit harder, a bit faster. Her body worn down by his as he relentlessly continued to take her.

"No regrets…"

Tell me. Tell me. Tell me.

"I have one, but it is an offshoot of another."

"What is it?" she asked, curious, raising an eyebrow.

"That I don't care what anyone thinks about what has happened and that…I didn't get what was mine when I first saw you. You were *always* supposed to be mine. Always, Rhapsody. I'm late, but I'm finally here."

What was mine? But you're finally here… So sexy….

He wrapped his arms protectively around her, tighter, and filled her. The sensuality of his moves overwhelmed her core, pushing her into a compact orgasm that tore her up.

"Ohhhhh! Uhhhhhh!" As the last waves washed over her, she bit into the side of his neck. Ravenous. She dug her nails into his back. Drawing back, he pushed forward, over and over and over again, right behind her, exploding deep into her warmth. Moments later, he kissed her forehead as his body finally relaxed. Together, hand in hand, they walked into the bathroom and showered, spread soap on one another, laughed, talked, joked and made love again under the stream of hot water. The day was getting away, tip toeing out of their reach, and they no longer cared. Soon however, exhaustion grabbed them and stopped them in their tracks, though it had been a good run. They dressed, kissed and parted ways once more, promising to spend more time together the following day…

"WHY ARE YOU asking me about this again?" Rhapsody stood in place as she watched Dane wave to her and drive off into the distance. She was prepared to take her evening jog after they'd spent time sitting on the bench, holding hands and simply talking. A peaceful, beautiful time which was what she desired above all. Now the recent memories were soiled as she cradled her cellphone and Melody's voice rang out, screeching like the motorcycle wheels that had just passed by.

"Because you said you'd be here!"

"I did no such thing. Melody. Why in the hell would I come to a party of yours when every time you invite me to something, you either ignore me, talk down to me, or make obnoxious jokes at my expense to impress your friends? I told you the last damn time that I wasn't attending anymore."

"Well, what am I going to do now?" She huffed. "I told them I had a singer."

"Oh, so now you want me to sing and play the piano for your guests like some trained monkey when you just told me not too long ago I wasn't all that talented. You know what, Melody, yeah, we need to talk. I am so sick of your shit."

She was met with brief silence.

"What?! You have some nerve, Rhapsody! I told—"

Rhapsody looked up at the clouds and held her forehead. "I…don't…care who you told what, this, that and the third! My life doesn't revolve around your schedule. I am sick and tired of the way you talk to me, treat me, and I am sorry that sometimes I let you make me stoop to your low, pathetic level!"

"Who are you calling pathetic?!"

"If the designer shoes you love so much fit, wear it! You never say 'thank you' for anything I do for you. These past few weeks you have treated me worse than usual, really letting me know that you don't give a damn about me. I won't stand for it anymore. I will no longer be the sister, the *person*, because I *am* a person, Melody, contrary to how you treat me, that you can just shit on. You think you can say anything you want to me, treat me any ol' kind of way, and I will still be here for you. It's *over!* I should have thrown you out of my life long ago! This has been a long time coming, you—"

"Let me tell your ass something, Rhapsody! You are a—"

"Better woman than you, for finally pulling the plug on this bullshit! Blood is thicker than water, but I can't tell. I've been treated better by a feral alley cat than by my own sister. Until you learn how to act, and as much as this hurts me..." Rhapsody's voice quaked. She tried so desperately to control her sadness, blending it in with sheer anger and a sense of release, to no avail. "I want nothing to do with you, Melody! Nothing!"

Rhapsody ended the call, her entire body shaking. The interaction had been so unnerving, she slumped down into the grass, her heart beating harshly. She gripped her shirt as she drowned in so much emotional pain. It had been necessary—Melody was a cancer, and Rhapsody was the patient and doctor on call who had to perform the risky surgery, extracting her from her own life like the ailment that she was.

"Oh God," she moaned as she gathered herself and stood back on her feet. After a while, she began to jog, her white Nikes hitting the pavement, pounding it as she seethed with anger but also cried a bit, on the inside…

Several weeks later…

DANE SAT IN the large chair in the vast room decorated in rich burgundy and gold, his hands gripping the intricate hand-carved arms as he looked at the men before him. The long-awaited meeting had been granted and still in a semi-daze, he held tight on his surroundings, regardless of the cursed stares being tossed his way by many of the priests dotting the room, some of which he'd never exchanged more than pleasantries with. Fr. Kirkpatrick, dressed in black vestments, and the bishop, peering from over small spectacles, dissected him with their piercing eyes, staring at him as though he were a dirty, rancid smudge on all that was holy. The process began, and twenty minutes later, he was still being grilled.

"…So, that is why I've applied for a permanent leave of absence, all of it, my faculties…"

"We will have to do a thorough investigation. Who else have you done this with?" he asked angrily.

"No one," Dane answered sternly, his anger growing tighter, harder, and about to explode from him at any moment.

"We don't know that. There could be *other* women, and we'd be in the line of fire for a scandal. You've broken your vow of celibacy, and from what you told us, it almost seemed premeditated, Fr. Caruso." Fr. Kirkpatrick's words cut him down like a tree, leaving nothing but a jaggedly serrated stalk.

Now, he was Fr. Caruso…no longer just 'Dane' or his 'pretend' Grandson. It stung.

Dane briefly turned away, trying to curb his tongue from making the situation even more volatile.

"I have done nothing wrong. By *your* law yes, but the law of my heart, no."

"You made vows! They are now broken...broken vows..."

In exchange for wedding vows...

"The priestly laws were broken, Fr. Caruso when you consummated your relationship with that woman. However, I want you to think about this long and hard."

Dane had been completely honest, laying his cards on the table without getting into graphic detail. He walked in, took a seat and told them, without skipping a beat, that he had fallen in love, had fornicated and wanted out. *NOW.*

"Christ called me to the priesthood. He didn't call me to celibacy, lack of intimacy and loneliness. Those are the rules, and since I can't change them, I can only change *me*...and I," he pointed to his chest, declaring it to the world, "I am ready to move on. I was forced to go to this level by the Church, because you will not allow me to keep my vocation while maintaining a romantic relationship, and ensuing marriage. This isn't some fling, or me trying to sow my wild oats. This is a woman I see as my future wife."

The room grew quieter as he pleaded his case, tried to drive it home.

"I am not blaming you, *any* of you, for me being physically intimate with my girlfriend," he said earnestly. "I made that choice intentionally, for a number of reasons I won't be discussing here since it is a private matter, but I *do* blame the Church for all the turmoil I've had to endure regarding the fact that I only had two choices in order to stay active as a priest—hide the relationship, which I refused to do, or break it off, which definitely is not going to happen. These rules are unrealistic. Priests do not have to be lonely and devoid of female companionship in order to do our jobs. It is archaic, man-made, severely flawed, dare I say warped and unnecessary."

Mumbles and irritated chatter began. Some of the priests looked enraged.

"Fr. Caruso." The elderly bishop coughed into a napkin, balled it tightly into his palm and continued. "Loneliness is a struggle many priests and clergy have faced. It doesn't lessen the seriousness of your actions. Instead of keeping this as a friendship, to help lesson some of that, which is understandable, you became physically affectionate and intimate, according to your own admission, and you do not appear concerned about the ramifications. You are one of our most beloved priests, and I wish you'd talked to someone before taking it this far. Since you don't want a disciplinary hearing and don't wish to stay, we are at the point of no return and must proceed with your removal."

"I warned you, Fr. Caruso." Fr. Kirkpatrick looked solemnly disappointed, hurt indeed. "I, too, wished you'd talked to someone, came to me," the old man's hollowed eyes glossed over, "and admitted you were struggling to the point that you'd do this, go this far. I tried to intervene before this happened. I sat down and spoke to you."

"Yes, I remember, and I appreciated your concern."

"Apparently not..."

"Fr. Kirkpatrick," Dane narrowed his eyes and steepled his hands as he leaned slightly forward, "I respect you, I really do. You are a mentor to me, and I do appreciate that, please believe me. However, because I did not do as you said doesn't mean I am a bad person or didn't appreciate you taking the time to express your concerns to me." He offered a smile. "I would like to say, for the record, that at the time of our discussion, the relationship had not escalated to the level that it is at now.

"I made a conscious decision to do such after weighing all of the implications and how I envision my life to be in the future. I thought about your advice, long and hard. I rolled it over in my mind, everything you said to me, *every word* of it," he paused, "but I have to do what is right for me and," he shook his head, briefly closing eyes, "living like *this,* is not how I wish to continue. God knows I worship Him, and give *all* glory to Him. My religious beliefs are *exactly* the same, except for this one issue. I do not have to sacrifice the joys of being a husband and a father in order to prove to God that I love Him, or that I am faithful. I can love and be faithful to *one* woman on order to prove it, and God would rejoice in that. It's just that simple."

Steel crept in Fr. Kirkpatrick's eyes. Dane surmised this was because of some sort of shame, a sense of failure, due to him in some ways having hand selected Dane to work at his parish. His gut instinct had been correct; Dane was a hit amongst his brothers in the order and the congregation. He did the things others didn't wish to do, simply to help another. He rarely missed a Mass, even when ill, and conducted prayer groups at all times of the day and night. He was dutiful to others and people trusted him and leaned on him. When he'd conduct the sermon, the church would be filled, no seat left empty. He had a way of speaking to people, of reaching down deep, getting into their hearts, as if he, too, had walked a mile in their shoes.

Now, Dane had fallen from grace. He'd done the unthinkable and worst of all, some may confuse his lack of remorse for smugness. He refused to feel something that he actually didn't, and although he knew the politically correct things to say, he wouldn't go there. He would no longer allow *anyone* to pressure him into keeping secrets, or telling lies. The jig was up, game over.

"I can't help that I fell in love. It happened, and quite frankly, I'm a better man for it. I am not the least bit sorry about falling in love with the Church, and *now*, with a woman. Some of you sit in judgement of me, but I believe some of you envy me, too." His statement caused eyes to buck, men to look away in disbelief, and some to cross their arms indignant-ly, as if somehow, looking into *his* eyes would confirm their own struggles with the same dilemma. Prove him right. Likely, he wasn't the only one in there who'd not only fallen in love, but made love to someone, and the hypocrisy sickened him. Yes, he was in the hot seat, but they would continue to burn.

"We will begin the laicization process," the bishop an-nounced, his tone calm and dry. "You must resign all ecclesiastic offices you hold, Fr. Caruso, immediately."

"He will die without his indult…" he heard someone say.

"You are not to teach nor serve at any Catholic schools you were formerly designated. You will be considered a layman from this moment forward. Do you understand me, Fr. Caruso?"

Dane nodded, "Yes, Your Excellency, I do."

"Far too lean. He should be ashamed!" a voice called out. He looked around sharply, trying to see where it derived from.

"Nothing but lust!"

"Quiet! That is enough!" Fr. Kirkpatrick stated. The old man's voice commanded attention, as he loudly shouted out, a burst of emotion no one saw coming. Dane looked at the man. Their eyes locked—and he could sense a shield of protection coming from his mentor. Though he was angry with Dane, and would never say in front of the spectators what was *really* in his heart, that moment, that one declaration, to stop the verbal assault, let Dane know that in spite of it all, the man loved him.

The proceedings continued until finally, Dane left with a written notice that gave him thirty days to find another residence, though he was told verbally to take his time. His heart was heavy. There were so many people he wouldn't see anymore, and he'd been made out to be a pariah to others. He had plans to visit the hospital, and say goodbye one last time to the sick people that relied on his prayers, but with the passing of his dismissal he was prohibited from doing so. There would be rumors, sordid gossip, sympathetic people, and those that were quick to judge. His lack of remorse, he knew, was what caused so many to see him as darn near demonic. He viewed his love for Rhapsody as a sacrament, not a sin.

Wrath was coming; he was expecting it, unflinching. He'd given this so much thought that he knew, deep in his heart, there was no other way for him to be truly happy. He had to choose one lover over another, and he chose *her*.

CHAPTER TWENTY-FIVE

Many weeks later…

"MY NAME IS Dane Caruso and I am a recovering alcoholic, anime addict and fornicating ex-priest. Please don't be alarmed about the controversial anime confession."

The crowd erupted in laughter, clapping loudly as he stood on the vast, creaky stage gripping the microphone. He'd sought a therapist that specialized in transition therapy from the priesthood, and it made a world of difference. In the course of those sessions, the man said he had a gift of humor, and it may be advantageous to use it for a myriad of reasons—one being, Dane enjoyed making people laugh but even more than that, it was another form of therapy for himself. He was able to laugh at himself, and turn it into something even bigger and brighter.

"Two prostitutes were driving around town with a sign on their car that read, 'Two Prostitutes for one hundred dollars.'"

A cop sees 'em and pulls them over, saying they can't do that and if he sees that sign again, they'll be arrested. One of the prostitutes says, 'But that's not fair, there is another man driving around with a sign on his car that says, 'Jesus Saves'. The cop said, 'But that's different. That's religious.' And then he walks away. The next day, the same two prostitutes are out with a different sign; this one says, 'Two Angels Seeking St. Peter, one hundred dollars.'"

The crowd lit up in laughter, amid claps and whistles.

"You know, priests are just like everybody else."

A heckler yelled out, "No you aren't!"

"Yes we are, look; let me give you an example. One day a man was driving down the road and saw a priest trying to hitch a ride. He normally didn't pick up strangers, but felt since it was a priest, he probably should. So the priest gets in, and off they go. A little ways further, he sees a lawyer standing on the side of the road. He immediately sped up to try and hit him, but remembered the priest in his car and swerved, barely missing him. He heard a thud anyway, and panicked. He didn't see anything, and figured it must've been something else and kept going. He looked at the priest and apologized, 'I'm sorry, Father. I almost hit that lawyer.' The priest looked at him and said, 'It's okay, son. I opened my door and got him on the way past.'" The crowd exploded in laughter and applause.

"I gotta girlfriend now," he continued. "Her name is Mary…" A burst of applause rippled through the crowd. "That's not the joke!"

Dane continued the rest of his set, becoming more animated and loose as each joke rolled off his tongue. He felt in his element, and it was great to let off some steam.

"I want to thank all of you for letting me entertain you

tonight here at the Comedy Castle." He sniffed, looked down reflectively at the stage then back out at the audience. As he stood directly under the beam, he turned toward Rhapsody, who sat off to the side of the room on the edge of her chair, cloaked under dark purple shadows and a red, warm glow. She refused to sit up front, didn't want him to become nervous or choke, but she was still visible, and for that, he was thankful.

"I just want to say one more thing before I get off this stage. One of my favorite quotes that embodies my journey in life right now comes from a man by the name of Francois Mauriac. It is: 'To love someone is to see a miracle invisible to others.'" He paused. "That's what I experienced…that is what helped me to get where I am today. Speaking to you all, enjoying this time together. It takes a special person to look beyond your past, and see your true potential. It takes someone devoid of conventional rules, to give someone a chance that society and religious dogma has already written a map for and pigeon-holed.

"It takes someone open minded to love you with all that they have inside of them, regardless of the obstacles and the 'what ifs'. Someone took a chance on me." He stared at Rhapsody, kissing her with his sweet words. She turned away; smiling, blushing, and it warmed his chest with pride. He focused back on the audience. "She saw past my title, my living arrangements, and saw me for me and that is what God does for us; that's what a good, true friend will do for you, and your soul mate, too. I'm not trying to give you guys a sermon, just to tell you to appreciate the people in your life, the ones that love you and would do anything for you. The love of your life will believe in you, even when you don't believe in yourself. Guys, thanks for believing in me and coming out tonight! Goodnight everyone!" Dane threw up his arm, waved goodbye and exited the stage.

A soft applause began, then became louder and louder until some were on their feet, whistling. He could hear it as he rounded the back of the club, and it was music to his ears...

Several weeks later

"Mmmm hmmm." Rhapsody scratched her taupe covered head wrap, digging her nails into the fabric to try to satisfy an unstoppable itch. She smiled at Dane as he rubbed her feet while they lazily enjoyed their Saturday afternoon together. The scent of chicken chili percolated from the stovetop, bubbling, the lid making a light, clanking noise every now and again. "So it's just a six month lease?" She asked as she left to turn the food down, and return right back.

"Yeah, I will take you over there tomorrow." He sighed. "Right now, they are painting it but let me tell you the perks. It is two bedrooms, the master is absolutely huge, exposed brick walls. Really nice. It will suit me just fine."

"Dane, your schedule is crazy now. I don't know how you have time for all of this. Between you going back to school, your volunteer work, the local comedy clubs and your job at the crisis-center, I don't have any idea how you even have time to sleep. Pass me a cookie, please." She grinned as he paused, pulled an Oreo from a Ziploc bag, placed it between his lips and made her lean forward to get it. Before she escaped, he planted a kiss on her lips.

Over the last month, she'd watch the man she adored with all of her being come even more into himself, as if he'd been reborn. He'd moved out of the rectory and found a beautiful apartment in a historic district of Detroit to rent. He loved it so much; he made an offer knowing he couldn't move in until the renovations were complete. Even through all of that, he invested time into their relationship though free time was sparse. Every moment he had, he used wisely and he ensured she was with him, at each opportunity. She stared at him as he applied more pressure on the soles of her feet. She loved how he lit up, discussing his plans for the future. Sometimes he truly didn't know, but he enjoyed the journey of simply living and trying to find out anyhow.

Every day was an adventure, and he thanked God many times daily in her presence, for allowing him the opportunity to go back to school and enter a doctorate/ PhD program so that he could teach philosophy and ethics as a professor. He knew it wouldn't be easy, but he never expected it to be. The job at the crisis call center enabled him to still assist people, and he was darn good at it. From the person thinking of committing suicide, to the teenager upset about a broken heart, he handled them all the same—with empathy, compassion and understanding.

He's such a good person, she kept thinking to herself, over and over. Those eyes of his were far more than just beautiful; they truly were windows to his soul. Crystal clear, blue—an open oasis for the entire world to see. He no longer hid from himself; he embraced every part of his being, the good bits and the parts still in need of development and fine-tuning. She'd never been treated so well in a relationship, and at times, she thought she may be dreaming. She could *trust* this man. There were no worries about who was calling him, if now that he had his 'freedom wings' he was also seeking other female companionship. She knew where his loyalty lied and where his heart trailed and she surely followed.

"…And so, the biggest bathroom has a tub *and* a shower. I wanted the tub for us." He winked at her and gave a naughty grin. Smiling, she reached for her ringing cellphone.

"Hello? Oh, hi Jacob, so great to hear from you. No, I'm just here with Dane, hanging out. Cookin' a little something for our lunch. What's up?…What!…" Dane shot a look at her, raised a questioning eyebrow.

"What is it?" he whispered, gently gripping her baby toe.

Bringing her finger to her mouth, she gestured for him to wait. "Of course! Yes…Yes! Okay, no problem. I will call you back. Thanks!" She disconnected the call, snatched her legs off of her boyfriend's lap, lunged toward him and gripped him by the shoulders. "You aren't going to believe this. I just got a call from an associate of mine, Jacob Reynolds, who works at the Mango."

"The Mango? That little club on Braxton you sing at sometimes?"

"Yes!" she screamed, dashing to the kitchen again, forgetting she'd already turned off the food in her euphoric haste. She returned to the living room practically out of breath, a plastered grin on her face. "Their Friday night group, 'Stairwell', has been invited to perform in Paris in a few months and they want me to go with them! It is for an entire week, all paid! I've always wanted to go to Paris!"

"This is great news, baby." He reached for her, hugging her tightly before releasing her, then placed his warm, soft lips on her cheek. "Is there anything I can do to help?"

"Go with me! Oh, and do you know French? 'Cause I sure as hell don't!" she said, giddy, wringing her hands together.

"Oui, Oui!" he teased, then took her in his grasp once

more, this time kissing her so passionately, she went limp in his arms.

He groaned in her ear as he led her down onto the couch and positioned himself just so, between her thighs. Rhapsody closed her eyes and sighed as he ran his lips over hers, then cupped the side of her neck as he kissed down the front of her chin. She whimpered when he trailed his fingers down the side of her body, ever so slowly, bunching the fabric of her long white shirt. His soft hair brushed against her chin as he explored downward, downward, downward. Rhapsody looked toward the ceiling, happy as can be.

This is bliss…

And then she closed her eyes as his knuckles gripped the sides of her leggings, and a cool breeze soon touched her exposed skin. Panties gone too…thighs parted…

"Mmmm!" Raising her arms, she gripped the armrest behind her.

Soft lips on her wetness…he was taking her down…down…down….

And he wouldn't stop, for several more hours…

"YOU REALLY CAN'T say you'd blame her, I mean, come on Rhapsody!" Dane laughed and shook his head as he held her hand, their steps in sync through shaded paths flanked by trees into open land, under streams of warm sun.

The leaves were turning colors; vibrant green to star burst orange and ruby red. They made their way along the narrow walking trail to the lake, where a few ducks moved about, the place supremely serene.

"Well, I told you what happened. I told her to not talk to

me anymore. Of course Mama intervened," Rhapsody grimaced, "but I've refused her calls and I finally answered, figuring she was calling to apologize. Yeah, right!" she rolled her eyes, "Now that Mom told her I am going to Paris, she wants to be buddy buddy again. Melody has a lot of nerve."

"And this is a surprise, how? You know how she is," he said in a pacifying tone. "And you keep expecting her to change or be different."

Rhapsody shot him a look, then turned to contemplate the matter. "Well, you *did*…"

"I did what?" They stopped walking and faced each other, standing so closely that they were almost stepping atop of each other's feet. Wrapping his arms tightly around her waist, he cinched her to him, fastening the woman so close so she'd never escape.

"*You* changed, is what I was saying. You became different."

"No I didn't. I just became what I *always* was all along."

She nodded and sucked her bottom lip, wrapping her hands around his neck, drawing further into him, as if craving the comfort. He grew warm as she pressed that plush mouth that he so adored onto his, and before long, their tongues danced together as she ran her fingers through the back of his hair.

"I love you so much," he managed, when they finally pulled away from one another. "Do you know that?"

"I suspected it," she teased as he took her hand and led her closer to the lake. "I love you too, Dane. Very much."

They both faced the waving water, hearing the peaceful aquatic sounds, quietly watching two swans make their way across the rippling water from the slightly cool breeze. It was a perfect sixty-seven degrees. The sun still showed occasional favor, warming their frames beneath the shells of the light-weight jackets. After a while, he turned to her, took both of her hands in his, and got in front of her. She looked at him inquisitively.

"Rhapsody, I can't complain. I'm blessed and though things haven't been easy, I really like my life now. I enjoy it. I look forward to it each and every day, and you are the main reason why."

He stared into her beautiful ebony eyes. Flashes of the songbird from high school entered into his mind…moving like in a worn reel of film. He saw her bopping past him, her dog-eared books cradled to her chest.

"You are the song in my heart, and I can't imagine not waking up to it, and going to bed to the sweet music of your spirit each and every night. I need you, Rhapsody. So, because of that, I've come to an important decision. I just hope you feel the same way about it as I do," he shrugged and looked over his shoulder, composed himself as a ball of emotion swelled in his chest, then back at her, "I have no doubt that if you give me this chance, this honor, you won't regret it."

He dropped to one knee and dug in his jacket pocket, feeling a slight throbbing in his head as he battled a bit of scattered nerves. Pausing briefly, he closed his eyes to try to get through the moment. He heard her gasp as he opened his eyes. Though he didn't look up at her face, he watched the breeze move her yoga pants to and fro, and her legs began to shake. The poor thing was rattling like an old Plymouth with a dragging muffler. He glanced back up at her. The sun cut through the trees, blinding a part of her face, and illuminating the other, making her shine like a brand new coin. He removed the oval four carat diamond ring, set in platinum; the sparkle competed with the sun's rays.

"So, I ask you," he said, his voice cracked, his heart beating fast. "I ask you, if you would be my wife, Rhapsody. Will you marry me?"

"Yes, Dane…Oh my God! I wasn't expecting this right now, I really wasn't!" she cried as he got to his feet.

He took her left wrist and slid the ring on her finger, then linked hands with her as they continued their walk in silence— both speechless, caught up in the moment. They tightly embraced, and turned back toward the lake. The two swans floated past, side by side, drifting away until they could no longer be seen…

RHAPSODY CROSSED HER legs and gritted her teeth as she sat on the worn, yellow chair in her mother's living room. The television was on, showing the evening news. Melody re-entered, her lips twisted and a look of disgust across her face as she nonchalantly handed Rhapsody a glass of punch. Taking a sip, Rhapsody glared at the woman as she slumped down in a chair across from her. Meanwhile, their mother was sound asleep in her bedroom.

"So," Melody cast a discerning eye, "what's this about?" She rolled her eyes as her wrist went limp. "When do you call a meeting over Mama's house? You must feel important." She smirked.

"You were late, so I already told her first and now I'm going to have to repeat myself. Trust me, if it weren't for Mama, I wouldn't be telling you a damn thing right now. She *asked* me to."

Melody shrugged. "I had things to do, Rhapsody. Believe it or not, the world doesn't revolve around you," she taunted, using her sister's former words against her.

"So, you're still mad because I said you couldn't go to Paris with me and not to talk to me until you changed your attitude? You know, you are more than welcome to go on your own. I don't owe you *anything*. I'm over your drama, Melody."

Melody's eyes turned to slits. "I never ask you for anything, Rhapsody. You said you were going to Paris, I asked if I could tag along and you said, 'No'. I guess you couldn't wait to try and get me back for some unforeseen injustice you think I did to you."

Rhapsody shook her head and yawned, looked at the television briefly, then back at her sister.

"I didn't call you over here to argue. I called you to tell you that I am getting married. And for the record, I will be spending my honeymoon in Paris. The timing lined up well. Regardless, this is a waste of time. I should've just saved you the trip and me the energy. Next time, I will tell our mother that I can't do this with you, no matter how much she wants us to get along." Slamming the half empty cup down on the coffee table, she got up, threw her army green bag over her shoulder and marched to the front door.

"Wait…wait a minute, Rhapsody," Melody called out, her voice cracking.

Rhapsody stopped and looked over her shoulder, fully expecting to hear more bullshit. Instead, she was met with a somber expression—her sister sitting there, folded up and her face ashen with concern.

"Come back and sit down please, Rhapsody."

Rhapsody hesitated, then made her way back to her chair

and sat erect, on the edge—just in case the next thirty seconds proved she'd get more of the same, she'd make a quick and hasty get-a-way.

"Look," Melody looked down at her folded hands, her perfectly arched brows knitted as she ran her thumb up and down the inside of her hand. "We need to talk…we have a lot of stuff between us, things I didn't want to talk about."

"And why now all of a sudden have you decided to act like an adult? My wedding plans should have had nothing to do with it," Rhapsody snapped.

"It does…because, well, I feel like I may lose you now, so I need to say something. I should have done this a long time ago. You were right about some of the things you said. I have not been good to you, Rhapsody…I know it's true."

Rhapsody wasn't buying it. She wanted to say something smart, something petty, to make Melody hurt the way she'd hurt her so many times, but she rose above it, clutched her arms, fixed her eyes on the woman across from her and kept her lips securely pursed.

"I love you, Rhapsody. I know you may not believe that, but I do. I also worry about you sometimes." Melody looked toward her sister, as if she were waiting to be asked, *'Why?'*

"No, I don't believe that." She rolled her eyes before she could stop herself.

Melody ignored her and continued. "I do, because well, you are very spontaneous. You just do things, you know? You just rush in. A part of me, I guess," she shrugged, "was kind of jealous about that. I never had the nerve to travel all around the world like you, or to let my heart lead me. You dated musicians, talented men with no money."

Rhapsody gritted her teeth and turned away.

So help me God…

"I don't mean it like that!" Melody smiled as Rhapsody shot her a glance. "It's all coming out wrong. Look," she slapped her thigh, "I mean, you dated from the heart. You didn't look out for your future."

This is the improved version of the last statement?

"Melody, here is a little something about me you don't seem to understand. I make my own future. I accept my mistakes and the people that try to get one over are eliminated from my life, period. I wasn't always this way. Let's just tell the truth. You were right when you said I had my head in the clouds. Sometimes I did."

"Well, that's *something* we can agree on then." Melody flaunted a condescending grin.

"I've grown up, I've changed. I used to allow people to stay in my life, people that misused and abused me but that is over," Rhapsody continued, refusing to allow her sister to get her off track with her childish antics. "I know better, I can't allow that to happen anymore. I have to learn from my past, from my mistakes. I've met some great people, I've met some not-so-great people, they all served their purpose. Life is to be lived, and that is what I do."

They shared a moment of silence.

"Yes…life *is* to be lived, and I was planning to go to Paris with you, to try to reconnect with you, Rhapsody, not to get a free trip. That is why I kept calling, but as soon as I said that on the phone, you thought I was trying to get over. I didn't know…I didn't know you had honeymoon plans as well."

Rhapsody looked at her for a moment, trying to put her sister's words on a mental gauge of sincerity. She wasn't sure which way they teetered; that would require further investigation. "At the time, we didn't have honeymoon plans there. Dane hadn't even proposed. Now, we will be spending an additional week there after the concert is over."

"Dane...so I finally get a name." Melody grinned and pointed at her sister, eyes squinting. "I knew you were dating someone all along! Mama held your little secret. You were just actin' different. You smiled more."

"Yes, his name is Dane, and he is my fiancé." Rhapsody couldn't help but smile as the words dripped out of her mouth.

And we have a wedding date. Do you?

But she kept the snide thought inside, instead, trying to be more open to the conversation. Trying not to let old habits rule her.

"Well, tell me about him, what does he do? What does he look like?"

"Before we get into all of that, Melody, I'd rather you finish telling me what you were going to initially. You know, about us and our relationship." Rhapsody lounged back in the chair, holding her knee with folded hands as she glared at the woman dressed from head to toe in a pink jogging suit and little pink diamond stud earrings to match.

Melody sighed and looked at her sister for the longest, no words coming from her mouth.

"Is it really that hard, Melody? Well, I love you very much, okay? I don't understand why we fight all the time, but I can say with one hundred percent certainty that usually it isn't my fault on how this mess gets started."

"Let's not place blame here," Melody interjected.

"Of course you'd say that, being the instigator nine times out of ten." Rhapsody's raised an eyebrow and shook her head in disbelief.

"Do you want to be right? Fine then, Rhapsody, okay." Melody rolled her eyes.

"No, Melody," she said, trying hard to keep her voice down so as not to wake their mother. "What I want is some damn acknowledgement! Some ownership! Some accountability!" She poked her knee with her index finger, driving the point home. "Whenever I have screwed up, and I knew about it or if I didn't, but it was brought to my attention, I'd apologize. I cannot remember the last time you said some messed up shit to me and owned it. I'm tired of it. I want my sister back but it is more important to me to be treated like a human being, than anything else. I won't jump over and through hoops just to get along with you. I won't walk on eggshells. I don't bend over for anyone but I let you get away with far too much. I suppose I trained you on how to treat me. I am still going to be *me*, Melody." She pointed to her chest. "You don't understand how I think, or why I do the things that I do, and that's fine. I'm not asking you to but I do expect for you to treat me how you'd want me to treat *you*!"

The anger, rage and sorrow merged into one, forming into a tight knot that caught in her throat. She tried to keep her bones from jumping in her flesh, to no avail. Her body shook like a vibrating volcano and her mouth brimmed full of lava covered words—hot, molten, ridden with anger. Words that could only bring tears.

"Rhapsody, I'm sorry if anything I've said has hurt your feelings." Her sister's voice broke through the pounding of her own heart. "I could sit here and lie, and say I never meant to hurt your feelings at any time, but we both know that isn't true."

"But why, Melody?!" her voice cracked as she tried to rein herself in. It hurt so badly. Rhapsody knew she was no angel, but when it came to her family, she tried to do right by them.

"I don't know…" Melody looked away, averting eye contact.

"I don't believe that."

Melody shifted in her seat, as if ashamed.

"It's Mama, okay?" Her sister glared back at her and for a split second, Rhapsody was certain her usually stony eyes had glossed over with fresh tears. Before she could confirm, she turned away, again, possibly composing herself, then glanced back her way. "You and Mom had music in common, your singing, the piano. The whole family would talk about you, how great and talented you were. No one said *any*thing about me…" Melody looked down into her lap.

Rhapsody's heart broke a million times over as she listened.

"I didn't have any of that. Mama really loves you, Rhapsody. I'm not saying she doesn't love me, too. I know she does…but…she enjoys her time with you. I know it sounds silly, I sound like a baby, but I can't help how I feel. It has been going on most of our lives, and I resented you for it. It just got to the point that I couldn't take it anymore. It felt like," she shrugged, fidgeting, "it just felt like she favored you over me—like you two had a special bond that I could never touch. I felt like the odd man out. I had to do something to differentiate myself, and in the process, I ended up pushing my sister away." Her bottom lip trembled as she looked down into her lap, scrubbing her palm with her thumb.

"But sometimes we'd get along fine, Melody. Hell, sometimes, it was like we were the best of buddies. This is confusing to me."

"Because, Rhapsody, I'd try…I really would," she said with a wounded expression. "And then I'd get upset again. Mama would be braggin'," she waved her hand dramatically in the air, "'Rhapsody got such 'nd such award, Rhapsody is performing at the playhouse, Rhapsody did this and that, she never talked about me that way…'"

They were silent for a moment, before Melody took a deep breath and continued.

"I know it sounds cliché, but it was me, not you. Yeah, we're different, different as night and day, but I love you." And there it was, a single tear escaped her sister's eye. Before it had a moment to wet her perfectly made-up face, she swiped it away, as if it were an annoying gnat. "I love you, and I admire you. You have guts. I think you're foolish sometimes, but shit, you're brave, a hell of a lot braver than I am." She chuckled. "And look at you…the man is marrying you, making it official. I'm still waiting. Everyone knows Adonis ain't shit."

Rhapsody smiled weakly and tried to form words and thoughts in the electric atmosphere. A breakthrough had been made; what she'd secretly prayed for had finally been granted.

"Melody, you, me, Grandmama may she rest in peace, and Mom, we're all we had. We're all we got! Wasn't anybody else there. We lost our father. You remember him a bit better than I do. We shared clothes, toys and secrets that only sisters would understand. Looking at you was like looking in the mirror. I always wondered, 'What did I do to her to make her hate me so much?' And it haunted me. I mean this from the bottom of my heart. *Whoever* else came into my life and left, I didn't lose sleep over, but you?" Tears brimmed in her eyes now, too. "You were right here, but so far away. I had wondered what I'd done to cause this. I'm glad to know now that it wasn't something I wasn't aware of. You're just an asshole."

They both looked at each other and burst out laughing.

Melody nodded in agreement. "Exactly," she said, doubling over with mirth. "And I want to thank you for telling me that."

"Sorry, but you know it's true, I love you, nonetheless, and thank you for finally talking to me. I'm just glad this is out in the open now."

"Well," Melody said after a pause. "I really am sorry, and I want to start over, okay?" She slowly rose from her chair and walked toward her. Rhapsody looked up at her sister and extended her arms. The two hugged tightly, smiling brightly at each other like two best friends who hadn't seen each other in years. "I love you, girl…"

"I love you too, Melody. So much." She patted her back.

After a while, Melody returned to her seat and wiped her eyes with the back of her hand.

"This doesn't mean I won't still go *in* on you." She winked.

"Oh, I know, and it doesn't mean you won't get it right back."

They both nodded and grinned.

"Now, tell me about Daaaaaaannnnne!" She batted her eyes teasingly.

"Melody, he is unbelievable!" Rhapsody fell back in her chair as if she were awe struck. "He's amazing. I love him *so* much. I don't think I have *ever* been this in love with someone before." Her heart made a flip at the thought of him.

"I can see it all over your face…you got it *bad*. Nose wide open," Melody remarked, crossing her legs. "Okay, chop!

Chop!" She clapped her hands. "Back to what I asked you before. What does he do? What does the damn man look like? Come on, give it to me."

"Right now he is a Crisis Counselor and he is in a double program. He qualified for a program at the University. It is hard, but he is finishing his Masters and PhD simultaneously. He will be teaching at the university, hopefully, after he graduates." She hesitated. "Before that, he was a priest."

Melody's face went from a full-out grin to a look of complete confusion.

"What the hell did you just say? The last part." She twirled her finger her way, as if rotating an invisible bracelet.

"Yes, you heard me right." Rhapsody looked down in her lap, laughing, as she toiled with a loose strand from her light gray knitted shirt. "He was a priest for about eight years."

"Oh my God," Melody said, her mouth agape—this from the kind of woman who scoops up gossip in a single bound. "So, the first thing he does is he goes and finds him a girlfriend after leaving. This is too funny!" She cackled. "Shit, if I were a priest or nun, I'd do the same damn thing."

"Uh, actually, no. He was still a priest when I met him… Well, got reacquainted with him. He actually went to high school with us but he and I never spoke. That school was so big, you may not even remember."

The silence in the room was deafening. Rhapsody was about to ask Melody if she needed help picking up her jaw from the floor.

"Only *you*, Rhapsody!" she finally said as she fell back laughing, her arm hanging lazily off the side of her chair. She laughed so hard, a vein protruded in the side of her neck. "Only *you*! You have brought a priest *down*, single-handedly tore the Catholic Church up! Got that man speakin' in tongues! Shame on you!" she teased, her face turning red.

"I promise you it wasn't like that," Rhapsody protested, trying to stay serious.

Rhapsody went on to tell their love story, in full, giddy detail—from the very beginning. It felt so good to get it all out, to air the dirty laundry that really wasn't as soiled as it appeared. By then, both sisters were huddled on the floor next to one another, the television off and their shoulders pressed together—accomplices, confidantes, just like old times. In that moment, they *truly* looked like sisters, like best friends, their arms intertwined, they eyes reflecting one another—mirror images. Mending and healing had begun, as well as enjoying one another—going back to the basics.

The icing on the cake was the squeaking of their mother's bedroom door right before it closed, and Rhapsody realized the woman had heard the entire exchange. And the sight had probably been just as uplifting to her, more than for them—to see the two of them together, sharing this healing moment in time...

CHAPTER TWENTY-SIX

"RAISE YOUR GLASSES! My brother, the priest, is gettin' married!" Anthony joked, his face twisted into a sarcastic grin, causing all of their friends and family in the house to burst out in laughter. Even their beaming mother turned red and looked down at the recently shampooed butter cream carpet. She'd gotten the house together for the special occasion, taking two weeks to scrub from top to bottom and decorate it just right.

Dane raised his glass of iced sparkling water with a thick slice of lemon inside, while Rhapsody wrapped her arms around his waist and buried her smile into his brown leather bomber jacket.

"And this is the part where Dane's big obnoxious Italian family embarrasses him, in stereotypical fashion!" Joseph, who'd drunk one too many, slurred.

His declaration brought on applause and a wide smile from Rhapsody's mother who sat in a grand chair at the head of dining room table in the Caruso home. Dane's mother had insisted she sit there. It was not an option. It had been predetermined.

Dane carefully placed his glass on the table and wrapped his arms around his fiancée while people continued to laugh, joke and engage one another. He delicately caressed her hands, slowly running his fingers up and down their length. Every now and again, he'd catch a glimpse of Daisy who loitered by the dining room bay window, smiling, but seemingly lost in thought. Her missing husband and children were not unnoticed. It was rare for her to come out without her family, and he could see that something was heavy on the young woman's mind. He'd asked her twice if she was okay and she forced a grin and a nod, telling him she was perfectly fine and simply there to congratulate him on his pending nuptials. He turned back to Joseph, who was now relaying an embarrassing story that he'd begged him not to share.

"And then…" Joseph's eyes narrowed in his beet red face, and the prominent vein in the middle of his forehead strained under the skin. "And then Dane told Mom that he didn't put the pile of steaming crap on the neighbor's steps, that I did it."

"What a crock of shit!" someone screamed, causing loud guffaws.

"And where did he get the crap from? Huh? We didn't have a dog then!" More laughter erupted.

"Dane, you didn't!" Rhapsody laughed as she peeked over his arm. He looked away in shame for he knew, since the incident, that that the story would haunt him for the rest of his life.

"Can you remember Mom's face, Anthony? She was mortified!"

Dane stood a bit taller, grinning. "That kid shouldn't have

stolen my football!" He felt Rhapsody shaking with laughter behind him.

"He was grounded for an entire week. Anthony and I taunted him, telling him what a great time we were having outside playing and all the cool desserts we got after dinner." Joseph counted off his fingers, "Strawberry cookies, chocolate cake, lemon meringue pie, yeah, with the fluffy, home-made whipped cream and Dane's favorite—"

"Pineapple cheesecake, you bastards!" Dane yelled in mock anger. "Joseph kept coming to my door, saying in a creepy voice, 'Weeeeee gooooot cheeeeesecake, booboo boy!'"

The room exploded in more laughter; this time Rhapsody's mother giggled so hard, she had to grab her glass of water from the table for relief.

After a while, the crowd simmered and returned to more mundane conversation as they moseyed around the first floor, drifting in front of the television set to a low volume, as people continued to drink cold beers and offer more congratulations.

Rhapsody left Dane's side when her sister bustled through the door with a shiny yellow gift bag and her new bright green Coach purse on her arm.

"I'm so sorry, everyone! I got caught up at work!" she announced, as if everyone had been stewing over her absence.

Dane immediately turned his attention away from his father and walked swiftly over to his soon-to-be sister in law. Rhapsody took the heavy bag from Melody's arm, and watched her sister flirt shamelessly. Melody gripped his arm and cocked her head, allowing her freshly relaxed, shoulder length tresses to sweep her shoulders. With a broad smile, she flashed her pretty white teeth as she gave him the once over.

"So I finally meet Dane!" She gave him a big hug, then

stood back, holding him by the wrists as she gleamed up at him, all gums showing.

Rhapsody put her hand on her hip and smirked after clearing her throat. Melody shot her a look, winked, and continued on as if her performance was stellar.

"It's nice to finally meet you." she said, her voice airy and extra feminine. A total put on.

"It is a pleasure to meet you as well." Dane smiled at her sincerely. He looked from one to the other. "You two look just alike." He shook Melody's hand. Rhapsody caught how he kept trying to politely break free from her grip. Finally, Melody let go, briskly grabbed Rhapsody's arm and scurried her away toward the steps…

DANE GRINNED, WONDERING how two people could look so alike yet be so different. Yet, he was happy they had reconciled, and that the two shared a much better relationship. Left alone, he looked back into the dining room, searching for his father. He moved through the crowd of people, and finally spotted the old man speaking with his cousin, both holding cold bottles of beer. Close by, his mother was busy clearing the table to set out an assortment of desserts, mints and coffee.

Dane tapped his father's shoulder. "Alright, so before I had to leave, you were telling me how the New York Giants were better than the 49ers," he ribbed, fully expecting his cousin Carlo's horrified expression. Carlo was obsessed with the 49ers, and this was a sure way to stir the pot.

"Dane, stop it! I did not!" His father laughed lightly then louder when he caught his nephew's angry expression. The conversation then turned to random topics until Dane felt a tap on his back.

He turned around. "What's up, babe?" He looked into Daisy's eyes. "Oh, hey sis, what's up?" He placed his hand on her shoulder and felt her body shaking under the purple cotton of her shirt. Bending down to her ear, he whispered, "Let's go somewhere and talk, okay?"

She didn't look up at him, simply nodded and let him take her by the hand out of the room. Rhapsody, Melody and their mother, stood huddled together, laughing away.

"Hey baby," he called out. "I'm going outside for a second. I'll be right back."

Rhapsody nodded and turned back toward her family as he walked out hand in hand with his baby sister.

"SO." THEY SAT on the steps and looked out onto the quiet street, the night air sweet with late summer barbeque aromas, the front yard dotted with leaves that stirred in the breeze. "Are you finally ready to tell me what's going on, Daisy?"

She looked down into her lap. "I'm thinking about leaving Rob. Filing for divorce."

Dane sighed and grabbed her hand, appreciating the quiet of the night.

"I wasn't going to talk to you about this, ruin your engagement party. I'm so happy for you."

"Well, thank you, Daisy. You're not ruining my party."

"Dane, when Dad told us about you leaving the priesthood, do you know what my reaction was?"

"Disgust," he half-teased, causing her to laugh.

She shook her head. "No, I think I was the only one that

thought, 'Finally…finally he is free.' And I envied you."

Dane looked at her contemplatively. He ran a hand across his face, then scratched his neck and gripped her tiny hand a bit tighter.

"Do you…think it's a sin?"

"Do I think what is a sin, Daisy?" he asked inquisitively.

"All of it. Divorce…to be…attracted to…never mind." She turned away, her complexion reddening.

Dane knew if she couldn't even admit the truth to herself, she'd never be able to admit it to anyone else, either. And then of course there were the children to contend with. Divorce with young children is never easy, not for anyone. There'd be lawyers, so much 'what if', so much possible shame and alienation.

"Well." Dane scooted a bit closer to her and wrapped his arm around her waist as a tear fell down her cheek. She quickly wiped it away, keeping her head bent. "I'm not God, Daisy. Now, as far our religion, divorce is not something God wishes to see happen. From a human standpoint, I'm sure there are reasons where it is justifiable, even in His eyes. I'm not even sure I'm the right guy to ask about divorce right now because," he offered a warm smile, "I am admitting that I am on cloud nine and it might skew my views right now, I am newly in love and so a part of me is like—work it out with him, you owe it to the kids, and yourself, but then," he kissed her cheek, causing her to smile, "another part of me is like—yeah, file for divorce. I don't like Rob, I don't like your husband, never have; he never treated you right and he is irresponsible. He's a neglectful father, and he's rude." He shrugged, looked up at the star-studded sky, then back at her. "So is it really fair for me to weigh in on this? Probably not. I'm not objective but then there is the other piece of this puzzle."

He felt her stiffen next to him. She drew her legs closer together.

"I'm the only one that knows the truth still? No one knows about your relationship in college but me?"

She nodded.

"...and when you talk about sin, *which* sin is worse? Living a lie? Lying to yourself and to others about who you really are, or the act itself, you know? I really can't say, Daisy, but I can offer you this. I will love you, no matter *what* your decision is. I love my nieces and nephews and I know that this has been hard for you. You don't want to disappoint anyone, trust me, I get it." He released her hand and rubbed her back affection-ately, comforting her. "Where are you at in all of this?"

She shook her head and folded her hands together. "Dane, I really don't know. I envy your courage to leave it all behind and follow your heart. I don't have those sorts of guts. And now, I've lived a lie, but, I do love my husband, or at least I did. I'm confused. I do know that my feelings, my sexual orientation," she paused, "God it sounds so strange even saying that, but I just tried to ignore it. I've been so unhappy, Dane I don't think I can keep living like this."

They shared a moment of silence.

"How long have you known?" Dane quietly asked.

"Honestly? Since I was about fifteen."

Dane nodded as he reflected over Daisy's behavior as a teenager. Nothing really stuck out as a tell-tale sign, but there were tiny things, *small* things, like a poster of Madonna on her wall. That was common, nothing alarming, but there was a lipstick stain mark right over Madonna's lips. No one seemed to notice or say anything, but Dane had seen it. He'd noticed.

They sat there for several minutes, not speaking, just shar-ing the space as she sorted through the pain and denial, all in her head.

Dane took her hand and gripped it, and then a bit tighter. He briefly looked back at the house, the lights dancing on the inside from people walking past the windows, conversations brewing, muffled laughter coming through the closed door and windows.

"Daisy, you have to be *you*. Nothing will ever turn out how you want it until you are true to yourself. Whether that is simply admitting the truth to yourself once and for all, and being proud to be that person and leaving it at that—or delving deeper where you actually change your marital status and all that entails, that is entirely up to you. But the first part to being okay lies in *here*," he pointed to her heart as she slowly lifted her head and made eye contact with him. "It's knowing who you are and being at peace with it. That's all. It's hard, I understand that, but we create the most pain for ourselves when we deny what is going on, deep in our hearts."

Moments later, they stood, and he gasped when she suddenly gripped him and hugged him tight. Returning her embrace, he placed his chin on the top of her head, and lightly swayed with her.

"I have a lot to think about, but you helped. Thanks," came her muffled reply as she smooshed her face into the front of his jacket, still gripping him with all of her might.

"You do have a lot to think about, but never be ashamed to love yourself, Daisy. God is our judge and God is about love, so you must not hate yourself, even if that self-love is *not* well received by others. God gave us free will, so don't let others govern over you where their own fears and feelings become *your* God. No one deserves that position in your life, *no one.*"

Tears streaming freely down her face as she brought her

hands to his chest, and gripped the leather in her hands. He felt nothing but love and pity for her circumstances. Though the small woman had been a thorn in his side for most of their childhood and adult years, he knew the little girl deep down inside of her, and she was lovable and gifted. She'd been living a lie, and it ate her up alive, turned her into a calloused, sarcastic and at times mean-spirited individual—all because she didn't want to let their parents down, God to despise her, and the world to judge her. Her eyes, brimming with emotion, told him so much.

Thank you for keeping my secret all of these years…

Thank you for loving me in spite of how I've treated you over the years…

Thank you for giving me the courage to explore the true me, again…

"And I want to tell you, Dane," she finally said, "that I'm sorry…"

No more words were needed to bridge the gap between them. Her spirit reached out to his at that moment, and he thanked her for it. She didn't need to cut herself open and bleed at his feet. The 'sorry' was for many years of verbal sword fighting, knit picking and angst. Daisy was his own personal 'Melody', and he understood the creature on a basic level—she was a little dog with a big bark, and her bite hurt her more than anyone else. Her core was good, but she'd wrapped it in protective clothing to keep the bad stuff away. But if one is wrapped too tightly, the bricks on their wall too high and the locks on their door too complex, nothing bad gets in—their mission has been accomplished—but nothing good can get through, *either…*

CHAPTER TWENTY-SEVEN

"YOU ARE A selfish, selfish, man, Mr. Caruso!" Rhapsody turned the thick, glossy pages of the wedding magazine and made herself comfortable on the brand, spanking new China red sofa. A garish thing—loud, whimsical and sexy— and he'd allowed her to move the monstrosity inside of his home until they relocated into their own house together, after the wedding.

"So, we are down to two houses now and I just need you to make a decision, Rhapsody. I know decisiveness is not your forte, but time is ticking." He tapped his wrist, pretending his watch was there.

"Selfish!" Rhapsody hissed in mock indignation as she flipped to another page featuring sage and salmon napkin holders. "I don't like this color combination. This is what Melody said I should have. She is ridiculous. I'm not doing it." She sneered at the glossy photo.

"Don't change the topic. I'm not selfish for not wanting

you to go on your little jaunt tonight and stay here with me for some evening delights." He sat across from her, running his hand across his chest, bunching the thin fabric of his white V-neck shirt.

"You see." She peered at him from over the top of the magazine as she shifted onto her side. "This is what happens when a full blooded male goes without sex this long and finally gets a woman. You just lose your mind!" She snapped her fingers, trying to keep the smile on her face to a minimum. "I am not your sex slave, Dane. I should be free to walk about the cabin," she teased as she pulled her shirt further down, exposing her ample bosom.

"What a load of bull! You are the one that has been after *me* the last two or three times." He laughed as he pointed an accusing finger at her. "I can cite examples if you wish...*detailed* examples."

"I plead the fifth," she said calmly as she turned another page.

Dane shoved his hands in his pockets, suddenly serious. "Rhapsody, I need to talk to you about something."

She looked up at him. "Yes, what is it?" she asked as she set the magazine down beside her.

"Look, you know I have no issue with our religious differences. Matter of fact, it has helped me as a person. I still believe how I believe, however, and as I've told you many times, I don't want you to change to be like me. I'd only want you to become Catholic if you wanted to."

"Yes, I understand that."

"Well, there is one thing though, honey." He sighed. "I really want to get married in a Catholic church. I want to have a traditional Catholic wedding. I'm not asking you to attend church with me every Sunday or anything like that, but—"

"Dane—"

"I just needed you to know that—"

"Dane—"

"This is really important to me and—"

"Dane!" Rhapsody yelled, then burst out laughing. "You're not listening to me, sweetheart. I've been trying to tell you that that is fine, and I have absolutely no issue with it. I know who I am marrying, give me more credit than that. Someone like you doesn't suddenly lose their values and beliefs simply because they've fallen in love. You are just being true to yourself, and how could I expect you to be anyone but you? That's why I love you."

"Well," he said, smiling, "that was much easier than I thought it would be. Um, one more thing."

"Yes?" she asked, her eyebrow raised.

"Since you've agreed to this, I'd like us to go to classes. It is called a Pre-Cana course."

"What's that?" She tucked her feet beneath herself and listened intently.

"Well, they are premarital courses that cover topics like conflict resolution, finances, couple prayer and sexual expectations. Those are just to name a few."

"So, it is like regular premarital counseling, basically?"

"Well," he shrugged, "yes, that is about right, but there is a difference from the standpoint that it focuses on Catholicism and emphasizes some of the issues that are important to us. For instance, birth control may be brought up. We will probably be asked about family planning and what we intend to do about it. Now, not all of us are in agreement about birth control but most Catholics that I know believe it is not God's will for us to utilize things such as birth control pills and condoms to prevent pregnancies. Life is precious and intercourse is for the bonding between husband and wife, as well as procreation. We rely on what we call 'natural family planning', the rhythm method, to help control how large we want our families to be."

He didn't miss the smirk on her face. "You know that doesn't work for all families, right? The woman's period could be irregular, and other things could go wrong, too."

"Well then, that's God's will, in my opinion, Rhapsody. If a pregnancy occurs that we may have been trying to avoid, then to me, it just means that child was meant to be here. I am not going to set up a barrier to stop them from being conceived. Now, obviously, you have some concerns about this. I wasn't trying to turn this into a discussion about birth control, but sure—we can talk about it, we should. I need to hear what your concerns are, and why, so we can work through this. We should have talked about this a long time ago actually and this is a prime example as to why we need this counseling, honey."

He sat down next to her, took her hand in his. Her affectionate gaze settled on him.

"I agree. It's kind of like we've been overwhelmed by so many other things, we haven't had all the discussions we need to have."

"Well, yeah, and there was a lot going on. We've talked about a lot of things, that's good, but I think we may have been distracted by everything going on within and outside of our relationship, *due* to our relationship, we didn't address some issues in an effort for resolution."

"Right, I can see that now." She sighed. "We seem to have a sense of how the other feels, so I suppose that left a sense of comfort, like, I knew you wanted a lot of children, I could sense it, but we never spoke about it. I also didn't know you felt this strongly about birth control but I had a suspicion you didn't want me on it."

"Right. We are in tune with one another, and that is what has carried us this far but it may not be enough to avoid all the pitfalls. That is where talking more specifically about it and getting Pre-Cana courses comes into play. Let's look at this for a minute."

"I'm all ears."

He gathered his thoughts while drawing lazy circles with his thumb on the back of her hand.

"I have been away from dating and relationships for a long time prior to you. That left me a little clumsy in that regard. We fell in love with one another, and those emotions took over. Because of our unusual start, we didn't do what most other couples do, or should do, which is talk all of this stuff out. We are from different faiths and belief systems. We are also an interracial couple, so with all of that, we definitely need to get some things ironed out, come to some concrete understandings, some agreements...like the whole family planning issue."

"Well, I tell you one thing." She smiled up at him. "My suspicions about your feelings were obviously right regarding that and this explains that strange face you made that time."

"What strange face?" He frowned.

"The one you made during the first time we made love when I told you I was on birth control."

He grinned and briefly looked away. "I guess...I know it seemed hypocritical, but yeah, it bothered me. I didn't want you to feel like I was trying to boss you around or anything like that and I didn't feel like I was in any position to talk about my beliefs when I was clearly going against them at that moment. I wanted you in *that* way, so" he shrugged, "it just didn't seem appropriate for me to say anything right then."

"I can respect that. We will definitely need to discuss this more, Dane. I don't want to take a chance on only using the rhythm method, especially with as active as we are, and you don't want to wear condoms or for me to stay on the pill so we need to come to some sort of resolution."

Dane nodded in agreement.

"Well, since we are discussing this, let's just jump right in and get it out there. How many children *do* you want? I know we both would like kids, we discussed this beforehand, but we really never got specific. So that there are no surprises, throw a number out there."

"Two."

"Two?! That's it?!"

Rhapsody laughed. "Dane, something told me you'd try to turn me into some one-woman nursery. How many did you have in mind?"

"Five, maybe six."

"Oh hell, no!" She cackled.

"Okay, well let's come to a compromise." He crossed his arms. "What is your counter offer?" his eyes twinkling.

Rhapsody mulled it over for a few seconds. "I tell you what, I can give you three and a pet. Deal?"

"A pet?" He snickered. "Three? Okay, deal. You may change your mind and want more though, you never know," he said optimistically.

Rhapsody shook her head. "I might, but I doubt it. I have no uncertainty that you'll conveniently forget about this discussion years from now and try to talk me into more."

"Now it is my turn to plead the fifth." He smiled. "Now, regarding the classes, they usually last for six months, but we are getting married in three. I have spoken to an older friend of mine however, who is also a priest. He is a really good guy, has been a priest for over twenty years, and he is willing to help us out here since I told him that the honeymoon was already booked. He will also marry us. I think you will really like Fr. Jones. I explained our situation, he understands it completely. He knows you are not Catholic. We will, however, have to have three months of post-marital counseling to make up for the missed ones. That was our deal. Is that fine?"

"Of course it is, and I think it is a good idea, Dane. I'm actually happy that you suggested this. It surely can't hurt. Pre-marital counseling is always a good idea in my book. I want this marriage to work, I want it to last. I love you."

"I want the same, and I love you too, sweetie." His heart swelled. "Okay, great. I will give Fr. Jones a call. He is over at St. Geneviève-St. Maurice. He was holding the wedding date for us, just in case. It is a nice church, Rhapsody, and he is looking forward to helping us."

"Is that the church over there on Jamison?"

"That's the one."

"Okay, I know where you are talking about. I am glad you finally said something! I wanted to get the invitations made next week and we still hadn't come up with a venue. I'm glad that's settled."

"Well," he exhaled, his heart soaring, "this is a big relief."

Unable to sit still, he got back out and paced the room, hands in his pockets. Rhapsody picked her magazine back up and flipped through a few pages. She made a face as if smelling something rancid and rotten. "You ought to see this dress! Now who in their right mind would think this is a nice wedding dress?!" She turned the magazine around to show him, stirring the vanilla candle scented air. "It looks like a big, cheap white napkin from some fast food joint that has been wrapped around her body. Check out the price tag, Dane! They want over twenty grand for a dress that should have 'Denny's' written across it. This white wedding dress mess is for the birds. I want a black dress, or red."

Before he had a chance to fully view the gown that caused her such dismay, she snatched the magazine back around, licked her finger, and turned another page. Her expression softened when she looked at something apparently more to her liking, then the phone rang.

He picked up. "Hello...yes, this is he..." Rhapsody kept her nose deep in the magazine. He snapped his fingers, garnering her attention. "Yes, yes, of course...just a moment, please. No, you aren't interrupting anything."

Rhapsody's loosely wrapped teal and gold scarf unraveled when she tilted her head in curiosity. She tossed her magazine on the couch and began the artistic process of retying her hair wrap.

"Babe, can you put the phone down after I get in the bedroom please?"

She nodded, a slight look of bewilderment on her face. Dane entered the master suite and closed the bedroom door behind him. Taking a deep breath, he made his way over to the phone and picked it up. He waited a few seconds, then heard Rhapsody hang it up. He gripped the black receiver and sat down at the foot of his king-sized bed.

"I know you're probably surprised," Fr. Kirkpatrick offered with a nervous chuckle. "But, I'd been meaning to contact you sooner."

"Well, yes, I'm a little surprised right now."

Dane cleared his throat and tried to choose his words carefully. It was almost unheard of, under the circumstances, for such a situation to occur. Fr. Kirkpatrick had been cordial to him during his last days at the rectory, even offered a hearty handshake, but no soft goodbyes, hugs or pleasantries beyond the 'hello' and 'good morning' were exchanged. Matter of fact, the man had been a bit withdrawn, as if he was unable to even look Dane in the eye at times.

Dane had gone to his office, on his last day, only to find that Fr. Kirkpatrick was unwilling to open his door, though he knew the man was inside.

His heart flooded as he felt anxiety over the phone, the fear of a potential show-down. Maybe the man was calling to see if Dane was still sure about his decision—perhaps thinking that possibly now, he had gotten his 'carnal lust' out of the way. Dane's imagination soared as silence steeped between them.

"I am surprised you were home. Your uh, cell phone number has changed I see. I called that first, then I realized it was no longer your number once someone else answered. I contacted Fr. Daniels who I'd heard had seen you not too long ago, and he had a current number for you."

Boy, word gets around fast.

"I see, okay…" Dane ran his hand along his jeans, wanting the man to just spit it out, come clean, say what he called to say so they could move on with their lives.

"I heard you were getting married, Dane." Fr. Kirkpatrick cleared his throat and coughed. The older man always paused after his rough coughing spells, so he gave him space and waited patiently. "Congratulations."

"Thank you, Fr. Kirkpatrick."

I would have liked for you to marry us, but that obviously will not happen.

Dane bit down on the sudden anger sweltering inside of him.

Fr. Kirkpatrick paused, cleared his throat again.

"I'm calling because, well, I wanted to tell you something that I should have told you before you left."

The bedroom door slowly swung open and Rhapsody stuck her head in.

She smiled at him, mouthing, "Is everything okay?"

He smiled back, winked and mouthed back, "Yes."

She nodded and closed the door behind her.

"Okay, go right ahead," Dane offered as he reached down and slid his sneakers off and let them thud on the floor. Then he lay back on the bed, slid a hand under his head and settled onto the comfort of the caramel and ivory duvet.

"When I saw your lady friend attend the church that after-noon, I noticed her from the back of the room." He sniffed. "It was crowded that Sunday. It always was when you'd speak, so we'd put in the previous Sunday's announcements that you'd be speaking, sure of a good turnout. Regardless of that, I notice new visitors in the crowded sanctuary because I like to take the time later to introduce myself and invite them to return. I knew I hadn't seen her before."

Dane continued to listen, his interest piqued.

"Before you spoke to her, when you reached the end of the sermon, I noticed she began to move in her seat, and I saw how she looked at you, a familiar look, like she knew you, and she had a big grin on her face." He coughed. "She was in the back of the church, but she looked at you like the sun rose and set on you." He paused. "Then, as people were leaving, she approached you and I saw how you looked at her in turn, Dane." his voice dropped a few octaves, "…that's when I knew without a doubt, that she was the woman the others were speaking about, the one that you had been seeing. I saw the look on your face, and I knew she wasn't *just* a friend. I knew from the way you looked into her eyes that you were in love with her, possibly even before *you knew*, of that, I'm not sure."

Dane chewed his inner jaw, hanging onto every utterance from the man. His muscles tightened then relaxed as he tried in vain to understand where the conversation was going. He was growing impatient, but his interest urged him to stay the course and not interrupt.

"In any case, I watched you and knew that you were in deep. You weren't doing or saying anything in particular, it was just the way you two looked at one another and…you held her gaze a bit longer, and touched her a bit more. I *knew* that look so…I took matters in my own hands to try and address the whole situation with you."

"Yes," Dane said blandly, "I remember the talk at the mall, Fr. Kirkpatrick. Well, that is all water under the bridge now." He'd had about enough, so he sat up and scratched his head, ready to get the conversation over with. It appeared to him that the man hadn't accepted things had changed, *he'd* changed, and he was not going to offer any flowers at the funeral of his priesthood.

"Yes, it is water under the bridge but I want you to know something. I was *you*, Dane. I was you, in 1989."

Dane's throat felt itchy, as if he'd eaten a walnut and fragments of it refused to be swallowed, irritating his pallet on its scratchy way down.

"My wife had been dead for years and I was deeply entrenched in the Church out of duty, because my heart followed the calling and it was a welcome reprieve. Then, this woman came, a widow, and I looked at her and she stopped my heart." He paused. "She was one of the most beautiful women I'd ever seen, about five years my junior, but had the heart of a child and the mind of a wise person. She was witty, faithful, loved God, and she was in a world of pain. She came to me for counseling, and we fell in love, Dane...we fell madly in love, and I was so ashamed." The man's deep voice rattled.

Dane stood now, his mouth pressed to the receiver, so close, he was afraid Fr. Kirkpatrick would hear him breathing more loudly than usual. Emotions traveled over the line like fresh wounds, like a new coat of paint right over the old man's beating heart.

"I prayed and prayed, Dane. I prayed to God to please deliver me from the feelings."

I'd done the same, but God knew I really didn't mean it...

"He didn't, Dane. The feelings stayed so I packed my things and left. I left that parish without another word to her and started fresh at another church. Many years passed, but the problem wasn't solved. Moving away didn't make me stop loving her. I felt terrible, Dane. Not for falling in love, but for the way I left things with her. I loved her, and she loved me."

The silence stretched between them for a while.

"We didn't take the relationship to a physical level, beyond kissing, though it was tempting, but my heart was wrapped around hers so tightly that we were killing each other. I was mortified because I also felt like in some way I was cheating on my late wife. I wrote this special woman poetry, beautiful words from my soul." His voice trembled. "I told her things I hadn't told another person on the planet. We confided our deepest secrets."

This sounds all too familiar...

Dane knew exactly what the poor man was talking about—that need to purge oneself into the world of your soulmate, to be cleansed and purified, through and through.

"And I just left because I knew I'd have to choose between the Church and her, and I chose the Church, Dane."

Was it his imagination or was Fr. Kirkpatrick crying? The way the man's voice shook—he'd never heard him that distraught, so sad and sullen.

"I'm sorry for your pain," Dane offered. "I suppose you made the choice that was right for you, Fr. Kirkpatrick. We chose differently, for the same situation, and neither of us is right or wrong, we just made the decisions that made sense to us, that would lead us to where we felt God was taking us." He sighed, still trying to take it all in.

"That's just the thing. To this day, I don't know if I made the right choice, Dane. I did what I thought I was *supposed* to do...but I'll never know now for certain." He cleared his throat and continued. "So, when I told you to not continue to see this woman, I realize now, it wasn't just out of me looking out for you, as I convinced myself at the time. No, it was because I was reliving history through *you*, and it scared me. A part of me smiled when I saw that meeting notice to the bishop Thayer and myself! I smiled, Dane! I knew that you too, were ready to make a choice. I knew in my heart what you were about to do, and I knew you'd get what I never got. A second chance at love!"

And then, the tears flowed on the other end of the phone. Fr. Kirkpatrick was not an emotional man, and this tore at his heart, reached down to his center and pulled and tugged on it for dear life.

"Before you even uttered a word," he kept going, his voice trembling, "I figured out what that meeting was about. Dane, you were leaving us to go follow your heart, because the heart wants, what the heart wants! I could see the distance in your eyes, from days before, weeks actually. You were already disconnecting, just going through the motions. You'd made peace with yourself and your decision, and you were respect-ful, but strong, and adamant! You went on, helping others, carrying out your duties, but you had a new peace about you— you glowed. You didn't choose her over the Church; you chose love over the parish. God bless you, young man, my dear grandson, and God bless your new bride!"

And just like that, the phone call ended…

Dane just sat there, his world spinning. No wonder Fr. Kirkpatrick had protected him in the meeting. He'd been in his same shoes. It all made sense now, the way the man was paying close attention to him, looking for the signs, noticing things others would have easily dismissed. Like the day in the church garden when he'd seen them having lunch, his expres-sion grave. But now Dane realized the man wasn't angry with him, he was simply sad. Through him, he'd seen the second chance at love lived out right before his old, tired eyes, and it made all those aged feelings resurface, as if they were brand new. Pain rekindled, remembered, lest he forget, like the host dipped in Jesus' blood for the Holy Communion. In that man's eyes lived great sadness, which he'd mistaken as a nasty glare. He'd meant no harm to Dane, he simply wished he could do it all over again too, and have a second chance at love…

RHAPSODY LEANED AGAINST the off-white barricade of the small hallway in the church. Her white, form fitting, mermaid-style long gown with a sky blue sash wrapped around the waist was a sight to behold. She'd paired it with the perfect mixture of sensuality, modernity and playfulness. She pushed the lacey fringe from her veil away from her eyes, and continued to daydream. The bride-to-be had forfeited the notion of a blood red dress, though Dane hadn't necessarily spoken against the idea. However, his raised brow gave away his opinion loud and clear. Regardless, she loved that he hadn't tried to talk her out of it, but her mother sure did and she just so happened to fall in love with the damned white thing, hanging there all pretty, dazzling, making her swoon in the tiny bridal shop.

Melody kept running around, barking at everyone and telling them who was supposed to be where and how it wasn't too late for a few of the bridesmaids to be cut out of the wedding. And she meant it. She'd given the photographer a few choice words as well once she discovered him outside the church taking a drag off his cigarette, loitering a bit too long while everyone waited to take preliminary photos. Her voice carried, too, but sounded so comical, causing Rhapsody to chuckle versus become annoyed.

Rhapsody tapped her foot; the satin light blue slipper shined under the light as she waited anxiously for the whole ordeal to be over with. She was looking forward to the marriage, not the ceremony, although she didn't mind the big party that was soon to follow. But most of all, she just wanted Dane in her arms, forever. They'd played an emotional cat and mouse game, and though it was necessary and unavoidable, she was simply happy to finally have her prize. The night beforehand, she could barely sleep as the butterflies multiplied in her stomach. She hadn't felt that giddy since she had sung the first time in front of a huge audience, garnering standing ovations. The exhilaration and momentum of the day could barely be captured. It felt like a blur, and she wobbled a bit, feeling restless and a little nauseous as she wrung her hands and twisted and turned with anxiety.

This was it. She was getting married. Her sister's voice boomed in the background as she stood by a side door of the church dining hall entrance, desperately needing a moment alone and some fresh air. The days got shorter as the weeks migrated further into the season; Autumn was waving her goodbyes while the winter knocked on the proverbial door. They'd been lucky that day to get a high in the 50s, and for Michigan, that was considered a real treat.

She startled when she heard his voice. It was faint, a distance away, but she knew that laugh, and it instantly calmed her. Soon, Melody was standing beside her, her chest heaving and hoing as she gripped her clipboard. Rhapsody looked at her and burst out laughing.

"Girl, I should have never agreed to let you plan my wedding!" Rhapsody shook her head in disbelief. "I fired the other lady because you insisted on doing it, and now look at you? About to hyperventilate and fall the hell apart, blood pressure probably sky high."

Melody punched her sister affectionately in the shoulder and burst out laughing.

"These women don't know who they are dealin' with!" She puffed, putting her hand on her hip. "Your little friend Tyra decided she needed to eat some chicken wings before she walks down the damn aisle in a light blue dress with a plunging neckline! Really?! Where do they do that at?!"

Rhapsody laughed and watched the trees sway from the light wind. "I heard Dane speaking. Is he around here still?"

"He was, I sent him away. He tried to act brand new, like he didn't know you were in the vicinity. It has been a hell of a task keeping you two out of each other's vantage point." Suddenly, Melody's head snapped to the right. "Hey!" She clapped her hands loudly. "That table doesn't belong there!"

She stormed off, her bouncy curls swinging with each stomp as she made her way toward two men with a look of total fear on their faces. Rhapsody grinned and turned back out the doorway.

Sighing, she slipped into a daydream, one filled with warm kisses from Dane's lips all over her body...

CHAPTER TWENTY-EIGHT

"COME ON, MAN!" Anthony barked from the full parking lot, almost no spaces left. Boasting arched ceilings and stained glass, the St. Genevieve and St. Maurice Church was a gorgeous setting for such an occasion. Members of their family from all over the country, even their Great Aunt who was ailing, came to celebrate the special day. Regardless, Dane kept close to his brothers. For once, he needed their support instead of the other way around.

"I am! Shut your pie hole. I had to get Dane's cufflinks. He left them in the car."

"Fine, hurry up." Anthony twisted his lips as he adjusted his necktie. "Stop wasting time, we need to get back to him before he passes out," he said, laughing.

"He did look kind of out of it, didn't he?" Joseph smiled as the two brothers approached Dane, who stood in the near distance.

"I can hear you two, you know!" Dane called out with a

sheepish grin. He danced around and jumped on the spot, as if needing to go the restroom.

Joseph tapped his shoulder and handed him the cufflinks. "You got ants in your pants? What's going on?"

"It's a nervous habit to burn off extra energy."

"Well, stop it, it looks weird!" Anthony teased as he eyed himself in a nearby window. "So, we're just going to stand out here, huh? This is stupid. I'm thirsty. Why can't we go back inside?"

"Because my crazy sister-in-law said I almost ran into Rhapsody too many times, and she wants to make sure I don't see her before the wedding. So I was forced to come out here."

"Oh, who cares! It is getting a little cold out here, let's go in." Anthony pushed past his two brothers and reached for the double doors.

"What do you think you're doing?" Melody hollered as she stood there like a linebacker, the trusty clipboard in hand and a look so heinous and menacing, it would cause a rabid dog to gallop away and hide.

Anthony stared back at his brothers, disbelief on his face. Dane smirked while Joseph snickered.

"...I guess nothing..." Dane caught a quick glimpse of Margie and the children walking between the back pews through the stingy slice of open door.

Wow. She came.

"That's *right*. Now stand back. I will come get you when it's time." And with that, Melody snatched the doors closed them in his face with a loud thud.

"Are you sure she and Rhapsody are related?" Anthony snarled as he walked back up to the duo. "What a bi—"

"Don't say it!" Dane cackled. "Come on, I know she is hard to deal with, but I don't want anything disparaging said about her, just be cool, okay?"

"What? What kinda cockamamie bullshit is *this?!* You're not a priest anymore, so why do you care if I call her what she is?" Anthony smirked. "Rhapsody is fun, laid-back and sweet. Her sister is—"

"Just your type!" Joseph ribbed. "You need someone like her, someone that could keep you in your place! Keep you in line. Make you grow up."

"There are too many people milling about out here." Dane looked around at all the parked cars of their friends and relatives who were already seated inside, minus a few stragglers who came intermittently and tapped him on his back on their way inside. "I just don't want anyone overhearing you call her that. We are all family now, so we just need to accept the good, the bad, and the—"

"Bitchy!" Anthony spat as he lifted his eye toward Dane, then back at Joseph, "And it would be a cold day in hell when I'd get down with a woman like Melody."

"Ahhh, you protest too much," Joseph teased, tapping Anthony on the shoulder.

Just then, the doors slowly opened back up. Melody stood there in her form-fitting gown, her hand on her hip. "Alright gentlemen, I have everyone lined up. You're on!"

"OH MY GOD." Dane's eyes glossed. A woman with a golden voice sung the 'Ava Maria.'

He contemplated wiping the darn wet things away before they dripped down his face, ruining the calm he'd worked so hard to obtain in the last ten minutes, but he lost his cool. Rhapsody practically floated down the aisle, hanging on to her uncle's arm. The flash of cameras continued and the sniffling from Rhapsody's mother made his heart thump. All so heartfelt, emotional, and it blended in with Daisy's tears of joy on their behalf.

"Thank you, God," he whispered, his lips trembling. He felt himself fall apart, wanting to kneel down at her feet as soon as she stepped onto the platform. Fr. Jones stood there proudly, holding the Bible in front of him and waiting for everyone to take their seats.

After a few words, two short prayers and the candle lighting took place, their vows were exchanged. The ceremony was quiet and seriousness loomed in the air. No one said a peep as the two gathered on their knees in prayer before the priest. Dane so appreciated this. He was certain that Rhapsody had no idea how much this meant to him. During their counseling, not only was she respectful, she remained open-minded and discovered that Fr. Jones was able to speak to her about their faith in a way that he hadn't. He wasn't convinced she'd be baptized in the Catholic Church, and he was fine with that, but he knew she had an even greater respect for his beliefs than she had previously. She was now prone to ask even more profound questions.

Shortly, they gathered to their feet to recite their vows.

"I, Dane Caruso, take you, Rhapsody Thomason, for my wedded wife, I promise to be true to you in good times and in bad, in sickness and in health. I will love and honor you all the days of my life."

"I, Rhapsody Thomason, take you, Dane Caruso, for my wedded husband, I promise to be true to you in good times and in bad, in sickness and in health. I will love and honor you all the days of my life."

He wanted to kiss her so badly, but he resisted as the priest began to speak again. Soon, the wedding drew to a close. He was so proud of her. His wife had done everything as if she'd been raised in the Catholic Church as well, and it touched him in the deepest part of him that she'd done all of this for him, stating it was a small sacrifice. He'd *never* forget this, not simply the day, but everything up until this point and what it signified. He knew in his heart without a shadow of a doubt, that this woman was brought into his life to be with him at this very moment—in holy matrimony.

Suddenly, the lights flickered on and off. People looked around murmuring amongst themselves.

Hmmm, maybe a storm is coming. The weather had promised to be clear though.

In a matter of moments, Dane was instructed to kiss his bride. He turned to her and carefully lifted her veil from her face, exposing the features he coveted.

My God, she is so beautiful...

He placed his hand at the side of her face, slightly bent to reach her lips, closed his eyes and placed a delicate, soft, sweet kiss on her lips. When he stepped slightly away from her, he could see the tears rimming the bottom of her eyes. He quickly turned away, trying to avoid being choked up as well. But he couldn't stay away from her glance long for he looked back at her, showing his joy with a bright smile, and before anything could be said, he whispered, "We did it, baby...we made it!"

The wedding reception...

RHAPSODY LOOKED OUT into the crowd, smiled and waved, her grin probably as large as her mother's, who had a beam on her face that would light up a whole planet. It was time she unwrap a little surprise she had in store for her new husband. As the people mulled about, drinks in hand, chatter high under the large, sparkling chandelier and children flocking close to the chocolate fountain, she decided now was as good a time as any.

"Attention, everyone!" called out the D.J. as he spoke into the microphone, and a semi-inebriated Melody clanked her fork against her glass to help usher attention toward her sister. "We have a special treat for you, tonight. The bride, Rhapsody Caruso, would like to sing a song for her new husband, Dane, so let's give her a round of applause!"

Their friends and family clapped loudly as she took front stage and center, leaving a look of surprise on Dane's face. He stood close by his brothers, the three in a small football type huddle, his broad shoulders bumping into Joseph's while he held a wine glass filled with water in his hand.

Rhapsody cleared her throat, and then the music began to play...

HE HAD NO idea what she had planned. Rhapsody kept the reception plans a secret for the most part. She'd allowed him to have the wedding he so needed, and he, in turn, allowed her to have the reception party that she desired. He looked forward to see what she'd had up her sleeve and now, his curiosity was getting the best of him. His eyes focused on two women, both dressed similarly in blue pants suits with silver accents, who headed toward the platform with microphones, along with three musicians.

"Dane." Rhapsody breathed in and out, nervous, emotional. "When I speak, you know sometimes the words come out jumbled. Occasionally I find it hard to express myself to you."

"No, you pretty much say exactly what you think, each and every time, and your feelings are quite clear." And he was serious. This caused an uproar of laughter. Rhapsody smirked and rolled her eyes.

"Anyway, smarty." More laughter came through from the seated family and friends. "When I sing though, everything, at least for me, feels crystal clear."

Dane nodded in understanding.

"So, I want to sing you a song that I love, that reminds me of how I feel about you. The lyrics are simple, but, they sum it up so well."

On the floor near the D.J.'s set-up, white petals strewn about with light blue ribbons made a tapestry of beauty across the platform. He looked at her, catching the first notes from the instruments playing, clean and pure.

"I Love Me Some Him…" she began, singing Toni Braxton's song while the two women joined in, singing the background vocals.

Dane chuckled lightly with others around him as he heard someone shout, "Sing it, girl! You love you some him! Yes ya do!"

Rhapsody smiled and slowly swayed back and forth, the ceiling lights catching the glimmer in her eye, making them sparkle even more as she hooked each note just so, with her sultry intonations. Dane floated in the sweetness of her voice, overjoyed that he now would be able to hear it anytime he desired. When she finished, the room burst with applause.

Dane cleared his throat as the music died down and every-one, besides the occasional giggle or cry of a child, went quiet. He approached Rhapsody, took her hands into his own and looked deeply into her eyes—bright, a tad moist—just enough to let him know how much this beautiful woman was truly in love with him.

"I was not expecting this, tonight. Thank you."

Rhapsody nodded and placed a small, soft kiss on his lips.

"I can't sing, but I feel compelled to respond to that. So," he looked at the crowd of people then back at her as he took the microphone from her hands, "I just want to thank everyone for coming out tonight and celebrating this im-portant day with us. Today is a Saturday, a cool, early winter day. Many people are enjoying a football game right now, the Detroit Lions are—"

"Yeeeaaaaaahhhhh!" someone cheered.

"Right." Dane smiled, looking out in the crowd then back at Rhapsody. "Playing, dinner is being eaten, kids are getting ready for bed and Saturday night dates are being made. But, you all are here with us, and we appreciate that." He paused as he gathered his thoughts. "At this time, last year, I would have been conducting a service, working at a soup kitchen or helping someone that attended the church. That was honora-ble, that was good." He glanced at Fr. Jones, who smiled at him and nodded in understanding. "…and *this* is also honora-ble and great, because right now, on this particular Saturday, I married my soulmate, my better half, a woman who had eluded me, and I eluded her, long ago, while I stared at her through a tiny window of a door during her high school choir rehearsals."

The crowd hummed, dripped in good cheer.

"She should have called the cops on me for stalking, but," he grinned, "it was just one of those things. Nothing came of that; we never even spoke and now here we are…" His voice cracked, the last words caught in his throat. He quickly wiped his left eye and continued. "Here we are, married now, after years of not seeing one another. A chance meeting in a park… I was down on my luck…and God…God sent me what I needed most, an angel…"

Out of his peripheral vision, he noted several people dabbing at their eyes.

Even Rhapsody's eyes were now glossed over to the point that she could no longer ignore it. Her sister leaned in front of her, and efficiently dotted at her face while Dane continued.

"I had everything I could have wanted. Friends, a place to stay, people who enjoyed my company, a chance to study God's Word for a living and for my soul's earnings, and He even made sure I was financially blessed in the midst of this. But, it still wasn't enough. There was one thing missing…" He took her hand and paused briefly when her hands started to tremble in his grip.

"God knew what I needed; I didn't even have to ask. But I did ask, I just didn't know that He would exceed my expectations like this." Swallowing, he took a moment to regain his composure when the emotions got too high. "I prayed to God for answers, for Him to show me, to please tell me what to do. At that time, there was no Rhapsody in my life…and then there she was, just like that." He snapped his fingers.

"So yeah." He squeezed her hand, and tilted her chin upward, exchanged a passionate glance with her. "I'm blessed beyond measure. I love you so much, Rhapsody. I loved you from the moment I realized I couldn't imagine life without you, and that nothing else mattered if you weren't with me. I will spend my entire life showing you how much I care and how honored I am that you chose *me*, when I know you could have had any man you wanted, but you chose *me* to be your partner in marriage."

Rhapsody smiled at him as Melody ran her hand lovingly across her sister's back.

"I promise to listen to you. I promise to not go to sleep angry, to talk out whatever disagreements we may have. I promise to be a good father to our future children. I promise to love you during all situations, good and bad, because you loved me at my worst…" His voice cracked then. He briefly closed his eyes and swallowed past a big lump. He felt his brother, Joseph, lightly brush against him and pat his shoulder, giving him comfort.

Then he looked out at his mother, who was crying through her happiness, tears streaking her plumped cheeks but covering a bright smile beneath.

"You were designed for me, *made* for me. You're my Eve."

He took both her hands and brought them up to his mouth, kissing them. "One day, a priest walked into a park. He sat down on a bench, and decided that he hated his life to the point that he was simply going to be alive for a little while, but not really live. And then he heard something…a melody; it touched him before the singing started. You see, because he heard the song in her heart, before she hummed or uttered a word. How could I give up," he smiled sadly as he looked deeper into her gaze, "on life with that sort of feeling now weaving its way into my soul? After hearing such a miracle? Somewhere inside of me, I *knew*, I was hearing the voice of my future wife…"

He could hear several people crying.

"I knew, on some primal level, and that is what made me want to give myself a chance to obtain peace at last. With you, Rhapsody, I never feel like I can't be myself, like I can't make it. I never feel like I have to pretend or put on a show. You saved my life, and I will spend the rest of it treating you as you deserve until God takes me away, and then after that, I want Him to promise me that when you're time comes, you'll be right by me in heaven, because I need you *now* and forever…"

The audience ahhed as he stole a quick kiss on her cheek.

Someone in the crowd murmured, "That was beautiful, Dane."

Just then, the lights dimmed, as they had at the church, and the room was bathed in shadows.

"What the?" Anthony called out as he looked around. "That's the second time, how weird."

Melody immediately marched toward the back of the room as everyone watched her. She flicked the switch. "I don't know what happened, maybe it is the breaker. The light is in the upright position."

And as quickly as it happened, the lights popped back on, bringing a sigh of relief.

"Someone didn't pay the light bill!" Anthony joked, causing an avalanche of laughter.

The party continued and soon, the search for a dry eye in the house came up empty, mission impossible.

No longer able to control himself, Dane urgently pushed his body into his bride's and heard her hitch her breath. He forced Rhapsody to rise on her tippy toes as he folded his arm around her back, brought her waist to his, and had her in his loving, quixotic grip, for all to see.

The crowd came alive with applause and it wasn't long after, Dane was stealing more sensual kisses in the corners of the vast, crowded dance hall with the music blaring, people dancing and eating cake. How could he help it, even if his behavior had the priest and his mother blushing and pretending not to witness such a wondrous and affectionate display...

Two days later...

"WHAT IS IT with women and over packing?" Dane complained as he hoisted his wife's bags out of the taxi, soon retrieved from the porters who greeted them at the nearby winding steps of the Hotel de Crillon, in the heart of Paris.

"Well, for my big debut, I wasn't sure what I'd wear. I need options, honey!" she batted her eyes dramatically.

Dane smiled and took her hand as they made their way inside.

"Oh my God!" she gasped, looking around in amazement. "The photos didn't do it justice. Dane, I can't believe you got us this place!" She turned around in circles, like a ballet dancer on auto pilot.

Dane grinned, overdosing on her exuberance. "Now you know I had to have us honeymoon in style. Besides, I have to share an evening with Paris, on our honeymoon, so they can enjoy your talent. This way, at least, when we get back to the room, things will be set up just how I want them," he said, winking.

Soon, they checked in and entered the elevator to their chamber. Lights reflected on the marble and gold walls and mirrored doors, as if they'd gone inside a crystal ball. Cupping the back of her neck, he pulled her close and stole a passionate kiss, slicking his tongue inside of her mouth. Rhapsody gasped when the doors opened on the seventh floor and they exited the elevator. It had been over three weeks since they'd last made love. Wedding plans and the long flight right after the wedding reception had taken their toll. He'd had enough. Dane was ready to unwrap his 'wedding package'.

They made the quick jaunt to their hotel room to find the door slightly ajar and the porters setting their luggage down. After exchanging pleasantries, Dane tipped them and they left.

When he turned back around, he caught Rhapsody repeat the performance from the lobby and giving their suite the once over. Looking around in awe, she ran her delicate fingers across the furniture and looked around the room, decorated with wine, gold and ivory drapes and bedding.

He took off his jacket…

Then his crisp white shirt…

All the while, she continued to move about, commenting about the décor, her back toward him.

He hooked his thumbs in the waist band of his pants; they hit the floor…

"Dane, you have to see this view!" She opened the thick curtains, allowing the setting sun to spray a mellow yellow inside the room.

"Oh, I can see the view just fine. *You* need to see the view, too…"

"I can, but if you come over here you'll notice that there is—" She turned around and stopped short at the sight of him. "You just couldn't wait. We've not been in here for more than five minutes."

At her side in mere moments, he ignored her laughter and made quick work of discarding her clothes, stealing kisses as he unhooked her bra. Then, he lowered her naked body onto the freshly made bed covered with little chocolate heart candies.

"Dane!" she said, breathless. "Baby…put the 'Do Not Disturb' sign on the door, just in case."

Don't stop me. No one is coming, baby…

But he relented. Racing to the bathroom, he snatched a plush white towel, wrapped it around him, and did as asked. In lightning speed, he'd locked the door back and returned to her, running his lips ruggedly up and down the side of her neck, making her coo as he used his knee to quickly push her legs apart. She trembled beneath him, fevered, but he continued to remind himself to take his time as his body grinded into hers and his kisses were unceasing, never yielding. Her bare, warm thighs cocooned him. She moved her lips across his cheek and beard, and ran her long fingers through the back of his hair. Her breaths came harsh and short, the longer they caressed.

"My wife," he murmured between kisses to her shoulder and collar bone. "You're all mine…"

He briefly looked into her eyes, catching a sweet smile, a secret smile just for him.

"I'm all yours, Dane," she said softly.

"You better be." He glanced lazily at her, watching her mouth open in shock then curve into a naughty grin.

"Hmmmm, possessive now, are we?" she crooned, as if she were about to break into song.

"Always have been…just more willing to show it…to claim *you*."

"Mmmm," she cooed, closing her eyes, as he pushed his pelvis hard into hers, teasing her, working her up, letting her feel his love growing against her taut stomach.

"My second chance…" He brought his face directly over hers. She sighed and purred as he kissed her, softly at first, but then more demandingly with each kiss, with each heartless tease of his rhythmic hip twist. "Never letting you go…*never*…"

"I don't want you to." She gripped him hard as he slipped lower, taking her nipple into his mouth, going over it meticulously, lick by slow lick. He rubbed the other, his fingertips pushing into the softness until soon, he felt the rigid, dark flesh peek as her arousal from his handy orchestration made it stand at attention. She purred in his ear and ground into him in smooth moves, matching his tempo.

"I'm going to make love to you, as if we never have before."

Then she gulped dramatically, and both burst into ripples of laughter…

*D*AMN, *HE GIVES good love*…

The way his beautiful blue eyes hooded and his soft lips brushed against her skin drove her insane. Linking her hand with his, high above her head, she surrendered to the rhythm of him bumping steadily into her pelvis.

He knew what he was doing. Teasing her, working her up into a frenzy, slowly but surely. She glanced off to the side, taking note of the silver bucket of chilled non-alcoholic champagne with two wine glasses slid snugly against it. Trails of icy condensation trickled down the pale pink bottle, slowly trekking, mimicking the pace of his tongue gliding up and down her earlobe. Fastening his arms around her waist, he took her lips again, sucking her bottom one with due pressure, soon slicking his tongue into her mouth. Warm breath from his mouth entered hers while she trailed her fingers down his back.

Dane reached down and slipped two fingers slowly inside of her, working them expertly on her G-spot.

Is this what long abstinence, does? He is so good…

And she meant that. Dane was an excellent lover—a man of high endurance, sensitive, considerate, dominating and skilled all at once. He made sure she was receiving pleasure as well, not stopping until she got what she needed, what she desired. He served her, and seemed to get highly intoxicated off her excitement.

"Mmmm, I think you're ready." He breathed harshly in her ear.

Reaching between their bodies, he gripped his shaft. She opened her legs wider for him, closed her eyes and braced herself as he entered her.

"Yes… this is what I needed, baby." He moaned, rising on his hands, looking down at her while she lost it. It didn't take long—he'd worked her up in a long, torturous state, making her body bend to his thrusting command.

"You like it, baby?" He smiled at her, knowing she did. She patted him lightly on his chest, on his pecs that glistened with sweat. He increased his pace before she'd had a chance to respond.

"Yessss!" Her body tensed as the orgasmic waves drowned her in sweet relief. He drove deep within her, his mouth on hers, his tongue echoing the moves of his hips, until she tumbled down the mountain of delight.

"Mmmmm!" they moaned in unison.

And her body did his bidding. He was so rough, yet so tender, his thrusts demanding, strong, and forcing her to submit.

"I'm going to make you have another one." Before she could grasp what he'd said, he reached between them, thumbing her clitoris as their bodies pressed together, and finally, she lost it once again, in epic proportions.

"Oh God!" Gritting her teeth, she pushed her head back into the pillow. He kept steady on her, driving her mad, using his fingers as if she were piano keys begging to be played, one solitary note at a time.

"Mmmmm! Dane!" He had her where he wanted, deep under his spell, and she did just as he'd said. She fell apart in his arms. She didn't know where her passion started and blended into his, but she felt him responding and opened her eyes to verify her findings. He was staring down at her. Not gawking, not smirking…but love was written all over his face. A wave of pleasure overtook her. She screamed out as he lunged deeper within her, breathlessly, urgently. His low, throaty growl—masculine and raw—roused her senses. He was so close, and she wanted nothing more than to feel it inside of her. Finally, she got her wish as he mumbled incoherently, gripped her hips, and came inside of her, filling her with the fluid from his love.

Sated, he fell down on her and she buried her face in his neck, relishing the moment as his body relaxed and his breathing slowed to a crawl. She strained a bit to get a glimpse of him, a big smile on his now sleeping face. She didn't dare disturb him, he'd earned the right to slumber and she knew that she, too, had better take the opportunity to nap, because Dane would be awake in about twenty minutes, ready, willing and able, to do it over again and again…

CHAPTER TWENTY-NINE

The following evening…

"ARE YOU SURE this looks okay? Maybe I should go back to the hotel and change into the red outfit! I think we may have just enough time."

Rhapsody stood backstage in the huge auditorium, her nerves visibly in overdrive, and the words that rolled out of her mouth proved it. Dane had never seen her like this before. They'd been having a blast, but within the last hour, his cool, calm and collected wife had turned into a mass of gelatin right before his very eyes. She continued to toil in front of the mirror, doing double takes and messing with the curls in her hair. He'd taken her to the Louvre and the Arc de Triomphe earlier that day to help her relax before her performance, but instead, she'd almost passed out of breath on the winding steps of the latter once they reached the top. However, it was well worth it as they observed the glorious view of the entire city. They'd stopped at a quaint café that served the best apple tart pastry she'd ever indulged in, and she resisted the urge to get another, believing it may force her tummy to poke out a wee bit too much.

"You look beautiful, honey." He stroked her back protectively, while musicians whirled past them, stage handlers screamed to each other in French, and a performer on the stage sang his last song. "Now look." He swirled her around to face him. "Everything is going to be just fine, better than fine. You've performed for big crowds before! No need to be nervous. You have this under control."

"I know." She smiled shyly. "But...this time, it isn't just me, you know? People are depending on me. I'm a fill-in."

"Fill in, shill in." He shrugged and rolled his eyes dramatically, causing her smile to widen. "You were *born* for this. They are in for a real treat. Now," he looked toward the slit in the curtain, from where a thin trail of light blazed through, "do you want me to sit back here, or take my seat in the audience?" He rubbed her exposed back, her long, silver form-fitting gown hugging every curve. She looked like a seductress encased in glistening ice and diamonds.

"Wherever you want, Dane. Just knowing you're close to me is enough." She winked at him, her features relaxing.

"Then I tell you what. I will sit out in the audience because my seat is pretty close to the front. That way, you can look at me in case your nerves get to you, but we both know how you are—as soon as you are out there, doing your thing, you will be fine."

She hooked her arms around his neck and kissed him affectionately.

I knew that was where she wanted me to sit. I know you, baby...

He smiled a smug smile over her shoulder as he hugged

her, kissed her once more and left to take his seat…

DANE STEEPLED HIS fingers and leaned forward as the lights dimmed. He dusted the shoulder of his black tuxedo as he looked around one last time before the faces turned into mere shadows. His entire core heated, taking on the stress of five men. The damned place was overwhelming, but there was no way he'd feed into her fears. He now saw his original assessment was untrue. This was the biggest crowd she'd ever played in front of and though the words were unspoken, key industry players, music producers and managers with clout would be occupying the seats.

Rhapsody hadn't uttered a word of it, but he'd heard her mother talking about it the day before their wedding. What endeared him the most was that his new wife didn't seem as nervous about that aspect at all. The biggest concern was the fear of letting a friend down…but that was Rhapsody, just one of a million reasons he loved the woman so very deeply. He heard her practicing in the bathroom since they'd arrived. She said the acoustics in their hotel lavatory were magnificent and he never grew tired of her singing the exact same verses, over and over, trying to perfect them 'just so.'

Finally, she floated onto the vast stage where at least twenty musicians lined up, all dressed elegantly. She stood in the middle, with the spotlight shining down on her, a platinum bumble bee clasp from her mother in her soft, shiny curls, and her bottom lip glossy—the deep, rich burgundy lipstick making them appear extra succulent. He tried to stave off any carnal desires and stay in the moment, but it was hard to do as he visually traced her plunging neckline, a pearl drop necklace pointing directly to the spot he often rested his head on after a marathon of lovely afternoon lovemaking sessions.

And he'd made her weak at the knees that morning, too – it was truly breakfast in bed. Between kisses, passionate thrusts and laughter, they'd find themselves at each other all over again, almost unable to break free. He loved that their beautiful time of sharing one another was oftentimes peppered with comedy. He couldn't recall one time they'd made love when a joke wasn't shared, or something whimsical didn't take place—they were so comfortable with one another.

When she gripped the microphone, he pushed the thoughts away and focused on her. Her brilliant wedding band and engagement ring created a rainbow prism that danced around under the illumination.

A cluster of women, background singers, stood a bit closer to her. Rhapsody lazily looked over at them and said, "Salut beauté!" causing the audience to burst out in applause.

She said it perfectly… 'Hello, Beautiful!'

Dane had been working with her on her French. He was far from an expert, but he'd learned enough for his missionary trips in several parts of Africa to get by.

"Je suis contente d'être ici."

Great job, baby! 'I'm happy to be here'

She took a deep breath, closed her eyes; dazzling him. She gripped the microphone and then, her eyes slowly closed and her lips parted…

"Remember those walls I built… Well baby they are tumbling down…" she belted out, and the audience cheered, suffocating the next few lyrics of Beyonce's, *"Halo"* in their applause.

Dane listened intently to the song he'd heard a thousand times, yet tonight, it sounded brand new. The music carried her notes away, hitting them perfectly, while the background singers brought out the gorgeous tones of her voice. Awe-struck, he sat captivated by the entire show and fell even deeper under her spell. It felt as if the woman was singing directly to him, and he knew, that she actually was.

"…I can see your halo…"

More time passed, but he never wanted the song to stop, and neither did the audience as they stood to their feet and belted a thunderous applause that was almost deafening. Her voice gave the song new depth, new meaning, her special touch that made it vibrate deep within the audience's souls, moved the room to at times zombie like silence—she'd stolen them, all of them.

You did it again, Rhapsody. You make people feel things they never knew were possible by your God given gift of song. That's your present to mankind; you are a musical genius, a prodigy to the entire world.

He smiled proudly at her, catching her gaze. In response, she tilted her head slightly to the side, paused and blew him a kiss before she went into her next song.

She's got it; she's okay now…

You've got them in the palm of your hands, sweetheart…

A week and a half later…

"Boooo!"

"Hey baby!" Dane threw his hands up as the cool night air ruffled their hair. He walked backwards from her, the Eiffel tower glowing brightly behind him. "We've been here two weeks; we do have to eventually get back to reality. You act like I wouldn't want to keep this majestic ride of ours going, you know I would, but you've got your work, and—" his voice trailed as he offered her a sympathetic smile.

Rhapsody sulked, then smiled devilishly before feigning anger again. "But I want to stay here forever. I don't want this to be our last night here!"

Dane grabbed her in his arms, pinning her arms down to her sides. She pretended to want to be free as he landed a perfect kiss smack dab on the middle of her forehead.

"You act like we can never come back again. Of course we will be back. I'll bring you here every single year if you want."

"Will you?!" She smiled gleefully, the child in her reborn. "I know we already extended our trip and can't do that again, but it's just so beautiful here. The people, the food, they appreciate my music! Did I mention the food?" She chuckled.

He ran his fingertips through her hair as it blew around under the darkened sky. "Yes, I will and yes, you did." He kissed her again, this time on the lips...soft...perfect. Tracing her ears with his fingertips, he looked down in her beautiful eyes—eyes that looked back up at him with the same intensity.

"What?" she asked softly, her smile warm, melting him, shielding him from the chill.

"Sometimes I still can't believe it."

She smiled a bit wider, waiting for him to continue, to explain himself.

"We talk about anything and everything and sometimes my mind wanders. I try to not do that, but it does. I look at you talking, smiling, hear you laughing, and all I can think is, 'How in the world did I get this lucky?' I look at you sleeping next to me. I put our hands together, my wedding band against your engagement ring, and...and I just can't believe I'm married to such a beautiful person, such a *wonderful* person, with a heart like I've never seen. In some ways we are opposites, some people may find it confusing while others think it is beautiful. I don't think we're that different at all."

She nodded in agreement, and a reddish glow spread across the apples of her cheeks. He loved that.

"I never knew I could feel like this about anyone. I just want to do everything for you, give you the whole entire world, if I could. Rhapsody, I love you so much." His voice shook, no matter how hard he tried to control it, so he quelled it by kissing her again, and again…until their tongues glided back and forth against each other's, slow, wet and warm.

She held him tight in front of the flashing Eiffel tower that turned shades of turquoise, cerulean and yellow. With that magnificent structure as witness, they lavished one another with the passion spilling fourth from their hearts, the kind that Paris was known for eliciting. He felt at home…at peace, content, loved, beloved, adored, respected, admired, cared for, lusted after, and wanted so desperately.

He felt it in her kiss, in her song—their hearts sung a duet, time and time again. He could feel it in her words, the way the woman made love to him, the tears she occasionally fought when he'd surprise her by doing something zany, romantic and unexpected. He showed her he was the 'real deal', crossed the long bridge to her heart. She'd thought him *safe* at first, that he couldn't break her heart because he'd promised it to the Catholic Church; in that, she felt security, but deep down, he knew she'd wondered, daydreamed of something *different*, something *more*, before their lives had changed completely.

He was okay being the first to admit it—he had to see if she was God's answer to his dilemma, he had to take a chance, and no doubt, it had been the best decision of his entire life. Their attraction for one another surpassed the physical. Their deep, entrenched soul connection had been barb wired together, super glued, tattooed, and cemented. His feelings for Rhapsody were a true testament of God's creation of love between two people who were solely designed to share their lives together and should they miss that first opportunity, they would be allowed to revisit the occasion.

And this time, *this time*, they reached for it with both fists, daring anyone to try and tear them apart…

Two weeks later…

"BABY, I GOTTA run around the corner back to the hardware store."

"For what?" Dane asked as he pushed the much detested red couch she coveted off center in their house. "I can go, just stay here and—"

"No, I want to go because the last time I trusted you to run an errand for me, you returned without what I wanted, but fifteen other things!" She laughed as she grabbed her bag and softly closed the door behind her.

After a few minutes, Dane fell into exhaustion. He walked sluggishly into their new kitchen, wiped the sweat from his brow with the back of his hand and opened the refrigerator, praying that the iced teas he'd purchased from the store were finally cold. He ran his thumb against one of the cans, tore it from the plastic six-cylinder divider, cracked it open, and downed it.

"Where in the world are the heating and air-conditioning people?"

It is the dead of winter, yet it is so hot in here!

There had been problems with the new thermostat, and he

was eager for the repair company to arrive. He looked around the home from his vantage point as he leaned against the black granite counter. The house was big, spacious, clean and beautiful… perfect to raise a large family in. Their dream home—five bedrooms, four full and two half baths, a master-suite, picture-perfect, seemingly right out of a magazine and a kitchen fit for the finickiest of chefs. He wanted her to have it, she deserved it. She never asked, and at the end, she still couldn't decide between that house and another. At the final hour, she kissed him and told him to choose…so he did.

He picked the one that had enough bedrooms to accommodate all the children he wanted to have with her, big family gatherings and holiday parties. He chose the house that had a larger plot of land, the one that had its own private pond, filled with small fish and ducks. It reminded him of Mies park, their courtship, and having a piece of that in their own backyard was too irresistible to pass up. There was yet another reason for the large plot of land. She didn't know why, and she wouldn't, until her birthday. Dane had laid out plans to have a music studio built on the grounds for her, and in their haste to pack and move about, he had to tell her the great news while they were in the moving truck—she'd landed a record deal. They'd be heading back out to Paris in the next couple of weeks to go over the details but she'd be recording from the United States. So much had to be done in a short time; it was a stressful, but exciting ride.

He tossed the can in the recycling bin and made his way up the steps. Each step he took echoed in the empty house, and he imagined it filled with friends, family and the pitter patter of little feet. When he made it into their bedroom, he cast his gaze over the far left corner where five boxes lay stacked atop one another. He zoomed in on the second to last of the stack—the box from Josh. Once and for all, he marched over and retrieved it, holding it with both hands. After all this time, emotion still got the better of him. There still wasn't a day that had gone by when he hadn't thought about the man. He grabbed a nearby box cutter, squatted on the floor by the box, and sliced it open, then began the process of removing the items that Josh had placed inside of it during the last week of his life.

First, their high school year book. Dane flipped through it, laughing at all the notes Josh had written—sarcastic notes, funny notes; circled girls in red meant the young lady was hot, circled in blue meant not so much. He reached back inside the box and pulled out a smaller container. Inside was his old favorite earring, a small white gold ball that he bequeathed to Josh on his final evening of drinking and debauchery before entering the seminary. He rolled it around between his forefinger and thumb, then attempted to place it back inside a long forgotten hole in his left earlobe that he was certain had closed. Much to his surprise, after a bit of finagling, it went in.

Next, he pulled out an empty bottle of whiskey that made him pause. Then, he saw a letter at the bottom of the box, sealed, with his name written across it in faded black ink, in Josh's handwriting. He sniffed and drew his knees upward as he continued to sit on that floor, surrounded by cases, bubble wrap paper and a bunch of books for home decorating Melody insisted they keep. A chill came over him, and an urge to break down and let the pain out. But finally, he sucked it up, slid his thumb under the flap of the envelope and removed the handwritten letter addressed to him:

Dane,

If I know you as well as I think I do, you are reading this significantly later than when I wrote it.

Dane paused and burst out laughing as one tear trailed down his cheek. He looked down and continued to read.

Now that you're reading it, let me tell you, 'Hey Man!' I'm telling you, even though I'm not there yet, I KNOW I love it here in Heaven. You should come and visit me sometime; I think priests get a discount to the all-you-can-eat buffet.

Dane shook his head.

Dane, you are my best friend. You spent most of your time lately trying to get me cured, trying to find someone to make it all better. I kept telling you to stop, but you wouldn't listen.

Dane's grip on the letter tightened as he made his way through it.

You wouldn't listen and I know why. It's because you love hard, and you think the sky is the limit! And it is! But no one said this was the end, bro! I will see you again, and we will do what we always do, get together and act completely foolish!
I love you.
Now, I want to tell you something that I was afraid to tell you to your face. You can't kill me if I'm already dead.
God, please forgive me, but Dane, just because you are good at something doesn't mean it is your calling. Let me rephrase that, just because you are good at something, and you are called to do it, doesn't mean it is your lifetime destination. Let me just say what I need to say to you, because you need to hear it. You are

one of the best speakers I've ever heard. Your sermons aren't boring, they are funny and they hit people close to home. You make people actually want to attend church instead of stay at home. Do you know why that is? It is the very same reason you may need to get ready to move on...

I know what you've done; you know what I've done. You know all about my problems, my past, you know my history inside and out, and since we share this, we know each other better than anyone else on this planet. Maybe I know you better than you know your own self sometimes, and vice versa. But what I'm sure of is that you're so good at giving passionate sermons, because your heart beats so damn loud, man! You are so alive; you were born to be seen! Please don't be angry, Dane.

I do think you are a great priest; that is the whole reason for this admission, actually. But, we used to talk about when we'd get married, where we'd live, our jobs and all this other stuff, and I know you told me you were fine with that being gone, but I never really bought it, Dane. You were going through a lot at that time in your life, and I think you felt you owed it to God to serve him in that way. It was noble, but inside, I questioned it. I know you bought it, and I knew you wanted it, so I let it go, but now that I have nothing to lose, I need to tell you the truth.

And here is what I think is going to happen. I think you are going to get to the point where you want the same dreams we discussed as kids in high school. Dreams never really die, Dane. We just push them aside. They always resurface sooner or later. Those dreams and desires are going to come back and gnaw at you. I think that you will fall in love, Dane. I don't know when, and I don't know with who, but you are going to fall in love and get caught up in some shit.

Dane couldn't help but burst out laughing. He covered his

eyes with his hand and held the letter with the other. In the loud laughter however was pain, deep pain welling in his chest. He lost his breath as the crying grew louder, soon replacing the quiet tears altogether, until finally, the pain turned to relief. Sweet relief that the man he adored, his best friend in the entire world before Rhapsody entered his life, knew exactly what his future held before he'd even imagined it!

I'm telling you, I can just feel it. Just like I knew when you were going to get that C on the midterm exam in Mr. Gracey's class because he hated your guts, regardless of all that brown-nosing you were doing to try to sweet talk him into a B. I know this, too.

"Josh, you're something else…" Dane smiled, shaking his head.

You are going to meet someone, it will be innocent. Maybe she attends the church, that would make sense. Hell, I'm not psychic, I just feel it in my heart—but you will meet her, and you won't be able to take your mind off of her and you know what, Dane? Why should you? The best part of me is my children. The most important person to me in the world is Margie. It sickens me that you can never have that, when I know you want it. That is what I hate most about being sick and dying. Not the pain I am in or the medicine and all that other bull, it is the fact that I won't be physically with my family anymore. That is what upsets me the most! Until our faith allows you to do what we both know you need, you will never be at peace. The last few visits I had with you, before telling you about the cancer, you were just going through the motions. I wasn't convinced you actually knew anything was wrong, but I knew something was wrong. You weren't yourself. Man, you were dying right in front of me.

I had cancer, but you were dying, Dane. Once again, you've been sacrificing yourself to make other people happy. You may hate me after you read this. You might rip this letter up into a million pieces and tell yourself it isn't true, but that will just prove that you know it is. I just want my best man who stood with me at my wedding, who carried my drunk ass across an entire football field at three in the morning, the same dude that let me have a girl that liked him better than me, to be happy. You stepped out of the way and let me have her anyway and she became my first love. I just want that same man to have what he deserves!

This isn't right, Dane. You deserve better than this. I want you to get married in a big ass church to a beautiful woman and have a honeymoon somewhere in Europe, maybe Italy or France since you like Paris so much. I want you to have a big house filled with fancy furniture, and a bunch of happy kids that are just as wonderful and silly as you are! You are smart, funny as hell and you would give your life for a stranger. The world needs you Dane, and you deserve to be happy, too.

Dane threw the letter down and sobbed so loudly, he thought his chest was going to burst. He took a moment or two to compose himself, picked it back up and started again.

Do you know why I put that empty whiskey bottle in there? That is the bottle of whiskey we shared the night my girlfriend left me to move away. Marilyn Lopez, the girl that had eyes for you, but she fell for me anyway. First love. We drank that entire thing and you kept telling me everything would be okay as we got drunker and drunker. I have no proof, but I bet you've started drinking again…a nip here and there. I know you, Dane.

You usually held your alcohol well, so it was kind of hard to tell, but some of the times we've talked lately, you didn't seem right. I believe you'd been drinking, and I believe you are depressed. If I'm wrong, I apologize, but I don't think I am. You rarely got sloshed; you would do just enough to take the edge off, from all the shit you dealt with that no one else knows about. It's time to stop this, Dane. It is time to stop being everything to everybody, but yourself. The bottle is empty! There is no more medicine to make the demons, as you called them, go away! It's just you, and a mirror. Don't piss this opportunity away. You still have a beating heart, blood in your veins, and ambition. You're healthy and fully capable. You can do this. I just want you to be happy and you clearly aren't. Only you can change that.

Wet tear drops fell on the letter as he continued to read.

I pray to God that you follow your heart. If your heart really is with the Church, being a priest, then please try to find it in your heart to forgive me. If anything I said is true though, please, think about it long and hard. I may not be there physically with you any longer, but I want to dance at your wedding, man, and if you ever have one, I will be there. I promise. And to prove it to you: remember that scary story your dad used to tell us about the haunted mansion? I will do that. I will flick the lights on or turn them off, then turn them back on.

Dane thought his heart had stopped as he re-read the line over and over again, recollecting how the lights at his wedding did in fact mysteriously go out, then again at the reception hall. Two different venues, yet the exact same experience. Josh obviously wanted to make it perfectly clear that he was in fact there. He swallowed deeply before he could move forward with the letter...

I'll do that just to let you know that I see you, and I was there and you can scoot Joseph over, because I'm the best man!

"God, Josh." Dane laughed lightly, feeling both sadness and joy.

So, anyway, that's what I needed to say to you, Dane. I needed to say it and I could only rest easy after it is all said and done, knowing that I had gotten it off my chest. I'm sorry if what I've told you in this letter is upsetting to you, but I love you, and sometimes the truth hurts but real love, the kind that you deserve, rarely even leaves a blemish. I want you to have that, Dane. A family is not overrated. If anyone deserves it, it's you.

Love Always Until I see You Again Mr. 'Great Dane' The big Dog of Michigan!

Josh

Dane wasn't certain how long he sat there with the whiskey bottle in one hand and the letter in the other, but his wife's gentle touch on his shoulder brought him into the present.

"Dane," she whispered, "What's wrong? I've been calling your name for over five minutes and finally found you up here behind all these boxes. You look really upset, baby, what happened? What is the matter?" With her index finger, she gently wiped a small tear from the corner of his eye.

He looked at her, put the letter and empty bottle in the box and grabbed her close to him. "Nothing, nothing is wrong at all, baby. Everything is just right!"

CHAPTER THIRTY

Three years later…

"SO THAT'S IT for today. Please read chapter twelve for the test next week and we will discuss British empiricism and contemporary cognitive science on Monday."

Dane watched his students gather their belongings and head out the classroom. He was looking forward to the weekend after this long, dreary Spring Friday, and he wanted to get home to his family. But as he gathered his computer and books, he was startled by a knock at the door, and then it suddenly swung open.

"What are you doing here?" His heart still flipped when he laid eyes on her or heard her voice, and now even more so as she stood holding their eighteen-month-old daughter, Sophie, in her arms. "I thought you were really busy, you know, with the new record release coming soon. I was going to rush home to see what you cooked so I could wolf it down and cuddle with you two on the couch." He grinned.

She drew closer and planted a firm kiss on his lips, then he ran his hand over Sophie's thick, black curls with little white bows adorned in them and kissed her cheek.

"Hi, DaDa!" she squealed.

"Hi, sweetheart." He leaned down and kissed the little girl once more.

"Well, we thought, *instead* of that, we'd take Daddy out to dinner for his favorite pizza." She looked at Sophie, bouncing her in her arms. "Ain't that right, baby doll?" She grinned.

"Sounds like a plan to me, finding your way to my heart through my stomach. See? I'm easy to please."

"Oh, this isn't about you, honey. That's just an excuse. This is for *me*. These cravings I am having are ridiculous. Your son is greedy as hell! Did you take a good look at him on the sonogram from last week's doctor's visit? He is *huge*! I will be glad when he is out of my stomach. He is killing my back and I can't get a good night's rest. He thinks my uterus is a twenty-four hour night club." she laughed as she ran her hand over her protruding belly.

"Yeah, blame it on our son, he isn't here yet to defend himself. I think you like being up late, watching all those silly programs on Cartoon Network at three in the morning." he teased.

They laughed and spoke quietly to one another as he grabbed his bag, placed the strap over his shoulder, and took his wife's hand. A hint of seduction glimmered in her mahogany eyes as they walked out of the college classroom door.

While heading toward the exit, a poster of 'Jesus Christ Superstar' caught his eye. The way it was drawn for the play advertisement reminded him of the statue in the parish he'd served. Dane had experienced peace, *total* nirvana, for the first time in his life after falling in love, head over heels, with Rhapsody. As they continued to walk hand in hand, he reflected on that final night when he'd packed up his belongings in the rectory and walked out those church doors for the final time.

He'd stood there, looking at the golden statue of Jesus nailed to the cross that he'd prayed before thousands upon thousands of times, the candles still lit from his silent prayers only moments before. He stood there, staring into Jesus' eyes, the pain etched hauntingly on the Savior's carved face. Dane clasped his hands and lowered his head humbly and said one simple sentence before he left St. Michael's forever to go forth and claim his new life once and for all.

"Please forgive me Father, for I have fallen in love." And then he turned and walked away, into a new life filled with sobriety, passion and serenity in his heart forevermore…

~The End~

A WORD WITH THE READER

When I sat down to write this book, I kept telling myself, "You are going to get in serious trouble." Though it is a work of fiction, I fully understood as a person that stays up on current events that there are three subjects in the world that people kill for: Race/Ethnicity, Power/Hierarchy/Classism, and Religious/Spiritual beliefs. Some would even argue the first two are actually tied together. If you want to start a storm, those are your three best bets and here I was, grabbing two out of three and telling a love story to boot. Due to the sensitive subject matter, I felt it was imperative that I speak to devoted Catholics, as well as do my own research.

Some of the people I spoke to were actual friends. I knew the nuisances touching their lives, shared with them both personal matters and more mundane, run-of-the-mill conversations. We were 'friendly', so to speak, so it made getting the information much easier. I then took time to study the world of a priest and there is no one story for each man who has this vocation, and falls in love. Every one of the stories I found is different, just like you and I, but the testimonies I read during my research regarding such matters were at times heart breaking, inspiring, or danced somewhere in between. This book is about love.

It is about acceptance and dissecting oneself to get the message and receive the answer to the old adage, *"Why am I here? What is my purpose?"* It is about finding beauty in the presumably socially and politically hideous and acceptance of the seemingly unforgiveable. It is the story of an intelligent, devoted, attractive Catholic boy who grows into a man, but not before being crippled by the weight of others personal demons resting on his shoulders and when he can stand straight and tall, the world around him looks vastly different than from his previous stooped position.

There are real 'Fr. Danes' in the world. I respect them, and wish for a day when, like the hero of this story, they will no longer be pressed up against a wall to make such a choice between love, and, well…love.

Thank you,
Tiana Laveen

AUTHOR BIOGRAPHY

USA Today Best-selling novelist Tiana Laveen writes resilient yet loving heroines and the alpha heroes that fall for them in unlikely happy-ever-afters. The author of over 75 novels to date, Tiana creates characters from all walks of life that leap straight from the pages into your heart.

Married with two children, she enjoys a fulfilling life that includes writing, drawing, and spending quality time with loved ones.

If you wish to communicate with Tiana Laveen and stay informed of new releases, please follow her on social media platforms and visit her website:

www.tianalaveen.com

Made in the USA
Middletown, DE
23 October 2024

63187020R00241